D0307574

THE MIDNIGHT HOUSE

ALSO BY ALEX BERENSON

The Silent Man

The Ghost War

The Faithful Spy

THE

MIDNIGHT HOUSE

———

ALEX BERENSON

HUTCHINSON

London

Published by Hutchinson 2010

2 4 6 8 10 9 7 5 3 1

Published by arrangement with G.P. Putnam's Sons, a division of the
Penguin Group (USA) Inc., New York

First published in Great Britain in 2010 by
Hutchinson
Random House, 20 Vauxhall Bridge Road,
London SW1V 2SA

www.rbooks.co.uk

Addresses for companies within The Random House Group Limited can be found at:
www.randomhouse.co.uk/offices.htm

The Random House Group Limited Reg. No. 954009

A CIP catalogue record for this book
is available from the British Library

ISBN 9780091931094 (Hardback)
ISBN 9780091931100 (Trade paperback)

The Random House Group Limited supports The Forest Stewardship
Council (FSC), the leading international forest certification organisation. All our
titles that are printed on Greenpeace approved FSC certified paper carry the FSC logo.
Our paper procurement policy can be found at:
www.rbooks.co.uk/environment

Mixed Sources
Product group from well-managed
forests and other controlled sources
www.fsc.org   Cert no. TT-COC-2139
© 1996 Forest Stewardship Council
FSC

Printed and bound in Great Britain by
CPI Mackays, Chatham, ME5 8TD

FOR THE MEN AND WOMEN OF CITY HARVEST,

WHO BRING FOOD TO THE HUNGRY

ACKNOWLEDGMENTS

Thanks to my family for their thoughtful criticism; to Neil, Ivan, Leslie, Tom, and everyone else at Putnam and Random House UK for all their hard work making these books real; to Heather and Matthew for their advice; to Larry and the *Times* for keeping me around, and to Deirdre for catching the mistakes even the copy editors miss. Most important, thanks to Jackie, my lovely wife, partner, and friend.

And, finally, thanks to every reader who came this far. John Wells wouldn't exist without you. As always, e-mail me with comments, suggestions, or criticism at alexberensonauthor@gmail.com. With the volume of e-mail I'm now getting, I can't promise to respond to every note, but I pledge to read them all.

Then Moses lifted up his hand and struck the rock twice with his rod; and water came forth abundantly, and the congregation and their beasts drank.

—Numbers 20:11

PROLOGUE

ISLAMABAD, PAKISTAN. JUNE 2008

To the worst place in the world."

"The worst place in the world."

George Fezcko and Dwayne Maggs raised their glasses and drank. The going-away party was over. One by one, the ops had said their good-byes and disappeared. Only Fezcko and Maggs were left. Fezcko, the guest of honor, leaving Pakistan after four years as deputy chief of station. And Maggs, his best friend at the agency.

The clock on the wall said 1:30, and they'd been drinking since dinner, but Fezcko felt solid. Maggs had gotten hold of a half-dozen Omaha steaks and two racks of ribs. The meat had soaked up most of the scotch in Fezcko's belly.

Though not all. Fezcko put his head against the cool wood of the conference table and hummed tunelessly: "'We few, we ragged few, we motley crew . . .'" He trailed off. He couldn't remember the rest of the song, or even if there was a rest of the song.

"Mötley Crüe," Maggs said. "Dirty deeds, done dirt cheap."

"That's AC/DC."

"Marine recon, too."

"Why does it always go back to the marines? By now everyone in this country knows you're a jarhead. All one hundred fifty million."

Fezcko tapped Maggs on the forehead. "Tattoo it right there. The few, the proud, the stupid."

"You wish you coulda been a marine," Maggs said. "Berkeley boy. You wouldn't have made it through the first week of basic. Eaten up and spat out."

Maggs was the station's director of security. He was short and wide and strong, arms as big as an average man's legs. Fezcko had thinning curly hair and wild black eyes. In college he'd played bass for a band that had almost broken out. They shouldn't have gotten along. But they did.

"A marine? I wish I coulda been Tom Brady."

"The Islamic Republic of Pakistan. Land of the free, home of the suicide bomber. Bet you miss it already," Maggs said.

"What's not to miss? The earthquakes. The weather. The fifteen pounds I put on 'cause it's too hot to run outside." Fezcko poked at the belly he'd gained.

"Can't blame Paki for that. That gym in the basement is pretty good. As you'd know if you ever visited."

"I like to run outside."

"How about the women? Those beautiful Paki women."

Fezcko sipped his scotch. "Black-and-blue with the ugly stick," he said. "I never should have let Marci divorce me. Maybe if our security officers didn't lock us in the embassy all the time, maybe then we'd find out what those burqas are hiding. Can't even go down the block to the Marriott for a going-away party. It's a *Marriott,* for God's sake."

Indeed, because of the risk of terrorist attacks, the agency barred employees in Pakistan from gathering at hotels and restaurants. Maggs had refused to make an exception, even tonight.

"Don't mind getting you killed, but there's got to be a reason,"

Maggs said. "You know better than me, they aim for that Marriott once a month. I know who you're gonna miss. The army and the ISI"—the Inter-Services Intelligence agency, the Pakistani secret police. Between them the two services more or less ran Pakistan.

"The army and the ISI. The ISI and the army. I'll tell you something about the ISI and the army."

"Yeah. Give me the speech. With feeling. Like I haven't heard it a hundred times before."

"The Egyptians, the Saudis, when they lie to you, they do it with a smile. Pour you tea, tell a story that takes an hour, and when they're done you're about ready to fall for whatever they're spinning. These guys, they just yell, like if I give you this nonsense at high volume it won't sound so ridiculous. They aren't all bad, maybe, but most of 'em . . ."

"Remember when they won that cricket match and almost burned down Karachi?"

Fezcko looked into his glass. "You really think Paki's the worst place in the world?"

"Somalia's bad."

"Worse than this?"

"Hotter. And blacker."

"You think you can say that just 'cause you're black? Insult your African cousins?"

Maggs smirked. "I can say it because I'm a marine."

"Let's drink to Somalia, then," Fezcko said. "The even-worse worst place in the world."

"Somalia. See you there."

"Three years. It'll be like that movie with the French chick—"

"I always knew you were gay, George—"

Fezcko struggled for the memory lurking in his alcohol-fogged brain. "Ethan Hawke. Julie Something—"

"Gayer by the second."

"Before Sunrise," Fezcko said triumphantly.

AND THEN HIS PAGER buzzed.

He pulled it off his waist, squinted at it. The scotch had blurred his eyes, and he didn't recognize the numbers. Then he did. *36963.* Code for "call me now" from Nawiz Khan, a division chief for the ISI. Fezcko slid the pager across the table to Maggs.

"Nawiz?" Maggs said. "Wants to wish you good-bye."

Fezcko didn't trust the ISI, but he did trust Khan, since a blown raid in Peshawar two years back. He and Khan had had to shoot their way out of an apartment. Khan took a round in the left thigh that night. He still favored the leg.

Fezcko stood, feeling the steak and the ribs twist in his gut, and headed down the hall, shielding his eyes from the fluorescent lights. He touched his thumb to the fingerprint reader beside the door of his office. Inside, he sat down heavily on the edge of his desk and called Khan.

Who answered after a single ring.

"Fezcko," Khan said, somehow making the name sound glamorous. The years he'd spent at university in London had given him a soft English accent.

"Nawiz?"

"May I speak freely?"

"You asking if this line is secure? Yeah, it's secure."

"Also if you are as drunk as you sound."

Fezcko laughed. "Not quite. Though it's been a long night."

"It has been a long night for me as well, George. But I have something you will want to see."

Something or someone?

"Both."

"Big?"

"If you're asking me, am I in line for your fifty million dollars"—the CIA's reward for the capture of Osama bin Laden—"the answer is no. But my friend, I wouldn't have called at this hour if this wasn't worth your while. You may want to let your CT team know as well."

CT was agency lingo for the practice known publicly as extraordinary rendition. The letters stood for "collection and transfer," snatching suspected terrorists from their home countries and holding them in American custody.

"My CT team," Fezcko said. "That's me and Maggs. As you know."

"My men will make the arrest, then. And I will give them to you as a going-away present."

"'Them'? What are you doing to me, Nawiz?"

"The question you should be asking me is what am I doing for you?"

"We gonna need a G-five for this?" A Gulfstream V jet, capable of carrying a dozen passengers halfway around the world without refueling, and thus the preferred method of transport for renditions.

"I think so. These men, it's best if they leave Pakistan."

"Man. You couldn't have given me a little notice? I need an hour, make some calls."

"And drink some coffee."

"That, too."

"One hour. No more."

"One hour."

BUT NINETY MINUTES PASSED before Fezcko and Maggs rolled out the side gate of the embassy in a black Nissan sedan. The car looked stock, but its windows were bullet-resistant and its doors were reinforced with steel plates. It wasn't as sturdy as the armored Suburbans that the ambassador and the chief of station preferred, but it would stop an AK round and it didn't attract attention.

In the passenger seat, Fezcko tried to rest, while his bodyguard, an ex-Ranger with the unlikely name of Leslie, drove. Maggs was in the back, playing a driving game on his iPod, his preferred method of relaxation before a mission. He seemed to have sobered up immediately. Fezcko wished he could say the same. Even after three cups of coffee, he was hardly in peak form. Before he left, he had gotten a definite maybe for a rendition from Josh Orton, the assistant chief for the Near East Section.

"I'm going to need more details," Orton had said, from his desk seven thousand miles away at Langley.

"You think?"

"Don't get pissy with me, George. You know the rules." Since 2006, the agency had become much more reluctant to authorize renditions, although they still took place.

The Nissan swung out of the Diplomatic Enclave, the high-security zone in eastern Islamabad that was home to the American embassy and other foreign missions. The night air was surprisingly cool for June. A breeze fluttered through the trees along Constitution Avenue.

After Pakistan gained independence in 1947, its military leaders decided to create a new capital city that would be easier to control than Karachi, the original capital. The result was Islamabad, a million-person city that Pakistanis called Isloo. With its boulevards, parks, and office towers, Isloo wasn't a bad place to live, at least compared to the rest of Pakistan. The city reminded Fezcko of Charlotte, his hometown—though Charlotte didn't have a mosque that could hold three hundred thousand worshippers.

The Nissan turned southwest on Nazimuddin Road, leaving the Diplomatic Enclave behind. Rather than giving names to the neighborhoods, Islamabad's planners had divided the city into zones identified by numbers and letters. Sixty years later, the system had stuck. Fezcko and Maggs were headed for the I-10 zone, a lightly built area on the southwestern edge of the city.

Fezcko's phone trilled.

"Are you standing me up?"

"Nawiz, please. We're on the way." Fezcko hung up, wondering at the urgency. Khan wasn't a nervous guy.

Ten minutes later, the Nissan pulled up outside an unfinished concrete building. A rusting white sign identified the shell as the "Future Center of the All-Pakistan Medical Commons." As Fezcko stepped out of the Nissan, the building's steel front door creaked open. A trim middle-aged man limped out toward him.

"*Salaam alekeim*, Nawiz."

"*Alekeim salaam*." They hugged, clapping each other tightly on the back.

"If I didn't know better, I'd think you were friends," Maggs said.

"Come," Nawiz said. "I'll show you your going-away present."

INSIDE, A BIG OPEN ROOM with a floor of hard-packed dirt. The air thick with dust and the stink of diesel smoke. A noisy generator powered strings of Christmas tree–sized white bulbs tacked to the walls, giving the place a strangely festive feel. In the corner opposite the generator, two men played checkers on a cheap folding table. Three more napped at their feet.

"Your crack team," Fezcko said.

"Merely conserving their energy." Khan handed Fezcko a long-lens photograph of a truck, a Mitsubishi ten-wheeler, the cab metallic blue with a spiffy beige stripe painted horizontally beneath the windshield. "Abu Zaineb Textile Manufacture (PVT) Ltd" was stenciled in black on the cargo compartment.

"Nice truck," Fezcko said.

"Such insight. I see why you've been promoted."

"Is Abu Zaineb Textile real?"

"We can't find the name. Though that's not dispositive, you understand."

"'Dispositive,'" Maggs said. "Mighty big word for a Paki."

Khan waved off Maggs and handed Fezcko another photo, this one centered on a pair of men standing beside the truck. One wore a white *salwar kameez*, the long tunic and pants favored by many Pakistani men. The other was younger and dressed Western-style, in jeans and a red T-shirt that, strangely, had a Batman logo stamped on its front.

"You know them?"

Fezcko shook his head.

"This one." Khan pointed to the man in the *salwar kameez*. "His name is Asif Ali. He is a cousin of Jawaruddin."

Jawaruddin was Jawaruddin bin Zari, a thirty-four-year-old from Peshawar who was wanted for numerous terrorist attacks, including four bombings in Peshawar and the killing of two American aid workers in Karachi. He was a member of a terrorist group called Ansar Muhammad that had first turned up in 2006. In Arabic, *ansar* literally meant patrons, or supporters, but the word was usually translated as warriors—in this case, the warriors of Muhammad. The CIA didn't know much about Ansar Muhammad, though the agency had picked up hints of connections between the group and the ISI. Some analysts at Langley believed the ISI was using the group to carry out anti-American attacks in Pakistan and Afghanistan. In any case, bin Zari was a high-value target. Capturing him would be a coup for the agency, at least until his successor popped up.

"Asif's an actual cousin? Or more like a good friend?"

"You've reached the limits of my knowledge, George. He was introduced to my men as a cousin. We didn't perform a DNA test."

"And he's part of Ansar Muhammad?"

"Based on what I'm about to show you, it seems likely."

"What about the other guy? Batman?"

"We don't know. Probably a driver."

Khan handed across a third photo, this one focused on the Mitsu-bishi's cargo compartment, which was filled with oil drums and plastic sacks. A fourth photo focused on the sacks, which were stamped "Highest-Quality Nitrogen Fertilizer." Khan didn't have to explain further. Ammonium nitrate and fuel oil were the basic ingredients for truck bombs.

"These were taken where?"

"Peshawar." Khan lifted his eyebrows, as if to say *Where else?* "Two days ago. My men learned that Asif Ali would be at a restaurant. They followed him, took these photos. Dumb luck."

"Your men learned how?"

"The usual way. A friend of a friend of an enemy."

"That like a cousin?" This from Maggs.

"I'd like some details on the sourcing," Fezcko said.

Khan lifted his shoulders a fraction of an inch: *Too bad.*

"Where's the truck now?"

"Approximately fifteen hundred meters"—about a mile—"from here. It arrived yesterday. I had hoped that bin Zari or someone at his level might visit the operation in person. But I think now that moment has passed. And I think we ought to move quickly."

Fezcko understood. The ISI was so ridden with Qaeda sympathizers that it was only a matter of time before the terrorists learned that Khan and his men were tracking them. Most likely very little time.

"Heck of a nice truck. Shame to blow it up. You know the target?"

"We're all targets, George. Terrorism hurts us all." Khan moved his lips, pretending to smile. "Roderick White arrives tomorrow for meetings with our president. He seems a likely candidate."

Fezcko rubbed his forehead, wishing his going-away party had been some other night. How had he forgotten that Sir Roderick White, the British foreign minister, was coming to Islamabad? "That sounds ambitious."

"You know our friends are optimists. And even if they don't reach him, they know that whatever they do will get extra attention tomorrow."

"Maybe they'll have help to get through a checkpoint or two." Fezcko didn't have to specify that the help would be coming from inside the ISI. "Who else knows about this, Nawiz?"

"Omar is the only one I've told." Omar Gul, an assistant director in the ISI's Counter-Terror Division. Sometimes known at Langley as the "Counting on Terror" Division. The CIA viewed Gul as the only reliable officer in the top ranks of the ISI, not least because he'd survived three assassination attempts in four years, the last of which had cost him his right eye.

Fezcko saw why Khan was so anxious to move. "You want to do this now. Get them out before the sun comes up. You and Omar are the only ones who know. Tomorrow, the next day, you come back on that truck, a big show. It's empty, and you tell your buddies that the bad guys disappeared."

Khan nodded.

"Then whatever we get from them, maybe even some names inside your shop, nobody knows but you."

Another nod.

The plan was at least one step past risky. Maybe all the way to stupid. Renditions usually required approval from senior-level officials on both sides. Now Khan wanted to grab two men on the fly. They weren't in some village on the North-West Frontier, either. They were five miles from the Pakistani parliament. If something went wrong, if they got caught tonight, the Pakistani government wouldn't be able to ignore what had happened. Khan would go to jail. There would be anti-American riots.

If anyone but Khan had made the offer, Fezcko would have rejected it outright for fear of a trap. But he trusted Khan. And the deal was tempting. Anything they could do to clean up the ISI would be valuable.

"We don't have a plane in country," Fezcko said, trying to buy time. "Where will we keep them?"

"Here."

"No problem getting them out?"

"Not if you get a jet in today to Faisalabad." A city about 150 miles south of Islamabad.

Fezcko nodded at Maggs. They stepped to the other side of the room. "Thoughts?" Fezcko murmured.

"Nothing you don't know."

"Too good to be true? Setup?"

"Not from him. You know my rule."

Maggs's rule was that you couldn't trust anyone in the ISI until he'd taken a bullet next to you. It was a good rule. And just like that, Fezcko decided. "All right," he yelled over the generator to Khan. "We're in. Let me see about that G-five." *And some authorization,* he didn't add. For this operation, winks and nods wouldn't do. He wanted explicit approval, in writing.

Behind the building, he called Orton on his sat phone.

"I was hoping it wouldn't be you," Orton said.

"Am I interrupting you, Josh? Gotta pick up the kids from soccer practice? Maybe a manicure?"

"Just tell me."

Fezcko did.

"Tricky," Orton said. "If the ISI isn't going to know about it, we're going to have to keep this one quiet. There's only one place for them to go. And that takes special authorization. Have to call the Pentagon."

"No excuses," Fezcko said. "Yes or no." He hung up.

WHILE THEY WAITED, they grabbed body armor and M-4s from the Nissan and suited up. Khan and his men did the same, though their own gear was less fancy, vests and AK-47s. When they were done, Khan's squad packed into a windowless white van tucked behind the building and rolled off. Fezcko and Maggs and Leslie followed in the Nissan.

The Mitsubishi truck was easy to find, parked beside a Toyota 4Runner in front of a two-story concrete house in a district that mixed residential and light manufacturing. The house had a strangely Art Deco look, lime-green with a white roof. It belonged in Miami, not Islamabad, though Fezcko had seen similar color schemes in Pakistan before. Splashy paint jobs grabbed attention from cracked ceilings and leaky pipes. The house seemed deserted, no lights or movement inside. There were walls along the property lot but none in front.

They rolled by without slowing. To the west, the city petered out. A mile down, Khan's van parked behind a tall brick warehouse. Khan stepped out, tapped a cigarette out of the flat silver case he carried. He lit up, dragged deeply, exhaled twin jets of smoke from his nostrils.

"You blow any harder you'll have liftoff," Maggs said.

"Let me guess," Khan said. "Marines smoke three cigarettes at once. Because one at a time wouldn't be manly enough."

Fezcko laughed. "Now you're getting it, Nawiz."

"So that's the place," Maggs said.

Khan nodded.

"Anybody watching it?"

"My men installed a PTD"—a presence tracking device, also known as a bug—"on the truck in Peshawar. Two of my men are monitoring it." Khan tilted his head toward the second floor of the warehouse, where a cigarette glowed behind a window. "The truck hasn't moved since they arrived yesterday."

"Who owns the house?" Fezcko said.

"Property records show it belongs to a family that lives in Karachi. We don't know if they're connected or if they even know it's being used."

Khan unrolled an oversized map, a street-by-street grid of the district. The map's corners rolled up, and Khan's men grabbed bricks to weigh it down.

"High-tech," Fezcko said.

"My Predators are in the shop." Khan circled the target house in red Magic Marker, and for fifteen minutes he walked his squad and Fezcko through the raid. The plan was simple, based on simple assumptions: that the doors of the house wouldn't be reinforced or booby-trapped, and that they would be facing at most four men inside. Khan's squad would handle the main assault, breaking through the front door and firing gas grenades to flush out the men. Fezcko's team would circle the house, wait for the jihadis to escape through the back door. If they didn't come out in sixty seconds, Fezcko and Maggs would go in the back.

When Khan was done, Fezcko pulled him aside.

"Too many guesses, Nawiz. If this gets ugly, we're underpowered. No radios. Layout's a mystery. This is how you get hurt."

Khan wrapped an arm around Fezcko's shoulders, put his face to the American's ear as if he planned to whisper a declaration of love eternal. "Are you walking, George? Taking your ball and going home? Tell me now so I don't waste more time. We have to do this before the sun comes up. Go on back to Langley. Another American hero."

In the cool night air, Fezcko felt himself flush. A cheap shot, sure, but there was truth behind it. His tour here was done. Khan's would never be over. He pushed Khan off, less than a shove but more than a friendly tap, and walked away. The soft, brown mud of the parking lot sucked at his boots, and he tried not to wonder whether the soil was a metaphor for the quagmire of the endless war on terror. He stood behind a corner of the warehouse and called Langley. "Anything yet?"

"The good news is the plane's in the air," Orton said. "The bad news is that the DDO's not happy. But I have a conditional okay."

"Conditional on what?"

"On your certifying that there's imminent risk of attack."

The message from Langley was clear: *Right back atcha. You want to play cowboy, go ahead, but don't expect us to cover your ass from eleven time zones away on an hour's notice.* "Can you say career ender?" Fezcko mumbled into the night.

"What?" Orton said.

"I said put it in writing. My name."

"George—"

"Whatever you have to do. Do it." Fezcko hung up, barely resisting the urge to smash the Iridium handset into the mud.

———

THE RAID WENT BAD before they even reached the house.

When Fezcko nodded to Khan, they pulled on their gas masks and grabbed their gear and rolled out east over the rough asphalt at eighty miles an hour. The house waited for them, still and silent.

Then the lights inside flickered on. Fezcko felt as if he'd been punched. He wondered if they should abort, but it wasn't his call. Anyway, letting the guys in the house get to the truck would be a very bad idea.

Khan's van swung off the road and stopped a few yards from the front door. The van doors opened, and Khan's squad jumped out. The two biggest men carried a knocker, a thick steel pipe with handles attached.

Khan's men sprinted for the house, Khan hobbling behind on his bad leg. Then the stuttering recoil of an automatic rifle sounded from the roof and the officer in front of Khan stumbled down.

"So much for surprising them," Fezcko murmured inside his mask. Adrenaline had burned through the last of the scotch in his blood. He felt alert and ready. Alive. He'd have a story for the grandkids at least. *I ever tell you about my last night in Pakistan?* Assuming he survived, of course. He slipped out of the Nissan, knelt behind the door. Rounds smashed into the window, and Fezcko was glad for the car's armor. *Where's the shooter? Find the shooter.* Based on the angle, the guy was on the right side of the roof, close to the corner.

Fezcko leaned around the door, raised his M-4, fired a four-shot burst at the front corner of the roof, trying to push the guy back. In the brief calm that followed, the wounded ISI agent pushed himself up and hopped toward the safety of the van.

Khan's men smashed the knocker into the front door. It shook but held. Fezcko wondered if it was reinforced.

Now the men inside the house were firing jihadi specials, long bursts on full automatic that tore through the night and shattered the front windows. The racket sounded impressive, but the shots were basically unaimed, and Khan's men stayed cool. Again they rammed the knocker into the door. This time it gave a couple of inches. Now they had a rhythm going, bang, bang, bang, a horizontal drumming—

The door twisted sideways and gave. Fezcko caught a brief glimpse of a green-painted room inside, before the lights went out. Khan and his men huddled around the front door.

Fezcko lifted his mask. "Stay here," he yelled to Leslie. "Watch the front door, make sure nobody gets out this way. Take out the shooter on the roof if you can."

"But—"

"Stay. That's an order." He looked at Maggs. "Back door!" he yelled. He lowered his mask and sprinted along the side of the house, keeping his head down. A window exploded over his head. He half dove, half fell, grunting as he banged an elbow against the side of the house. Clods of dirt covered the plastic face shield of his mask. Rounds thudded into the wall above him and shards of concrete cascaded down. *How many guys were in there, anyway? Did they have grenades?*

Fezcko grabbed for the CS grenade on his belt, pulled the pin. He lifted the handle and tossed it through the steel bars of the blown-out window above his head. If things got worse, they would have to forget taking anyone alive and just smoke the place. Maggs ran by, doubled over but somehow staying on his feet. Fezcko wiped off his face shield and scuttled after him.

Inside the house, men shouted at one another in Pashto. A man yelled *"Allahu akbar! Allahu akbar!"* and a long burst from an AK ripped through the night.

The left-rear corner of the house had a square notch cut into it, offering cover from the side and back walls. Fezcko hid in the notch and peeked around the corner. The rear of the house was unpainted and unfinished. The property sloped down from front to back, so the back door was a couple feet off the ground. There were no stairs. Anyone inside would have to jump out. But for now, the back door was closed. Beside the door, thick plastic sheeting covered a window frame. As Fezcko watched, rifle fire tore apart the plastic and a trail of CS gas leaked out. Someone coughed viciously, stopped, and then coughed again steadily.

Then the back door swung open. A man looked out. Not one of Khan's squad. A jihadi. He leaned forward, craned his head left and right, but Fezcko and Maggs were hidden in the notch and he didn't see them. He jumped out, stumbled, righted himself, and began to run across the back lot. He was barefoot and wore a jean jacket and sweatpants. No gun, as far as Fezcko could tell.

Maggs stepped out and raised his rifle. Fezcko pushed it aside.

"Alive." They sprinted after him.

The jihadi ran for a gate at the back-left corner of the wall. He tugged it frantically as Maggs and Fezcko closed on him. Locked. He tried to climb over, but he was big and slow. Maggs jumped up, tugged him down, threw him onto his stomach. Fezcko put a knee on his shoulders and pushed his head down into the dirt. Maggs pulled his arms behind his back and cuffed them. Then Maggs straddled his legs and cuffed his ankles together.

"Hog-tie?" Maggs said.

"Do it."

Maggs pulled off his belt, thick black leather, and ran it between the two sets of cuffs and tied it so the prisoner was on his belly with his legs and arms leashed together. Fezcko gave the guy a quick dose of CS in the eyes. He howled at them in Arabic and blinked furiously. Tears streamed down his cheek. Given enough time, he might figure out a way to slip off the belt. But even then he'd have his arms and legs cuffed. And with his eyes on fire, he'd have a tough time going anywhere.

SO THEY LEFT HIM in the corner, yelling, and ran to the house and took up positions by the back door. The door was swinging free. Fezcko grabbed it and pinned it against the outside wall and peeked inside. He couldn't see anyone, just construction materials, wood and bricks and cartons of tiles. Then the quiet scraping of a man trying not to cough. He seemed to be on the left side, hidden behind a half-finished wall.

Maggs sent a CS grenade skittering into the room like a duckpin bowling ball. White smoke filled the room like dry ice rolling onto the dance floor at a sweet sixteen, and the coughing started again, harder this time. Maggs pointed into the room and then at himself: *I'm going in. Cover me.* Fezcko held up three fingers, two, one. He swung his rifle into the doorway and fired three shots into the darkness.

Maggs levered himself up, jumped inside, ran for the coughing man. As he did, four shots, small-caliber, echoed inside the room. Maggs shouted in pain, the exclamation muffled through his mask, and thumped down.

Fezcko double-checked the seal on his mask, jumped inside. A round crashed into the wall beside him. *Damn it.* He dropped to the floor, tried to get oriented through the smoke. He could hear the guy coughing but not see him. Maddening.

He crawled across the room and lay next to Maggs, who pointed at his right leg. Blood puddled underneath the calf. Maggs made a snapping motion with his hands, indicating that the shot had broken his fibula, or his knee, Fezcko couldn't tell. Fezcko pointed toward the door—*Let's go; we'll wait him out*—but Maggs shook his head.

Then something dark flew out of the white smoke, twirling toward them—

Grenade—

Fezcko tried to squirm away—

And realized he was looking at a pistol. The gun clattered at his feet. He grabbed it, racked the slide, checked the clip. Empty.

A man stood up, wraithlike through the smoke, hands in the air. Maggs raised his M-4 and was about to shoot, but Fezcko pushed the gun down. The man coughed violently, his body shaking with each breath. He stepped toward them slowly, one hesitant foot after the next. He was surrendering. Either that or trying to get close enough to them to blow a suicide-bomb belt. But the belts were thick and obvious, and this guy was wearing only a T-shirt. So Fezcko let him get within five feet and then popped up and grabbed him.

He shoved the guy out the back door and wrestled him down to the pebbled lot behind the house. The guy landed face-first, and all the air went out of him. Fezcko grabbed his bushy black hair and ground his face into the rocky soil. Then he chopped the guy three times in the neck for what he'd done to Maggs. Also to make sure he wouldn't be any trouble. Though the guy didn't look like much of a threat. He was shaking, and a trail of spittle covered his thin black beard. And he was young, maybe seventeen. But he had been popping off at them with that snubnose.

Fezcko patted the guy down and flex-cuffed his ankles so he couldn't run and turned back to grab Maggs. But Maggs had already crawled out and was leaning against the side of the house on his good leg. The smoke inside was thinning, and the action had eased. No one was shooting, and the ISI men were yelling at one another in Punjabi as they cleared rooms on the second floor.

Fezcko pulled off his mask. "How's your leg?"

Maggs shrugged.

"No marine crap," Fezcko said. "If you're bleeding out, I'd like to know."

"I'll live. Lucky my running-back days are over," Maggs said. "And lucky he only had a .22. Shoulda let me shoot him."

"Next time."

In the corner of the lot, the second captive lay on his stomach. The guy's nose and mouth were foaming, and Fezcko wondered if he'd gone overboard on the CS. He pulled off Maggs's belt and dragged the prisoner to his feet. The guy's face was slack, his eyes wild and red. Fezcko mopped him up with a corner of his shirt. And realized he was looking at Jawaruddin bin Zari.

HE FROG-MARCHED bin Zari to Maggs.

"Got my belt."

"That's not all."

Maggs took another look at the slumped-over mess in the jean jacket. "Is that—"

"I believe it is."

Maggs raised a hand and they high-fived. Juvenile, maybe, but Fezcko didn't care. They'd just caught one of the most wanted men in Pakistan.

A breeze picked up, dragging tendrils of the CS in their direction. Fezcko caught a whiff and began to cough. After a few seconds the breeze faded, but he kept coughing, until the cough turned into a laugh. He sat down beside Maggs.

"What?" Maggs said finally.

"Been one hell of a going-away party, hasn't it?"

Ten minutes later, the smoke had cleared enough to allow Fezcko to enter the house without his mask. Six jihadis had been in the house when the raid started. Four were dead. Khan's squad had shot two on the ground floor, the others on the stairs. In turn, Khan had taken four casualties, one dead, three seriously wounded.

"Not how we planned it," Fezcko said to Khan.

"I should like to know who tipped them. Maybe our new friend can tell us."

"How will you explain what's happened to your squad?"

"Leave that to me. Just promise, if you get anything from these monkeys, you'll pass it on."

"Done."

THEY PUT HOODS ON the prisoners and threw them into the back of Khan's van and rolled into the dark. By sunrise they would be halfway to Faisalabad. Before noon the plane would be at the airport, and by sunset bin Zari and the second prisoner would be somewhere over the Black Sea. After that . . . they would be in God's hands.

God's, and the agency's.

PART ONE

1

A chauffeur.

That's what Jack Fisher was, when you came right down to it. A chauffeur.

He didn't mind, not too much.

When the new administration came in, he read the politics like everybody else. The rules were changing. The lawyers were putting their noses everywhere. Anybody too close to the black stuff might have a tough time. And he'd been close. Very, very close. And things had gotten messy at the end, for sure. But nobody could say they hadn't gotten the goods in the Midnight House.

So be it. Let the big brains weigh what they'd done, the pros and cons, the morality of it. Fisher didn't have an opinion. He wasn't a big brain. He slept fine. No bad dreams. Even if Rachel Callar had tried to give him some of hers. And look what had happened to her. Fisher didn't have much sympathy. As far as he was concerned, she was a coward who'd gotten what she deserved. But, Callar aside, after the freedom they'd had, he wasn't planning to ask some twenty-eight-year-old lawyer "Mother may I?" when he wanted to make a detainee stand up straight. Nope. Not interested.

So Fisher quit, took the deal they were offering, the extra severance and the enhanced pension. A lot of the guys in 673 had reached the same conclusion. Which was probably how Langley and the Pentagon wanted it.

Even with the pension and the severance, staying retired wasn't an option for Fisher. Not with two ex-wives sucking him dry. He thought about working security for a company like General Electric or Boeing. Would have taken him about two days to get a job. The multinationals couldn't get enough former CIA operatives.

But after twenty years of working for the government, Fisher didn't want to swap one bureaucracy for another. He wanted to work for himself for a change. And live in California, like he always said he would. He'd grown up in backwoods Maine, a crummy little town called Caribou, halfway between Canada and nowhere. Some of his friends liked the winters, hockey and skiing cross-country, but Fisher wasn't one of them. For as long as he could remember, he'd thought of California as the promised land. He printed up some fancy business cards: Jack B. Fisher, Fisher Security Consulting. Moved to Berkeley with wife number three. And rented an office in the Mission, a formerly down-and-out neighborhood in south San Francisco that was now as fat and happy as the rest of the city.

Fisher figured he'd start with freelance work for guys he knew at Kroll and Brinker. Jobs that were too small for them, too messy, that pushed the limits of the legal. He wouldn't mind those jobs. In fact, he'd like them. He took out ads on late-night local cable and posted on Craigslist and waited for the calls to come in. But with the economy lousy, business was slower than he'd expected. After a couple months, he wondered if he might wind up at GE after all.

Then this gig dropped into his lap. He was sitting in his office, trying to think of ways to get his name out, when his cell phone buzzed. He didn't recognize the caller ID. He answered anyway. He always answered. Couldn't afford to piss off any potential customers.

He'd probably work for his exes, if they'd hire him. Ex number one, anyway. Number two was a real piece of work.

"Jack? It's Vince. Heatley."

Fisher had gotten into a small-time poker game, mostly dollar-ante stud, with a bunch of retired FBI agents. Vince Heatley was a regular, former special-agent-in-charge of the San Jose office, now running security for George Lucas. Heatley was a solid guy, tight-assed for Fisher's taste but no worse than the average Fed. He usually lost a little but didn't seem to mind. Which probably meant he had money.

"Free for a drink?" Heatley said.

"If you're buying," Fisher said. And wished he hadn't. He sounded desperate.

"Meet me at the Four Seasons."

OVER A COUPLE OF BEERS, Heatley outlined the deal.

"Ever heard of Rajiv Jyoti?"

Fisher shook his head.

"He's a VC," Vince said.

"He's Vietnamese? Sounds Indian."

"You really are new in town. No, a venture capitalist. You know, they invest in tech companies, start-ups. Rajiv was early in Google. He's worth maybe a billion now, a billion-two. Depends on the day."

"Nice."

"He's looking for a new head of security. And he loves ex-govs. FBI, military. He'd probably get hard just at the idea of a CIA op."

"What happened to the guy who was working for him?"

"Gone to work for Larry Ellison. The CEO of a company called Oracle."

"I've heard of it," Fisher said, though he hadn't.

"Ellison's richer than Rajiv. Heck"—only Mormons and FBI agents said heck instead of hell, Fisher thought—"Ellison's richer than just about everybody. Point is, Rajiv's friends with George, and he's been bitching to George about needing a new guy. George asked me if I had any ideas. I thought of you. You seem solid, and I know your business—I mean, I know the economy isn't great."

"Personal security." Not exactly what Fisher had imagined when he quit Langley.

"You might like it. Someone like Lucas, these *Star Wars* fans get freaky about him. He really needs the protection. But Rajiv, outside San Francisco, nobody's even heard of him. Probably he's never gotten a threat in his life. He likes the idea of having somebody around, is all."

The job sounded less and less appealing. "What's he like?" Fisher said.

"These guys all have egos, but from what I see he's low-key, better than average. You wouldn't have to live at his house, anything like that."

Fisher sipped his beer. "I'll think about it."

"Before you say no, the money's great. Rajiv told George he was paying his old guy two and a quarter a year. Now he figures he's got to up that. I think for you, if he likes you, he might go to two-seven-five."

"Two hundred seventy-five thousand dollars." The rent on Fisher's office was five grand a month, every month. And the electricity, and the insurance, and the phone. And the alimony. Never forget the alimony. His exes sure didn't. Suddenly, working for a venture capitalist didn't seem so bad. "You think he'll like me?"

Heatley coughed into his hand. "Before I called you, I checked in with a couple guys I know at your shop."

"You backgrounded me? Guess I'm not surprised."

"Anyway, I don't think you should have any problems. So? Interested?"

"Maybe," Fisher said. "Long as I don't have to walk the dog."

AND HE DIDN'T. Jyoti was all right. Not exactly a bundle of laughs but quiet and even-tempered. He spent most of his time tapping away on his iPhone. Plus, the job came with a few perks. Billionaires hung together. Fisher went to a party on Ellison's yacht, *The Rising Sun*. Yacht wasn't even the right word. The thing was a cruise ship. Five hundred feet long. He met Arnold Schwarzenegger at a fund-raiser and sat with Mark Cuban at a Warriors game. Jyoti even leased him a car, a beautiful silver Lexus LX600h sport-utility, by far the nicest vehicle that Fisher had ever driven.

The work wasn't tough, either. So far, Jyoti had called Fisher at home only twice. Once on Halloween, when kids egged the gate of his mansion in Sea Cliff. The second time after his wife's poodle escaped. No kidnapping, no extortion, not even any stealing by the housekeepers.

Fisher's biggest complaint was that the job was too easy. He hated being bored. He figured he'd work for Jyoti another year or two, until he'd saved a couple hundred grand and the economy turned up, then go back out on his own. Or maybe work for Halliburton someplace like Nigeria, for a couple of years. Though his wife would have a fit. Not that it mattered. He'd never been too good at listening to women.

But Jyoti did have some quirks. The most annoying was his insistence that Fisher come to Sea Cliff every morning to pick him up for the drive to his office in Atherton, in Silicon Valley, twenty miles south of San Francisco. Jyoti said he liked the certainty of know-ing that Fisher would be outside his house every morning. He said the drive would give them a chance to talk over the day's security arrangements. Fisher knew the truth. The truth was that Jyoti liked having a former CIA agent drive him to work.

So Fisher was a chauffeur. And that didn't bother him.

Okay, maybe it did. A bit. But for two hundred seventy-five thou-sand dollars a year, plus medical and dental and a one-hundred-thousand-dollar hybrid, he would suck it up.

Sometimes he wondered what the guys from 673—his old unit—would make of his new gig. They knew he was in San Francisco. He'd even told a couple of them he was working for a billionaire, though he'd made the job more interesting than it really was, hinting he had gotten into high-stakes corporate espionage.

And here he was, at 7:05, parked outside Jyoti's front gate. Ten minutes early. Jyoti was precise. If he said 7:15, he meant 7:15. He expected the people who worked for him to be precise as well. Fisher didn't mind. He'd never needed much sleep. He got up at 5:15 and was out of the house by 6:00 to head over the Bay Bridge and into San Francisco. Assuming he didn't hit any accidents, he usually had time to stop for a smoothie and a coffee—no bacon and eggs for him, not anymore.

Of course, by the time he reached the mansion, the smoothie and the coffee had to be gone. Jyoti didn't like food in the car, especially not in the morning. He liked what he called a "sterile environment." No crumbs, no newspapers, no radio except NPR on low. Nothing except a bottle of chilled Fiji water in the center console. After eight months with the guy, Fisher had reached the considered opinion that Jyoti was kind of a puss. Still. Two hundred seventy-five thousand dollars.

IN FRONT OF THE GATE of Jyoti's mansion, Fisher cut the engine. "Global warming, Jack," Jyoti had said. "We must conserve where we can." Fisher had restrained himself from pointing out that Jyoti could save even more gas by trading in the six-thousand-pound Lexus for a smaller ride to work. Billionaires didn't appreciate backtalk.

Jyoti had one other quirk. He insisted that Fisher be armed. So Fisher dusted off his old Glock and got himself a concealed-weapons permit. Even Berkeley could hardly deny that a former CIA agent might have a legitimate need for protection.

Jyoti's mansion sat on two acres in Sea Cliff, probably the most exclusive neighborhood in San Francisco. It didn't look like much from the front, flat and wide and two stories high. But the property opened onto a priceless view of the Pacific and the Golden Gate Bridge. Though maybe priceless wasn't the right word. Fisher had checked the property records, found that the place was assessed for 21.5 million dollars. It had a squash court and a pool. The rooms were stuffed with high-end Indian art, bronze Buddhas and paintings of fierce-looking gods. Jyoti knew how to live, Fisher gave him that much. He knew how to stay married, too. His wife wasn't much of a looker, but he seemed devoted to her, never even checked out other women. Fisher would have to ask him the secret sometime.

Seven ten. Another cool San Francisco morning, fifty-five degrees with a touch of fog. By mid-afternoon the city would be in the low seventies, the Valley a bit warmer. Perfect for a hike or a mountain bike ride—Fisher had seen the first biker of the day go by just a couple of minutes before, headed up the hill toward Golden Gate Park, then turning out of sight.

Fisher took a quick check of the Lexus, making sure it was clean, no papers or receipts in sight, the leather in the front passenger seat showroom-new. Jyoti liked to sit up front with him, his nod to Fisher's equality. Fisher appreciated the gesture. He would have appreciated even more not driving the guy to work.

HIS CELL PHONE RANG. A blocked number. He looked at it, decided not to answer. He didn't want to be on the phone when Jyoti showed up. He sent the call to voice mail and tucked the phone away.

A few seconds later, it rang again.

Blocked again. Strange. He flipped the phone open. "Hello."

"Jack." The voice was unfamiliar, eerily high-pitched. Fisher wondered if they had a lousy connection or if the guy was disguising his voice. "Jack Fisher."

"Who's this?"

Silence.

Fisher hung up. He looked at his phone irritably, as though it were a misbehaving dog.

For the third time, the phone rang.

"Jack Fisher?"

Again the unnatural voice. Fisher reflexively slid his hand toward his shoulder holster, then realized he couldn't hold the phone and grab the pistol. He stayed with the phone.

"Who am I speaking with?"

"Look to your right. At the house."

Fisher leaned right, looked out the passenger-side window. Nothing. Suddenly he knew he was in trouble. *Gun. Now.*

He dropped the phone on the passenger seat. He reached his right hand across his body, trying for his shoulder holster—

And a tap on the driver's-side window twisted him back.

No.

A pistol. With a silencer screwed to the barrel. A gloved hand held the gun and—

He'd fallen for it. Look right. He should have looked left, why hadn't he looked left—he couldn't die like this, it was impossible, not now, not as a goddamn *chauffeur*—

He didn't hear the bullet, and he didn't see it, of course. But he felt it, a rush of fire in his lungs. His training told him he had to go for his pistol. The pistol was his only hope. But the pain was too much, especially when a second bullet joined the first, this one on the left side of his chest, tearing a hole in his aorta. Suddenly Fisher felt an agony he could never have imagined, his heart clutching helplessly, unable to pump, crying its bitterness with each half-finished beat.

Fisher screamed but found that the sound he made wasn't a scream at all, merely a whimper from high in his throat. His head flopped forward. His tongue lolled out. The world in front of the windshield raced away from him as if he'd somehow put the car—no, himself—in reverse at a million miles an hour.

The door to the Lexus was pulled open. Fisher sagged sideways in the seat. Already the pain in his chest was fading. But he wasn't dying quickly enough for whoever was holding the gun. Fisher felt the touch of the silencer against his temple. He turned his head, tried to pull it away, but the pistol followed him.

He knew now he would die. He wasn't even afraid, too far gone for that. In the fading twilight of his consciousness, he understood he was being mocked. The shooter wanted him to know he was dying as helplessly as a lobster boiling in a too-small pot. Even so, Fisher wished he could understand why death had found him this way, wished someone would tell him. And so he opened his mouth and asked, or tried to ask, or imagined asking—

The third shot tore open his skull and scattered his brains over the Lexus's smooth leather. The shooter looked down, making sure that Fisher was dead. Unscrewed the silencer and tucked away the pistol. Looked up and down the empty street. Noticed the phone on the passenger seat and, the only unplanned moment in the whole operation, reached across Fisher's body and grabbed it. Switched it off so it couldn't be traced. Closed the door of the Lexus and smoothly walked away, to the mountain bike propped against a utility pole a half block down. Start to finish, including all three phone calls, the murder took barely a minute.

AT 7:15 PRECISELY, Rajiv Jyoti walked out of his front gate, tapping away on his iPhone. He reached for the door. Then he looked at Fisher. And screamed and dropped his phone and trotted shakily around the Lexus. He opened the door carefully, even in his distress wanting to be sure that none of Fisher's blood wound up on his six-hundred-dollar hand-tailored pants.

Jyoti wasn't a doctor, but he could see that Fisher was beyond help. He looked at the body and up and down the empty street, wondering why no one had heard the shots, wondering if whoever had killed Fisher would be coming back for him, wondering if he had been the real target. The seconds stretched on and still Jyoti stood motionless, until the drip of blood on the pavement shocked him to life. He ran back into his front yard, slammed the gate shut, and ran into the house.

Then, finally, he dialed 911.

2

The trail wasn't much, faded white chevrons every hundred yards, their paint hardly visible in the cloud-beaten light. They beckoned John Wells up the mountain halfheartedly, with New England reserve. Come or don't, it's all the same to us, they said. Their lack of enthusiasm didn't bother Wells. He stalked upward, eating ground with long strides, ignoring the mud sucking at his heels. A clot of clouds covered the sky, and a moist wind blew from the north, promising rain or even snow.

Wells hadn't dressed for snow. He had deliberately left himself exposed. He wore jeans, Doc Martens, a T-shirt, a light wool sweater. Wool socks were his only concession to the weather. He didn't mind being cold. In fact, he wanted to be cold. But he didn't want to lose a toe to frostbite.

Wells wasn't properly equipped, either. He was thinking about camping overnight, but he hadn't brought a sleeping bag or tent, only a cotton sleep sack and a foil blanket. No stove, only a bag of dried fruit and PowerBars. No GPS, only a torn map, a compass, and a penlight. His gear fit easily into his blue daypack.

And no gun. Not a sleek black Beretta, not an old pearl-handled Smith & Wesson, not an M-16 or a 12-gauge. No knife, either. No weapons of any kind. His Glock and Makarov were tucked away in a lockbox at his cabin. Since coming to New Hampshire six months before, he'd touched them only twice, to clean them.

For twenty years, Wells had surrounded himself with guns. He'd put them to use in Afghanistan and Chechnya and China and Russia, Atlanta and New York and Washington. Now he was trying to imagine life as a civilian.

But he had to admit that more and more he found himself missing the feel of the pistols in his hands, their heft and balance, especially his favorite, the Makarov, an undeniably lousy gun but one that had seen him through any number of tight spots. He understood now why ex-smokers said they missed the physical act of smoking, of flicking lighter to cigarette, as much as the nicotine itself.

WELLS WASN'T ALONE on the trail. Trotting three steps ahead was his new companion. Tonka, a lean, agile dog, with a long snout and a thick brown coat. She banged her bushy tail against tree trunks as she climbed, sending Wells a single message: let's go, let's go, let's go. She was part husky, part shepherd. In his too-thin sweater, Wells might have a rough night if the snow came down. Tonka would be fine.

Wells had rescued her from a shelter in Conway three months before, a couple of days before she was scheduled to be put down. She took a shine to him immediately, jumped onto the bench beside him and nuzzled against his shoulder. Wells had always gotten along with animals. People, not so much.

"Found her tied to the fence outside, no name tag, no chip," the woman at the shelter said.

"Chip?"

"A lot of them have ID microchips implanted now, under the skin.

That way we can trace them to their owners even without their tags. This little lady, she didn't have a chip."

"That happen a lot? The abandoning, I mean."

"More than you'd think. 'Specially now. People have to choose between their kids and their dog, dog's gonna lose. You can see she's been cared for, she's not afraid of people. She's a good girl. I don't think they, the owners, wanted to do this. Though who knows?"

"I'll take her," Wells said.

"Just like that?"

"Why not?"

"Dog's a commitment. Ever owned one before?"

"Growing up."

"You live around here?"

"Berlin." Berlin was about fifty miles north of Conway. "Moved in a couple months back."

"Do you travel a lot?"

"Once in a while," Wells said.

"And you're sure you'll be able to take care of her, Mr. Cant?"

Wells's new driver's license and credit cards identified him as Clarkson Cant. Every time he had to use them, Wells imagined Ellis Shafer smirking. Shafer, his sort-of boss at the agency, a man with the sense of humor of a not-so-naughty ten-year-old. Wells had almost demanded a less ridiculous alias before deciding not to give Shafer the satisfaction.

"Yes," Wells said evenly. He refrained from pointing out that the dog would surely choose him, whatever his flaws, over the alternative.

The woman looked Wells over, considering his patched-up jeans, shaggy hair, and half-grown beard. Finally she nodded. "Okay. Fill out the papers, pay the fee, she's yours."

Wells and the dog had gotten along fine ever since. She'd been a boon companion during the winter, which had been harsh even by the standards of northern New Hampshire. For two straight weeks in February the temperature stayed below zero, a lung-burning, skin-sloughing cold that kept Wells inside except for runs to the grocery store and stretches of wood chopping. Wells loved working the ax. The sky was bright blue and the air bone-dry, and the logs split easily under the blade. Tonka, no dummy, watched from inside the cabin. He couldn't pretend he was entirely alone. Trucks rumbled distantly and snowmobiles whined along the creek trail. But Wells didn't mind. In fact, he liked being reminded that the world was still there, with or without him.

A YEAR BEFORE, Jennifer Exley, Wells's fiancée, had almost died in an assassination attempt aimed at Wells. In the aftermath, she'd demanded that he quit the agency. Wells couldn't. But he couldn't accept that he'd lost Exley, either. So he'd fled Washington, fled her. Though even Shafer, never known for his tact, was too polite to use that word.

For months he backpacked through Europe and Asia, bunking in hostels alongside students half his age. Then he rented a cabin in southwest Montana, where he'd grown up. But after a week, he left. Heather and Evan, his ex-wife and son, lived in Missoula with Heather's second husband. Their proximity disturbed him. He wanted to make amends with Evan, at least announce his presence to the boy. Take him out for pizza. But the simple act of picking up the phone, asking to speak to his son, left him shaking his head.

Years before, when he'd last talked to Heather, she'd told him she wouldn't let him parachute in and then disappear again. At the time,

Wells understood. The agency had been on the verge of declaring him a terrorist. These days no one would question his loyalty to the United States. His judgment maybe, but not his loyalty. But he knew Heather's feelings hadn't changed. Quit the job, she would tell him. Come back to earth and then we'll talk. Just as Exley had.

Only Wells couldn't quit. He wished he could tell himself that his sense of duty and honor wouldn't let him. And those fine words were part of the reason. But only part. In truth, he feared being bored. Feared, he supposed, that one day people would ask him, "Didn't you used to be John Wells?"

No, he couldn't quit. But he wasn't ready to work again—not yet, anyway. So no to Exley, no to Heather, no to Evan. He would be alone.

He left Montana, headed east, to the Presidential Mountains of New Hampshire. Wells remembered his surprise when, as a freshman at Dartmouth, he'd first seen the Presidentials. He'd imagined that mountains in the East were hummocks. But Mount Washington towered nearly a mile over the valley to its east. And its weather was fierce. The observatory at its peak had measured the highest wind ever recorded, 231 miles an hour. If the Sawtooth Mountains were out, the Presidentials would do.

Wells rented a two-room cabin on a gravel road in Berlin, a little town just north of Mount Washington. He had twelve acres to himself and a woodstove for heat. The place also came with DirecTV, and Wells had to admit that he watched more television than he'd planned. Still, he plowed through a couple books a week, mainly biographies. Jackson, Lincoln, Rockefeller, Churchill, great men facing great obstacles. War, slavery, depressions global and personal. No women, and no religion. Not the Bible, not the New Testament, not the Quran. In his cabin, alone, he wanted the tangible consolations of the world as it was, not the uncertain promises of paradise.

For the same reason, he worked out incessantly. He turned the cabin's second room into a miniature gym. Every weekday afternoon he turned on the television—okay, he'd admit it, he watched *General Hospital* and then *Oprah*; he wasn't proud of himself, but the truth was the truth—and spent an hour running and an hour lifting. On Saturdays, before the winter got too nasty, he hiked Mount Washington, carrying a frame pack loaded with twenty-pound bags of dog food. In the winter he substituted a three-hour climb on the treadmill, eight thousand vertical feet.

A mental renaissance came along with the physical. In his first months without Exley, he'd awoken more than once certain that she was beside him. When he reached for her and didn't find her, his mind refused to accept her absence. He told himself that his fingers were lying, that she really was with him. As though he were an amputee insisting on the presence of a lost arm or leg. Then he would wake fully and feel the same emptiness he'd felt when he'd learned his mother had died and been buried while he was eight thousand miles away.

Slowly, though, his dislocation and loneliness faded. He still missed Exley badly, but part of him was happy that he was no longer hurting her. She'd made him choose, her or the job, and he'd chosen. One day, if they were meant to be, they would be.

As the days got longer and the worst of the winter faded, Wells felt his thirst for action returning. Hard as the job had been, it had given him the chance to see worlds most people couldn't even imagine. Years before, during the worst sickness of his life, he'd had a dream—a vision, really—that the guns he carried were part of his body. He couldn't put them down even at the cost of losing his chance at Heaven. Wells was no fan of tarot cards or psychics, but he had never forgotten that dream, or doubted its truth. He couldn't stay in

New Hampshire forever. Soon enough, the call would come, and he'd have to answer.

But for now he was free. And so this morning, with clouds hiding the sun and the wind whistling from the north, he had decided to brace himself with his first big hike of the new year. He hedged his bets slightly, choosing to go up Mount Adams, slightly lower and easier than Mount Washington. He packed his daypack and offered Tonka two cans of her favorite high-protein food. She knew where they were going without being told. When he opened the cabin door, she headed straight for his Subaru WRX, her tail wagging wildly. Then she stood against the front door and tried to open it herself.

NOW HE WAS CLOSING on the peak of Mount Adams, scrambling over trees that the winter's winds had torn down. He hopped over an iced-over stream and landed in a thick patch of muddy snow that dirtied his jeans. As he reached the final stretch, a cold drizzle began, matting down his unkempt hair. Tonka had changed her mind. She looked up at him, asking wordlessly why he'd brought her out in such weather.

"You wanted to come. I warned you."

The last half mile the trail turned to scree, loose rocks and boulders. Wells pulled his gloves from his pack and climbed hand over hand. He was cold now, cold through and through, and he loved the gray sky above and gray rock below, loved everything around him. He was free. If he slipped and broke a leg on this mountain, if the weather turned ugly and somehow he died up here, the earth wouldn't care. He was in a mortal battle, and yet he didn't have to hurt anyone to win. He needed only to survive.

His legs chilled and lungs aching, he reached the summit and surveyed the mountains around him. To the south, the mass of Mount

Washington dominated. To the north, the range fell off sharply, and the narrow path of a river, probably the Upper Ammonoosuc, was just visible through the brown bark below. The trees had not yet budded for spring, and the valleys beneath Wells were almost monochrome, a mix of gray and white and flat dark green from the pines and firs, the only flashes of color coming from the cars and trucks rolling on Highway 2.

Tonka bumped against his legs and whined quietly, telling him that he might be enjoying this communion with nature, but she was cold and wet and wanted off the mountain.

"I thought you were tougher than this, bud," he said. "You're the one with the fur coat."

He reached into his jacket for a PowerBar, gave half to her, swallowed the other half in two ungraceful bites. Still the dog's tail drooped.

"All right," he said. "I get it."

Wells took a final survey of the land. And realized he wasn't alone. Several paths climbed Mount Adams. Wells had come up the west face, the main trail for day hikers. But the mountain could also be reached from the northeast or the south, on a path that was part of the Appalachian Trail. A hiker had just popped out from a ridge on the northeast side of the mountain, a couple of hundred yards away.

"Just a sec," Wells said to Tonka. "Let's see."

He was surprised anyone else had braved the weather, more surprised when the hiker turned out to be a woman. She was much better equipped than he was. She carried a solid frame pack with a tent attached and wore a red jacket and jeans and boots and a floppy hat to keep the rain away. She was tall and solidly built and moved confidently up the mountain. When she got close, she waved and gave him a friendly gap-toothed smile. He wouldn't have guessed a woman

THE MIDNIGHT HOUSE | 43

alone up here would be so confident meeting a strange man and a strange dog. Then he saw the pistol holstered on her hip, half hidden under her jacket.

"Nice day for a hike," he said.

"Isn't it, though?"

"Least you dressed for it," Wells said. "I was gonna stay out overnight, but the dog says no."

"You blame the dog?"

"For everything."

She reached out a hand and they shook through the gloves. "I'm Anne."

"John," he said, using his real name for the first time in months. He nodded to the dog. "This is Tonka."

She smiled again. Despite the frigid rain, Wells felt a sudden warmth in his groin. He kept holding her hand until finally she let go. "Hi, Anne."

"What's a nice flatlander like you doing in a place like this?"

"Is it that obvious?"

"You have all your teeth."

"Is that joke allowed?"

"For me."

"I've been living in Berlin the last few months, but I'm from D.C."

"And came to New Hampshire for the winter. Bold. Stupid, but bold."

"I got a great deal on a cabin. Frostbite included."

"I'll bet."

She smiled, and Wells realized he wanted very badly to keep the conversation going. "How about you?" he said. "I take it you're a native."

"Conway." Conway was about forty miles south of Berlin. "I like being up here when it's quiet. No city slickers to spoil the view."

Wells nodded at her pistol. "Looks to me you could clear the trail whenever you wanted."

"I don't shoot anyone who doesn't deserve it."

"Fortunately, that leaves plenty of targets."

"My ex-husband, for one."

Now they were flirting, Wells thought. A deliberate mention of an ex-husband had to count as flirting. Though he wasn't totally sure. He hadn't flirted in a long time. Tonka let out a growl that turned into a deep bark, and he decided to quit while he was ahead. "She has better sense than I do," he said. "We should get going."

"Sure."

"Maybe I could take you for a hike sometime."

She laughed.

"I'm sorry. Too cheesy?"

"Much, much too cheesy. How about this? I had a reservation tonight at a cabin past Mount Washington. But the weather's so crummy I might change my mind. You know Fagin's Pub?"

"In Berlin."

"None other. I might stop by tonight."

"You might."

"I might. You should, too."

"I'll do that," Wells said. "On one condition."

"What's that?"

"You leave your gun at home."

3

The Accord was hidden behind a Silverado. It backed out fast, its driver as anxious to get home as everyone else, and Mike Wyly almost bashed it. He jammed his brakes and horn, and jolted to a stop a foot from its trunk. Its driver waved, a halfhearted apology, and went back to her cell phone. Wyly had half a mind to give her a talking-to, but he'd been speeding, too. And she was cute.

Instead, he waved back and followed her down the ramps of the giant employee parking garage at Universal Studios, six levels of concrete, thousands of cars. He wondered if he'd ever get a pass to park on the lot. These endless left turns were a pain. Especially in a '67 Mustang convertible without power steering.

Life was strange. If anyone had told Wyly two years ago that he'd be worrying about parking passes, he would have . . . well, he didn't know what he would have done. Probably just laughed. Back then he'd been in the middle of the most secret war the United States had ever fought. Now he was wondering if he had enough points to join the Screen Actors Guild.

Wyly eased out of the garage and onto Lankershim. He fired a stream of dip-darkened spit into the Coke bottle in the passenger seat and plugged his iPod into the Mustang's radio, an aftermarket addition, the only part of the car that wasn't genuine Ford. The smooth twang of Brooks & Dunn poured from the backseat, and Wyly looked into the warm night sky. Another day done. Eight thirty-eight p.m., according to the iPod. Twelve hours' work. With the overtime he'd made close to five hundred, pretax. Not bad.

When Wyly quit the army, he figured on staying in North Carolina, his home state. Working security in Charlotte. Then his wife, Caitlin, told him they were moving to Los Angeles. She'd always wanted to be an actress. She was twenty-four now, and if she waited any longer, she'd be too old.

Caitlin certainly had the looks. She'd been in a "Girls of the ACC" spread in *Playboy* five years before. But she couldn't act her way out of a paper bag. Wyly had seen her try. He told her she would miss her family and friends; she could act in Charlotte.

No dice. She told him she'd divorce him if he didn't "support her dream, help her reach her potentialities." He'd always been "an avatar of failure" for her, she said. *"Potentialities"? "Avatar"?* Wyly didn't even know what an avatar was, and he was sure Caitlin didn't, either. He could always tell when she'd been talking to her sorority sisters.

He should have let the marriage come to its inevitable sorry end right then. He'd hardly seen her for two years. Still, he wasn't ready to give up. And he figured he could work security in Los Angeles as easy as Charlotte. They could live by the ocean. He'd learn how to surf. So off to California they went.

But Los Angeles was more expensive than either of them figured. They got stuck renting in Chatsworth, the northwest corner of the Valley, a five-room house for $1,625 a month. Robbery. As for surfing, the traffic meant that they were an hour from the beach, on a good day.

To nobody's surprise but her own, Caitlin didn't land any gigs. To help pay the rent, she started waitressing at a restaurant called the Smoke House, by the Warner Bros. studio lot. A month later, barely three months after they moved to California, she told Wyly she was leaving. She'd met her soul mate. He made the mistake of asking *Who is he?* and got the dude's résumé in return. Bart Gruber. He made the kind of movies that went right to the video store. Gruber had convinced Caitlin her career would take off if she would let the world peek at her C cups in his next movie, *The Smartest Girls in the Room,* something about lesbian scam artists. Even worse, Caitlin had convinced herself she was in love with him. Probably the best acting she'd ever done.

Wyly was through arguing. Thank God she hadn't listened when he told her, that first year together, that they should have kids right away. He dragged her suitcases out of the bedroom closet.

"Careful," Caitlin said, when he started tossing her clothes onto the bed. "A lot of that stuff is new."

"Now I know where your money's been going."

"Mike. Aren't you even going to fight for me?"

A single tear ran down her cheek. Typical. Now that she was an actress, she wanted some drama. He almost laughed. "Fight for you. No."

"Because you never loved me."

"No, Cate, I loved you, best I could considering we've hardly seen each other. I don't think you ever loved me. And I'm not inclined to take on a fight I'm bound to lose. But I do feel a tiny bit bad for you. You oughta marry a doctor back home, like Cindy and Sandy"—her favorite sorority sisters. "Put those tits to use before it's too late. You're gonna whore, get yourself paid."

"Michael Steven Wyly. I won't let you speak to me that way." She hauled off and slapped him across the face. He let her. If he grabbed back, she'd probably call 911. He did not need a domestic violence charge on his back.

"Listen to me here," he said. "I know you don't think so, but I'm looking out for you. You wind up staying out here too long, these guys like Geller—"

"His name's Gruber—"

"They're gonna use you up. Go home while you still have it."

"I love California."

"Love. Sure. That word again. You wouldn't know love if it gave you a hundred bucks to suck it off." He guessed he was angrier than he knew. He'd never said anything like that to her before.

She tossed back her hair and tried to slap him again. "You're a pig, Michael. Bart says you're a Fascist, just like the Germans."

Wyly felt his heart race. For a few seconds they were both quiet, and then he spoke, slowly, carefully. "This guy I've never met says I'm a *what*? Like the *who*?"

"He says you and your unit, what you did to those detainees, it was criminal and you should be in jail—"

Wyly took a breath, stepped away from her so he wouldn't do something he'd regret. They were in deep waters here. "What did you tell him about me, Caitlin? You know I don't talk about that." Not now, and not ever, Wyly didn't add. He didn't talk about it, and he didn't think about it. Different guys had different ways of handling it. He'd decided as soon as he got out that the best way for him would be just to forget it. That plan was working pretty well so far.

"I said you were on an interrogation unit. That's all." She sounded defensive. Then her face hardened. "I didn't have to tell him anything else. He says everybody knows what you did. He says we broke the Geneva convention—"

"You know what the Geneva convention is, Cate? You have any idea?"

"He says you embarrassed the whole country—"

Ugly words went through Wyly's mind, slurs about this guy Bart, but he didn't say them. He wouldn't give her the satisfaction. He summoned his Ranger discipline and kept his voice even.

"He doesn't know what it was like over there, and you don't, either."

"Just like Apu Grab, Bart says."

"You mean Abu Ghraib? You don't have a clue."

"I know you think I'm stupid, but I have a college degree, Michael. Unlike you."

"Physical therapy is not a college degree. Even if NC State says it is. Tell your boyfriend we were interrogating top level terrorists. The guys who pulled the strings. Not random Iraqi farmers who got caught in raids."

"Just answer me one thing. If you're so proud of what you did, how come you never talk about it? How come you always change the subject?"

And despite himself, Wyly was carried back to the barracks in Poland. He pushed the images out of his mind. Past was past. "I'm a soldier, Cate. I did what they told me, my superior officers. That's how it works."

"Bart said you'd say that. You were the muscle, you followed orders. He said that's an old story."

Wyly stepped toward her, raised his hand high. Then he turned away, grabbed a T-shirt and shorts and his running shoes. Los Angeles had a chain of gyms called 24 Hour Fitness. He'd joined a couple of weeks back. If he wasn't going to get arrested for assault, he needed to get out of this house.

———

HE RAN SEVENTEEN MILES that night, stayed on the treadmill until 2 a.m. When he got home, Caitlin was gone. A month later they finalized the divorce, a quick no-fault that split their assets—the two cars and the four thousand dollars in their savings account—right down the middle. Wyly celebrated by going to Hollywood and going home with the first girl drunk enough to say yes. She didn't have Caitlin's body, but she was a much better lay.

A week later, he saw a posting on a military-only chat board looking for ex-soldiers to do stunts on a television show. He thought maybe the post was a scam, but he applied anyway. It was real. And he got the job.

Now he was working regularly. Making decent money. Enough to pay the rent on the house and have a few bucks left over for this Mustang. Nothing fancy, a gunmetal-gray convertible with the six-cylinder engine. He would have liked a V-8, but he couldn't make the math work. The odometer on this one read eighty-five thousand miles, which probably meant one hundred eighty-five thousand. It needed a little bit of work, had some rust on the right quarter panel, but nothing major.

He got a loan from the friendly bankers at Wells Fargo and picked it up for eleven-five. After a couple of weekends, he had it running smooth. Of course, it was no good for anything longer than a trip to the beach. These old engines overheated in a hurry, and the six-cylinder was underpowered by modern standards. He needed a week to go zero to sixty. But he could run it back and forth to work, and that was all he wanted.

Yeah, he couldn't complain. California was all right. He thought about Caitlin less than he would have expected. A couple of weeks back he'd seen her at a club in Burbank, looking pissed, standing with another girl who could have been her twin. No guys around. He wondered if Gruber had dumped her already. He'd ducked out before she saw him, blown the fifteen-dollar cover. He had nothing to say to her.

Once in a while he remembered what Caitlin had said to him on their last night together. No, he couldn't say he was proud of everything 673 had done. Especially at the end. But he was done now. He lived in the Valley and played drill sergeant to overpaid actors, none of whom cared about his time in the army. If they asked, he said, "Yeah, I was a Ranger." People in Hollywood preferred to talk about themselves anyway, so most of the time he didn't need to say anything else. On those rare occasions when somebody pushed him for details, he'd say, "I wish I could tell you. But it's all classified. Maybe in fifty years."

WYLY STOPPED at an In-N-Out Burger, thinking he'd refuel, then head out to one of the bars near his house, have a beer, watch the end of the Lakers game. While he was waiting to order, he changed his mind. He was eating too much junk these days. He'd noticed this morning that he'd gained a couple of pounds. Out here, that mattered. Being an ex-soldier wasn't enough. He needed to look the part.

He pulled out of line, headed home. He had a date tomorrow night, a nurse he'd picked up at a Starbucks the week before. Girls out here were easy. He was pretty sure that if he paid for dinner and half listened to whatever she told him, they'd wind up back at her place. Playing doctor. Though he better not make that joke. He'd tried it with another nurse a month back. She hadn't laughed.

At the Safeway on De Soto, he picked up a premade salad and

low-fat turkey. The guys he'd served with would be laughing. So be it. If everything went right, in a year or two he might start getting regular acting gigs. He could deal with a few tasteless dinners.

Chatsworth was a dull middle-class neighborhood, built in the 1960s and 1970s as Los Angeles expanded into the northern end of the Valley. Houses here were packed tightly on small lots, separated by walls or hedges for privacy. Wyly made a left onto Lassen, a right onto Owensmouth, another left and right, the streets getting shorter and shorter, and finally swung into his driveway. The place had two narrow bedrooms, a galley kitchen, and a living room that barely fit a couch and a coffee table. Wyly didn't mind. After living for years in army housing, and then that barracks in Poland, he was just glad to have a place of his own.

He caught the very end of the Lakers game, then flipped on ESPN. At about 11:30, he was watching *SportsCenter*, nursing a Corona Light, and slapping mustard on the low-fat turkey to make it go down easier, when the doorbell rang.

"Yeah," Wyly yelled. "Who's there?"

"Domino's."

Wyly hadn't ordered any pizza. A month before, Pizza Hut made the same mistake. Maybe someone was pranking him. But as a prank, ordering pizza for someone was lame. The Pizza Hut guy left, no argument, when Wyly said he hadn't ordered it.

"Not mine," he said. He pulled open the door, saw the Domino's box—

And then his stomach was torn in half. The pain was worse than the worst punch he'd ever taken, not just his skin or his abs but tearing deep into his gut.

"Oh, God," he said. He dropped his beer and stumbled backward. His upper body jackknifed, closed on itself, as he instinctively tried to protect the wound. He put his right hand to his belly and felt blood, his own blood, trickling through his fingers. Barely a second had passed. Wyly didn't understand exactly what was happening, much less *why* it was happening, but he knew he was in trouble.

Wyly tried to raise his arm to defend himself, though he felt the power leaving his legs. In a few seconds, he'd be on the floor—

"No—" he said. "Ple—"

He didn't even get to beg. The second shot caught him higher up, breaking two ribs and tearing into his right lung. His muscles collapsed. He went down hard, no acting job, no slow-motion fall into the beer puddling on the clean wood floor. No noise from the shots. *A silencer.* The gun, the pistol, hidden under the Domino's box. Wyly got that much but no more. He understood the how, but not the who or the why. Wyly tried to raise his head and look at the shooter, the killer, since he knew now that he was dying, would be dead very soon.

Then the pistol spoke its lethal whisper twice more. Wyly twitched and died. Behind him, the ESPN anchors introduced *SportsCenter*'s top ten plays of the day.

THE SHOOTER SLIPPED the pistol, silencer still attached, into the empty pizza box, and pulled the door shut and walked to the Toyota in the driveway and slipped inside. And the car rolled out and disappeared into the blurry Los Angeles night.

4

BERLIN, NEW HAMPSHIRE

D*on't take your guns to town. . . ."*
Wells was pulling himself up a steep rock face, when Johnny Cash's voice erupted from his cell phone. The dream left him, and he found himself in his cabin. He couldn't remember why he'd been climbing, or what waited for him at the peak. He squeezed his eyes, hoping to recover the mountain. But the phone kept ringing—or, more accurately, singing—until Wells swept an arm across the bed-side table and grabbed it.

"Hello." The word stuck in his throat. His tongue seemed glued to the roof of his mouth. His pulse hammered in his skull, a met-ronome gone mad. He wondered how much he'd drunk the night before. Three beers, a couple shots. Hadn't seemed like all that much. He supposed he wasn't used to drinking.

"I wake you?" Shafer sounded amused. "Long night, John?"

Wells lifted his head, an inch at a time, peeked at the clock by the bed: 12:15. He hadn't slept past noon in at least twenty years. Then he remembered the martini. The martini had done him in. Anne had ordered it for him at last call, over his protests. *Shaken not stirred,* she'd told the bartender. Then she'd winked at him. He'd wanted to be irri-tated, but the truth was he'd been flattered. He'd told her who he was two beers before. She was twenty-nine, a cop in Conway, divorced two years before and remaking her life. She seemed amused that he'd wound up in a cabin in New Hampshire.

"Shouldn't you be in the other Berlin? Chasing Russians?"

"The cold war's over, sweetheart." *Sweetheart* said like a 1950s movie star.

"Germans, then. Back in high school, I wanted to go to Berlin, see the Love Parade."

"That big rave?"

"That big rave. I read about it, and it sounded like the coolest thing ever. Remember, I was sixteen. Instead, I got stupid, fell in love, married Frank Poynter, and now look at me. Stuck in a bar with a guy pretending to be John Wells."

"I *am* John Wells. At least I think I am."

"Sure you are. I bet you run this scam all the time." She laughed and kissed him. Even before the martini, they both knew she was going back to the cabin.

"WHAT DO YOU WANT, ELLIS?" But he knew, without knowing, what Shafer wanted. This call was overdue. He ignored the jackhammer in his skull and sat up. Anne reached out, ran a hand down his back.

"I want you," Shafer said. "Your presence is requested down here."

"Mmmph."

"Soon as possible. If you can tear yourself away from your social obligations."

Wells didn't bother asking how Shafer had guessed he wasn't alone. "Unless you want to send a plane, it's going to be tomorrow," he said. "That too late?"

"Tomorrow's fine."

Wells hung up. His first thought, he couldn't help himself: *Something wrong with Exley?* But Shafer would have told him. This was business.

Anne slid her hand over his chest.

"I have to go," he said.

She ignored his objection and pushed him down.

When they were done, they lay still for a minute. She got up before he did and reached for the rainbow-striped panties bunched under the bed beside his jeans. Fifteen minutes later, she stood at the door to the cabin and pressed a folded-up piece of notebook paper into his hand before she left. "My e-mail address," she said. "You're leaving town?"

"Looks that way."

"Gonna do some super-secret stuff?"

"Only kind of stuff I do," Wells said, trying to roll with her.

"All right, then."

"All right." Wells tucked the paper into his pocket. "Look, Anne, you probably won't believe it, but I don't do this kind of thing very often. This was my first time in a while—"

"No, I believe it. You were a little rusty last night."

He flushed. She laughed. "Don't worry. Much better this morning, especially for a man your age—"

"Ouch," Wells said.

"What I'm trying to say is, I had fun. Give me your number, maybe I'll take a trip to D.C. See the monuments. Isn't that what tourists do down there?"

He found a pen, scribbled his cell number. "There's no name on it."

"Of course there isn't."

She kissed him on the lips, ran a hand through his hair, walked away in her battered hiking boots, her blue jeans cupping her ass.

Wells didn't expect to see her again, but he found himself waving as she got into her Silverado and rolled off. She had style.

TONKA DIDN'T LIKE WATCHING him pack. She tugged at his jeans as he filled his duffel bag. He would have to bring her to Langley, he realized. He didn't know how long he'd be gone, and he could hardly take her back to the pound. He grabbed her bowls, her treats and toys, and threw them in the Subaru beside his bag.

He took one final look around the cabin. He didn't feel overly sentimental. It had served its purpose, given him a place to hide and to heal. From the bedside table, he grabbed the book he'd just started, a biography of Elvis. It had been Elvis or Gandhi, and Wells hadn't felt like Gandhi. And thinking of Gandhi reminded Wells of what he had almost left behind. He reached under the bed for the lockbox with his pistols.

HE STOPPED ONLY ONCE on the drive down, for a tankard of 7-Eleven coffee and a jug of water. Somewhere outside Philadelphia, the hangover lost its grip on him and he settled in his seat.

He spent the night in a no-tell motel outside Washington. He assumed Exley was in the house they'd once shared. The motel room stank of smoke, and the bed was bowed like a hammock. Wells brought Tonka in with him, and they slept on the floor back-to-back.

When he reached Langley in the morning, the gate guards didn't want to let him in. Aside from the agency's own bomb sniffers, dogs were not allowed on the campus. Wells told them it was just for a few hours, they'd be doing him a favor. He didn't have to tell them that after the last couple years, he had a few favors coming. They hemmed and hawed and made a couple of calls and finally waved him through.

"JOHN—" SHAFER BARELY STOOD before the dog jumped on him. On her hind legs, she was nearly as tall as he was. He ineffectually tried to push her away. She licked his face, eager to play. "I was gonna say I missed you. But this is a new low. I cannot believe you brought a dog in here."

"Her name's Tonka. And she likes you."

Shafer pushed the dog aside and hugged Wells. Wells always felt awkward at these moments. Male affection baffled him. His dad had been distant, taciturn, not exactly cold but unemotional. Unflappable. A surgeon, in the best and worst ways. Wells had followed his example, packed away his emotions. Even as a teenager, playing football, a sport where passion was not just tolerated but encouraged, he had resisted showing off. When he scored, he handed the ball to the referee without a word. As his high-school coach liked to say, quoting Bear Bryant: "When you get to the end zone, act like you've been there before."

Now Wells reached down, patted Shafer's shoulders before disengaging himself. He tapped Tonka's flank. "Come on, now. Over there." He pointed to Shafer's couch. The dog reluctantly complied.

"It's good to see you," Shafer said. "Even if you look like a survivalist. With the beard and the flannel. And this ridiculous dog."

I am a survivalist, Wells didn't say. *Survival's my specialty. Though the people around me aren't always so lucky.* Shafer's desk was covered with army interrogation manuals, some classified, some not, as well as what looked like a report from the CIA inspector general. Wells decided not to ask. He'd find out soon enough.

"Actually, you look about ready to head back to Afghanistan," Shafer said.

"That what this is about?"

"Closer to home. I got the outlines this morning, but I don't have details. Duto wants to fill us in himself." Duto, the CIA director, Wells's ultimate boss.

"Vincent Duto? What a pleasant surprise."

Wells and Duto didn't get along. To Wells, Duto was a martinet who saw agents as interchangeable parts, pawns in a game that was being played for his glory. And Wells knew that Duto saw him as valuable but uncontrollable, a Thoroughbred with Derby-winning speed and an ego to match. Duto had said as much, leaving out the second half of the analogy: We'll ride you until you break a leg, John.

"Then off to the glue factory," Wells said aloud.

"What?"

"Wondering why Duto wants to brief me, instead of letting you do it."

"He misses you."

"Do you trust him, Ellis?"

Shafer's only response was a grunt. The question didn't merit an answer.

"Really," Wells said, not sure why he was pressing the issue. "Do you?"

Shafer sat on his desk—and knocked over a bottle of Diet Coke. He hopped up like he'd been scalded. Wells grabbed the bottle while it was still mostly full and set it on the coffee table.

"Still have your reflexes," Shafer said.

"I try." Wells didn't mention the endless games of Halo he'd played in New Hampshire, trying to stem the inevitable decline in hand speed that came with age. He didn't know if the games would do him any good in a gunfight, but he was an impressive killing machine on planet Reach.

"You can't say you trust Duto or don't," Shafer said. "His value system doesn't include trust. Your interests overlap, he's your friend. He may even tell you the truth. Once he stops needing you, that's that. It's like, I read about this Hollywood producer, he wrote two memos every time he made a movie. One about how great the movie was, the other about how bad. When the movie came out and he saw how it did, he decided which memo to keep. It wasn't that one was right and the other was wrong. They were both true, until they weren't. Get it?"

"I get it was a stupid question."

Shafer's phone rang. He listened, grunted, hung up. "Let's go," he said.

They walked out of Shafer's office, Tonka trotting after them. "Can I make one request? Can we leave the dog here?"

"Not a chance."

DUTO MET THEM in the executive quarters on the seventh floor of the New Headquarters Building, a conference room down the hallway from his suite. Wells guessed Duto had been warned about Tonka and didn't want the dog in his office.

Duto had upgraded his wardrobe in the year Wells had been gone. He wore a blue suit that fit like it was hand-tailored, a white shirt, and a crisp red tie.

"Running for something?" Wells said.

"You're going to want to shave that beard now that you're back in civilization, John."

Despite his distrust of Duto, Wells found himself strangely relieved that the man was still in charge. At least they didn't have to pretend to be friendly. "And this is Tonka," Wells said.

"She trained any better than you?"

"I wouldn't say so."

"Too bad. Can we start, or you have any other pets I need to meet?"

They sat. Tonka sighed and lay down at Wells's feet.

"Ellis got a little bit of this earlier, so I'll start with you," Duto said. "Ever heard of Task Force 673?"

Wells shook his head.

"Joint army-agency group. Interrogated terrorists, high-value detainees."

"I didn't know we and the army ever did that together."

"Everybody's fighting the same war."

"What Vinny means is that Rumsfeld kept pushing into our turf, and creating these teams was the only way to protect it," Shafer said.

"Anyway, starting in 2004, we had a bunch of these squads. They went through various permutations, different names and squad numbers."

"Translation: we and the army kept wiping them out and reconstituting them to make it harder for Amnesty or Congress or anyone to follow the thread," Shafer interrupted. "I wish I could answer your questions, Senator, but Task Force 85 doesn't even exist."

"Do you want to explain, or should I?" Duto said.

"You go ahead."

"Thank you, Ellis. In late '05, when the Abu Ghraib blowback was really bad, we eliminated all the black squads. But then at the beginning of '07 we put one more together. Six-seven-three. The final iteration. Ten guys. Seven army, three agency. It ran out of Poland, a barracks on a Polish base there."

"Okay," Wells said, picturing the setup: the concrete building at the edge of the base, the one everyone pretended didn't exist. Planes landing late at night, guards shuffling prisoners in and out.

"The army picked the commander. A colonel with a lot of experience in interrogations. Martin Terreri. And because of all the pressure we were under from the Red Cross and everybody else, we saved 673 for the toughest guys. This was not for routine cases."

"Because of the tactics they were allowed to use."

"In general, the way it worked, detainees came to 673 one of two ways. Some were in the system already—say, in Iraq—and somebody decided that they needed more pressure. The others, they were sent direct after capture."

"Ghosts," Shafer said. A ghost prisoner was a detainee whose existence the United States refused to confirm to outsiders, like lawyers or wives or Red Cross monitors.

"But not entirely. They were all in the system," Duto said. "Legally, they had to be."

"Got it," Wells said. "Who oversaw Terreri?"

"Nobody, really," Duto said. "Six-seven-three, they were kind of ghosts themselves. Theoretically, Terreri reported to the deputy commander of Centcom"—Central Command, which oversaw all army operations in the Middle East and central Asia. "At the time, that was Gene Sanchez."

"Isn't Sanchez a lieutenant general? A colonel reporting to a three-star?"

"That was intentional. Sanchez wasn't keeping a close eye on 673. It wasn't on his org chart. The point was to let these guys do what they needed to do. In reality, the intel got chimneyed straight to the Pentagon."

Chimneying—sometimes called stovepiping—meant moving

raw intelligence straight to senior leaders instead of sending it through the normal analysis at Langley and the Pentagon. In theory, chimney-ing saved important information from being lost inside the vortex of the CIA and gave decision makers the chance to judge it for themselves.

"So, short version of the story, this 673 was a black squad with a straight line to the Pentagon," Wells said.

"Pretty much."

"They report to you also?" Shafer said. "Or anyone on our side?"

"Not directly."

"What does that mean, Vinny?"

"We saw the take after the army."

"Even though you had guys on the squad?" Wells said.

"That's right."

Wells didn't get it, and then he did. "You didn't like this squad. But you wanted to be sure you were involved, just in case they wound up with something good. You put a couple guys in, nobody important, protected yourself from whatever it was they were doing, but made sure you had a hand in the game."

Duto was silent and Wells saw he'd scored.

"Always so clever, Vinny. Always playing both sides."

"Guess you never broke the rules the last few years, John. Always please and thank you. May I go on, or you have more ethics lessons?"

Wells laid his hands on the smooth polished wood of the table. He stared at Duto, and Duto stared back. The triple-thick windows and carpeted floors of the seventh floor swallowed conversations. Only Tonka's panting spoiled the room's silence.

"Vinny," Shafer said. "You might take a different tone. Since it's possible none of us would be here without John." A reference to the bomb that Wells had stopped a year earlier.

"We would have found it," Duto said, without any conviction.

"We were close." He tugged his tie loose, opened his briefcase, pulled out a folder, a physical effort to put the conversation back on track. "Like I said, 673 reported to the army, but we got their take." Duto opened the folder, slid across a sheet with ten names on it. "Anybody on there ring a bell?"

One name jumped at Wells. Jeremiah M. Williams, a soldier he'd met at Ranger training fifteen years before. "Jerry Williams," Wells said. "I knew him a long time ago. Nice guy. Quiet. My ex-wife said something funny about him once. I can't remember when it happened. But I remember her telling me he was built like a Greek god. You know, we'd just gotten married, so it was sort of a funny thing for her to say, but she was right. He was. Like a black Greek god. I'll never forget it."

"Your wife met him; you were friends with him."

"Friendly." Williams was tough to get close to. Or maybe Wells hadn't tried.

"But you didn't stay in touch."

"When I started here, I didn't stay in touch with anyone from the army."

Wells wasn't sure why he was going into so much detail about his non-relationship with Jeremiah Marquis Williams. Maybe to explain to himself how he'd gotten to this point in his life with so few people he could trust.

"He was a good man, Jerry. The type of guy who made training easier. Always pulled more than his weight." Even as Wells said the words, he realized they sounded like a eulogy.

"He's the only name you recognize?"

"At first glance. Where is Jerry these days?"

"Missing."

"Jerry's missing? All those guys are missing?"

"Jerry's missing. Presumed dead. The other six names with the asterisks, they're dead for sure."

Now Wells wished he hadn't jerked Duto's chain by bringing the dog. Headquarters brought out the worst in him. Acid rose in his throat. Another good soldier dead.

"How?"

"In order. Rachel Callar killed herself in San Diego ten months ago. Overdose."

Duto handed over two photographs. The first showed Callar in her army dress uniform. She was pretty and trim, her brown hair cut in bangs that covered her forehead. A practical-looking woman, freckles and a wide chin.

"Six-seven-three had a woman?"

"She was the squad doctor. A psychiatrist."

The second photo had been taken by the San Diego police at the scene of Callar's suicide, a plastic bag pulled tight over her head. Wells passed the photos to Shafer without comment.

"Husband found her," Duto said. "No note, but no reason at the time to believe it was anything but suicide. She was in the army reserve. Had done a couple of tours in Iraq, counseling soldiers there. Three months later, two Rangers, the most junior guys on the squad, were killed by an IED in Afghanistan."

Duto slid across three photographs. The first two were similar, shots of broad-shouldered men in camouflage uniforms, both smiling almost shyly. The third focused on a blown-out Humvee, its armored windows shattered, smoke pouring from its passenger compartment.

"This one, we don't know if it was related to the others—it was on a stretch of road where another convoy got hit the next week. Still, they were part of the squad, so it's possible."

"First the doctor in San Diego, then the two Rangers in Afghanistan," Shafer said.

"Correct. Then we're back stateside."

Duto handed Wells two more photographs, the same macabre before and after. The first was a standard CIA identification shot. A paunchy man in a sport coat, striped tie, thick black hair. The second photo, a D.C. police shot. The same man, faceup on a cracked slab of sidewalk, dress shirt stained black with blood. His wallet sat open and empty on the curb, a few inches from his shoes.

"Three months after that was Kenneth Karp. Shot in D.C., east of Logan Circle, four months ago. About one thirty in the morning. Outside an ATM. He was one of ours, so it was reported to us, of course, but nobody made the connection. The cops figured it for a robbery gone bad, and so did our security officers. The ATM tape doesn't show anything."

"He live in D.C.?" Shafer said.

Duto shook his head. "Rosslyn. Next question, why was he pulling five hundred dollars from an ATM in the District in the middle of the night? There's a strip club a block from the bank. Karp had a weekly poker game in Adams Morgan. Apparently he had a routine. Leave the game at one, make a pit stop, get home at three. Wife never knew."

"He did the same thing every week?"

"That's what his buddies told the cops."

"Somebody could have figured out the routine, waited for him."

"In retrospect, yes. At the time, we had no reason to think so."

"What'd he do for 673?" Wells said.

"He was the senior translator," Duto said. "Spoke Arabic, Pashto, Urdu."

Duto handed over a photograph, a bald-headed black man whose uniform stretched tight across his massive shoulders. Jerry Williams. No second picture, since Williams was missing, not dead.

"Williams's wife reported him missing in New Orleans two months ago. Last seen at a bar in the Gentilly district. North of the French Quarter. He retired last year, after the squad broke up. He knew Arabic from his Special Ops training, so he worked with Karp on the translations. He was having marital problems, and the cops down there didn't look too hard for him. If he's alive, he's laying low. He hasn't been seen since, hasn't used his ATM card or credit cards, hasn't called his family, hasn't flown under his own name. The cops haven't officially ruled out his wife, but she's not a suspect."

Wells looked at the smiling man in the photograph and wondered if he was dead. "Let me make sure I have it straight. Callar, the doctor, hangs herself in San Diego. The two Rangers die. Nothing happens for a while. Then Karp dies here. Then Williams disappears in New Orleans."

"Correct," Duto said.

"Five missing or dead from a ten-person squad, nobody put it together?"

"Why would we? A suicide, an IED in Afghanistan, a robbery, a missing person. Four army, one agency. Hard to see a pattern. Until this."

Duto slid two more sets of photographs across the table.

"Jack Fisher and Mike Wyly. Both killed two days ago. Fisher in San Francisco in the morning. Wyly in Los Angeles near midnight. Both shot at close range. No witnesses, and even though they were in residential areas, none of the neighbors heard shots. The cops are assuming a silencer."

Duto didn't need to explain further. Silencers were illegal, and good ones were hard to come by. A silencer meant a professional, or at least a semiprofessional, killer.

"Same gun in both shootings?" Shafer said.

"Yes. Same as the one that got Karp, by the way."

"Who were they?"

"Wyly was a sergeant, a Ranger. Good guy, by all accounts." He looked like a good guy to Wells. Tall, blue-eyed, big square jaw. He belonged on a recruiting poster. At least in the before shot. The after wasn't so nice. He lay sprawled across a bare wooden floor, eyes dull, his hands covered with his own blood. Four shots in his torso, two in the abdomen, two up high in the chest. The shooter had wanted to be sure.

"Where was this?" Wells said.

"His house, the San Fernando Valley. He'd just gotten divorced. The cops talked to his ex, but she has an alibi. Given the pattern of the shootings, there's no reason to believe she's involved."

Wells handed the photos of Wyly to Shafer. He looked at Fisher, who was bald and offered a smile that revealed prominent canines. Wells hadn't remembered the name, but the face was familiar.

"Rat Tooth," Wells said. "I kind of liked him, but that was a minority view."

"Rat Tooth? You knew him?"

"He was an instructor at the Farm when I was a trainee. Even back then he was bald. Specialized in what he liked to call 'tactical physical arts.' Eye gouging, finger breaking. Halfway through, he disappeared. There were rumors he'd, quote/unquote, engaged in inappropriate physical contact with a trainee."

"Bingo," Duto said. "After that, we put him on the road where he belonged. He was in Colombia in the late nineties, the Philippines for a couple of years after nine-eleven. The places you could run without a lot of eyes on you. He liked it messy."

Messy. The second photograph of Fisher was messy. He was

slumped against a driver's seat, head torn open by a close-range pistol shot. His jaw was open, and Wells couldn't help but notice his teeth, long and sharp and nearly vampiric.

"Fisher had a reputation, I can't deny it," Duto said. "But he had his uses."

He was as much as telling Wells and Shafer that Fisher had been the squad's designated torturer. Though the United States didn't torture, Wells reminded himself. Torture was wrong. And illegal. So whatever Fisher had or hadn't done for 673, he hadn't tortured. QED.

"You put all this together yesterday?"

"The San Francisco police got the call on Fisher in the morning, two days ago. Once they figured out who he was, they got in touch with the FBI, which reached out to us. We didn't know if his murder was connected to Karp, but we figured we'd better check on the other members of 673. We called Wyly's house yesterday morning. An LAPD detective answered the phone."

"What about the other three guys, the rest of the squad?" Wells said.

"All safe. Murphy, the number two, still works for us. He's at CTC now"—the Counterterrorist Center. "Terreri, the colonel, he's in Afghanistan serving at Bagram. The last guy, Hank Poteat, is an army communications specialist. He's at Camp Henry in South Korea now. None of them have noticed anything off."

"Is Murphy under guard?"

"Yes."

"The FBI is leading the investigation?" Shafer asked.

"Correct. They've classified the murders as a possible terrorist attack. They're putting together a task force. We're assisting, and so's the army. But the Feebs have jurisdiction. No different than the Kansi shootings." In 1993, Mir Amal Kansi, a Pakistani graduate student, killed two agency employees near the main entrance to Langley. The FBI had led the investigation, capturing Kansi in Pakistan in 1997. He was convicted, sentenced to death, and executed in Virginia in 2002.

"And the local police departments are cooperating," Shafer said.

"Of course."

"So, John and me," Shafer said. "Help us out here, Vinny. Where do we fit in? Since we're not part of the task force, and the agency's got no jurisdiction anyway."

"I'll get to that," Duto said. "But first, let me ask, this sound like AQ"—Al Qaeda—"to you? Or any of the usual offshoots?"

"It's too subtle," Wells said. "Too much work for the payoff. It's not like shooting a Cabinet secretary."

"Did anybody outside know we'd set this squad up?" Shafer asked.

"You might have noticed, there's no shortage of articles about our interrogation techniques."

"But 673, were they ever mentioned specifically?"

"Last year, a jihadi Web site wrote about them. 'The American squad 673 are rabid dogs who must be exterminated.' Nothing specific about their tactics. Generic stuff. We have the pages cached if you want to see them. NSA tried to find the source, but it couldn't."

"We know how the squad ID number got out?"

"It was reported in Germany last year. A prosecutor in Berlin opened an investigation into our rendition tactics. But the names of the squad members weren't mentioned, not in the papers and not in the prosecutor's report. As far as we know, they've never leaked."

"Doesn't mean jihadis couldn't find them. Maybe they got help from somebody in Poland," Shafer said. "Or somebody in the prosecutor's office."

"There's another reason to believe it's Al Qaeda. Yesterday morning a group calling itself the Army of the Sunni posted a claim of responsibility online. It refers to the murder of Mike Wyly. Looks authentic. At the time it was posted, his death hadn't been reported. This morning the FBI backtraced the posting to a pay-per-minute computer at a Dunkin' Donuts in L.A. The kind where you literally feed cash into a box. But the place doesn't have cameras, and the counter guy doesn't remember anyone special."

"What's the posting say?"

"That the killings are revenge for the way we treat detainees. These sites are in Arabic, so the media hasn't noticed it yet. But eventually they will. You can see the headlines. Payback for rendition, et cetera."

"If it's true, it's got to be personal," Wells said. "I can't see why you'd pick these targets otherwise. Somebody who 673 interrogated and let go. But they're all in our custody, right?"

"All but two. One of them we can rule out. His name's Mokhatir. A Malaysian national, caught in the Philippines with three soda-bottle bombs, looked like the kind you'd use to take out a plane. He was in custody for a few weeks, had some kind of health issue. They sent him back to the Philippines. He died in detention maybe eight months ago."

"A health issue?"

"That's all we heard."

"How'd he die?"

Duto shook his head. *Dead is dead.* "If you care, ask the Philippine army. I wouldn't bother. The other guy is the one we need to find. Alaa Zumari's his name. We sent him back to Cairo two years ago, give or take."

"Halfway through 673's tour."

"Give or take. He was arrested in Iraq with a bunch of cell

phones and cash, suspected of being part of the insurgency. But 673 cleared him."

"Anybody over there tried to talk to him?"

"Tried, yes. Succeeded, no. The Egyptians lost him a few months ago. He's gone."

"Vinny," Shafer said. "I'm still not clear on what you want from us."

"I want you to investigate," Duto said. "Start with Alaa Zumari." He looked at Wells. "Go to Egypt, find him. If I recall, your particular skill set might come in handy for that."

The idea was implausible. Wells had burned the jihadis twice and couldn't see how he could get inside a third time. Even so, his pulse quickened. Aloud, he said only, "I'm guessing the FBI has about a hundred agents on this?"

"There are complexities here. Which they may not see."

"Just tell us," Wells said. "What you're dancing around."

"Because this is interagency, the FBI is reporting to the DNI"— Fred Whitby, Duto's boss, the director of national intelligence. The position had been created after September 11, when Congress and the White House decided a new Cabinet-level post was needed to oversee not just the CIA but the entire intelligence community. "I'm concerned that Whitby may not be giving the full picture to the Feds."

"Meaning?"

"I can't tell you more. At this time."

"You want us to sneak behind your boss's back—"

"He's not my boss, John."

"Actually, he is," Shafer said. In fact, the relationship between the DNI and DCI was still being defined.

"I run the CIA. Fred Whitby's got no operational authority here."

"Have I touched a sore spot, Vinny?

Always, Wells thought. At Langley, and all over Washington, the men and women at the top always focused their attention on power plays and turf grabbing, as if the world outside the Beltway didn't exist except as a kind of simulated reality, a way to keep score.

"You want us to interfere with the FBI," Wells said. "Operate on American soil. Which is illegal, last time I checked. And you won't even tell us why, exactly, except that you don't trust Fred Whitby. I didn't know we were such good friends."

"It's not interfering. It's piggybacking. I'll get you access to the 301s—" the reports that FBI agents filed after interviews. "The physical evidence. Lie-detector tests. After that, you do what you like. Say John wants to go to Cairo, find Alaa Zumari before the Feds or the Egyptians? Nobody can stop him."

"What is it you're not telling us?"

Duto paused. "Without going into details. These guys, they broke something important. Major security implications."

"Related to this Egyptian, Zumari?"

"No."

Wells and Shafer waited for Duto to go on, but he didn't. The silence stretched on. The room's air seemed to thicken. Even Tonka's breathing slowed.

"I can't tell you," Duto said finally. "Not even you two. Only about eight people in the country know the whole story."

"Vinnie, you know as well as we do, we're coded for everything."

"Everything here. These files, they're at Liberty Crossing"—the buildings a couple miles west of Langley where the office of the director of national intelligence had its headquarters. "And Whitby's holding them tight. He's not even planning to tell the FBI what I just gave you. The Feebs, they're getting the names of the squad members and the names of the detainees. Not their full records, just their names.

I think there are ten. Along with the barest outlines of the way 673 worked. Nothing more. Nothing at all about what they found. I think Whitby's making a mistake, and I told him so. But I'm overruled. So, yeah, I want you involved. Maybe I can feed you tidbits. The bureau comes back with a suspect, makes an arrest, great. They get lost, maybe you come up with something they don't, steer them the right way."

"And you embarrass Whitby and the FBI by doing what they couldn't," Wells said.

"You've gotten so cynical, John."

"At least give us access to the full detainee records—"

"I don't have them."

"Then no," Wells said. "Forget it."

"We're in," Shafer said.

5

W hy?"

"When the director asks, it's best to agree," Shafer said.

After the meeting, Shafer suggested they leave Langley, get some air. They were standing along the black granite wall of the Franklin Delano Roosevelt Memorial. Tucked behind the Mall, on the southwest edge of the Tidal Basin, the monument rarely attracted attention.

"New philosophy for you, Ellis," Wells said. "Whatever this game is, I don't want in."

"Let me explain something, John," Shafer said. "In five minutes you would have done it anyway. Here's how it would have gone. Duto would have said it was a chance for you to turn the page with him, build a new relationship. And when that didn't work, he would have appealed to your sense of duty, told you you needed to avenge Jerry Williams and the rest of the guys. That probably would have done it. And if it didn't, he would have challenged your manhood and you would have bitten in about half a second."

"No, he—"

"Yes, he. Because that's what I would have done."

Does Duto think he can manipulate me that easily? Wells wondered. Followed by, *Am I that easily manipulated?* Even now, after everything he'd done, he suspected that these men, Duto and Shafer, saw him as little more than a door kicker, playing the role they gave him.

Wells could have forced Duto to accept him as an equal. With his successes the last few years, he could have become deputy director of operations. He could have quit the agency entirely, moved over to the White House and the National Security Council. He could even have taken a job teaching, someplace like Georgetown, while he figured out his next move. But he knew he'd be bored out of his mind wearing a suit to work every day, running meetings. He belonged outside. But because he wouldn't accept more authority, Duto and Shafer didn't respect him.

Wells's pulse crept higher. He forced himself to smile, not to give Shafer the satisfaction of seeing the sting of his words. "You like the FDR?" Wells said aloud.

"Not so much. Too politically correct, don't you think? The Democrats wanted it, and then the Republicans stuck it in the back of beyond. And all this self-conscious inspiration. We should have kept to Lincoln and Jefferson and Washington."

"Where's Exley?" Wells said, apropos of nothing. And saying Exley's name made him think of Anne. He imagined he could smell her on his hands, feel her skin on his. Thinking about her made his mouth go dry. Yet, equally, he wanted to confess what he'd done to Exley. To apologize to her. And to make her jealous. Remind her of what they'd had. "How is she?"

"Ask her yourself. You know how to find her. I'm not involved. You're going to get back together, one of you needs to break already. Otherwise you'll just make each other miserable."

Suddenly a class of elementary-school kids, third or fourth grade, swarmed the memorial. Their teacher was barely old enough to shave, a hipster in black glasses, a well-meaning Teach for America refugee halfway between the Ivy League and law school. He was trying, but he could barely keep the kids in line. They bounced off one another, shifting foot to foot. Two boys ran off, chased each other around one of the marble benches at the edge of the memorial, playing at a gunfight. "You dead. Pump this shotgun on your head." The other boy ducked behind a bench, then raised an invisible rifle in both hands. "Shotgun ain't nothing. You the one *is* dead."

"Let's go," Wells said.

"Depressing."

"I hate watching it."

"I mean, the waste of ammo. These kids can't hit the side of a barn. And somebody needs to reload."

"Nice, Ellis."

"Can't let everything get to you. You got to be able to smile sometimes, the absurdity of it."

They left the kids behind, walked around the basin toward the Jefferson Memorial. A faint breeze fluttered off the stagnant water, carrying the muddy, briny smell that Wells would always associate with Washington. The swamp. A city that existed only as a kind of hotel for power. New York or Philadelphia would have been more natural sites for the seat of government, but the South wouldn't agree, back in the day. So here they were.

Wells supposed the United States had been lucky to have D.C. If the capital had stayed in the North, the South might have seceded a decade earlier, before the Union Army could bring it to heel. And if the South had broken away, at least three countries would have formed in the area now occupied by the United States—a North, a South, and a West. Then the United States wouldn't have been the dominant world power in the twentieth century. Perhaps World War I or even World War II would have ended differently. On and on the counterfactual history ran.

Kierkegaard was wrong, Wells thought. Life couldn't be understood backward or forward. In the end, humans depended on faith as armor. But Wells's own faith had faded. He didn't know where to look. He'd lived as a Muslim for a decade. But how could he rejoin the *umma*, the community of believers, after what Omar Khadri had done to him? Yet Wells was even more perplexed by Christianity, the religion he'd been raised in growing up. He found Islam's precepts easier to accept than Christianity's, the relationship with God more personal.

The wind picked up and riffled the basin's brackish water, scudding low waves against its concrete walls. Despite himself, Wells found himself looking for a fish in the pool. A fat, ugly carp or even a toothy pike. *Lord, just show me a pike that got lost on its way up the Potomac, and I will never question your existence again.*

No fish.

Wells shivered in the breeze. Duto had certainly ruined his mood.

"Cold?" Shafer said.

"Wondering if I should become a Buddhist."

"I don't think it would suit you. You know what you need, John? A mission."

"That what you think?"

"I knows you fancies yourself a deep thinker," Shafer said in a ridiculous southern accent. "But philosophy ain't your thing, John-boy."

"You were born an ass, you will forever be an ass, and you will die an ass."

"At least I'm consistent. You ever see Gandhi eating meat?

Barbecue? Pulled pork? A fat T-bone? Sirloin? Broiled in butter and served with a side of bacon?"

"I have no idea what you're talking about, but you're making me hungry, Ellis."

"Follow your destiny," Shafer said. "Put down the book, grasshopper. Pick up the gun. Can't kill nobody with a book."

Wells laughed. "When we get back to the office, I'm going to try. Then I'm gonna put you on a spit."

"Meantime, get to it."

"You really want to do this," Wells said.

"If nothing else, don't you want to catch whoever killed your friend?"

"You don't know he's dead."

"He's dead, John. Until proven otherwise. Let's find out who killed him."

"Simple," Wells said. "And if the truth turns out to be complicated?"

"We'll cross that bridge when we get there. Or burn it. Whatever."

"All right."

"So, Duto wants us to play detective, we play detective," Shafer said. "Spitball. Everything but the obvious, the jihadi connection. Save that for last."

"You know anything more about 673? Anything Duto didn't tell us?" Wells said.

"Only this: we and the army paid the members of the squad their regular salaries. But the expenses were financed by the agency through what's called a C-one drop. The squad got quarterly disbursements. No accounting of what happened to the money after that. No receipts, no oversight. It's very rare. Seven-three got close to eight million through these drops."

"Eight million for a ten-man squad. Not bad."

"No, it wasn't. Some went to the Poles who were running the base. Some for charter flights. Some for coms equipment, probably. Satellite gear, et cetera. But that's another possible motive. Maybe whoever was in charge of the money skimmed a couple million. Now he's worried the rest of the squad found out, so he's eliminating them."

"What I don't see, why kill the rest of the squad now? You're just calling attention to yourself. Doesn't make sense."

"I can't disagree," Shafer said. "Okay. Your turn."

"What about the woman, Rachel? The doctor. One woman, nine guys. Maybe she was having an affair. Two affairs. A love triangle."

"Then she gets home and one of the guys kills her? And makes it look like a suicide? Then starts in on the rest of the squad? Why now?"

"Same problem as the money," Wells said. "The timing doesn't work."

"Okay, this is the worst yet," Shafer said. "Say one of the members is actually a jihadi. Who worked for all these years for the agency. Or the army. Waiting to get put on this squad. And then, lo and behold—no. I can't even say it. It's so ridiculous."

"Try this. Coincidence. The doctor killed herself. Jerry Williams walked out on his wife. Karp got shot in a robbery—"

"Tell it to the guys who just got popped in San Francisco and L.A."

With that they stood and looked over the Tidal Basin. Two helicopters flew low overhead, most likely headed for the White House, as an overweight jogger huffed slowly along the path that circled the pool.

"Not the most productive ten minutes we've ever spent," Shafer said.

"What if—" Wells said.

"Just say it."

"What if, let's say, someone inside the agency or the Pentagon is embarrassed by what 673 did? Somebody high up?"

"So, they want these guys taken out? One by one? Okay, go with it. Six-seven-three was torturing detainees. They were dumb enough to keep evidence, videos or photos. And some senior official was stupid enough to put his authorization in writing. He's got a problem."

"Big problem. The kind that puts him in jail."

"Sure," Shafer said. "But that's a lot of stupid. And even so, the risk of taking them out is huge."

"People have been known to do dumb things when they panic."

"True. But play it the other way. What if Duto's telling the truth and 673 found something huge? Proof the Kremlin is financing terrorism against us. Evidence that the French were paying bin Laden before nine-eleven."

"Now someone's decided that the information is too important to risk a leak. And so it's time for 673 to go."

"In the immortal words of Avon Barksdale, 'They got to be got.'"

"Who?"

"Ever see *The Wire*?"

Wells shook his head.

"It's great. You'd like it. You're like McNulty, only less of a hound. So. Six-seven-three finds something big, gets the wrong people upset . . ." Shafer trailed off.

"Doesn't make sense, does it?"

"I never buy the big conspiracies. You know, half the time we can barely tie our shoes. And now we're saying the SecDef or the President or the Pope is taking out these guys one by one? That they're rubbing their hands together in the White House, whispering to each other, 'First San Diego. Then New Orleans. They know too much. Kill them. All of them.' Giggling. *Bwah-hah-hah*."

"The Russians," Wells said.

"The Russians do enjoy their conspiracies. They might be crazy enough to kill our guys this way. But if Duto and Fred Whitby think it's the Russians, why wouldn't they tell us?"

Wells couldn't think of an answer.

The jogger had reached them. She wore red shorts over her doughy white legs and a pale blue T-shirt with the University of Maryland terrapin logo. She kept her head down and avoided eye contact with them. Looking at her, Wells had a vague sense of déjà vu. He didn't know why. Then he did. She looked like a younger version of Keith Robinson's wife. Keith Edward Robinson, the CIA desk officer who'd spied for China and then fled for parts unknown, leaving his alcoholic wife, Janice, behind. Wells had met Janice only once, in a house that stank of hopelessness.

"You like her? Didn't think she was your type," Shafer said.

"She makes me think of Janice Robinson."

"Keith's wife?" Shafer looked again. "Yeah, I can see that."

"Never found that guy."

"No, we didn't. Probably buried in some jungle. He didn't strike me as having much candle left. Though some of these guys, they last longer than you think. Keep pouring out misery. On themselves and everyone else. You know she quit drinking, right? Janice. Just in time, too. She had about two ounces of liver left."

"Good for her."

"Maybe one day he'll send her a postcard, give us a chance to pay him a visit. No statute of limitations on what he did."

"He got to be got, right, Ellis?"

"Exactly right. So. Assuming we're out of wild theories. Let's go back to the beginning. Say it's a jihadi op."

"Tell me how they got the members of the squad."

"Bad opsec"—operational security. "Somebody in Poland found a flight manifest, didn't put it in a burn bag like he was supposed to. Or the guy they released, Zumari, he knew where they were operating, and after he got out, he went back and bribed somebody there. Or the Berlin prosecutor's office hates the agency and leaked the names."

"I still don't see it," Wells said. "But if you got the names, you could do it. And maybe this is how you would. One at a time. Quietly. Once you've killed three or four, you lift the veil, go public with it. Shove it in our faces. Revenge on the American torture squad."

"Makes as much sense as anything else," Shafer said.

"How do we find out if the names leaked?"

"We don't," Shafer said. "That's the FBI's job. I'm going to work on Duto, push him to open the records. Even if he can't give us the interrogation records, we've got to get more on the detainees. Names, nationalities, what we're holding them for. And I'm going to talk to Brant Murphy."

"The guy who still works for us."

"Yes. At CTC"—the agency's Counterterrorist Center.

"What's that leave for me?"

"You're going to do what Duto said. Go to Cairo to find Alaa Zumari. An encore performance. John Wells, back to his roots, under-cover as a jihadi. For one night only. Acoustic. It'll be fun."

"And how do I get to him if the *muk*"—short for mukhabarat, the

Arabic word for secret police—"can't? I got it. I'll ask Khadri and the rest of my buddies for references. Only they're all dead. I killed them, remember?"

Though in truth, Shafer was right. Wells wanted to go, to be undercover again, to speak Arabic, to hear the midday call to prayer roll through dusty streets.

"As it happens, I've got an idea on that."

6

The security at the big Egyptian hotels seemed good. It wasn't. At the Intercontinental, a blocky pink tower on the Nile, a low gate protected the front driveway, and a bomb-sniffing German shepherd nosed around every car. But a determined bomber could have plowed through the gate, Wells saw. The guards had AKs and pistols, but they didn't wear bulletproof vests. Wells wondered if the men he hoped to meet on this trip had made similar calculations.

Since the mid-1990s, dozens of terrorist attacks had hit Egypt, killing hundreds of tourists. Still, Americans and Europeans came here every day to gawk at the pyramids and visit the splendid tombs near Luxor. Wells wondered if they understood the resentments in the giant city around them.

Wells reached the Intercontinental's front doors and gave up his cell phone to pass through the hotel's metal detector. Inside, the lobby was air-conditioned, with a pianist playing at a black baby grand, its elegance oddly disconnected from Cairo's dirt and noise.

At the reception desk, Wells handed over his newly minted passport, which proclaimed him William Anthony Barber, forty-one, of Plano, Texas.

"Mr. Barber. You will be with us for a week."

"You got it, sweetheart."

The receptionist tapped on her computer, handed over his pass-port and keycard. "Room 2218. Please enjoy your stay in Cairo."

"Of course."

Room 2218 had two queen beds and a pleasant view of the luxury hotels and apartment buildings along the banks of the Nile. Feluccas, single-masted Egyptian sailboats that catered to the tourist trade, put-tered along the water, along with open-air cruisers that ferried tour-ists and even some native Cairenes between the riverbanks. Wells watched for a while and then pulled the curtains and closed his eyes. When he left this room again, the mission would begin in earnest.

HE SLEPT WITHOUT DREAMING and woke dry-mouthed but refreshed. In the bathroom, he stripped. A day earlier, at Langley, he'd taped a plas-tic bag to the back of his thigh. Now he pulled it off, trying not to take his leg hair with it. He showered and scrubbed, and when he was done, he looked himself up and down in the bathroom mirror. Despite the wounds he'd suffered on his missions, age had been kind to him. Being free to work out for hours every day helped, too. Only actors, pro athletes, and spies, perfect narcissists all, could devote so much time to their bodies. And, of course, he didn't have a wife or family or kids to distract him. Though that wasn't entirely true. Wells closed his eyes. His boy was a ghost to him. When this mission was done, he would go to Montana and insist on seeing Evan, whatever his ex-wife said. It was time.

Back in the bedroom, Wells popped open his suitcases. The first was filled with jeans, khakis, polo shirts, sneakers, even a Dallas Cow-boys cap. Just what the housekeepers at the Intercontinental would expect William Barber to be wearing. Wells neatly folded the clothes in his dresser and turned to the second, larger case.

It held a different culture's clothes. One brown *galabiya,* the simple robe worn by many Egyptian men. Two pure white dishdashas, the more elegant robes favored by Saudis and Kuwaitis. For his feet, heavy brown leather sandals. A cell phone with a 965 prefix, the code for Kuwait City. A thick steel Rolex. No self-respecting Kuwaiti man would be caught without one. Under all the robes, an expensive Sony digital video camera and a brushed-aluminum iMac.

Wells considered a *galabiya,* then changed his mind and decided on a dishdasha. Then he pulled the fake passport that the agency had given him from the bag he'd carried strapped to his legs. According to the passport, he was a Kuwaiti named Nadeem Taleeb. An Egyptian visa showed that he'd entered the country at Suez, on a ferry from Jeddah, Saudi Arabia. The passport came with Saudi entry and exit stamps to support the story.

Back at Langley, Mike Merced, a talkative twentysomething who was Wells's favorite document geek, had promised Wells that the passport would hold up to almost any inspection. "As long as you don't try to get into Kuwait with it," Merced said. "Though I don't know why anyone would ever want to go to Kuwait." Besides the passport, Merced had given Wells a wallet stuffed with Kuwaiti dinars and Saudi riyals, along with credit cards and a driver's license in Taleeb's name.

But Wells was missing one item that he normally would have considered essential. A weapon. He could have connected with the station here for a pistol. Instead, he was coming in dark. Not even the chief of station knew he was here. He'd chosen this course for two reasons. One was logical, one less so.

First, the Egyptian *mukhabarat* would have tails on all the station's couriers. Wells preferred not to risk blowing his cover before his mission even began. More important, this mission wasn't the kind for which a gun would help. If he wound up sticking a gun in someone's face, he'd already failed. No, to succeed in this mission, Wells would need to *become* Nadeem Taleeb. And Nadeem would naturally stay as far from the CIA as possible. So Wells wanted nothing to do with the agency. Now, as Nadeem, he flicked the television to channel 7, MBC, and watched an Arabic sitcom, talking back to the screen, finding the rhythm of the language for the first time in years.

After an hour, he rose, pulled the curtains. The sun was sinking behind the city. As the heat of the day eased, Cairo came alive. On the Nile, the boats flipped on neon lights and glowed red and blue and green. Couples and families and packs of teenagers filled the sidewalks on the Tahrir Bridge, savoring the breeze that fluttered down the river. Beside them, battered black-and-white taxis and boxy green buses filled the pavement. The sun disappeared entirely, and the sky darkened. From every direction, the calls to evening prayer began, eerie amplified voices that echoed through the city.

Wells turned east, away from the river—the orientation was easy enough, since the room faced straight west to the Nile—and fell to his knees and pushed his head against the carpeted floor and prayed. As Nadeem. As a Muslim.

A HALF HOUR LATER, he walked out of the Intercontinental's side entrance, carrying the larger suitcase. Before he could even get a hand in the air, a cab stopped.

"*Salaam alekeim*," Wells said. Peace be with you. The traditional Muslim greeting.

"*Alekeim salaam.*"

"Lotus Hotel," Wells said in Arabic.

"Come on, then."

Wells slipped in.

"Where you from?"

"Kuwait."

The driver was silent. Other Arabs often viewed Kuwaitis as arrogant. Then, as if realizing he might be missing an opportunity, the driver put a hand on Wells's arm.

"First time to Cairo?"

"First time."

"Tomorrow. I take you to the pyramids! Giza, Saqqara, Dahshur. All-day trip. Only two hundred fifty pounds"—about fifty dollars. "Give me your mobile number!" The driver was a bit deaf, or maybe he thought he could shout so loudly that Wells would have to agree.

"I'm here on business."

"I drive you around Cairo, then! Very good price."

"Maybe."

"Definitely!"

Wells didn't respond, and eventually the driver dropped his arm. They fought through traffic onto Talaat Harb, a brightly lit street crowded with clothing stores, restaurants, and travel agencies. The pavement ahead opened up, and the driver gunned the gas.

As he did, a woman in a burqa stepped into the road about fifty yards ahead. With her feet hidden beneath her black robes, she looked as though she were floating over the pavement on an invisible river. A very slow river.

The driver honked furiously. Still, the woman didn't hurry, didn't even turn her head to look at them, as if her robes were a force field that would protect her from harm. Finally, the driver gave in and slammed his brakes. The taxi, a cheap old Fiat, pitched forward on its springs and skidded to a stop just short of the woman. She walked on.

"Women," the driver said. "Crazy. How many wives you have?"

"Only one."

"Hah! And you a Kuwaiti! I have three. Three wives! And ten children!" The driver smiled at Wells with teeth as yellow and battered as the Cairo skyline. "How many children you have? Two? Three?"

"Eleven," Wells said, trying not to smile.

"Eleven?" The driver frowned. Wells wondered whether he would try to have another baby tonight, or maybe two, to retake the lead. "And only one wife? You keep her very busy! I have six boys! How many boys you have?"

"None."

"All girls and no boys! You need new wife, *habibi*. She wastes your time." The driver patted Wells's arm happily. He might not have as many children as Wells, but he had more boys, and boys were what counted.

At the hotel, the driver, still hopeful, pressed a tattered business card into Wells's hand. "Al-Fayed Taxi and Car for Transport."

"You call tomorrow."

"*Shokran,*" Wells said.

"*Ma-a-saalama.*"

"*Ma-a-saalama.*"

THE LOTUS HOTEL was eight floors of dusty concrete. The receptionist gave a bored look at Wells's Kuwaiti passport, took his credit card, and handed over the brass key—no programmable cards here—to room 705. The elevator was an old-school model, a metal gate on the inside. When Wells closed the gate and pushed the button for seven, it didn't move for a while and then ascended as huffily as a smoker in a marathon. His room was narrow and dark, with a creaking three-bladed fan pushing the stale air sideways. Wells stripped off his dishdasha and lay diagonally across the sagging double bed, his feet hanging off the corner. The perpetual honking from the street should have bothered him, but instead it soothed him. He fell asleep instantly.

He woke to the sound of the morning call to prayer, showered under a surprisingly hot stream, and slipped on his *galabiya*, feeling its loose folds envelop him. He lifted the mattress and slid the keycard for the Intercontinental into a tiny seam in its bottom, where it would be hidden from the most thorough of searchers. He peeked out the window. The street was temporarily empty, aside from a handful of teenage boys joking with one another. They looked as though they'd stayed out all night, smoking flavored tobacco from the tall water pipes Egyptians called *shisha*.

During the early twentieth century, Cairo had been one of the world's most cosmopolitan cities, a place where Muslims, Christians, and even Jews lived together peacefully. During World War II, brothels had operated openly just east of downtown, in a district Cairenes had jokingly called "the Blessing." Egypt's version of Islam was generally more moderate than that practiced to the east in Saudi Arabia. After all, Egypt's history long predated Islam. Its proudest moments had come not as a Muslim state but under the pharaohs. And almost ten percent of Egyptians were Christian.

In theory, Egypt still remained moderate today. The nation was the only big Arab power to have made peace with Israel. Women here were allowed to drive and didn't have to wear head scarves, much less burqas. Cairo was home to an English-language radio station whose announcers openly offered relationship advice. Alcohol was legal, and the city's big hotels even had casinos, though they weren't supposed to be open to Egyptians.

But in reality, Egypt had swung toward Islam since throwing off Britain's colonial yoke in 1952. High birth rates, government bureaucracy, and slow economic growth had left tens of millions of

Egyptians living in destitution in the vast slums in and around Cairo. Millions more aspired to the middle class but could not find decent-paying jobs despite college degrees. Many saw Islam as the answer to their country's crisis. Islamic charities fed and clothed poor families. Islamic courts offered quick decisions to people who couldn't afford to wait years to be heard by the overcrowded government court system.

But as they promoted charity and community values, Islamic leaders also stoked a fierce anger among their followers: at Egypt's government, at Israel, and at the United States, which supported both. The United States, so concerned about bringing democracy to Iraq but happy to look the other way when Hosni Mubarak, Egypt's president, rigged elections to stay in power. Egyptians called Mubarak "the pharaoh," not only because he had been president for almost thirty years but because he was trying to anoint his son Gamal as his successor.

Year by year, the radicals gained influence. Despite being outlawed, the Muslim Brotherhood, the most important Islamist political party, had won twenty percent of the seats in the Egyptian parliament in the 2005 elections—more than ever before. On the streets, too, the changes were obvious. Even in downtown Cairo, most women wore head scarves, and burqas were not uncommon. Alcohol had largely disappeared outside hotels and a handful of restaurants that catered to tourists. The calls to prayer grew louder each year. And except for the Egyptian Museum, the pyramids, and a few protected neighborhoods, tourists—or non-Arab foreigners of any kind—were almost invisible in Cairo. Despite its grinding poverty, the city was not particularly dangerous for locals. In fact, street crime was rare. But foreign visitors, especially women, faced constant harassment. And with the threat of terrorism vague but real, most tourists stayed off the streets.

Too bad, because Cairo was fascinating, Wells thought. After breakfast he'd walked around downtown, orienting himself, talking to shopkeepers to scrape the last of the rust off his Arabic. Now he was heading east along Sharia al-Azhar, a narrow road that ran under the concrete pylons of an elevated highway. The streets around him formed an area called Islamic Cairo. Almost all of Cairo was Islamic, of course, but this district was the historic center of Islam in Egypt, filled with mosques and madrassas. At its center was al-Azhar University, the second-oldest degree-granting school in the world, established in 975 A.D., hundreds of years before Oxford and Cambridge.

Around Wells, boys carried trays of tea and coffee to men who stood outside their shops. In Cairo, as in many Third World cities, the stores clustered by type. This stretch of road had nothing but textile stores, as though humans needed only brightly colored cloth to survive. The din was constant. Three-wheeled tuk-tuks and skinny 125cc motorbikes buzzed by, and shopkeepers incessantly shouted the praises of their wares.

"Best quality, best quality!"

"Extra-special!"

"Sir, sir! Take a look!"

And step-by-step Wells edged closer to his destination, a mosque a few blocks south, in the very heart of Islamic Cairo.

AN HOUR LATER, just in time for midday Friday prayers, he arrived. The mosque wasn't big or famous or even particularly old. It had yellow-painted concrete walls and a low minaret mounted with speakers to broadcast calls to prayer. It was the home mosque of Alaa Zumari, the would-be cell-phone mogul scooped up in Iraq and sent to Poland for interrogation by 673.

Wells could have gone straight to the house of Zumari's family, of course. His dossier had the address. But Zumari was missing. And his mother and father wouldn't exactly be eager to help a CIA agent find him.

The call to prayer blared. Wells shucked his sandals by the front door and joined the stream of men stepping inside. Islamic law barred artists from painting images of Allah, Muhammad, or even ordinary men and women. Such portraits were considered distracting and disrespectful to God's majesty. So the mosque had almost no decoration, though its mihrab—the nook that faced toward Mecca—was laid in an ornate pattern of black-and-white tile. With high ceilings and fans spinning overhead, the mosque was notably cooler than the streets. Unseen pigeons cooed from windows high on its back wall.

The mosque's central hall was nearly one hundred feet square, much bigger than it seemed from outside. Hundreds of men had already arranged themselves in front of the *minbar*, the wooden pulpit where the imam gave his weekly sermon. Muslims prayed five times a day, every day. But the Friday midday prayer was the week's most important service, the time when the community gathered. Most men sat near the pulpit, but some stayed back, the cool kids in class, leaning against the walls and chatting with friends as they waited for the service to begin.

Men streamed in, filling the hall. Wells estimated at least a thousand had already arrived. And this was just one mid-sized mosque. Some, like the Mosque of Ibn Tulun south of here, were open squares as big as a city block, capable of holding tens of thousands of men.

The room was notably warmer now, and the odor of a thousand sweating bodies filled the air. Men were supposed to bathe before the midday prayer, but many came straight from work. The men were mostly Arab, though a handful were black, probably Nubian

Egyptians or Sudanese from the Upper Nile. Many had faint bruises on their foreheads, a sign of piety. The bruising came from touching their foreheads to the ground as they prayed.

Suddenly the imam mounted the wooden pulpit and began the *Surah Fatiha*, the first verse of the Quran: *"Bismallahi rahmani rahmi al-hamdulillah . . ."* In the name of Allah, the most gracious, the most merciful; All praises to Allah . . .

The imam spoke beautifully, Wells thought. Even without amplification, his voice filled the mosque. He finished the *surah* and began his sermon. "Brothers. Allah tells us that we are not to call ourselves pure. Only he knows who is truly righteous. . . ." Good deeds would not please God if they were done for selfish reasons, he explained. "Actions are judged by motives."

As he listened, Wells remembered what he loved most about Islam, the strength and simplicity of its doctrines. The religion had five basic tenets: accept God and Muhammad as His prophet; pray five times a day; give to charity; fast during the month of Ramadan; and travel to Mecca for the sacred pilgrimage of the hajj. Anyone who followed those rules, or sincerely tried to, was a good Muslim.

The men paid rapt attention to the sermon. No watches were checked, no cell phones pulled out. Wells didn't know how long the imam spoke; his words flowed together as smoothly as the Nile. When he finished, the muezzin gave the *iqama*, a second call to prayer performed only at the Friday midday service.

The men in the mosque clustered together shoulder to shoulder for the *rakaat*, the core Muslim prayer. Side by side they dropped to their knees and touched their foreheads and hands and toes to the floor, a thousand men affirming God as Muslims had for a thousand years.

———

AFTER THE SERVICE, the imam stood beside the pulpit, clasping hands with men who'd come forward for advice or a benediction. Finally, the last of the worshippers left and the imam was alone. Wells intercepted him.

"*Salaam alekeim.*"

"*Alekeim salaam.*"

"Your sermon today was filled with wisdom."

"Thank you." The imam gave Wells a puzzled smile. "I haven't seen you before."

"I'm from Kuwait."

"You came this far to hear me preach?"

"I hoped you might help me find someone."

The imam glanced at the front of the mosque, as if he wanted to ask Wells to leave. But he said only, "Please, come with me."

He led Wells through a nook in the wall behind the pulpit and down a concrete corridor. His office was simple, square, and furnished only with a wooden desk and a bookshelf filled with Quranic commentaries. A barred window looked into a narrow alley. A heavy man with the full, bushy beard of a believer sat beside the desk, sipping tea. He hugged the imam, then looked suspiciously at Wells.

"*Salaam alekeim,*" Wells said.

The man let the greeting hang like an unwanted hand extended for a shake. Finally, he murmured, "*Alekeim salaam.*"

The imam nodded for Wells to sit. "Leave us, Hani," the imam said. "And close the door."

The man hesitated, then walked out. The imam regarded Wells across the desk.

"Your name?"

"Nadeem Taleeb."

"From Kuwait?"

"Kuwait City, yes."

"Where are you staying in Cairo?"

"The Lotus Hotel." Wells paused. "I understand why you wonder about me. When I arrived, I saw a man watching this place. He wore no uniform. But I'm certain he was *mukhabarat*."

"How do you know?"

"I know. He wore a black shirt and pants. He was drinking tea at the shop on the corner. The one that sells ice cream. He pretended to read, but he was watching your front entrance. Have your men check."

"Hani—" the imam said. The door opened, and the fat man scuttled in. The imam whispered to him.

"*Aiwa*," Hani said. Yes. He glared at Wells before he left.

"So, Kuwaiti," the imam said. "Who are you looking for?"

"Ihab Zumari." Alaa's father. "A friend told me he worships here."

"You should leave," the imam said. "Finish your tea and leave. I don't know what game this is, but I know it's dangerous. For both of us. I'm a peaceful man."

Wells pulled a pen and pad from his robe and scribbled on it in English and Arab.

"You use computers, sheikh? The Internet?"

The imam looked almost offended. "Of course."

"My apologies. Please. Look at this site. You'll understand. I'll come back tomorrow for another cup of tea. *Inshallah*"—God willing—"you'll see me. If not, I won't bother you again."

Wells slid the paper across the desk, stood, and walked out, leaving the imam looking at a single note. A Web address: Prisonersof America.com.

THE DIRECTORATE OF SCIENCE and Technology had done a good job, Wells had to admit. Two videos were up. They looked professional but not too professional, the interviewees giving long speeches about how they'd suffered as captives of the United States. One was supposedly an Algerian captured in Iraq in 2006 and released two years later, the second a Pakistani caught in Afghanistan in 2005 and let go in 2009. Both men wore bandannas to hide their mouths and had exceptionally common names: Mohammed Hassan and Ahmed Mustafa. They gave detailed descriptions of the deprivations they suffered. They spoke angrily but not so passionately that they seemed unhinged.

They were fakes, CIA employees, analysts in the Directorate of Intelligence. They'd agreed enthusiastically to the assignment, knowing that the interviews might be as close as they would ever get to the front lines.

The technical details were right, too. A commercial Russian Internet service provider hosted the site. Its content was uploaded through a Finnish server that guaranteed anonymity to its users. Even the IP address registration was backdated, so that the site seemed to have been up for months.

The site itself had a straightforward front page in English and Arabic: "Here you will find the stories of Muslims held captive. Here you will find the truth about the 'peace-loving' Americans." No over-the-top rhetoric. And, of course, no pictures of Wells as Nadeem anywhere. He wouldn't have been foolish enough to give up his anonymity.

WELLS LEFT THE MOSQUE and a few minutes later found himself on Sharia al-Muizz, a narrow street in the heart of Islamic Cairo. He took his time. If the imam had ordered him tailed, he wanted to show that he had nothing to hide. But no one seemed to be on him. After an hour of browsing the storefronts, he grabbed a cab to the Lotus. He would leave his room at the Intercontinental unoccupied tonight, the bed unmussed. The hotel wouldn't care unless his credit card bounced.

At the Lotus, he couldn't fall asleep for hours. During his time off, he'd forgotten the intensity, the perpetual vigilance, required for these missions. Finally he faded out. He found himself in a window-less room with Exley, interviewing her for the site. She wore a blue *hijab* and sunglasses and held a duck in her lap.

"Next question," she said in English.

"Did they let you pray?" he said in Arabic.

"I prayed for you, John."

"Please speak Arabic."

"You know I can't speak Arabic."

The duck quacked madly. Exley petted its feathers. "He doesn't mean to upset you, Ethan. He doesn't know any better."

"You named the duck after Evan? My son?"

"No. His name's Ethan. Not Evan. He's named after our son."

Wells was confused. "We didn't have a son—"

"We did. Would have, I mean. I was pregnant, that day Kowalski sent his men—"

No, Wells thought. It wasn't so. He knew she was lying. "Tell the truth, Jenny."

"You can't handle the truth," she said in Jack Nicholson's voice.

"Why can't you let me go?"

"I think you have it backwards, John—"

And with that, a strange scratching pulled him back to the world. Exley disappeared as he opened his eyes. The room was empty. He didn't know the time, but the city was close to quiet. He guessed it was between 3 and 4 a.m., the quiet hour, when only insomniacs and cabbies prowled the streets.

The scratching, again. Low and quiet. At the door.

Wells waited. Let them come. Nadeem Taleb wouldn't resist.

The door creaked open. Hani slid into the room, followed by a dark-skinned, wiry man. Hani flicked on the overhead bulb. He held a pistol, a small one. It looked almost silly in his pillowy hands. "No noise," he said. He gathered Wells's passport and watch and wallet from the nightstand and moved over to the window and tucked his pistol into his jeans. He flipped through the passport and set it aside. His movements were easy and purposeful, and something in them bothered Wells. Wells flicked his tongue over his lips in a show of nervousness. Then stopped, reminding himself not to overact.

"Get up, Kuwaiti. If that's what you are. Get dressed."

Wells rolled out, pulled on a *galabiya*. The wiry man rousted the room, pulling open drawers, rooting through Wells's toiletries kit, shining a flashlight under the bed, a cursory but efficient search. Wells watched in silence until the man reached the suitcase.

"It's locked," he said.

"Why?" Hani said.

"There's a camera inside."

"Open it."

Wells extracted a key from his wallet and unlocked the case. The wiry man pulled out the video camera almost triumphantly.

"Why do you have this?" Hani said.

"To film the interviews." Wells took a slightly aggravated tone, as if he could hardly be bothered to answer such a stupid question.

Hani held up Wells's Rolex. "You're a rich man, Kuwaiti. Why stay here? Why not the Hyatt, with your cousins?" The Cairo Grand Hyatt had paradoxically become the favorite of the Gulf Arabs who visited the city. Paradoxically, because Hyatt was owned by the Pritzker family, who were not just Americans but Jews.

"The Hyatt? So the *mukhabarat* can watch me come and go? Does that seem like a good idea, *habibi?*"

"Stuff your mouth with sand and see if you make such smart remarks," Hani murmured, to himself as much as to Wells. Again, his manner troubled Wells. A decade ago, in Afghanistan—and especially in the abattoir that was Chechnya—Wells had seen men who responded to any uncertainty with violence, the quicker and messier the better. Hani might be one of them. And yet he didn't seem angry or volatile. Perhaps he didn't want to be here, and the imam had forced the mission on him.

Hani pulled out his cell phone, typed a quick text, slipped it away. He tucked Wells's passport and wallet into his jeans. "Time to go."

"Where?" Wells wasn't expecting an answer.

But he got one. "You wanted to meet Ihab Zumari, Kuwaiti? Now you will."

OUTSIDE, A PEUGEOT 504 IDLED. A four-door sedan, boxy and black, with tinted windows. Hani ushered Wells into the back, tied a black bandanna over his eyes, tightly enough to ensure that light didn't leak through.

Wells lay back, closed his eyes, tried to sleep. He wasn't overly worried. Most likely the imam was just being cautious. And if not . . . he'd faced worse odds than this.

The car turned left, right, then accelerated. Even without the blindfold, Wells would have been lost.

"What's your name, Kuwaiti?" Hani said.

"Nadeem Taleeb."

"Where do you live?"

"Kuwait City."

"And why are you here?"

"To interview Alaa Zumari. You know all this."

"You're a spy."

"No more than you."

The back of a hand stung his face.

"Be careful, Kuwaiti."

Then Wells understood. The well-knotted blindfold. Hani's two-handed pistol grip. His strangely relaxed attitude. He was no jihadi, however many years he'd spent at this mosque. He was *mukhabarat*. Very good, but not good enough to eliminate the traces of his training.

And he, even more than the imam, must be wondering what Nadeem Taleeb was doing here. Behind his blindfold, Wells puzzled through the permutations. The Egyptians couldn't have penetrated his cover already. Cooperation between the Kuwaiti and Egyptian intelligence services was mediocre at best.

No. Hani didn't know who Nadeem really was. His best move would be to play along, to hope that Nadeem could get him to Alaa Zumari. The Egyptians were embarrassed to have lost Zumari. Even if they didn't want to arrest him, they surely wanted to find him again.

What about the imam? Did he know his deputy was an Egyptian agent? Could he be working for secret police, too? Wells guessed not, though he couldn't be sure.

The car stopped. A hand tugged him out of the car. "Turn, facing the car," Hani said. "Hands behind your back." His voice was close. Wells smelled the coffee on his breath, the stink of his unwashed skin. Wells held out his hands, and Hani slipped handcuffs around his wrists and frog-marched him toward a second vehicle, a bigger one with a diesel engine.

"Two steps here," Hani said.

As Wells reached the second step, Hani pushed him forward. He tripped, sprawled forward. With his hands cuffed behind him, he instinctively rolled onto his right shoulder to protect his face. Too late, he remembered that he should have rolled left. Two years before, he had separated his right shoulder, and then it had taken a terrible beating from two Chinese prison guards. He had rebuilt and strengthened the joint as best he could. Now he landed directly on it. It buckled up and came out of the socket with an audible *pop,* and Wells felt as if the joint were being prodded with a hot iron.

Through the pain, Wells remembered that Nadeem Taleeb had to swear in Arabic. *"Sharmuta, sharmuta,"* he said. The word roughly translated as "bitch."

Wells squirmed onto his left side, trying to relieve the pressure on his shoulder. The handcuffs worsened the pain, pulling his arm down and out of the socket. His breaths were coming fast and shallow, and he didn't know how long he could stay conscious.

Someone tugged off the blindfold. Wells found himself looking up at the imam.

"Are you all right, Kuwaiti?"

"The handcuffs—"

"Take them off," the imam said to Hani.

Hani hesitated, then reached for the cuffs, giving Wells's shoulder a final tug as he did. With his arms free, the pain was merely agonizing. Wells sat up, his right arm hanging limp. He was in a midsize panel truck. The imam and Hani sat beside him, a skinny middle-aged man in the corner. His hair was gray, unusual for an Arab. Wells recognized him from Alaa Zumari's dossier. Alaa's father, Ihab.

"Pop it in," Wells said to Hani.

"What?"

"My shoulder." Wells could fix the joint himself. He had before. But very few people had his pain tolerance, and they might wonder how he'd managed it.

Hani looked to the imam, who nodded. Hani grabbed Wells's arm at the elbow and without hesitation pushed it up and into the socket. Wells's body became a machine devoted to generating pain, the agony radiating across his chest. Then his arm settled in and Wells could open his eyes. He took two breaths, three, and then was able to move. He squirmed backward, leaned against the side of the truck.

"You are all right?" the imam said.

"*Inshallah,*" Wells said.

"*Inshallah.*"

Hani gave the imam Wells's Kuwaiti passport and wallet. The imam leafed through them. "You came to Suez. Why not fly?"

"At the airport, every passenger is photographed. It's best for me if my picture isn't taken. The pharaoh's men are everywhere."

"That man"—the imam nodded at the man in the corner—"is Ihab Zumari. The one you've come to see."

Wells braced himself to stand, but Hani put a hand on his left shoulder. "*Salaam alekeim,* Ihab," Wells said.

"*Alekeim salaam.*"

"I'm Nadeem Taleeb. I'm sorry to disturb your sleep."

Zumari nodded.

"Did you see my Web site? The videos?"

Another nod.

"Then you know why I've come to you."

"Tell me," Zumari said. His voice was low, each syllable measured. His dossier said he ran a small electronics store in a run-down

section of Islamic Cairo, but he looked and sounded more like a law professor.

"I want to talk to your son. Interview him."

"Why Alaa? It must be thousands of detainees who've been released."

"Only a few from the secret prisons."

Neither Zumari nor the imam looked convinced.

"You wonder why I do this. I'll tell you about myself. I'm not a jihadi. I pray, sure, but I never hated the Kaffirs. Back in the 1990s, I lived in France. I liked it. But five years ago, a boy I know, a friend's son, Ali, he went to Afghanistan. He wasn't really a jihadi. Not very religious. He went with the Talibs for the adventure, I think."

"Adventure," the imam said.

"Kuwait, it's boring. Office buildings, oil wells, desert. These boys have nothing to do but drive around all day. Not even a wife, unless they're rich. The sheikhs take three, four women each, and there's none for the rest of us. With the Talibs, they can fire AKs, throw a grenade. Pretend they're soldiers."

"You don't have children."

"I'm not a sheikh. I didn't have the money to marry. Anyway, Ali, the Americans caught him in Afghanistan and kept him for two years. Finally, they released him. When he came back, he told me how they kept him in a little cage. I think it made him crazy. He was so angry. At the Americans, the Kuwaitis, his own family."

"He was like that before he went to Afghanistan?"

"No. He was a regular boy. But once he came back to Kuwait, he wasn't anymore. He only ever talked of martyrdom. And then he disappeared. I found out later, he went to Iraq, became a fedayeen"—a martyr.

"A bomber."

"Yes. He killed himself outside a police station in Baghdad. Thirteen police died. And after that, I had the idea for these interviews. So that everyone will know what the Americans are doing. I know about computers and filming. But it isn't easy to find the men, or get them to talk. They may be home, but they aren't free. They know our police are working with the Americans and don't want to be embarrassed. And lots of them are just—" Wells spread his hands out, meaning *disappeared*. Then winced as his shoulder caught fire again.

"You should go to Saudi."

"In Saudi the *mukhabarat* are too good." Wells paused. "And your son, there's something else, another reason I want to talk to him. I heard he wasn't a jihadi at all. Just a man who wanted to set up a cellphone business. An innocent."

"You heard this? Who told you?"

"People see the videos, the Web site, and they e-mail me. Most of the time I can't confirm what they say. But this time I found someone who could."

"Who?"

"I can't tell you."

"Then I can't help you."

Wells looked to the imam. "It is best for all of us if I'm the only one who knows. For the same reason you took these precautions to pick me up."

"And my son's story—"

"He tells whatever he likes, as much or as little. I protect him, hide his face. Show just enough of him that people know he's real. The video takes one, two hours to make. Three at most, if your son has a lot to tell. I send it to the Web site, and you never see me again."

And along the way I'll find out if he knows anything about the murders, Wells thought.

"Even if I wanted to help, I don't know where he is," Zumari said.

"But you can reach him."

"I can try."

"Then please try."

They were silent as the truck rumbled on. Hani dialed his phone, spoke so quietly that Wells couldn't hear.

"Do you have anything else to tell us?" the imam said.

"No."

The truck slowed, then stopped.

"Kuwaiti," the imam said. "Your shoulder is all right?"

"I think so, yes."

The imam handed Wells his passport and wallet. "Then this is where we leave you. There's a ramp ahead. Take it down, go back to your hotel. Stay away from my house"—the mosque. "If we need to see you again, we will find you."

"I'm sure," Wells said. "I ask only this: whatever you decide—" Wells broke off.

"Yes?"

"Decide soon. It will be safer for all of us."

An air horn blasted through the cargo compartment. Hani pulled up the back gate of the truck. Wells saw they were on a highway, the traffic piling up behind them.

"*Ma-a-saalama,*" he said to Ihab and the imam. Peace be with you. Good-bye.

"*Ma-a-saalama,*" they said in turn. Wells jumped out the back of the truck. A wave of dizziness hit him and his knees buckled, but he stayed upright. Behind him, the truck rumbled off. He didn't turn to watch it go.

He found himself on an elevated highway, staring east, into the rising sun. To the north and south were endless zigzag blocks of misshapen concrete buildings. Many seemed unfinished, their roofs turned into dumps filled with half-melted tires and lumpy plastic bags of garbage. He must still be in Cairo, somewhere on the ring road that had once marked the outer edges of the city.

A Mercedes sedan nearly knocked him over. He turned to look for the exit ramp—and saw, looming over the city on a plateau to the west, the three great pyramids, just beginning to reflect the glow of the morning sun. Wells understood immediately why European adventurers had thought that they'd been built by aliens. They were immense, so much larger than the buildings around them that they seemed to be governed by entirely different laws of physics. Wells stared at them until a honk brought him back to the highway. He walked slowly down the ramp until the city swallowed up him and the pyramids.

HEADING BACK to the hotel, Wells saw the scope of the city at last. Close to twenty million people lived in Cairo, though no one, not even the Egyptian government, knew exactly how many. The shabby concrete and brick buildings went on block after block, mile after mile, unrelieved by parks or gardens or even palm trees. The place was overwhelming, ugly, primordial, Los Angeles without highways, Rio without the ocean. Year after year it had grown east and west into the desert and south along the Nile, swallowing every settlement in its path.

Wells had seen only one other city as big and dense, as noisy and smoggy: Beijing. But in Beijing the hand of the Chinese state touched every alley and dumpling stand. Beijing was order disguised as chaos. Not Cairo. Cairo was chaos, undisguised. Cairo lacked any organizing principle. Except Islam.

A minivan pulled in front of them, and the cabbie banged his brakes to avoid a collision. Wells stifled a groan as the seat belt grabbed his shoulder. The van, improbably enough, seemed to have a load of goats as passengers.

Suddenly, Wells badly wanted to find his way to the Intercontinental for air-conditioning, a hot shower, and a cold beer. He reminded himself that he'd spent a decade living without any of the three. No, he would go back to the Lotus, where he belonged. And as the traffic inched forward, he smiled to himself. The *mukhabarat*, the jihadis—he was back in the game.

7

The Counterterrorist Center was the CIA's fastest-growing unit. To make room for it, the agency had built offices in a subterranean maze carved from the foundations of the New Headquarters Building. The fight against Al Qaeda ate a disproportionate share of the agency's budget, so the new space had bells and whistles the rest of the CIA lacked: flat-panel screens, dedicated teraflop-speed connections to the National Security Agency and Department of Defense, and videoconferencing equipment capable of projecting in three dimensions. Somewhere, Osama bin Laden was quaking in his boots.

Or not.

Brant Murphy met Shafer at the main entrance to CTC, a miniature version of the agency's main lobby, two guards overseeing a bank of turnstiles. The official logic behind the secondary checkpoint was that CTC needed extra security because it so frequently hosted visitors from other federal agencies and foreign spy services. In reality, the second guard post was further proof that the unit held itself apart from the rest of the agency.

Murphy was handsome and compact, with deep blue eyes and close-cropped blond hair that had lost its grip on his temples and was fighting a rearguard action against its inevitable fate as a widow's peak. He had a firm two-pump handshake, friendly but manly. Shafer couldn't understand how Murphy had ended up with 673. Spending a year-plus in Poland interrogating detainees didn't seem like his idea of a great time.

"Ellis Shafer," Murphy said. He had a clipped Yankee accent, a relative rarity at the agency, which recruited more from the South and Midwest.

"Good to meet you," Shafer said. "I appreciate this."

"The pleasure is mine," Murphy said. He didn't look pleased. "If the director asks, I'm glad to accommodate. And of course your reputation precedes you."

"Follows me, too."

Murphy led them into a high-ceilinged conference room, the walls of which were lined with expensive black-and-white photographs of Iraq and Afghanistan.

"Nice digs."

Murphy looked around as if he'd never seen the photos before. "You spend as much time in here as we do, you hardly notice."

"Just like Poland?"

"Not exactly, but sure."

Shafer set a digital tape recorder on the table. "Do you mind?"

"And here I thought this was a social call. You don't mind, I'd prefer we keep it informal."

The room itself was almost certainly wired, but Shafer didn't argue. He slipped the recorder away, reached into his pocket for a pen and a reporter's notebook, its pages filled with an illegible scrawl.

"Tell me how you became part of 673."

"Have you seen my file?"

Shafer grunted noncommittally.

"So, you know a couple years back I did a tour in Iraq. Mosul. My COS"—chief of station—"there was Brad Gessen. Remember him?"

"Yeah." Gessen had been arrested for stealing 1.2 million dollars from a fund used to bribe Sunni tribal chiefs in Iraq. Starting in early 2006, the CIA and army had thrown cash at the tribes, hoping to turn them against the insurgency, or at least buy their neutrality. More than one billion in cash was distributed through the program, with only the barest accounting. Rumors of thefts were rampant. But only Gessen had been arrested, probably because he'd stolen so much money that some of the tribal leaders had complained to the army about the missing payments.

"Brad and I were tight," Murphy said. "I mean, I had no idea what he was up to—"

"Sure about that?"

"I don't appreciate that question."

"One-point-two million, and the guy was your boss and you didn't know?"

Murphy controlled himself, the effort visible. "There was a full investigation. The IG cleared me. But my career took a hit. Started hearing that I might get moved to Australia"—not exactly the agency's hottest theater. "So 673, when it came up, I figured it was a chance to turn the page. High-risk, high-reward, but we get the right intel, we're all heroes."

Shafer started to like Murphy a tiny bit more. The man hadn't sugarcoated this explanation. No talk of taking the battle to the enemy, broadening his experience. He'd made a clear-eyed analysis that going to Poland might rescue his career. He was a hopelessly ambitious careerist, but at least he wasn't pretending otherwise.

"And what did you do in Poland?"

"Ran admin and logistic," Murphy said, calm again. "Nine-person unit on a foreign base, plus the detainees, there's a lot to do."

I thought it was ten.

"I'll get to that. I handled our relationships with the Poles, set up the supply chain. When there was significant intel, I summarized it and passed it to the Pentagon."

"With so few men, how did you watch the prisoners continuously?"

"We had help from the Poles. They supplied food, picked up garbage, handled security around the building. At night they helped us monitor the cells."

"But they weren't actively involved in the interrogations."

"No."

"How often did you visit the detainees?"

"When necessary," Murphy said. "Like I said, it wasn't my role."

"And how were they treated?"

"As illegal enemy combatants. If they cooperated, they received more privileges, and if they didn't, they didn't."

"I'm sorry," Shafer said. "I didn't hear an answer."

"I told you, I spent most of my time on admin."

"The unit was short on manpower," Shafer said. "You were basically running a jail with a ten-man squad."

"Yes and no," Murphy said.

"How many detainees did you have?"

"Ten."

"And you'd hold one or two at a time?"

"Yes. Once we had three, but Terreri didn't like that. Said it was too many. And he was right."

"Walk me through a day in the life."

"The interrogations ran about eight, ten hours at a stretch. Two or three men were involved: the interrogator—that was usually Karp—and a muscle guy or two."

"So you could run two interrogations at once."

"If we needed to. But we preferred to go one at a time. As you know, the squad was all men, except for the psychiatrist, Rachel, Dr. Callar. The org chart, LTC Terreri was the CO"—the commanding officer. "I was XO"—the executive officer, the number two. "Karp was the lead interrogator. Jerry Williams did swing duty; he knew Arabic, so he could handle interrogations. And also he oversaw the three Rangers, who were the muscle. And then Callar."

"What about Hank Poteat?"

"He was technically part of the squad, but he was only there a couple of months, at the beginning. He helped set up our coms, and then he left. So that's everybody."

"It isn't, though," Shafer said. He flipped back through his reporter's notebook. "CO is Terreri. XO is you. Karp is the interrogator. Callar's the doctor. Williams and his three Rangers make eight. Poteat counts as technically part of the squad, even though he wasn't there long. That's nine. You forgot Jack Fisher."

"Right," Murphy said. "Fisher helped Karp with the interrogations. He would stay up late with the prisoners. If they wouldn't talk, they needed an extra push. Sometimes Jerry Williams helped. The Midnight House, we called it sometimes. Fisher, he'd tell the detainees when they got there, 'Welcome to the Midnight House.'"

"Funny."

"We were trying to take the edge off. Stuck in Poland for a year and a half."

"How tough was Fisher?"

"I don't know. Specifically."

"Friendly persuasion. Cup of cocoa. Tell me about your mother."

"I wasn't there."

"You were the second-in-command and you didn't know."

"I told you, I wasn't operational.

"You strike me as the type who prefers to lead from the rear."

Murphy stared at Shafer as if Shafer were a misbehaving brat he wanted to spank but couldn't. In turn, Shafer made faces at Murphy, raising his eyebrows, throwing in a wink.

"I'm sorry," Murphy said finally. "I didn't hear a question."

"Try this. Did the unit have internal tensions?"

"We were a small group living in close quarters in a foreign country. We couldn't tell anyone what we were doing. Of course, we didn't always get along. But nothing you wouldn't expect."

"Did you believe that the detainees were treated fairly?"

"From what I saw, yes."

"Did 673 ever uncover actionable intel?"

For the first time, Murphy smiled. "Definitely."

"What, exactly?"

"I can't say. Vinny Duto wants to tell you, it's his business."

"But it was valuable."

"You could say that."

Shafer made a note. "Fast-forward," he said. "The squad breaks up, a bunch of guys retire. You stay."

"With the intel we'd gotten, I wanted to see where I'd be in a year or two."

"Any idea why so many guys decided to leave?"

"Ask them."

"Guilty consciences?"

"I'm not a mind reader. Not now or then." Murphy looked at his watch. "The FBI's coming tomorrow, and I'm sure they'll be asking all the same questions as you, and more besides. Can we finish up later?"

"A few more minutes," Shafer said.

"A few."

"After you got back, did you stay in touch with the rest of the unit?"

"Colonel Terreri and I had lunch a couple times before he got sent to Afghanistan. I saw Karp upstairs once."

"How about Fisher?"

"Talked to him once or twice. No one else. It was an ad hoc deployment, and we got scattered."

"You didn't know what was happening to the unit. The deaths."

"Of course I did. We all heard about Rachel. Not right away, but we heard. Then Terreri sent me an e-mail that Mark and Freddy"—the two Rangers—"were KIA. Then Karp. By then we were all wondering a little bit. I remember saying to Fisher, 'What's the story? Somebody put a curse on us?' But we didn't know that Jerry was missing. I know it looks obvious in retrospect."

"You don't seem nervous."

"Should I cry for Mommy?"

"Can you think of any reason someone might be after the squad?"

"Beyond the fact that we put the screws to some bad actors?" Murphy drummed his fingers on the table. In contrast with his neatly tailored clothes, his nails were jagged, bitten nearly to the quick. "My ass on the line. I've thought about it. I don't know."

"What about Alaa Zumari?" Shafer said.

"I can't tell you anything that's not in the file."

"Haven't seen the file," Shafer muttered into his teeth.

"Say again?"

"I said I haven't seen it. Not yet."

"You'll have to work that out with Vinny."

"How about you walk me through it?"

How about not?

Shafer wanted to reach across the table and slap Murphy, but in a way he was right. Duto had started this charade, asked him and Wells to try to find a killer without the background information they needed.

"Any chance Alaa Zumari's connected to this?"

"If we thought he was a terrorist, we wouldn't have let him go."

"Maybe he lied. Withstood the pressure somehow. Could he have figured out who was on the squad? Your real names?"

"We were pretty tight about opsec. Never used real names with the detainees."

"The Poles? Could they have leaked your names?"

"Anything's possible."

"Could anyone inside the unit be responsible for the killings?"

"You asking if I'm the killer? I'm gonna have to say no."

"How about Hank Poteat? Or Terreri? Or Jerry?"

"I told you, Poteat wasn't part of the squad. The colonel's in Afghanistan. Jerry's dead."

"What if he's not?"

The question stopped Murphy. He ran a hand down his tie, flipped up the tip, looked at it as if the fabric might hold the answer. "Jerry had a temper. And he was having problems with his wife, we knew that. And he thought he deserved a promotion. He quit when he didn't get it. But I don't see him taking it out on us."

Murphy pushed himself back from the table. "Mr. Shafer. I hope you enjoyed this as much as I did. I have to get to work. I think of anything else, I'll let you know."

"Before you go," Shafer said. "Tell me about the C-one drop."

"What about it?"

"Eight million for ten guys for sixteen months? Nice work if you can get it."

"Two hundred grand a month to the Poles to rent the barracks and the guards. Payments whenever we landed a jet. A million for coms gear that we bought over there. Charter flights."

"You keep receipts?"

"Of course. We wanted to leave a nice long paper trail for all those congressional investigators. And the Justice Department."

"I take it that's a no."

"You take it correctly."

Shafer leaned forward in his chair, flared his nostrils like a terrier on the scent of a rat.

"Let me make sure I understand. You worked for a guy who stole one-point-two million dollars in Iraq. This squad, you're in charge of eight million. And you don't keep receipts."

"I got verbal approval for anything over twenty-five thousand dollars."

"From who?"

"Somebody in Sanchez's office, usually."

"Anybody keep records of those conversations?"

"Colonel Terreri knew where the money was going."

"Terreri. He's not dead yet, right?"

"You have something to ask, ask it," Murphy said. The vein on his forehead had popped out again, visible proof that Shafer's bluff had scored.

"Maybe I'll wait until tomorrow, when the Feebs come to town." Suddenly, Shafer understood. Every so often he had a flash like this, the pieces fitting together all at once. "Six-seven-three was your career saver? Guess again. You put in for it figuring on the unrestricted drop. Figuring you could skim. You saw Gessen's mistakes. And you would have gotten away clean, if not for the murders."

"Only one problem with that theory. It's been investigated. And

I've been cleared. No evidence of wrongdoing, and that was that. I've got it in writing. Now, you want to talk to me again, you call my lawyer."

Murphy pulled open the conference-room door, walked out, slammed it shut behind him hard enough to leave a hairline crack in its porthole-shaped window.

"New construction," Shafer said to the empty room. "Can never trust it."

8

CAIRO

For two days, Wells cooled his heels at the Lotus, leaving only for a quick trip to the Intercontinental. The move was risky, but if his room stayed empty too long, the hotel's managers might get nervous. Wells stayed an hour, long enough to muss his bed, take a shower, and have a brief conversation with Shafer on an innocuous Long Island number that routed through to the agency.

"Mr. Barber," Shafer said. "How's business?"

"I'm worried our client has another bidder. A local agency."

"Maybe you should work together."

"I think our needs are different."

"You're the man on the ground, so I defer to you."

"Your man in Havana."

"You've been reading again, I see," Shafer said.

"Despite your warnings."

"I recommend *The Comedians*. It's excellent. Anything else I should know?"

"Probably, but I don't feel like telling you."

Shafer sighed. "Your honesty, so refreshing."

"Have you learned anything new about my client?"

"No, but I did have an interesting talk with our friend Mr. Murphy," Shafer said. "I'll fill you in when you get back."

"Something to look forward to. How's Tonka?" After much protesting, Shafer had agreed to take the dog while Wells went to Cairo.

"She's developed a taste for the rug in the living room. Aside from
that, fine."

"She miss me?"

"Without a doubt. Every day she leaves a note at my door asking
when you're coming back."

"Good-bye."

Wells left his air-conditioned room unwillingly. No question, he
was getting soft. *"A luxury once tasted becomes a necessity."* Wells didn't
know who'd popped that kernel of wisdom—someone richer and wit-
tier than he, no doubt—but he had to agree. He needed to spend a few
months in Haiti or Sudan, unlearn his bad habits.

Back at the Lotus he passed the time watching Al Jazeera and
Lebanese soap operas. He figured he could wait a week, at most. If he
was right and Hani was a *mukhabarat* agent, the Egyptians would put
a tail on him soon enough—or just break down his door and arrest
him. Part of him wondered why they hadn't done so already. Probably because they didn't want to scare him back to Kuwait, blow their
chance at Alaa.

Or maybe Wells had gotten paranoid as well as soft. Maybe Hani
was just what he seemed to be, a dedicated Islamist who had nothing
to do with the police.

THE ENVELOPE APPEARED BENEATH his door on the third day, during the
call to afternoon prayer. Inside, a single sheet of paper: *1 a.m. Northern
Cemetery. Bring the camera. Nothing more.*

Wells read the note twice to be sure he understood. The Northern Cemetery was a huge and ancient graveyard east of the Islamic

quarter. Over the centuries, thousands of poor families had nested in the cemetery's mausoleums and built one-room houses over its graves. Space was precious in Cairo, and the dead didn't charge rent. Now, with fifty thousand residents, as well as paved streets and power lines, the cemetery was a city within a city, as crowded as the rest of Cairo. And so as an instruction for a meeting place, "Northern Cemetery" was strangely nonspecific, the equivalent of naming an entire neighborhood in an American city, like Buckhead in Atlanta.

Still, Wells had no choice but to obey and hope that the imam could find him. For dinner he had two plain pitas and two bottles of Fanta, the Egyptian version of his usual pre-mission meal of crackers and Gatorade, light and sugary and easy to keep down. And at 11:30, he slipped on his *galabiya,* tucked his camera into his backpack.

But at the door he stopped, took out the camera. He popped open the battery compartment and pulled out the flat black battery. Sure enough, a radio transmitter about the size of a nickel was taped to its underside. The bug was oldish, Russian, nothing fancy. Probably had a range of a few hundred yards, enough to help a search team track down a fugitive once he'd been treed.

Wells guessed that the *mukhabarat* had put the bug on the battery when he met with Hani and the imam. Wells was happy to be rid of it, happy his instincts were still sharp. Even so, finding it was a bad sign. For the first time since China, he was facing a professional secret police force. He reached a dirty fingernail under the tape and detached the bug. He'd toss it on the way to the cemetery, after he lost the tail that was surely waiting for him.

OUTSIDE THE LOTUS, the downtown streets bustled. Couples strolled side by side. A few even held hands. Discreetly, of course. A mother and a daughter, wearing matching pink head scarves, giggled as they bought Popsicles from a stooped man pulling an ice-cream cart. The lack of alcohol gave the streets a pleasant, relaxed feeling. The crowds were lively but not rowdy, the sidewalks free of broken bottles and shouting matches. And Wells walked, his hands at his sides, split from the ordinary lives around him by a wall only he could see. The curse of the spy, at once present and absent. He walked, and he wondered whether anyone was on him.

Build countersurveillance into your schedule. If you don't have time for it, you don't have time for the meet. Even if you don't think anyone's on you. Even if you're sure no one's on you. The life you save may be your own.

Guy Raviv, one of Wells's favorite instructors at the Farm, had given him that lesson a lifetime ago. Raviv had striking blue eyes and a smoker's hoarse voice and hair too black to be anything but dyed. He seemed to be in his mid-fifties, though he could have been older. My children, he called his trainees. My precious, precocious youngsters. He'd been introduced to Wells's class as a legend who had shucked whole teams of Stasi agents in East Berlin. Wells assumed that the story was exaggerated. Instructors at the Farm had a habit of embellishing their résumés, perhaps with the agency's encouragement. Far better for new recruits to believe that they were learning from stars than from failed ops put out to pasture.

But whatever Raviv had or hadn't done in East Berlin, he was a master teacher, as Wells learned firsthand when he and a team of recruits chased Raviv through the crowded streets of Philadelphia on a Saturday in July. Raviv lost them twice in two hours. He didn't run—*Please remember that anything more than a brisk walk is reserved for emergencies*—but he had what Wells's linebacker coach at Dartmouth called "quick feet," the ability to change speed and direction almost instantly. Coming back from Philly, Raviv stopped at a McDonald's on I-95 and distributed a full tray of bon mots along with his Happy Meals.

Your first goal is to make your pursuer show himself. He knows you. You don't know him. Before you can lose him, you have to find him. And give yourself time. Listen to the wisdom of Mick Jagger, children: Time is on your side; oh, yes it is. More time equals more moves. More moves equal more chances to make your pursuer show himself. Will you be eating those fries?

In retrospect, Wells was shocked that the agency had allowed Raviv near them. Langley had always been a tribal place, unfriendly to oddballs. In the 1980s, the agency had become especially macho, spending its energy and money running guns to tinpot Central American dictators, operations that didn't exactly match Raviv's skill set. Wells supposed that Raviv had survived the Reagan years by bobbing, weaving, and staying low to the ground, skills as useful at Langley as in East Berlin. He'd become an instructor around 1990, and by the time Wells's class of recruits arrived, he had his act perfected.

After his stint at the Farm, Wells never saw Raviv again. Wells always imagined he would. He tried to look Raviv up after he got back from Afghanistan. But Raviv seemed to have shed the agency. Wells assumed he was retired, living someplace warm with his wife. If he had a wife.

"Whatever happened to Guy Raviv?" he asked Shafer.

"Good old Guy," Shafer said. "Died. Lung cancer."

"When?"

"You were in Afghanistan. Maybe three years ago. Don't look so shocked."

"You're a sweetheart, Ellis. Real humanitarian."

"He smoked like two packs a day is all I'm saying. Pretty good at CS, though."

And that was Raviv's epitaph.

———

WELLS WALKED toward Midhan Tahrir, the heart of Cairo, a big, brightly lit square formed by the intersection of a half-dozen avenues. A pedestrian walkway ran under the square, leading to a subway station and offering a dozen exits—a nightmare for a surveillance team. Once Wells got underground, any tail would have to stay close or risk losing him.

At the square's northeastern corner, a waist-high railing blocked pedestrians from crossing at street level, forcing them to use the underground passageway. Wells stopped, apparently lost, as an old man walked slowly by. Wells touched his arm. *"Salaam alekeim."*

"Alekeim salaam," the man murmured, his voice barely audible above the traffic.

"Sorry to bother you, my friend. What street is this?"

"Talaat Harb. Of course. Very much so."

"I'm looking for the movie theater."

"The Cinema Metro?"

"Yes, I think so."

"This way." The man pointed up the street. "Past the next traffic circle. And then a few more streets. But I must tell you, there aren't any more films tonight."

"My mistake. *Shokran.*"

"Afwan." Welcome.

The man walked on. But the conversation had given Wells what he wanted. From the mass of pedestrians around him, he'd picked out five possible tails. Two men in dark blue *galabiyas,* their arms interlinked, walking slowly down Talaat Harb. A tall, light-skinned man in a striped blue button-down shirt, lighting a cigarette just a few feet away. Another, glancing at a shoe store as he dialed his cell phone. And a fifth, younger, drinking a Pepsi, casually watching the traffic roll by. They weren't the only possibilities, but they were the most likely.

Trust your instincts, Raviv always said. *Unless they stink, in which case you shouldn't.*

But then you shouldn't be in the field at all. So I'm gonna assume a certain level of competence here. And my point is, you have to guess. And always remember that most of the time there won't be anyone on you at all. You'll be playing a little game with yourself. And then sometimes it's the other thing.

What other thing? someone had asked.

If you're lucky, unlucky, however you want to look at it, at least once in your career you'll wind up with a whole platoon on you. Cars, motorcycles, helicopters. I know it seems impossible, but it isn't, not in Moscow or Beijing or Tehran or a few other places where these little games are taken seriously.

What do we do then?

Abort your meeting. Head for the nearest house of worship. And pray.

WELLS HOPPED the railing and picked through the slow-moving traffic on Talaat Harb. Across the street, stairs led to the underground walkway. Wells stepped down them, not quite running, the camera bouncing in his backpack. He made his way along the tiled corridors of the underpass, past a blind man selling packets of tissues, a grimy teenager wearing a New York Yankees cap. Wells turned right, left, and then jogged along a passage and up a stairway. He'd crossed all the way under the square, to its western edge. From here, a wide avenue, three lanes in each direction, ran west toward the Nile.

Wells stepped around the stairs, positioning himself so he could spot anyone coming up the steps without being seen himself. And sure enough the man in the striped blue shirt emerged from the passageway and jogged up the steps. His cigarette was gone, but he was the same man who was standing next to Wells on Talaat Harb.

Wells heard Raviv's raspy voice: *You found him. Now lose him.* Wells stepped onto the avenue as a bus passed, moving maybe fifteen miles an hour. He moved around the back of the bus, then sprinted along its left side, where its body shielded him from the sidewalk. He kept pace, barely. A taxi honked madly at him, and its passenger-side mirror whacked his ass. He stumbled in his robes but didn't fall. After thirty seconds, the traffic lightened and he crossed to the south side of the road.

The move was ugly and unsubtle, but it worked. Wells was two hundred yards from his pursuer, effectively hidden by the traffic. He kept moving, walking briskly to the Corniche el-Nil, a three-lane road that ran south along the riverbank. He reached into his pocket and tossed the bug into the Nile. It disappeared without even a splash. He looked back, but the tail seemed to be gone. He extended his arm. A battered black-and-white cab pulled over.

"The Hyatt," Wells said. The hotel was a mile down the Corniche. Before they reached it, Wells touched the cabbie's arm. "Stop here."

He paid, waited for the cab to disappear, waited for any sign he'd been followed. But here the Corniche was nearly free of pedestrians and the traffic flowed fast and freely. Wells reached up a hand, hailed another cab. "Northern Cemetery."

"Which part?"

"The entrance."

"It has many entrances." The cabbie looked puzzled but waved Wells in anyway.

As they drove, Wells closed his eyes and tried to think through the tail and the bug. They had to have come from someone at the mosque. Hani, most likely. Maybe someone else in the imam's office.

Possibly the imam himself. Whoever it was, Wells had to expect the Egyptian police to crash his interview with Alaa. He wondered if he should abort the meeting.

"Where are you from?" the taxi driver said abruptly.

Back in America, Wells had forgotten the Arab world's obsession with ethnicity, its never-ending tribalism. Me against my brother. Us against our cousins. Our family against the family next door. Our block against the next . . . and on and on, to infinity. Or at least this universe against the next.

"Kuwait."

"Ahh, Kuwait. Of course. You have business here? Maybe you take day off, I take you to the pyramids. Very exciting, very historical . . ." He was off and running, and Wells couldn't help but smile. One day he really would come back here as a tourist. He wondered who'd be with him. Or if he'd be alone.

THE CABBIE WAS STILL TALKING as they headed up a low rise. Ahead, the road seemed to dead-end at a wide avenue, almost a highway, six lanes of cars heading north and south. Beyond the avenue, a jumble of buildings loomed, darker and lower than the rest of the city. The cabbie pointed at them. "Northern Cemetery."

"I can't wait."

The cabbie drove through a short tunnel that ran under the avenue and opened into the cemetery. He stopped in front of four nut-brown men sitting in folding chairs, passing a *sheesha*.

Wells paid the driver, unfolded himself from the cab. The men in the chairs looked curiously at him as it pulled away, trailing diesel smoke. Hani wasn't among them, and Wells didn't recognize any of them from the mosque. They were arranged in front of a store whose shelves, as far as Wells could tell, held only cardboard boxes of spark plugs.

"*Salaam alekeim.*"

"*Alekeim salaam.*"

The men's *galabiyas* were gray with dust, their bodies limp, as if they had been sitting for so long that they were molded to the chairs. They could have been forty, or seventy. They struck Wells as the Egyptian equivalent of the old men who had—in the days before Wal-Mart and air-conditioning—sat in town squares in the South and watched the world go by.

"May I sit?" Wells asked the man on the far right. He seemed younger, or at least more awake, than the others.

"Sit, sit."

Wells plopped down. Based on the regularity of the traffic passing them, the road through the cemetery seemed to be a major route to eastern Cairo. Wells couldn't help feeling that running roads through a graveyard was somehow disrespectful. Yet did the dead prefer the loneliness of the immaculately maintained cemeteries in the United States? At least this way they were connected to the city where they had lived.

What nonsense, Wells thought. In truth, if this place proved anything, it was the foolishness of ghost stories. Wells didn't claim to know where the dead went. But he was sure they weren't here. Their bones might be, but their spirits were long gone.

The man next to him moved a few degrees toward vertical.

"I am Essam."

"Nadeem."

"You visit the cemetery?"

"Yes."

"Now? At this hour?"

"Why not?"

Essam didn't seem to know what to say next. He slumped in his seat, reached for the *sheesha*. Its coals were out. He whistled sharply. A very small and very dirty boy, no more than ten years old, emerged from the spark-plug store, carrying tongs and a brass brazier trailing white smoke. He plucked two red-black coals from the brazier, arranged them on the *sheesha*.

"You like to smoke?" the boy said to Wells. "Very good smoke. Apple, cherry, strawberry, melon—"

"No, thank you."

"Very good smoke." The boy tugged at Wells's *galabiya* with a small hand black with coal dust. "You Kuwaiti?"

"Not you, too. Shouldn't you be asleep?" Then Wells realized why the boy had asked. "Yes. Kuwaiti. You have something for me?"

The boy ran inside the store, reemerging with a piece of paper. "For you. One pound."

"Who gave you this?"

"One pound." One Egyptian pound was about twenty cents.

Wells gave him a pound, received the note in return. *"Keep walking,"* it said in Arabic. Nothing more. "Who gave you this?" But the boy had already gone back to spark-plug heaven.

"Who left this?" Wells said. "A fat man?" As an answer, Essam put the *sheesha* pipe to his mouth and took a long draw. He closed his eyes as the coals glowed red and the *sheesha* burbled happily. Wells stood, looked at the crumbling brick buildings around him, wondering if he was being watched, by the *muk* or the jihadis or both. But nothing moved.

Wells was gripped by a feeling he had never heard properly named, the sense that he could stay with these men for a thousand years, waiting for something to happen. Anything. And nothing would. Yet every moment would be as pregnant with anticipation as the one before, even as his feet took root in the earth, even as he turned into a living statue. The opposite of déjà vu. A state of permanent expectation.

"Good-bye," Wells said.

Essam exhaled a cloud of white smoke. "Come back. Smoke *shee-sha* with us."

I know where to find you, Wells didn't say.

"*Ma-a-saalama.*"

"*Ma-a-saalama.*"

THE STREET CURVED LEFT and then right. The dead were all around him—the living, too—huddled inside one-room mud-brick houses that reached the edge of the road. The neighborhood's poverty was obvious here. The houses had uneven holes for windows. Mangy dogs slept fitfully in garbage-strewn lots, their ribs visible under thin brown fur. At the sight of Wells, they stirred but didn't bother to stand.

Around the next turn, a narrow alley ran perpendicularly from the street. As Wells walked past it, a boy in dirty brown sweatpants hissed at him. "Are you the Kuwaiti?"

Kuwaiti. The magic word. The password for tonight's adventures.

"Yes."

"Follow me."

Wells turned down the alley, following the boy. This section of cemetery sloped north to south. They headed south, down a narrow staircase, concrete steps crumbling. The alley shrank as it continued, buildings pressing on both sides, leaving just enough room for two men to stand side by side. Wells wasn't happy. An ambush here would be lethal. He peeked over his shoulder but couldn't see anyone.

"How much farther, boy?" he said. The kid ignored him, trotting ahead.

THEY PASSED AN OPEN SQUARE filled with tombstones and one large mausoleum, the first evidence Wells had seen of an actual cemetery in the Northern Cemetery. Ahead, the alley swung left, a blind turn. The boy whistled and ran. *Here it comes,* Wells thought. As he made the turn, he felt rather than saw a man in a black mask stepping out of a hole in the wall behind him. He tried to turn, to protect himself, but something hard and metal crashed into the side of his head—

A sap—

His last thought—and then his legs sagged underneath him and he was out.

9

The letter was a single white page, typewritten, undated, no letterhead.

To: Robert Gates, Secretary of Defense

CC: Frederick Whitby, Director of National Intelligence

CC: Vincent Duto, Director of Central Intelligence

CC: Lucy Joyner, Inspector General, Central Intelligence Agency

Dear Mr. Gates:

This letter is in reference to the illegal activities of a unit operated by the army and the Central Intelligence Agency. Squad 673. This unit operated in Poland. Based at Stare Kiejkuty army base in eastern Poland. It had the job of interrogating "enemy combatant" detainees. Those known as high-value.

This squad 673 was led by COL Martin Terreri of the Fourth Special Operations Brigade. The second-in-command was Brant Murphy. A CIA officer. The unit had ten members. **You should know** that Brant Murphy and Colonel Terreri stole at least $1 million from the unit. They received kickbacks from **Europa West Aircraft** in return for hiring Europa West for Charter Flights. Flights **#11**, **#19**, and **#27** never took place.

Dr. Rachel Callar and other members of Squad 673 knew about the stealing by BRANT MURPHY and COLONEL TERRERI. However they did **not** profit from it. They did not want to report the leaders of the squad. **You should ask them!**

Also, the unit did do acts of torture on its detainees. Including Waterboarding, Electric Shock, Stress Positions, Prolonged Sleep Deprivation, **Mock Executions**. And other bad acts.

I am not making this up. For proof, here are the prisoner identification numbers (PINs) of the detainees:

3185304876—3184690284—4007986133—4013337810—4042991331—4041179553—4192578423—5567208212—6501740917—6500415280—7298472436—7297786130

I know the Department of Defense is a **law-abiding** and **ethical** institution. I appreciate your attention to these matters.

Thank you for taking the time to read this.

Not surprisingly, the letter was unsigned. The envelope carried a Salt Lake City postmark and the same Courier twelve-point font. No return address.

Four thick lines of classification were stamped across the top of the letter:

TOP SECRET/SCI/PLASMA/76G

NOFORN/NOCON

DISTRIBUTION BY DCI ONLY

And just in case the message hadn't gotten through: PRINCI-PALS ONLY.

Shafer read the letter through twice. He was examining it a third time when Lucy Joyner, the CIA inspector general, reached across the table. "Time's up," she said.

Joyner was a tall, round Texan whose curly hair was dyed a striking platinum blond. She investigated internal allegations of wrongdoing at the agency, a job that made her as popular at Langley as a police officer at a pro-hemp rally. She couldn't fit in, so she'd taken the opposite route. Her hair was defiance in a Clairol bottle. *We're here, we're the IG's office, get used to it.*

"I'm a slow reader," Shafer said.

She waggled her fingers at him, and he handed it over. They were in a conference room in Joyner's office suite, on the sixth floor of the Old Headquarters Building. A framed map of Texas hung on one wall, beside a photo of Lyndon Baines Johnson wearing a cowboy hat and holding his dog, Little Beagle Jr.

"Can I see the original?" Shafer said.

Joyner had shown him a high-resolution copy of the letter, which was locked in her safe. "Nothing on it," Joyner said. "No fingerprints or DNA. Whoever sent them was awful careful." Joyner hadn't lived in Texas in twenty-five years, but she sounded like she'd just gotten off a plane from Amarillo. Shafer wondered if she practiced at home. *Bar-be-cue. Fixin's. Largemouth bass.*

"What about the other letters?" Shafer said. "To Gates and Duto and Whitby?"

"Destroyed. I asked Duto about it; he told me his office gets all kinds of crazy mail. Can't check everything. Yeah, well, my office gets nutjob letters, too, but we know when one's real. And so do they."

"Except when they'd rather not."

"This conversation shouldn't be happening," Joyner said. "Lucky for me, you have that super-fancy clearance."

"They keep forgetting to take it away."

"So, I don't need permission to show you this. And I remember how they treated you after nine-eleven, Ellis. Which is to say I think we're on the same side. But most of what you want to know, I can't tell you. You have to go to the source for that."

"A couple of questions."

"Just a couple."

"Murphy told me you'd cleared him."

"Did he, now."

"I'm guessing that isn't exactly accurate."

"It is and it isn't."

"How far did you get?" Shafer asked.

"He came in for a prelim—"

"A prelim?"

"A preliminary interview. No lie detector, no lawyers. It's optional, but most folks agree to 'em, because if we can get our questions answered then, nothing gets into your file, nothing for the boards"— the promotion boards—"to see. Anyways, he came in. I showed him the letter, asked him if he could tell me anything. He said he couldn't. I asked him whether 673's records would exonerate him. He said it didn't matter, because they were DD-and-above clearance"—that only deputy directors and Duto himself could see them. "I asked him about the torture. He told me that he was administrative, didn't run interrogations. Then I asked him about receipts and he laughed. Literally. Laughed out loud. Asshole. That was it. He left. I figured I'd better check it out. But before I got anywhere, Duto called."

"When, exactly?"

"Maybe two days after I spoke to Brant. He told me to find

something else to do, that he was invoking the NSE"—the national security exemption, which allowed the director to overrule the inspector general and stop internal investigations if they were likely to damage vital national interests.

"Duto didn't tell you what was behind the NSE."

"He did not."

"And that was it?"

"I'm not like you, Ellis. I get a direct order from the director, I listen. I called Murphy, told him not to worry. A couple of days later, his lawyer called, told me that wasn't good enough, that Murphy wanted all records of the investigation destroyed."

"Smart."

"Yes. Too bad for him, I was able to tell him that wouldn't be possible, that I had to hold the letter because of the allegations of torture, et cetera. So the lawyer asked me to certify that I had cleared Murphy of any wrongdoing related to 673. As an insurance policy, he said."

"Without specifying what the wrongdoing actually was."

"Correct, Ellis." She paused. "So, I wrote it. Murphy had Duto on his side, and I figured it was more important to make sure this"— she looked at the letter—"survived. Then I locked that letter up and forgot about it. Though not entirely. I knew somebody would call. Sooner or later. Stuff like this doesn't stay down forever."

"You heard what's happened with 673," Shafer said. "The murders."

"The day after Fisher and Wyly got killed, Duto called me to his office. I knew something was up, because normally he prefers to stay as far from me as possible. Anyway, he told me. Said there was an investigation starting up."

"So, the FBI has the letter."

Joyner shook her big blonde head. "Not exactly. Duto asked me whether I'd talked to the bureau. I said, how could I have done that when you just told me there was an investigation going. Then he told me that he was not authorizing distribution of the letter to anyone outside the agency."

"Including the bureau."

"Correct. Nobody had the clearance, he said. I had the distinct impression he wanted me to destroy the letter, but he didn't come out and say so."

"Did he ask you to purge it from your memory? Eternal sunshine, et cetera?"

"Not yet. That's probably next."

"He tell you his logic for hiding evidence in a criminal investigation?"

"He did not. If I'd asked, no doubt he would have pulled out the ol' national security exemption, but I did not ask."

"And he didn't explicitly tell you to destroy it."

"You know Vinny Duto better than that, Ellis. That would have needed to be in writing, and he wasn't interested in having this in writing. And then, to my not quite surprise, you called." She paused. "Wish I could be more helpful, but that's pretty much all I have."

"Do you think there's a connection between the torture allegations and the theft?"

She tilted her head and clucked—*chk-chk.* "Aside from the fact that the same person's making them? No. I mean, Murphy was worried about the money. Less so about the torture. You'd expect it would be the other way around."

"It's a strange letter," Shafer said.

"Very strange. It reads like the writer didn't grow up speaking English. The bolding, the capitalized words. But I think all that's fake. It feels like it's from somebody inside the squad. I can't think how else anyone would have the specifics, the prisoner numbers.

"If you worked for a foreign intelligence agency."

"Maybe the Brits," Joyner said. "But probably not even. Now do me a favor, figure this out, since I'm not allowed to."

"I'll do that, Lucy. But I need something."

"Anything."

"Really."

"No. Not even close to anything."

"It would be very helpful to me if you could freshen up. As they say in Texas and other such genteel places."

She put a finger on the letter. "You can't have it, Ellis."

"It'll be right here when you get back."

"You're very fortunate to have that clearance." She stretched her arms over her head. "Well. I do believe I need to freshen up," she said. "Be right back."

She disappeared. And Shafer thumbed twelve ten-digit numbers into his BlackBerry:

3185304876—3184690284—4007986133—4013337810—4042991331—
4041179553—4192578423—5567208212—6501740917—6500415280—
7298472436—7297786130

The letter was just where she'd left it when she got back. Ellis wasn't. He stood, examining the L.B.J. poster.

"What's this about, Lucy? Texas pride or something deeper?"

"Wish I could tell you, but it's a secret I never share," she said.

"We seem to be heavy on those."

10

An ocean and a continent away, Wells woke to cool water trickling down his neck. He lay on a mud floor, his hands bound behind his back, shoes and camera bag gone. His head throbbed, and the base of his skull had grown a soft sticky lump. Two identical imams sat on two identical chairs above him, pouring water onto him from two identically cracked pitchers.

Wells closed his eyes and counted slowly to ten in Arabic: *"Wahid, itnayn . . ."* When he opened his eyes, he found that the two imams had merged into one. He moved his head carefully, taking in the room. It wasn't much, a ten-foot square with smooth, windowless walls and a single naked bulb above. He saw only the imam and Ihab, not Hani.

"Kuwaiti," the imam said.

"My name is Nadeem," Wells said. His voice was low and cracked. "And it wasn't necessary to hit me."

"You woke up quickly."

"I have a hard head. *Inshallah.* May I ask, sheikh? How did the boy find me? How did you know I'd come that way?"

The imam smiled. "He wasn't the only boy, Kuwaiti. All over the cemetery they watched for you."

"Where's Hani?"

The imam set down the pitcher, knelt beside Wells, squeezed

Wells's cheeks between his fingers. "Why do you care? You miss him?"

Wells hesitated. Should he speak badly of the imam's right-hand man? For all Wells knew, they'd been friends from birth and insulting Hani would cost him his shot at Alaa. But he didn't see any other move. "I don't trust him, your friend Hani."

The imam's eyes flicked to Ihab, then back to Wells.

"I don't know how long you've known him, but I fear he's one of the pharaoh's men. I almost didn't come tonight."

"Why would you say such things about my good friend?"

"I've dealt with *muk* before."

"Dealt with, Kuwaiti? Or worked with?"

Wells pushed himself against the wall, forcing himself into a sitting position before nausea overtook him. "I risked my life to come to you. And I've done what you've asked, everything. So, please, if you still don't trust me, let's end this charade." He turned to Ihab. "In the truck, you asked me why I'd chosen your son. Don't you see? I didn't choose him. The Americans did. Do you want him to tell his story? Because if you do, I need to speak to him tonight. I can't stay longer."

The imam squeezed Wells's shoulder. "Close your eyes, Kuwaiti. Sleep a bit." The two men turned off the light and left.

WELLS WOKE to find his hands free. A third man had entered the room. Deep-set eyes, a soft chin, close-cropped black hair, a gentle face. Alaa Zumari. He didn't look like a man who could have ordered a half-dozen murders.

The imam pulled a chair beside Wells. "Can you sit?"

Wells pushed himself up, took the chair. His stomach turned a somersault. He touched his skull, found his fingertips wet. He was still leaking.

"Salaam alekeim," Alaa said.

"Alekeim salaam. You're Alaa Zumari? I'm Nadeem."

His camera bag and shoes had materialized at his feet. He pulled out the camera, mounted it on the tripod. He turned on the camera, then turned it off.

"First, you tell me your story without the camera, Alaa. Then we do it again, on tape. It will go more smoothly."

"I understand," Alaa said. He was his father's son, quiet and collected. Wells wondered if his interrogators had misunderstood his composure as arrogance.

"How old are you?"

"Twenty-five. I was born in Alex"—Alexandria. "We moved to Cairo when I was six."

"Are you very religious?"

"Not so much. He"—Alaa glanced at his father—"always told me to study the Quran, study, study, but I didn't like it."

"How did you end up in Baghdad?"

"Four years ago, when I was twenty-one, I was a waiter in the Sofitel." The Sofitel was one of the bigger Cairo hotels, a tall, cylindrical building on an island in the Nile. "Sometimes I drove a Mercedes for a rich man who visited there with his girlfriends. A very rich man."

"An Egyptian?"

"Yes. I worked hard. I wanted to save money, to get married. I drove for this man a lot. After a year, his son, at the time he was nineteen, he came to me and said, 'Alaa. My father likes you. He trusts you. I trust you, too. I want you to go to Baghdad and start a mobile-phone business with me.' He said, 'You carry in the phones, and when you get there, you do an agreement with the Iraqicom'"—the biggest mobile-phone company in Iraq. " 'You buy minutes from them, a lot, millions. They give you a discount. Then you sell the phones with the time attached. If it works, we make a lot of money.' That's what he said."

"But he didn't want to go to Baghdad himself?"

"He's not a fool. Unlike me."

"So you said yes."

"It's a risk, okay, but I need the money. I said yes. He gave in fifty thousand U.S. and I gave in five thousand pounds." Five thousand Egyptian pounds, about one thousand dollars. "All my money. We bought five hundred cell phones, cheap ones, in Qatar. The rest of the money was to buy the minutes."

"And you went to Baghdad."

"Yes. Over the border through Jordan. Very dangerous. I didn't know how dangerous until too late. We drive in a convoy. Six cars, GMCs. Halfway through, the middle of the desert, one of the GMCs, it gets hijacked, the driver shot. The passengers kidnapped. Killed, probably. I don't know. But we were lucky, we made it to Baghdad. And my rich friend, he has found a place for me to stay, because the hotels are too dangerous. He has a second cousin there. Named Amr."

Alaa paused, hunched back against the wall, as if reliving his arrival in Baghdad.

"Have you ever been to Iraq?"

"Iraqis don't like Kuwaitis."

"Right. So. Baghdad. At first it seems okay. For a few days, I try to get an appointment with Iraqicom. But I can't. Then one night two men come to the house where I'm staying. Jihadis. Fighting the Americans. They heard about my cell phones. They say, you must pay us a tax."

"They heard. Who told them?"

"I don't know."

"Maybe Amr. Maybe your partner."

"I don't know!" For the first time, Alaa raised his voice. "So, they say, a tax. They take a hundred of the phones. And ten thousand of the money."

"Did you argue with them?"

"No one argues with these men. I think they would have taken it all, but the man I'm staying with, he stops them. And a few days later, they come back, take more phones, more money."

"You didn't want them to? You weren't there to help them? Tell me the truth."

"I went there to do business! After they come the second time, I call my friend to ask him, maybe I should just come home. He tells me to stay. Tells me, 'Stay with Amr. Do the deal. Sell the rest of the phones. We can still make money.' A very good friend." His voice was low and bitter.

"You couldn't go home?"

"They told me, don't try. They said they watch the bus stations, GMCs. They'll kill me if I try."

If the story was true, Alaa had been either betrayed by his host or, more likely, set up from the start as an unwitting courier. Wells imagined this quiet man in Baghdad in late 2007, with Iraq teetering close to anarchy. Markets and roads and police stations under attack daily. Wandering into the wrong neighborhood meant certain death. And Alaa, holed up in a house, unable to trust his host, waiting for the insurgents to return, and return again, until the money and the phones were gone and he was left with only his own skin to give them.

Unless, of course, he hadn't been set up at all. Unless he'd gone to Baghdad to deliver cell phones and money to the jihadis. But if that was his goal, why hadn't he dropped off his cache and gone back to Cairo to pick up another load?

"What happened next?" Wells said.

Alaa ran a hand through his hair. "What happened? Two days later, the Americans came. Many of them, maybe fifteen. It was the middle of the night. Amr went for his AK, and they shot him."

"Were there any Iraqis with them?"

"I don't think so, no. Just Americans."

By that point all the regular combat operations were joint Iraqi-American, so American-only meant a Special Forces unit.

"They tie me up and put a bag on my head and put me in a helicopter. They say I'm a jihadi, they're going to throw me out if I don't tell them the truth. I tell them no, I'm there for the cell phones, I don't know anything about the jihadis. The jihadis stole my money; they would have killed me if you hadn't come. But the Americans didn't believe me. When the helicopter landed, they beat me. This went on for a few days. I told them to look at my passport, my name. But they said they found a computer at the house with messages from Al Qaeda. They said Amr was a big man in the insurgency. To this day I don't know whether what they were saying was real. Amr never said anything about jihad to me. They told me, just tell us the truth."

"But you lied." Wells understood now how Alaa had ended up in 673's hands.

"I told them about what happened," Alaa said. "But I didn't say who sent me."

"You made up a name." Wells still wondered why Alaa had been so reticent to give it up, but he decided not to press. The answer would come.

"Yes. This was when I was still in Iraq. They beat me; they kept me in a room like this, no windows, very hot. Finally, I told them a name so they would stop. And they were happy; they stopped beating me. Then a few days later they got angry. They told me they knew I was lying and that I wasted their time. And they said they were going to send me someplace I wouldn't like. Then the next day they put a hood on me and tied my arms and gave me a shot—"

"With a needle—"

"Yes, with a needle. And I fell asleep, and when I woke up I was on a plane. And then I was somewhere very cold." Alaa shivered at the memory. "I don't know where. Since I got out, I tried to figure it out. I think somewhere like Germany. But maybe not."

"They never said."

"No. And I couldn't see anything about it, where they kept me. If I ever left the building, they put a hood on me. But it was Americans who ran it, I'm sure of that. It had a special name. They told me. They were proud of it. They called it 'The Midnight House.'"

"Midnight House."

"Yes."

"Do you know why they called it that?"

"They said it was always midnight for the prisoners."

"Were there a lot of prisoners?"

"Not that I saw. Mostly, I was alone."

"And they hurt you?"

"These men, they were much different than the ones in Iraq." He closed his eyes, took a slow, deep breath. "I know I must talk about it, what they did, but—"

He broke off. The room was silent, the only sound the faint buzzing of the bulb overhead. Somewhere outside, a dog barked fiercely.

"They told me, it's very simple to hurt you. And it was. They make me stand all the time with my arms out, make me stay awake, hit me with the electricity. They put me in a very small cell, so small I can stand only like this—" Alaa hunched over. And even though he held the position for only a few seconds, his face went slack in fear and pain, the muscle memory overwhelming him. He stood up, slowly.

"Nothing that ever left a mark," he said. "I would look at myself and wonder if I had dreamed it all. Yes, sometimes, when they stopped, brought me back to my cell and I fell asleep, I thought the sleep was real and the torture was the dream. I said, 'Allah, Allah, help me, help me escape these evil dreams, sleep in peace.' But he never helped. And you must see, they never stopped. Not like Iraq. In Iraq, the guards and soldiers, they came and went. They had many prisoners. But in this place, this house, it was only me, and they never stopped. And after a while, I don't know how long, maybe three weeks, I couldn't resist anymore. I didn't know if they would kill me or send me back to Iraq or what they would do, I only knew I couldn't resist."

"Anyone would have done the same," Wells said. "But what I don't see, even now, is why you protected this man who sent you to Iraq at all."

Alaa laughed, low and bitter. "Not to protect him. To protect my family. Do you know who it was, the man I drove? Samir Mohammed. He owns half of Heliopolis"—a wealthy neighborhood in northeast Cairo. "His daughter is married to Mubarak's grandson."

"And it was his son who sent you to Baghdad?"

"Do you see now, Kuwaiti?" the imam said.

Wells saw. The American government supported Hosni Mubarak, for all his flaws, because he was viewed as a reliable ally against radical Islam. If his family had been connected to the Iraqi insurgency, the outcry in Washington would have been immediate and intense. Congress might have ended the billions of dollars of aid the United States gave Egypt every year. And Mubarak would have lashed out. Angering a pharaoh was never wise.

What Alaa hadn't realized was that his confession would be so toxic that the agency and the army had no alternative but to bury it. Then, with no reason to keep him, they'd told 673 to let him go.

Amazingly enough, the truth had set Alaa Zumari free.

IN THEORY, Alaa might still be responsible for the 673 murders. But why? His captivity had lasted only a few months and had ended with his regaining his freedom. Now he simply wanted to be left alone. Nonetheless, Wells figured he should ask about the murders.

"Are you angry with the Americans?" he said.

"The ones who hurt me? Sure, I'm angry." Though Alaa's voice was even. "I wish that they would see how it feels. But not the woman. She was kind."

"The woman."

"One was a woman. A doctor."

"Did she talk to you?"

"Only a few words. I don't think she knew so much Arabic. But she had a kind face. That's the only way I know how to say it."

"Do you know what's been happening to them?"

"What do you mean?"

"This unit that held you." Wells paused. "They're dying."

"I don't understand." The surprise in his voice was genuine.

"They went back to the United States. And now someone is killing them."

"I don't believe it," Alaa said. "It doesn't make sense."

Wells was sure now that Alaa hadn't been involved in the killings. He couldn't be a skilled enough actor to fake this.

And then a distant high-pitched whistle breached the room, a long, warning cry. The imam stepped forward, cupped a hand around the wound on the back of Wells's head. "They're coming."

"I swear on the Prophet it wasn't me," Wells said. "Hani saw the note you sent. He works for them."

The imam's silence was answer enough. Wells wondered if they had time to escape. If the *mukhabarat* had seen the note, they knew he was headed for the Northern Cemetery but not exactly where. They had put a bug and a tail on Wells, figuring it would be easier to follow a Kuwaiti than the imam and Ihab, who knew the local streets. But Wells had lost his bug and his pursuer. Now the police were regrouping. They had tracked him to the *sheesha* café and were going from there.

"Leave," Wells said. "I'll go the other way, draw them off." But the imam seemed frozen.

Wells heard the distant thumping of a helicopter high above. Would the *mukhabarat* bring in a copter for this op? Apparently so. And no one would be surprised when Alaa was killed during the arrest. *A suspected terrorist died early this morning in a counterterrorist operation in eastern Cairo, Egyptian authorities reported. . . .*

No. Wells wasn't going to help the Egyptians kill this man, or send him back to prison. Alaa had suffered enough. Wells wondered briefly what the agency would make of his helping a fugitive who'd been connected to the Iraqi insurgency, and decided he'd care later.

Another whistle, this one closer. Wells stood, braced himself against the wall. He didn't know how far he could run, but he'd have to try. "Follow me or don't," Wells said to Alaa. "But decide."

Wells stepped out of the hut and found himself in the alley where he'd been sapped. Alaa followed. A helicopter buzzed overhead, but Wells couldn't see it. Good. Like the bumper stickers on eighteen-wheelers said, *If you can't see my mirrors, I can't see you.* American helos had see-through-walls radar, but Wells didn't think that technology had come to Cairo yet.

He pulled himself up to the roof of the one-room house where he'd been held, then squatted low and oriented himself. Alaa followed. They were in a tough spot. The cemetery was a long rectangle that ran more or less north-south. Its east and west perimeters, the long sides, were hemmed in by broad avenues that formed natural bulwarks, easily patrolled and defended. Getting to the northern or southern edges, where the cemetery blended more naturally into the the city, meant running a half mile or more through the alleys full of police, or over the rooftops—in full view of the helicopters. Two lurked over the cemetery, one to the north, one to the south, shining their spotlights in tight circles.

Despite the helos, Wells thought their best bet was to stay high for as long as possible. The rooftops were filled with debris and scrap metal. The police would avoid them and stick to the alleys. If Wells and Alaa could just get through the first cordon, they might be able to disappear.

Still bent over, Wells scrambled crabwise south along the rooftops. The helicopter to the south was shining its light in a slow, looping pattern, moving slowly north, trying to catch any movement on the roofs. It paused. Wells saw that a dog was caught in its beacon, barking madly upward. Then it moved on. Wells and Alaa reached a two-story building, a ruined mosque, with a low wall that offered concealment.

To the west, three motorcycles streaked along the avenue, their red-and-blue lights flashing, a flying patrol cutting the cemetery off from the city. In the alleys around them, flashlights popped up and disappeared. To the north, a whistle sounded. A man shouted, "You! Raise your hands!"

Between the helicopters, the motorcycles, and the men on the ground, one hundred or more *mukhabarat* officers had to be on this mission. Wells realized now that he'd unwittingly put Alaa in special peril. Lost in the Cairo slums, Alaa was no problem. But now that Alaa could tell his story to the world, the police were determined to find him.

Overhead, the helicopter closed in, the chop of its blades and growl of its turbine growing louder each second. A wave of nausea pulled Wells sideways, and he braced himself to keep from falling over. That crack on his skull was the gift that kept on giving. Right now he ought to be lying in a dark room with a compress against his head and a friendly nurse rubbing his shoulders. Forget the nurse. Forget the compress. He'd settle for the room. He almost laughed, then bit his tongue to stop himself.

He tried to stand and couldn't. Too dizzy. He couldn't get much farther.

"Nadeem," Alaa shouted. "It's coming."

"I'm going into the spotlight. Pull it away. You go south, get out of here."

"But—"

"Go."

Wells bit his cheek, hard enough to draw blood, hard enough to just himself with adrenaline. He stood and ran along the uneven wall of the mosque. He stepped down, into an alley. He jogged through a narrow archway and found himself in a courtyard filled with crumbling graves. The spotlight swung at him and night became day. So much dust filled the air that the light seemed almost liquid, white fire pouring down from the heavens, setting the gravestones ablaze.

Wells tried to dodge, hiding behind a grave, knowing he couldn't. The spotlight settled on him. He stumbled a few steps farther and then fell to his knees and raised his hands in surrender and waited for the police to come. He hoped they wouldn't shoot him on the spot. He hoped Alaa had followed his instructions and run south. He closed his eyes, let the furious thrum of the helicopter's turbine fill his ears and shake his skull until he disappeared.

The police found him quickly. They grabbed him and cuffed his arms tightly and marched him out to the avenue. Hani waited for him there, leaning against a black Audi sedan with tinted windows. He stepped forward, backhanded Wells hard, his gold ring digging into Wells's cheek.

"What trouble you've caused us, Kuwaiti," he said. "Now you'll be our guest. See our prisons firsthand. You can make your own video when we're done with you. Interview yourself."

"Sounds like fun," Wells said in English. "But I'm not Kuwaiti."

"No? What are you, then?"

"American. A CIA operative. Name's John Wells." His last card. His trump card. Wells would rather have avoided playing it. Not exactly *pukka sahib*. He wished he could have made a clean escape, avoided the nonsense certain to follow. But he had no alternative. He wasn't sure he could have gotten past the cordon tonight even if his skull was in one piece. His embarrassment was a small price to pay for Alaa's freedom.

Hani must have known Wells was telling the truth, because he slumped back, his mouth half open, a fisherman who'd just reeled in the biggest catch of his life only to watch it wave and jump off the deck and back into the ocean. "John Wells. You work for the CIA," he said finally.

"So they tell me, *habibi*."

PART TWO

11

The Gulfstream jet's itinerary had taken it at forty-one thousand feet over a half-dozen countries, all avoided by anyone with a lick of sense. Exceptions included oil workers, who made good money for their trouble, and Special Forces operatives, who knew how to take care of themselves. The natives, too. They didn't have a choice.

After leaving Faisalabad and climbing northwest over Pakistan, the G5 crossed into Afghanistan roughly at the Khyber Pass. For an hour it flew over the Hindu Kush, jagged snowcapped peaks glittering in the cloudless sky. Eventually the Kush gave way to the steppes of Turkmenistan, a vast expanse hardly touched by roads or cities. Even the most intrepid travelers rarely visited Turkmenistan. The country existed mainly as a bridge between more appealing destinations, nations with amenities such as oceans, reliable electricity, and the rule of law. The ultimate flyover country.

Had the jet kept on the same route, it would have entered Russia next. But the other men in the G5 preferred to avoid Russia. Instead, the jet veered left, over the Caspian Sea, a vast blue-black expanse broken only by an occasional oil platform. Then over Azerbaijan. The less said about Azerbaijan, the better. And into Georgia, not the former heart of the Confederacy but the former (and perhaps future) Russian republic.

After Georgia came the Black Sea, the jet chasing the setting sun at five hundred miles an hour, invisible to the trawlers and freighters dotting the water below. The Gulfstream had a range of more than six thousand miles, so fuel was no problem. Halfway across the Black Sea, the G5 doglegged northwest, a forty-five-degree right turn that took it to Ukraine.

Aside from a few bumps over Afghanistan, the trip was smooth for five of the seven men in the cabin. Wearing black sweatshirts, jeans, and steel-toed boots, they sat in the jet's leather chairs, keeping watch on the reason for the trip: the two prisoners who lay prone on the floor, legs and arms shackled, wearing orange T-shirts and diapers. Detainees were not allowed to take bathroom breaks during these flights.

In Faisal, the prisoners had received sedatives: two milligrams of Ativan, five of Haldol, and fifty of Benadryl, injected intramuscularly. Emergency-room psychiatrists called the combination a B-52 and used it to restrain psychotic patients. The Haldol caused extreme sedation and reduced muscle control. Essentially, the drug produced temporary paralysis. The Benadryl acted as another sedative, as well as a counter to the nastier side effects of the Haldol. The Ativan was more pleasant, a tranquilizer that reduced anxiety.

But the smaller prisoner didn't seem to be getting much relief from the Ativan. As the jet crossed into the Ukraine, he began to moan through his hood and toss his head side to side like a dog with a mouse in its jaws.

The men guarding him watched him silently and without sympathy. They didn't know exactly what he'd done, or even his name, but they knew he was a terrorist, else he wouldn't be on this plane.

The guards were ex-soldiers, now employed by a private security company called Ekins Charlotte. Little Eight Enterprises, a Maryland shell company, owned the jet. Little Eight's nominal president was

Tim Race, a former CIA deputy section chief. Retired now, Race lived near Tampa and spent his days fishing in the Gulf. As a favor to his old bosses, Race had signed certain necessary documents—aircraft leases, insurance forms, and corporate records. He did not know exactly how the agency planned to use the jet, though he guessed it wouldn't be for golf outings.

Little Eight put a legal veil between the CIA and the Gulfstream, though a veil sheer enough to allow the agency to track the jet minute by minute. Everyone involved with these renditions agreed that official U.S. government aircraft shouldn't be used for the transfers, though no one could fully explain why. The answer seemed to be a combination of secrecy and plausible deniability. Not to mention the faint but definite odor of brimstone attached to the process of stealing men from their homelands without the approval of even a kangaroo court.

AS THE JET PROGRESSED over Ukraine, the smaller prisoner began to hammer his forehead against the cabin floor. A kick to the ribs stilled him, but after a few rattling breaths he started again, regular as a metronome, the flat, dull sound echoing through the jet.

Joe Zawadzki, the former Ranger captain in charge of the transfer, grabbed the man's hood and held his head. Despite the Haldol, the prisoner's shoulders and neck revealed tremendous agitation. But he neither cried nor spoke. Zawadzki was holding a vibrating bowling ball. After a few seconds, Zawadzki let go. Immediately, the prisoner banged his head, harder this time. And again.

Zawadzki had been in charge on dozens of these flights, and he'd never had a prisoner seriously injured. "All right," he said. "Take off the hood, sit him up."

They pulled on latex gloves, flipped the prisoner on his back, stuck a pillow under his head so he couldn't do any more damage. Then Zawadzki pulled off his hood and tugged him up.

The prisoner's lip was split and his nose was bleeding, not a gusher but a steady flow from the left nostril. Zawadzki was glad for the gloves. He grabbed the first-aid kit and a water bottle. The prisoner shook his head side to side, sending a trickle of blood on the floor. If he kept up this nonsense, they were going to have to hit him with another dose of Ativan, or more Haldol. Zawadzki kept syringes in his pack.

He poured water onto the Paki's face, rubbed away the remaining blood with a gauze pad, taped a cotton ball into the prisoner's nostril. Zawadzki poured a few drops of water into the guy's mouth and waited to see if he would spit or swallow. He swallowed. The water seemed to have calmed him a little.

"Relax," Zawadzki said. "No one's gonna hurt you."

The prisoner seemed unconvinced. He opened his mouth wide. A shiny spit bubble stretched between his lips, popped, re-formed. He mumbled something, and then repeated it more loudly. It wasn't Arabic. Probably Pashto. Whatever it was, Zawadzki couldn't understand.

"Quiet or the hood goes back on," he said to the guy. "Come on, don't you speak any Arabic?"

"He only knows Pashto. I know what he's saying," the second prisoner, the fat one, said in Arabic through his hood. "Take this off and I will tell you."

Zawadzki pulled the fat guy's hood half off so his mouth was visible.

"He says his ribs are broken, that the Pakistani police broke them when they took us to the airport. They beat us in their van. Like the animals they are. And these drugs you gave us are very bad. Poison."

"Tell him he'll get medical care when we land.

"Is that true?"

"Yes." In fact, the guys running the detention center would make that decision. But Zawadzki wasn't going to explain that right now. "Tell him to relax. He's got to calm down."

"All right," the fat prisoner said. He craned his head toward the first prisoner, and the two men had a short conversation before Zawadzki pulled the hood back over the fat prisoner's head. But the talk seemed to have done the trick. The first guy was breathing more normally. Zawadzki lowered him to the floor of the cabin and laid him down. Probably better for his ribs that way, if they really were broken. Zawadzki didn't believe in hurting prisoners. His job was transport, not interrogation.

TOUCHDOWN WAS BUMPY. The runway needed to be repaved, but Szczynto-Symanty wasn't a working airport. It opened only for these ghost flights. The Gulfstream taxied for a minute before its engines spooled down and the jet halted. The copilot opened the cabin door. "Looks like you guys had fun," he said.

Zawadzki lifted the prisoner, shackled him again, and pulled the hood over him. The prisoner grunted and bobbed his head a couple of times, but the fight had gone out of him. For now. Zawadzki and another guard wrapped him in a black blanket and walked him to the cabin door and down to the runway. The other guards handled the second prisoner.

Outside, two black Jeeps and a Range Rover waited in the dark. Jack Fisher stood at the foot of the stairs. Zawadzki had run a couple of other prisoners to this squad over the last year. From what Zawadzki could see, they weren't afraid to knock the prisoners around a little bit, maybe too much. But that wasn't his business.

"Any trouble?"

"This one," Zawadzki said. "Knocking his head against the floor, got a bloody nose. Says the Paki police broke his ribs on the way to the airport." Zawadzki hesitated. "He needs medical treatment, maybe."

"Poor little angel," Fisher said. "You know, him and his buddy shot one of our guys last night." Fisher reached behind the prisoner and pulled up his shackled hands, dragging his arms out and back and twisting his shoulders in their sockets. The prisoner groaned. "That's right," Fisher said. "You weren't a good boy." He let go. The prisoner flopped down, nearly falling over. Zawadzki propped him up.

"Let's get them back to base, settle the paperwork there," Fisher said. "Get him a deep-tissue massage." He lifted the prisoner's hood. "Lemme get a look." He pushed back the prisoner's lips, looked at his teeth and nose like he was inspecting a horse.

"Banged himself up nice, didn't he? Good. Less work for us."

12

Wells came back to Langley spoiling for a fight.

He'd spent a night in Cairo locked in an empty office at the *mukhabarat* headquarters in Abdeen, while the Egyptians verified his identity. Oddly, the room was festooned with Egyptian tourist posters, their slogans in English and French: *Leave London behind, come to Cairo for Christmas! Les Pyramides d'Egypte: Une Merveille du Monde!* Wells dated the posters to the late seventies: the men wore mustaches and checked short-sleeve shirts, the women blown-out hair and brightly colored miniskirts.

He had just fallen asleep, his head on the desk, when Hani walked in and poured a bucket of freezing water over his head and down his *galabiya*. Wells was covered in so much dust from the cemetery that he didn't mind.

"I knew you were no Kuwaiti. I knew."

I did you a favor, Wells didn't say. *You were getting nowhere fast. Now you can blame me for this mess.*

"You knew I was *muk*," Hani said.

"I thought so."

"You should have told me who you were." Hani banged a flashlight against the desk, sending vibrations oscillating into Wells's damaged skull.

Wells sat up. "Did Alaa get away?"

"For now."

"Good."

This time Hani brought the flashlight down on top of Wells's head. Not a full swing, and not in the same place as Wells had been sapped. But more than a love tap. Wells counted Mississippis in his head until the ringing stopped.

"What did you want from him?"

"I can't remember."

"What did he tell you?"

"Mainly, we talked soccer."

Hani raised the flashlight over his head, turned toward Wells, measured his swing like a batter in the on-deck circle. One practice swing, another—

Then another swing, this one for real, the flashlight whistling through the hot, dry air at Wells's face—

And stopping just short of his left eye. Wells didn't flinch, didn't even blink. He burrowed into the core of himself and waited.

A thin trickle of sweat dripped down Hani's left temple. He stared at Wells and then sighed and sat on the side of the desk and lit a cigarette. "I'll be glad to have you gone," he said.

WELLS SLEPT FITFULLY until the morning, when Hani brought in a doctor—or a man in a dirty white coat who said he was a doctor—who poured rubbing alcohol on Wells's scalp, setting his broken skin on fire, and then taped a gauze pad to the wound. Hani was the only *mukhabarat* agent Wells saw. He guessed the case was so toxic that no one wanted to be near it. Day turned to evening, and finally Hani returned.

"You leave tonight."

Wells didn't argue.

At midnight they put a hood over his head and bundled him into a van. When they pulled it off, he stood on the tarmac of Cairo International, staring at the blinking lights of a Delta 767. Delta ran a flight to New York four times a week.

Hani took Wells's fake passports and the digital camera and arranged them neatly on the tarmac. He pulled a red plastic canister from the back of the van, splashed gasoline over the pile. He lit a cigarette and dropped it on the pile. The flames danced sideways on the tarmac, and the acrid smell of the camera's melting battery filled the hot night air.

"Burn, baby, burn," Wells said in English. "Got any marshmallows?" Hani hadn't given him food or water since his arrest, a full day ago now. He was unsteady, feverish, his temperature spiking and diving like a Blue Angels pilot showing off for a new girlfriend.

"Marshmallow? What is that?"

Wells poked at the dying fire with his foot. "That wasn't strictly necessary," he said. "Can I go now?"

"Unfortunately, I don't have a choice in the matter," Hani said. "Our American ally. But if you ever come back to Egypt. We have so many accidents in Cairo. I know how I would suffer if Mr. John Wells were hit by a truck."

"If I ever come back to Egypt, you'll be the last to know," Wells said. His voice tore his throat like ground glass. No more talking, in any language. He turned away and stumbled across the tarmac. At the jetway, he made sure to give Hani a wave.

FROM NEW YORK, he flew to D.C., where an army doc met him and stitched him up properly. The doctor told him he needed to spend a day at Walter Reed, but Wells turned him down. He took a cab to the apartment that Shafer had arranged as a crash pad and slept for eighteen hours straight.

When he woke the next morning, his fever was gone. He still had a headache, a dull pounding behind the eyes, but he felt just about human for the first time since the Northern Cemetery. Two messages waited for him on his cell phone, which he'd left in Washington. The first: "John. It's Anne. Hope you and my friend Tonka are all right. Wherever you are." She laughed nervously. "Don't shoot anybody I wouldn't shoot, okay? And call me sometime."

The second message was nothing but a few seconds of breathing, followed by a hang-up. Wells wanted to believe he could recognize the fluttering of Exley's breath. But the line didn't have a trace, so he had no way to know. He listened twice to Anne's message and three times to the hang-up and then saved them both.

He showered and shaved and sped to Langley, his headache growing more intense as he approached the front gate. For once, he wanted to talk to Duto. But when he got to Shafer's office, he found out he wouldn't have the chance.

"Duto going to see us?" Wells said. "Talk about Alaa Zumari? Tell me what an idiot I am, how I should have gotten the Egyptians involved from the get-go?"

"Nope."

"Have a full and frank exchange of views?"

"Nope."

"Because I've got a few things to say to him."

"I'm sure you do."

"He had to have known the details of Alaa Zumari's interrogation. Had to. That Zumari gave up Samir Mohammed. Why didn't he tell us? It's like he's deliberately inciting us."

Shafer cocked his head sideways and grunted.

"Are you trying to speak, Ellis? Because that's not English."

"Thinking." He tilted his head to the other side. No other response.

Wells lowered himself onto Shafer's couch. "You talk too much or not enough," he muttered. "I have no idea how she"—she being Exley—"survived all those years with you."

"I could say the same."

Shafer had only three photographs on his desk: him and his wife, his family together, and him with Exley, standing side by side in front of the polar-bear cage at the Washington zoo. Shafer held up his right hand with the fingers hidden, as if a bear had just chomped them. Exley's mouth was open in a wide O, a mock-horrified expression. The picture had been taken at least five years before, Exley and Shafer visiting the zoo with their families. A purely platonic trip. And yet Shafer's face betrayed a depth of emotion for Exley that ran past simple friendship. *Did you love her?* Wells wondered. *Do you still? Do you blame me for her quitting? Or am I just projecting?*

Shafer seemed to read Wells's mind. "You'll never be free of her as long as you work here."

"Maybe I don't want to be."

"Maybe you don't." Shafer turned the picture facedown on his desk.

"Meantime. Setting ghosts aside. I know you're angry, John, but I think we ought to wait on Duto until we have a better idea of the game he's playing. Because this whole thing just keeps getting stranger. While you were sunning yourself in Cairo, I was keeping busy." Shafer explained his meeting with Murphy and then the anonymous letter that Joyner, the inspector general, had gotten.

"You think Murphy was stealing?"

"Yes. But that's not the strangest part. The letter had twelve PINs. I copied them all."

"PINs."

"Every detainee gets a unique prisoner identification number, a ten-digit serial number. Most of the time, the PINs are matched to a name, date of birth, home country—the basics of identity. If detainees aren't carrying ID when we arrest them, and we can't figure out who they are, the PIN won't be matched to any biographical information. In that case it's called a John Doe PIN and the first three digits are always 001."

"Did 673 have any of those?"

"No," Shafer said. "They always knew at least the name of the person they were interrogating. But whether or not we have any biographical details, once a prisoner is assigned a PIN, it's entered in what's called the CPR. Stands for Consolidated Prisoner Registry. The worldwide detainee database. And the CPR includes everybody, without exception. If you're in U.S. custody, whether you're at Guantánamo or the black sites, you are required to be in it. Even the base in Poland. Which was called the Midnight House, according to Murphy."

"Zumari said the same."

"Must have been proud of their ingenuity if they were telling prisoners." Shafer sat at his desk and tapped keys until a blue screen with a white title appeared: *"Consolidated Prisoner Registry—TS/SCI/ BLUE HERON—FOR ACCESS CONSULT OGC—"* Office of the General Counsel.

"I got the passcodes two days ago," Shafer said. "In between explaining to Cairo Station why you were there and why you hadn't told them. You can imagine."

"If only I cared."

Shafer entered the codes. A new screen popped up, a black word on a white background. *Query*. Beneath it, a space for a name or a PIN. Shafer typed in a ten-digit number—6501740917. A brief pause, and then Alaa Zumari's name and headshot appeared on-screen. "That's him, right? Zumari."

"Yes."

Shafer flicked to the next screen, which had rows of acronyms and dates. "DTAC—that's date taken custody. CS, confinement site. Et cetera. You can see, he was arrested in Iraq by something called Task Force 1490. Then a couple of weeks in custody at BLD—that's Balad."

"Says BLDIQ SC-HVD."

"We do love our acronyms. I don't know for sure but figure it means something like 'secure custody, high-value detainee.' Then he's transferred to 673-1. We can safely assume that's the Midnight House. Then, a month after that, transferred back to Iraq, held again at Balad. This time not as a high-value detainee. They'd decided he didn't have anything. And two months after that, they release him. The final note is AT-CAI."

"Air transfer to Cairo International?"

"Probably. This match what he told you?"

"More or less."

"And you see, the record is confined to movements and detention sites. Nothing about what he actually said."

"I get it, Ellis. So how's this help us?"

"That letter to the inspector general. It had twelve ID numbers. Six of them, they're like this. Complete, with a reference to 673-1 as a detention site. Four of them, they have some gaps in time. And no mention of 673."

"And the other two?"

"See for yourself." Shafer typed in a ten-digit number: 5567208212. This time the screen went blank for several seconds. Then: Record not found. He retyped the code. Same result.

"And this is the other missing PIN." Shafer typed it in. *Record not found.*

"Ellis. You're sure—"

"I'm sure. They went right in my BlackBerry like the others."

"Maybe those two were fake." Wells knew he was stretching.

"Ten real and two fake. It's possible. Sure."

"Or they were so high-value that—maybe there's another database."

Shafer shook his head. "I checked. There's a couple guys like that, cases where we don't want to disclose anything about where we caught, where we're holding them. Even in here. But it's about four guys. And then you get something like this—" He typed in another number and the screen flashed: *Restricted/Eyes Only/SCAP. Contact ODD/NCS*—the office of the deputy director for the National Clandestine Service, the new name for the Directorate of Operations. "There's always a record. Precisely because we don't want guys to disappear from the system."

"But two of them did," Wells said. "How easy is deleting these records?"

"I don't know yet," Shafer said. "I'm guessing not very. And probably you've got to be very senior."

"Senior like Vinny. But then why get us involved?"

"Guilty conscience."

"Good one, Ellis."

"Truly, I don't know," Shafer said. "There's too many angles we can't see yet. You're sure Zumari's not behind the killings?"

"I'd bet anything. He's been hiding from the Egyptian police since he got home. And if you'd seen him—he's not a terrorist."

"Then it's all pointing the same way. Inside."

"Inside meaning somebody who was part of the squad? Or inside meaning bigger, like a conspiracy?"

"I don't think we know that yet."

They sat in silence, the only sound the hum of the computers under Shafer's desk. "So you don't want to go to Vinny?" Wells said eventually.

"Anything we tell him now isn't going to come as much of a shock."

Shafer was right, Wells realized. Even if Duto hadn't deleted the numbers himself, the letter to the inspector general would have tipped him. He knew much more than he'd told them.

"WE NEED TO GO BACK to the beginning, find out what we can about 673," Shafer said. He pulled a folder from his safe, handed it to Wells. "These are the individual personnel records for members of the squad. I warn you it's less than meets the eye."

Wells flicked through the file. The personnel files hadn't been put off-limits, because they predated the creation of 673 and weren't part of its record. They held basic biographical information on the members of the squad—names, unit histories, birthdays, home addresses.

"No obvious pattern," Wells said. "They're from all over. Mostly not interrogators."

"That *is* the pattern. Only four of the guys have experience handling interrogations. Terreri, the LTC who ran it. Jack Fisher. The lead interrogator, Karp."

"And my old buddy Jerry Williams."

"Even those four, they were all over the map. None of them knew each other before 673 was formed. It's all spare parts."

"You think we wanted a clean break from other units."

"Remember the legal situation at the time. Post–Abu Ghraib. Post-Rumsfeld. Pressure to close Guantánamo. The Red Cross accuses us of torturing detainees. *Torture.* That's their word. And it's the Red Cross. Not Amnesty International. Everybody knows the score. This stuff isn't supposed to happen anymore," Shafer said.

"But we still need intel."

"And we think we have to get rough to get it. So, we make this new group, a few old hands and a few new ones. They've got a connection to the Pentagon, but nobody's exactly responsible for it. That was the point. The whole reason for the structure."

"Maybe so, but these guys, they're not dumb. They would have wanted legal protection. There's got to be a finding"—a secret Presidential memo that authorized 673 to operate. "Even if they destroyed the interrogation tapes, or didn't make any, there's transcripts."

"Forget the records," Shafer said. A note of irritation crept into his voice. "They're gone. Focus on what we know." Shafer held up his fingers. "One: Ten guys on the squad. Six are dead, one's missing. Two: Millions of dollars can't be accounted for. Murphy and Terreri, the guys who allegedly took the money, are two of the only three to survive. Three: Two detainees have vanished. Their records, anyway. Four: Duto—maybe on his own, maybe on orders from Whitby—stopped the IG from investigating. And then, for some reason, pulled us into this to do our own investigation. Five: According to the FBI, the remaining members of the squad have airtight alibis. Terreri's been in Afghanistan for a year. Poteat's in South Korea, and like Brant Murphy told us, he wasn't part of the squad for long anyway."

"And Murphy?"

"He was at Langley last week when Wyly and Fisher were killed in California. Our own surveillance tapes prove it."

"Maybe he outsourced."

"Doubtful."

"Doubtful." Contract killers were popular in the movies. In the real world they were greedy, incompetent, and more often than not police informants.

Wells stared at the ceiling. Everything Shafer had said was true, but he couldn't see how it fit together. "What about the FBI inter views? Anything yet from them?"

"So far, no."

"There is one other mystery," Wells said. "Jerry Williams. We keep assuming he's dead. What if he's not? What if he disappeared because he got wind that someone was after 673?"

"There's another explanation," Shafer said.

"Not possible," Wells said. "I know Jerry."

"You *knew* Jerry. I asked Murphy about him. He said Jerry was disgruntled, thought he deserved a promotion, hadn't gotten it—"

"So, he's stalking his old unit?"

"Deep breath, John."

Wells nodded. Shafer was right. He liked Williams, but they hadn't seen each other in fifteen years.

"Either way, you've got your next move," Shafer said.

"Noemie Williams."

"Beats hanging around here waiting for FBI reports, trying to figure out what Duto's really up to."

"Amen to that," Wells said. "But do me one favor. Next time you talk to him, tell him to make the Egyptians go easy on Zumari if they ever catch him. I'd do it myself, but you know it would be counterproductive."

"Done. Can I run any other chores, my liege?"

"Mind holding on to Tonka a couple more days?"

"The kids like her. Anyway, I think she's forgotten all about you. Doesn't even know who you are anymore."

"I'm going to pretend I don't get that analogy."

13

Three months left on the tour. As far as Martin Terreri was concerned, it couldn't end soon enough. He was done with Poland. Sick of the whole damn country.

Terreri was sick of their living quarters. The Polish government had given his squad two barracks in Stare Kiejkuty, a military intelligence base near the Ukrainian border. The Poles on the base shared a mess hall with Terreri and his men and provided overnight security for the prisoners but otherwise kept their distance. The hands-off attitude was the reason that the United States had chosen to operate here. But the freedom came at a price. Terreri had never felt so isolated. They could leave for day trips, but the Poles required them to return each night, since they hadn't cleared Polish immigration and officially weren't even in Poland. And ironically, they lived under harsher conditions than American soldiers almost anywhere else. Bases in Iraq and Afghanistan had the amenities that U.S. troops had come to expect: decent grub, live satellite television, well-equipped gyms. But the Polish army wasn't much for creature comforts. The showers had two temperatures, scalding and freezing. The food in the mess was sometimes fried, sometimes boiled, always tasteless.

Terreri was sick of the Polish countryside. Not that all the women here were ugly. In Warsaw they were gorgeous, a magic combination of blue-eyed Saxon haughtiness and wide-hipped Slavic sensuality. But the peasant women aged at warp speed. They wore ankle-length dresses to hide their boxy bodies and sat by the side of the roads selling threadbare wool blankets. They had stringy hair and tired, stupid eyes. The men were worse, sallow, with faces like topographic maps and brown teeth from their cheap cigarettes. They rode sideways on diesel-belching tractors, pulling bundles of logs on roads that were more pothole than pavement. No wonder the Russians and the Germans had taken turns beating up on them all these centuries.

Terreri was sick of being alone. He'd promised to e-mail Eileen and the kids every day. He'd even attached a Webcam to his computer for video chats. But the calls, the instant messages, the seeing-without-touching of video, they made him more depressed, reminded him of what he'd left stateside. He almost preferred the old days, when being on tour meant checking in for five minutes once a week.

Terreri was sick of his squad. The Rangers were fine. But the CIA guys, they weren't soldiers. He could tell them what to do, but he couldn't *command* them. He couldn't give an order, get a salute, and know that what he wanted would be done quickly and without question. That instant response was the essence of military discipline. The CIA guys didn't have it. He had to negotiate with them, explain his decisions to them. A pointless chore. And Rachel Callar, the doc, she was about two minutes from turning into a real problem. She didn't have the stones for the job. Literally or figuratively.

Terreri was just plain sick. Probably because he wasn't sleeping right or exercising right or eating right. And because of the dirt and lead and chemicals in the air, the stale gray clouds that coated his tongue with a metallic tang that he couldn't shake no matter how much Listerine he swigged. For a month he'd been fighting a sore throat, a low fever. Callar said he had a virus and antibiotics wouldn't help. But she was a shrink, not a real doctor, even if she did have an M.D. What did she know about treating sore throats? He bitched at her for antibiotics until she gave him a course. The meds didn't help his throat, but they gave him diarrhea for a week. He didn't tell Callar, didn't want to give her the satisfaction, but he knew she knew.

Most of all, Terreri was sick of the work. Which surprised him. He'd been in the interrogation business since 2002. He'd run a squad in Iraq in 2004, when the army and the agency were just learning how to break guys. When Fred Whitby came to him, told him about 673, told him the army and the agency wanted him to run it, he'd jumped at the chance. He believed in the mission. They were doing what couldn't be done at Guantánamo. Not with the lawyers and the reporters bitching and even the Supreme Court getting involved. The liberals could complain all they liked, but sometimes you had to let the bad guys know they weren't in charge anymore and the ride was going to hurt.

What he hadn't expected, though maybe he should have, was that he'd finally lost his taste for wrangling these jihadis. In the last six months, he'd burned out, plain and simple. He was sick of playing Whac-A-Mole with them. Of their lies. Of their historical grievances. Of hearing about the perfection of the Quran and the greatness of the Prophet. They all were reading from the same script, and none of them had any idea how boring it was. They were by and large a bunch of jerk-offs who ought to be herding sheep. But they considered themselves soldiers because they'd gotten a couple of weeks of training with AKs and grenades. The real geniuses, the big winners, they could mix oil and fertilizer to make a truck bomb, something any tenth-grader with a chemistry book could do. They thought that made them terrorist masterminds.

Terreri, he'd never been a cop, but he figured he knew how those

LAPD officers in South Central felt. He was wasting his life with a bunch of losers who didn't understand anything except a closed fist. When this tour was over, he was done with interrogations.

Being here did have a few compensations. Like at no place else he'd ever been, Terreri had free rein. Nominally, he was on special assignment for General Sanchez, but Sanchez had made clear from day one that as far as he was concerned, 673 was nothing more than a line on an org chart. The intel went up to the Pentagon and only then was funneled to Centcom. Basically, nobody in Washington or at Centcom headquarters in Tampa wanted to know anything about their tactics. They wanted only intel.

Terreri agreed. In 2003, 2004, lawyers for the CIA and army spent a lot of time talking about what was legal and what wasn't. Lots of conference calls, lots of memos. Lots of ass-covering. Now some of those memos had wound up on the front page of *The New York Times*. The less in writing, the better. Instead of a list of do's and don'ts, Terreri had a simple two-page document—a secret memorandum signed by the President.

> I hereby authorize Task Force 673 to interrogate unlawful enemy combatants, as defined by the Department of Defense, using such methods as its commander deems necessary. I find that the operations of Task Force 673 are necessary to the national security of the United States. Pursuant to that finding, as commander-in-chief of the United States, I find that the Uniform Code of Military Justice does not apply to the members of 673 for any actions they shall take against unlawful enemy combatants. . . .

> Task Force 673 shall operate only outside the states and territories of the United States. Outside those states and territories,

only the Uniform Code of Military Justice and not the laws of
the United States shall govern the actions of Task Force 673.

In other words, 673 was in legal limbo, exempt from both military and civilian law in its treatment of detainees. Of course, they
weren't completely off the radar. Their detainees were listed in the
prisoner registry, and eventually most of them wound up in Guantánamo. So Terreri's men had to be sure that they didn't do too much
visible damage. Still, they had plenty of room, and Karp and Fisher,
especially, had found ways to take advantage of it.

Then there was the money. The army's accountants were strict.
But the CIA was funding this operation, and the CIA had different
rules. In fact, as far as Terreri could see, when it came to spending
money on black projects, the CIA had no rules at all. Brant Murphy,
who handled logistics for the squad, never turned down a request for
gear. He bought flat-screen TVs, computers, even a couple of Range
Rovers for prisoner transport, quote/unquote. Still, the money was
piling up. At this rate, they'd have two million bucks in their accounts
when the tour was done.

Murphy had told Terreri that a month back, late on a Thursday
night, in his office, as they knocked back pints of Zywiec, the local
beer. It wasn't half bad once Terreri got past the faint formaldehyde
smell.

"Two million?" Terreri said. "You serious?"

"Yeah." Murphy sucked down his beer. "There's something else,
too."

Terreri took a sip, waited.

"Nobody'll care if we send it home," Murphy said. "Fact is, they
won't even notice it's gone."

Murphy hadn't said any more that night, but Terreri could guess where he was going. Soon enough they'd have another conversation. The only question was how much they would lift and how'd they'd split it. Terreri wouldn't feel guilty. The agency was practically begging them to skim.

SO TERRERI HAD A million reasons, give or take, to slog through the last couple of months of this job. But now he had to deal with Jawaruddin bin Zari. Their newest problem. The worst mooch they'd had yet. Since he'd arrived a week before, they'd treated him decently. Terreri's orders. He always gave the detainees a chance to talk. But bin Zari had made clear he wasn't interested. He seemed to want to provoke them into getting tough.

So be it. Terreri buzzed Jerry Williams in the basement. "Major. Please take prisoner eleven"—bin Zari—"to room A."

"Yessir. Full shacks?"

"Hands and hood only, unless you believe he's a risk."

Ten minutes later, Williams and Mike Wyly led bin Zari into a cinder-block room, white, twelve feet square, lit by a hundred-watt bulb. A steel conference table and two steel chairs, all bolted to the floor, were the room's only furnishings.

Bin Zari didn't complain as Williams pushed him into a chair and snapped shackles around his legs. Only then did Williams uncuff him and tug off his hood. Bin Zari blinked, opened and closed his hands. A week of confinement hadn't shaken his self-assurance. He appeared calm, almost bored. He had heavy, round features and relatively light skin for a Pakistani, more beige than brown. His slack skin and big lips promised decadence. He could have been a nightclub promoter in London, a hash dealer in Beirut.

"Jawaruddin bin Zari," Terreri said in Arabic. "We captured you in June in Islamabad. Put you on a plane. Now you're in what we call a secret undisclosed location. I know you understand me. I know you speak Arabic."

Terreri let a minute go by. But bin Zari remained silent.

"We've treated you with dignity."

"Is that what you call breaking my friend's ribs? Injecting us with drugs?"

"What happened to you before you arrived, that wasn't my doing."

"Have you given him medical treatment?"

"Not your business," Terreri said. "But yes, we have. Tell me, have we not treated you fairly? Would you have done the same for us? In return, I ask only that you answer our questions. Which you have not done."

Silence.

"You may be asking yourself, 'Why is this American wasting his breath? Is he so stupid as to think I'm going to speak?'"

Terreri dropped the safety on his pistol, snapped back the slide to chamber a round. Bin Zari's eyes widened, but his breathing stayed steady. Terreri raised the gun, pointed it at bin Zari's face.

"My friend. This speech is for me. Not for you. So that when we hurt you, when we break you, I won't feel guilty. I won't say to myself, 'Maybe we didn't give him a fair chance. Maybe he would have talked on his own.'"

"Do it, then," bin Zari said.

Terreri flicked the safety on, put the gun back in his holster.

"You think I'd kill you, Jawaruddin? No. We want what's in there." Terreri tapped his temple. "That fat head of yours. Your organization, your e-mail addresses, your contacts in the ISI, your safe houses, all of it. And you're going to give it to us."

Bin Zari shook his head. And smiled, his wide lips spreading into a rubbery grin. Terreri felt a bloom of rage surge into his chest, his heart taking three beats where one would do. This fool. His bravado, real or fake, would lead only to more agony. *You're going to make us hurt you. Why are you going to make us hurt you?*

He was so tired of this.

"Your choice." Terreri nodded to Williams.

"Full shacks?" Williams had seen this speech before.

"Nice and tight."

Williams pulled the hood over bin Zari's head.

THREE MINUTES LATER, Terreri sat alone, staring at the empty chair across the table. He laughed, a low chuckle. His rage had faded. That poor deluded asshole.

Then the door opened. Terreri found himself looking at the shrink. Rachel Callar. Another irritation. From the start, Terreri had wondered if she was tough enough for the job. But Whitby had insisted that they had to have a real doctor, preferably a psychiatrist. And Callar had volunteered. Before she'd signed up, Terreri had interviewed her, asked her if she understood what she was getting into.

She told him about a private she'd met in Iraq, a guy from the First Cav, two kids and another on the way. Guy's name was Travis. An IED hit his Humvee. He walked away with a bad concussion and a broken hand. But the other guys in the Humvee both got wasted. The gunner's leg landed in Travis's lap. Travis blamed himself for getting hit. He couldn't eat, couldn't sleep. When he closed his eyes, he heard his gunner cursing him out. His hand healed, and he wanted to get back to his squad. Callar told him, "We're gonna send you stateside, get you the help you need." Three a.m. on the day he was set to go home, he put his .45 in his mouth and blew his head off. Left a two-word note: *I failed.*

"I let him down," Callar said. She told Terreri she was tired of playing defense, trying to fix guys. This way she could be part of the fight, get the intel that they needed to save lives.

The story bugged Terreri. He wasn't seeing the connection. She wanted in on interrogations because this guy offed himself? But they had to have a doctor, and she said she'd move to Poland. So he signed her up.

She'd been fine the first four months. But then something had happened. Okay. Terreri knew what had happened. They'd had a problem with this nasty little Malaysian named Mokhatir. He'd come to them from a raid in the southern Philippines. A Delta/Philippine army team had caught him in an apartment with three soda bottle–sized bombs that looked just about right for taking down an airplane. The other two guys in the apartment had been killed, so Mokhatir was all they had. He wouldn't talk, and after a month the Deltas sent him to the Midnight House.

He insisted he hadn't made more than three bombs. Karp and Fisher hadn't believed him. They'd pushed him harder than any prisoner they'd had before. Over Callar's objection, they'd locked him in the punishment box for fourteen hours straight. When they opened the cell, Mokhatir couldn't move his legs or left arm. At first they thought he was faking, malingering, but after a few minutes they realized he wasn't.

When they called for Callar, she said he'd had a stroke, probably the result of infective endocarditis. Bacteria had built up in a heart valve and caused Mokhatir's blood to clot inside his heart. Then the clot had traveled to his brain, blocking blood vessels there and causing a stroke. Callar said he needed to get to a hospital for real care, but

Terreri refused, told her to do what she could on the base. Without an MRI or CAT scanner or clot-busting drugs, she was reduced to the basics. She gave him aspirin and antibiotics, kept him hydrated, elevated his legs. She knocked down the infection, and eventually the clot seemed to break. A few days later, Mokhatir regained the use of his arm. But he never walked again. After a month, they put him on a plane, sent him to the Philippines, said he'd had a stroke, cause unknown.

The day after they flew him out, Callar knocked on Terreri's door, said they needed to report what had happened.

"To who," Terreri said. "Whitby? Sanchez? You think they care?"

"He's permanently disabled."

"He's got a limp."

"He can't walk."

"One of those bombs of his had blown up in his face, he'd be disabled."

"Colonel—"

"Major, I have heard your advice, and I will consider it. Anything else?"

"No, sir." Callar didn't argue further. But her attitude changed. Twice since then, she'd interfered during interrogations, made Karp and Fisher pull detainees out of the punishment box. The squad had to have a doctor, so Terreri couldn't dismiss her. But she was yet another reason this deployment couldn't end soon enough.

NOW SHE WALKED into the interrogation room, sat across from Terreri. "Colonel."

"Major."

"You seem tired."

"So do you." Tired, and getting old like a local. She seemed to have aged a decade in the last year. And lost about fifteen pounds. She wasn't bad-looking, but her skin was tight on her face and her arms painfully thin.

"Why were you laughing just now, Colonel?"

He considered blowing off the question. Then decided, might as well tell her.

"Jawaruddin was in that chair just now. Playing tough. I was thinking what we're going to do to him, and it seemed funny."

"Why did it seem funny?"

"Figuring out how to break guys without leaving a mark. It's a strange way to spend your life."

"Are you uncomfortable with the idea of hurting him?"

"Are you?"

"That's not an answer."

"The answer is no. I'm plain sick of these guys. That's all."

"Do you think you've lost the ability to empathize with them? Does that bother you?"

For the second time in five minutes, Terreri found himself laughing. She didn't say anything. He laughed as long as he could. Then his laughter petered out and they stared at each other in silence.

"That's about the stupidest thing I've ever heard," he said.

"Why?"

"You really are a shrink. I say you're stupid, and you say why. I don't want to empathize with them. I want to break them. If you can't handle it, you let me know."

"We both want the same thing, Colonel. But I see disturbing tendencies in some of the interrogators. Even in you. I'm worried about depersonalization."

Terreri felt his stomach tighten, rage bubble up. This woman, this *reservist* with some fancy letters behind her name, telling him what to do.

"Three months left and we're done. I don't need this crap right now, Major."

"Sir. Three months is a significant length of time. I am responsible for monitoring the mental health of the members of this squad. As well as the physical health of the detainees."

"That speech you gave me when you signed up, that private you didn't save. Guy who decided to find out how a bullet tasted."

"Travis."

"Travis. That was his name. Now, Travis, he got depersonalized. He *depersonalized* himself with a .45. And I warned you it wasn't going to be easy, but you signed for it, and now we're almost through. Jawaruddin bin Zari, we caught him with a truck bomb. His buddy Mohammed put a bullet in one of our guys. Your job is to help us get these men to talk. You understand that?"

She didn't say a word. Just nodded. *Good.* Terreri had enough to worry about. They were going to go hard at bin Zari, and she was going to have to be involved. Whether she wanted to be or not.

"Thank you for your concern, Major. You are dismissed."

14

NEW ORLEANS

Noemie Williams and her sons lived in a two-story house in Gentilly, the northeast corner of New Orleans, near Lake Pontchartrain. During Katrina, levees had failed on both sides of the neighborhood. The floodwaters had topped ten feet.

Even now, even at night, the scars from the storm were obvious. The house beside Noemie's was vacant, plywood over its windows, a jagged crack slicing through the bricks on its front-right corner. A lot one block down was simply empty, no sign that a home had ever existed on it. On another, only a poured concrete foundation remained. Traffic was sparse and pedestrians nonexistent, though a few blocks south, toward the Ninth Ward, an open-air drug market was in full swing. The neighborhood made Wells think of a proud old man who'd had a heart attack and hadn't decided yet whether to try to rehab or lie back and let nature take its course.

Noemie Williams was fighting, though. Her house had a fresh coat of white paint and what looked like a new porch, complete with a rocking horse painted red, black, and green. She had asked Wells to come at 10 p.m., saying she needed to put her sons to bed. He gave her a little extra time, knocked on her door at 10:15. She slid the dead bolt back immediately, and he realized too late that when Williams said ten, she meant ten.

The door pulled just an inch, a soft creak, chain still on the hook. Wells flipped open his wallet, showed her his identification.

"May I?" she said. Wells handed it through the crack in the door. She glanced at it, handed it back, opened up. She was tall and light-skinned, cornrows tight across her skull. She wore cropped black pants and a black T-shirt with "Forever New Orleans" stenciled in gold on the chest. The lines on her forehead said she was at least forty, though she had the legs of a woman a decade younger.

"Sorry I'm late."

"Sit." She nodded to the living-room couch, protected by a plastic cover. In the reports of their interviews with her, the FBI agents wrote that Noemie Williams had been "calm and composed." Wells agreed already.

"Get you anything?" Noemie said. She had the marbles-in-mouth south Louisiana accent: half Birmingham, one-third Boston, one-sixth Bugs Bunny.

"I'm fine."

"Chicory coffee? Local specialty. Along with po'boys and heart attacks. Got a pot brewing." Indeed, the sweet smell of chicory filled the house.

"If you're having some, sure."

Noemie disappeared, leaving Wells to examine the room, which was decorated—to a fault—in the motif of proud African American. On one wall, posters of Martin Luther King Jr. and Muhammad Ali shared space with family pictures. Another wall was given over to a framed poster of Barack Obama standing in front of the White House.

Noemie carried in a tray, two steaming mugs of coffee and a jug of milk, along with a plateful of cookies. "Come to Louisiana, you will get fed," she said. The cookies were lemon and sugar and cinnamon, and fell into buttery pieces in Wells's mouth. He had to make a conscious effort to stop after three of them. The coffee had a bite that pulled Wells back to Pakistan, tiny cups of sweet, strong coffee brewed in battered metal pots, half sugar and half crunchy grounds, the only antidote to the chill of winter in the North-West Frontier.

"So, you knew my husband."

The past tense jumped at Wells. Jerry Williams was missing, not dead. Officially, anyway.

"We were friends. Trained as Rangers together."

"That was a long time back. Before he met me."

The windows were open, and a light breeze stirred the humid air through the curtains. But the city around them was anything but romantic. Police sirens screamed down Elysian Fields Avenue, four blocks away. Somewhere overhead, a helicopter buzzed.

"Lot of action," Wells said.

"Bangers banging. This neighborhood's not too bad, but the city's so small you can't get away from it. Unless you live in one of those mansions in the Garden District. Doesn't matter, anyway. Soon enough, another 'cane will make our acquaintance and even us Louisiana lifers will have to admit this place isn't meant to be. And that *will* be a shame." She closed the window and pulled the chain on the ceiling fan.

"You and Jerry have three boys."

"Asleep. Or pretending to be. Maybe reading comic books under the covers. Long as they're reading."

"What are their names?"

"Unfortunately, Jerry was a member of the George Foreman school of naming. The boys are named Jerry Jr., Johnny, and Jeffrey."

Wells couldn't think of any way to spin that.

"Every so often he'd have an S-A-N moment, and that was one."

"S-A-N?"

"S for stupid, A for ass, and N for a word I don't use around white people, no matter how well I know them. And I don't know you too well."

"You seem pretty calm about what's happened."

"The boys are used to Jerry being gone. He shows up tomorrow, they'll think this was just another mission. No need to upset them just yet. Though we're two months on. They're wondering."

"You don't think he's coming back."

"You don't shine it up before you spit it out, do you? No. I do not. Let me tell you why. We were having some troubles, no two ways about it. But Jerry Williams, Major Jeremiah Williams, he was very conscious that he was a man with three sons. A *black* man with three *black* sons. And everything that entails. Very conscious of all those boys whose daddies never even see them enter this world. You see those posters." She nodded around the room. "My husband insisted on them. He would not have walked out on his boys. Whatever happened to him, he's not with us anymore."

Her voice had stayed even through this explanation. Now tears sprung from her eyes, slid down her cheeks. Wells put his hand on her shoulder.

"Mrs. Williams—"

But she shook him off and walked out of the room.

Wells shifted on the couch, listening to the fan rustling overhead, and tried to figure what he'd done. Someone else—Exley, say—could have asked the same questions without inciting such a ferocious response. But Wells seemed to have lost his sense for the give-and-take of human interaction.

Noemie stepped back in.

"I'm sorry," Wells said. "I can come back.

"Just ask your questions, Mr. Wells."

"Let me start again, then. You were married in, what, '99?"

"Correct. You knew Jerry before that?"

"In Ranger training. You know, I was gone awhile."

"I know who you are."

"But before I went to Afghanistan, I remember him saying he was getting married, his wife was ten times as beautiful as he deserved."

Noemie gave him the tiniest of smiles.

"You're from New Orleans?"

"No. Came here for college, got my degree in social work from Tulane. After I met Jerry, we jumped around base to base. But I always wanted to come back. Last year, when Jerry retired, I told him after all that time in North Carolina and Texas and what all, he owed me. He didn't want to, but eventually he agreed."

"But you are from Louisiana."

"Grew up in Lafayette. Couple hours west of here on the Ten. Mom was black and dad was white, which accounts for this cracker accent. They were both from this swamp town, Morgan City, deep in the bayou. Back when they met, it wasn't so safe for a white boy and a black girl to be in love down there. Though better that than the other way around. So, they moved to Lafayette. The metropolis. You know how to tell the size of a town in Louisiana?"

Wells shook his head.

"Count the McDonald's. Morgan City only has but one McDonald's. Lafayette has a whole bunch of 'em. Are you married, Mr. Wells?"

"I was." Wells felt the need to say something more. "The job sort of took over."

"Uh-huh."

There was a whole speech in those two syllables, Wells thought. "Tell me about Jerry's last tour, in Poland."

"A few months before, he'd gotten back from a deployment in Afghanistan. I was worried they were going to send him there again. He wouldn't have argued. He wasn't the type to say no. Then he got this call, a special assignment in Poland, working with detainees."

"You know why they chose him?"

"In Afghanistan, he'd done some interrogations."

"How did you know?"

"I was, I am, his wife. He told me enough; I got the picture. They were trying to put a new unit together, one that wouldn't have any connection to the old squads. Or Guantánamo. One that could run more or less on its own."

"That's about right."

"I know that's right, Mr. Wells. I wasn't asking."

"Did you mind having him over there?"

"Matter of fact, I didn't. Figured he was safer in Poland than any-where else."

"But did you have a problem with what he was doing, the inter-rogations?"

"These men who want to blow us up? Kill my husband? And then they cry for lawyers soon as we catch them? Start talking about their rights? You are not seriously asking me that."

"Jerry felt the same."

"Of course."

"But not everyone on the squad agreed. Somebody thought they were going too far." Wells was guessing, chasing the defensiveness in her voice.

"That what somebody told you?"

"Yes," Wells lied.

"I don't know all that much about it. But I do know there were arguments. And they got worse as the tour went on. My husband, he went over there with the attitude that they didn't have to give these guys feather pillows. I don't got to tell you, Mr. Wells. If there's one person who knows, it's you. But it's strange, 'cause he came back with a different attitude."

"Like how?"

"It's hard to explain." She edged away from Wells on the couch, turned to look at him full-on. "Mr. Wells. Do you think my husband did something wrong? If you do, tell me now."

"Look. Somebody's killing the squad. We don't know why. The logical assumption is that it's because of something that happened over there. So, we need to know what that was. And there's only three guys left from the squad, not counting Jerry, and they aren't talking much—"

"Why—"

"Maybe they're worried they're gonna get prosecuted for torture. And the records of what they did, they're buried deep. So, the best bet is talking to you and the other families. You have my word, whatever Jerry did, I'm not after him. I'm not a cop or FBI. I'm working for the agency, and only the agency, to figure this out. And I'm a friend of your husband's. I know it may not seem that way, since we've never met before, but believe me, Ranger training, the guys in your unit, by the end you either can't stand the sight of them or they're friends for life. And Jerry was a friend. If he'd called me two months ago, said, 'I'm in trouble,' I would have been on the next plane down, no questions asked. That's just how it is."

Not a bad speech, Wells thought. Even if the reality was more complicated. After fifteen years, he probably would have asked at least a couple questions before buying his ticket. But Noemie seemed to like it. She patted his arm, leaned in.

"I'm telling you, I don't know much."

"Anything."

"They were rough. And I think near the end, something went wrong."

The FBI interview report didn't have anything like this from her. Wells waited. "What gave you that impression?" he said finally. "Something he said?"

"He changed. The last couple months, he didn't want to talk. Stopped e-mailing. He was hiding something, like he was having an affair. But Jerry would never have done that. Anyway, it was Poland."

"He never said anything about what had actually happened?"

"No."

"What about the information the squad developed? Did he ever talk about that?"

"No."

"Mom-mom!" From the second floor. A boy's voice.

"Jeffrey," she said. "He has nightmares. Since Jerry's gone. He knows what's up. The others don't, but he does."

She hurried upstairs.

I don't got to tell you, Mr. Wells, she'd said. *If there's one person who knows, it's you.* Was he a torturer? A killer, yes. But never a torturer. Though he'd come close, that night in the Hamptons with Pierre Kowalski, the arms dealer. Another bit of unfinished business. Close to a year before, Wells had found himself outside Kowalski's mansion in Zurich, pacing, hand on the Makarov tucked into his pants. Then he'd walked away. He'd made a deal with Kowalski, and he'd keep his word. For now.

NOEMIE RETURNED, trailed by a small boy, a miniature Malcolm Gladwell, a shock of curly hair springing from his head. His T-shirt, printed with a caped Will Smith from the movie *Hancock,* reached to his knees.

"This is Jeffrey," she said.

"Hi, Jeffrey. Did you like *Hancock*?"

"Mommy wouldn't let me see it!"

"Touchy subject," Noemie said.

Jeffrey tugged on his mother's pants. "I'm sleepy, Mommy."

"If you're sleepy, why weren't you sleeping?"

"Want to sleep in your bed."

"You know that's not allowed." She put him on the couch, settled beside him. He curled into her lap, his face just visible.

"Please."

"Go to sleep here, and when you wake up, it'll be morning. Deal?"

Jeffrey nodded happily.

"We're going to go from twenty to zero. Promise to be asleep by zero."

"Promise."

"Close your eyes. Twenty, nineteen . . ." She rubbed his forehead as she counted, and by the time she was done, the boy's mouth had dropped open and his breathing was as steady as the fan overhead.

"You're a magician," Wells said.

She glanced at her watch. "Anything else you need to know, Mr. Wells? I should get him to bed."

"Tell me about what Jerry was like when he got back."

"He was quiet, not talking much."

"And you read into that what?"

"I told you. That something happened he didn't want to talk about." She leaned back against the couch. The boy in her lap stirred, and she ran a finger down his arm to calm him. "One time." She broke off, and Wells waited. "One time, I got home early from work, and he was reading a book about the Nazis. When I saw him with it, it was like I'd caught him looking at I don't know what. He tried to hide it from me double-quick. I asked him about it, and he told me to mind my business. Which was not usual for him, even at that time. But I let it go. And I never saw the book again."

"The Nazis. Do you remember the name of the book?"

"I do not."

Again the boy stirred in her lap, and again she soothed him. "All right, Mr. Wells. I think it's time for this one to go to bed. Me, too."

"Just a couple more questions."

"A couple."

"You said a while back, you two were having problems before he disappeared. What was that about?"

"I loved Jerry, and I know he loved me. But like I said, he was different when he came back. And after we moved here, he had a tough time finding work. I guess I figured, a major in the Special Forces, a man like that could always find a job, even in New Orleans. But the corporate stuff—there's not a lot of companies down here for that work. He did some bodyguard work, but he wanted to be a director of security somewhere. Thought he'd earned that. He told me we should move. I wanted him to give it time. It'd hardly been six months. New Orleans can grow on you."

"But you're sure he wouldn't have walked out."

"I'm sure."

"The night he disappeared?"

"He told me he was going down to the market, pick up a six-pack. He'd been drinking more, too, since he got back. That was around seven p.m. Ten or so, I tried to call him and he didn't answer."

"Were you worried?"

"It'd happened a couple of times recently. So, no. I wasn't happy, but I wasn't worried. Figured he was on the corner, hanging out. Watching dice get rolled. When midnight came and he didn't come home, I decided to see for myself. So, I put my shoes on and I slipped my little .22 in my purse—"

"You have a gun—"

"Mr. Wells, you think those bangers out there care about Mace?" She laughed, her voice losing an octave and filling the room. *"Mace? This is New Orleans. Mace?* Anyway, I went out there, and Harvey, who runs the market, he said he hadn't seen Jerry in a few hours, said he had himself a quart of Budweiser and went off to the Pearl, a few blocks away."

"The Pearl?"

"The real name is, I believe, Minnie's Black Pearl. But everyone just calls it the Pearl. A high-class establishment. Get shot in there for wearing the wrong hat. I was in no mood to visit the Pearl, so I went home. I figured Jerry would get home eventually and we would have it out, say some things that needed saying. Like my daddy said, sometimes a big storm clears the air. Though my daddy was full of it."

"But Jerry never came home."

"He did not. And the next morning, soon as the Pearl opened at eleven, I went over there, showed them the picture, asked if they knew him, and that S-A-N bartender, he started in with, 'We don't snitch around here.' I said, 'I'm not the cops, I'm the man's wife,' and you know what he said. He said, 'That might be worse.' So I said, 'Look, my husband didn't get home last night, and if you don't tell me what you know, I will stand outside your bar tonight shouting about Jesus and sinners until you're the one calling the cops to get rid of me.' And so I found out what they knew, which was hardly worth the trouble. Jerry drank until eleven, by himself. And then he left. Said he was going home. And that was it. He left the Pearl and turned to smoke."

"So, you called the cops?"

"They said Jerry was a grown man and that if he didn't turn up in a couple of days I could file a missing-persons report. Which I did, soon as I was allowed. The detectives talked to the bartender down there for about five minutes and then forgot it. I begged *The Times-Picayune* to write something, and after a month they finally did, some little thing that didn't even have his picture."

"Too bad he wasn't an eighteen-year-old girl."

"You mean a *white* girl. With blond hair and a big smile. CNN would have been all over it then. But I don't think it matters, Mr. Wells. I think he died that night."

"Why?"

"My husband, you know how big he was. I don't think anybody would take a chance keeping him alive. Too easy for him to mess you up."

Wells couldn't disagree.

"Something else, too," she said. "I think he knew whoever did this. I don't think it was Al Qaeda or any of them rats."

"Why?"

"Nobody would go at him straight up, see? Look at the man. And Jerry wouldn't just be getting in a car. Come on, even little kids know better. So, no, it had to be somebody he knew, make him drop his guard."

"The others, they were shot with a silencer," Wells said, thinking out loud. "Somebody could have done it on the street and then taken his body. Not a lot of lights out there."

"They were killed all different ways, though. The woman, the doctor, somebody snuck into her house, made it look like a suicide," Noemie said. "Somebody been *creeping*."

"Last question."

"You already got your last question."

"I promise. I don't want to upset you again, but—" Wells hesitated. She nodded to him. "Is there any chance that Jerry's the one behind this? That he's faked his own death. You said he was upset—"

"I said he was in a mood. Come on, Mr. Wells. You knew my husband. You cannot be serious. He was angry that he didn't get a promotion, angry that they made him retire. He wasn't a killer."

You're wrong, Wells didn't say. *He was a soldier. A Ranger. He was nothing more or less than a trained, professional killer.*

Just like me.

"And now I have to put this boy in his bed," Noemie said. She picked up Jeffrey, put him over her shoulder. His eyes blinked open, and he looked suspiciously at Wells.

"Thank you, Noemie. If I have more questions, can I call you?"

"Uh-huh. And if you check out the Pearl, keep your back to the wall. They don't like white people much in there."

"I don't blame them."

THE PEARL WAS CHEAP and flashy, Hennessy posters on the walls, faded red vinyl booths, and a half-dozen Mercedes hood ornaments hanging from the ceiling. Wells didn't get any smiles when he walked in. Not from the bartender, a tall, skinny man with a Saints cap pulled low on his forehead. Not from the three boys in the corner booth who wore identical gold studs. Not from the two old heads deep in conversation at the bar. And not from the woman in the silver bikini dancing listlessly on the back counter to the heavy slow sounds of rap that sounded like it was being played at half speed.

Whatever had happened in Poland had upset Jerry Williams more than a bit, Wells thought. The Pearl wasn't a place Jerry would have favored when Wells knew him. Wells debated staying, forcing the issue, maybe taking a seat with the boys in the booth. But what was he trying to prove? He would come back tomorrow and get the same stiff non-answers about Jerry Williams as the New Orleans cops.

"You lost?" the bartender said.

Wells shook his head. "Thanks."

"Thanks for what?" the bartender said. Then, under his breath, "Dummy."

Wells knew he ought to walk away. But after Cairo, he was in no mood to get pushed around. "I'll take a Bud," he said.

"We're all out."

"Miller."

"Out of that, too."

"Then a gin and tonic. Tanqueray." A half-full bottle of Tanqueray sat on the back counter directly across from Wells.

The bartender turned down the music. "You dumb or just playing that way?"

"There's no call for this."

"Go back to the Quarter where you belong." He took two steps toward Wells, his hands loose at his sides.

Wells turned toward the door, as if he were leaving. Then he spun back and with his right hand grabbed the bartender's skinny left arm and pulled him down onto the scarred wood of the bar and knocked off his glasses. Wells stepped forward and with his left hand reached down the bartender's back for the pistol that he knew would be tucked into the man's jeans. He grabbed the pistol, a Beretta knockoff that fit snugly in his hand. Still holding the bartender down, he turned to cover the room. The action had taken less than three seconds, and the kids in the corner hadn't moved. Yet.

"You are either a cop or a damn fool," the bartender mumbled. "And I know you ain't no cop."

Wells let go of the bartender's arm, stepped back from the bar. "Slowly. Put your hands on top of your heads. All of you."

They complied. Wells knew he didn't have long. Soon enough, one of the bangers would do something stupid, and then he'd have blood on his hands for this stunt.

"Quicker you answer my questions, the quicker I'm gone. I'm trying to find a friend of mine. He came in here for a beer a couple months back. Been missing ever since. Named Jerry Williams. Big guy. Ring any bells?"

"That what you hassling me for? I told the cops, I don't know nothing about it, said the bartender."

"Jerry and I were Rangers together. Now he's missing. This is the last place anybody saw him. Do me a favor, answer my questions, I get out of here."

Unwillingly: "Ask what you gotta ask."

Wells tucked the pistol into his jeans. "Ever see anybody with Jerry?"

"Not hardly. He drank quiet. Put a twenty on the bar, nod when he wanted a hit. He put out two twenties, then I knew he needed some relaxation. Once or twice, late night, we got to talking; he told me he was a vet. Said nobody understood what it was like over there, you had to be there. Nothing more."

"He ever say anything about disappearing, getting out of New Orleans?"

"Not to me."

"He seem nervous ever? Like somebody was after him?"

The bartender shook his head.

"Ever talk about his wife?"

"Men don't come in here to talk about their wives."

"And you're sure nobody ever struck up a conversation with him?"

The bartender hesitated. "There was a guy, came in once or twice around that time Jerry was here. Never saw him since. It struck me, 'cause he was white."

"Could you recognize him?"

"I reckon not. Like I said, he was here twice at most. I think he was tall."

The kids in the corner booth were grumbling at one another, waggling their heads. Time to go. "You have a nice night," Wells said.

"Gimme back my gun." Wells backed away. "Come on, man. I answered what you asked."

"It'll be in the river. Hope you can swim."

Wells pulled open the front door, backed out. He scuttled around the corner, then ran for his car, waiting for footsteps. Shots. But nobody came after him, and the sighing of the city was all he heard.

AT 7 A.M. the next morning, his sat phone jolted him awake. No mystery about who was on the other end. Only Shafer and Exley had the number, and Wells was fairly certain Exley wasn't calling him at this hour.

"How'd it go?"

Wells filled him in.

"I think she was straight with you?

"I do."

"And he's dead?"

"Most likely."

"Anybody else for you to talk to down there? Girlfriend, anyone like that?"

"I don't think so. He didn't have many friends down here. What about you?"

"Getting some threads here. Mainly about Whitby. Looks like our director of national intelligence knows more about 673 than Duto let on at first."

"How's that?"

"You know how Duto told us the intel from the Midnight House went to the Pentagon? He neglected to mention that Whitby was on the other end."

"Say again, Ellis?"

"Whitby ran the unit where Brant Murphy sent his reports. It was called the Office of Strategic and Intelligence Planning. Big name, but there were only three people in it. Whitby, a deputy, and an assistant. When Whitby left to become DNI, the Pentagon closed the office, took it off the org charts. It's not exactly a secret, but you have to know where to look. I'm not sure the FBI knows about it. Though they must."

"How'd you find it?"

"Amazing but true, Duto told me. I went to him about the missing prisoner numbers, and he told me he didn't know anything about them. He told me it was Whitby who made him kill the inspector general's investigation into the letter. Then he told me that Whitby had been in charge of 673 at the Pentagon."

"Back up, Ellis. Why did Whitby make Duto stop the IG investigation?"

"Duto says Whitby wouldn't tell him."

"Whitby made Vinny Duto end an internal CIA investigation and didn't tell him why. And Duto agreed? That's impossible, Ellis. Duto would never do that."

"Normally, I'd agree with you. But this isn't a normal situation."

"What are you saying, Ellis?"

Twelve hundred miles away, Shafer sighed. "Whitby's got a lot of juice, and I'm not sure where it's coming from. Let's talk about it in person."

"I'll be back this afternoon. We need to talk to Duto and Whitby. No more pussyfooting."

"Not yet. First, I need to talk to the NSA. They're the ones who ran the registry. Find out if they have anything on the missing detainees. Meantime, you go to California, talk to Steve Callar. Rachel's husband."

"Why would Callar talk to me? It's not like Noemie. I don't know him. Or his wife."

"I'll send you the FBI interviews. You'll see. I checked. American has a flight to Dallas at nine thirty, on to San Diego at noon."

"Thanks for letting me decide for myself," Wells said.

But Shafer had already hung up.

15

There is actor and acted upon, you understand, Jawaruddin? In this room. And I'm the actor. Which makes you the—work with me here—the acted upon."

In his right hand, Kenneth Karp held a stun gun, a sleek gray box no larger than an electric razor. He pushed a button on its side. A tiny lightning bolt arced between the prongs at the gun's head.

Karp was skinny, with wiry black hair and dark brown eyes. When he got excited, his hands twitched and words poured out. He was excited now, pacing the room. Angry. Or pretending to be. With Karp, the distinction could be difficult to make.

Jawaruddin bin Zari, the object of Karp's attention, sat shackled to a chair. Steel chains wrapped around his chest, forearms, and shins. A U-shaped band of steel extended from a rod behind the chair, holding his head in place. Unlike Karp, he seemed calm, his breathing steady.

The room around them was cinder-block, no decoration of any kind. With one exception. An American flag filled the wall in front of bin Zari. He could escape it only by closing his eyes.

Karp finally stopped pacing, knelt beside bin Zari, ran a hand down his biceps. "For ten days now, you have been our guest," Karp said, speaking Arabic now.

"Guest," bin Zari said. He hardly moved his lips. His voice was soft, nearly inaudible.

"Yes, guest." Karp pulled a half-dozen grainy photographs from the file folder on the table behind bin Zari. He held them up one by one. "Your truck. Your truck bomb. Very nicely put together. The house where we arrested you. Three Paki army uniforms, found inside the house, genuine. Three army identification cards, also genuine. And a pass for the building where your president was to meet White"— Sir Roderick White, the British foreign minister. "This wasn't just any operation. This was well planned. Well organized. The heart of Islamabad. A senior British official. And you would have pulled it off, if not for bad luck."

Karp put the photos aside. "Yet when we ask you, you tell us you don't know anything about it. Where's the pride of ownership? The pleasure a man takes in his craft?"

Bin Zari shifted sideways, clanking his chains against the chair.

"You don't respect us enough even to lie to us. Make something up. Pretend to answer our questions."

A tiny smile flickered across bin Zari's face.

"The idea of lying pleases you. Let me tell you again. You don't want to be in this room. This is not a good room. You don't want me to ask you questions. You don't want to be the acted upon. So I'll ask you one last time. We both know you didn't put this together alone. Who gave you the security plans? The uniforms, the ID cards?"

Silence.

"Are other elements of your cell still operational?"

Silence.

"Do you want me to hurt you?" And without waiting for an

answer, Karp jammed the stun gun into bin Zari's jowls. Bin Zari screamed and the muscles in his neck bulged, but the restraints held him tight. Karp counted aloud. "One Miss-iss-ippi. Two Miss-iss-ippi. Three Miss-iss-ippi . . ."

At five, Karp stopped, stepped away from the chair. Spittle ran down bin Zari's chin. He reached out his tongue to wipe it off and then seemed to change his mind. He pulled back his tongue and snapped his mouth shut.

"Here's what you're thinking. You're thinking, *I can get used to it. I'm strong. I'm not Craig Taylor*"—the aid worker bin Zari had kidnapped and killed in Karachi. "I'm a son of the Prophet. They can't break me with a stun gun."

Karp knelt beside bin Zari. "What you don't understand. You might get used to this." Again, Karp jammed the gun into bin Zari's neck. Zari tried to pull his head forward, but the band around his temple held him tight. He squeezed his eyes closed, grunted, as the electricity poured into him.

"I've got a hundred different ways to hurt you. They all hurt in a different way. It's not a fair fight."

Karp left the gun in place until bin Zari screamed and his eyes rolled back and he slumped into the side of the world. Only the thump of his pulse in his neck proved he was still alive. Karp reached under bin Zari's chair for a plastic gallon jug, uncapped it, poured it over bin Zari's head.

Bin Zari snapped awake. The fear in his eyes flared and faded as fast as cheap fireworks. "Do it again," he said, his lips barely moving. "Again."

"I'm going to let you think things over," Karp said. "Don't go anywhere."

———

ONE FLOOR ABOVE, Rachel Callar watched Karp at work on twin closed-circuit television screens that ran a live feed from the interrogation room. Hank Poteat had installed the room's cameras before leaving Poland for Korea. They offered high-quality video, almost high-definition. Callar could see everything. She could see they were losing themselves. They were all id, no superego. She didn't know anymore why Terreri had brought her here. He didn't respect her or listen to her. None of them did. Now they were heading for *Lord of the Flies* territory. They'd been here too long. Each day they dug themselves in deeper. Soon enough they'd be using a conch shell to decide who could speak.

Callar's dad was a doctor, an oncologist who specialized in lung cancer. He'd always wanted her to follow him. Doctors were respected, he told her. Doctors were educated. Doctors cheated death. He didn't mention that doctors lived in Beverly Hills and bought new BMWs every year, but then she could see that for herself. She spent her first semester at Berkeley painting and then gave in and went pre-med.

Her second year in med school, the pressure got to her. She stopped sleeping. She lay in bed jamming her brain with beta cells and lipoproteins. She tried to memorize the pages of her textbooks exactly, as though her mind were a hard drive that could store every word. She was afraid to stop studying, afraid she'd flunk out. Or worse, would kill a patient because she hadn't studied enough. *Her fault, her fault, her fault . . .*

Anyway, she stopped eating.

An itty-bitty case of anorexia. She'd had one in high school, too, like at least half the senior girls, but she was more serious this time around. She started by skipping dinner. More time to study. Then she decided that lunch would be her only meal. The rest of the day, she restricted herself to water, coffee, and sugarless gum. At lunch she had a green salad, no dressing, a couple of croutons, a cup of yogurt, and berries on the side, maybe eight hundred calories in all. Very healthy.

She lost forty pounds in three months, went from one hundred fifty to one hundred ten. People told her she looked good. Then they told her she looked great. Then they told her maybe she was getting a little thin. Then they stopped talking to her about it, and she knew she was in trouble. But she felt great. In total control.

She finished the year, went back to Los Angeles for the summer. She was sitting in a bikini by the pool of her parents' house when her mom got home from yoga, saw her, and started to cry. Her parents convinced her to spend six weeks in a "facility" that specialized in the treatment of eating disorders. "It's called the New Beginnings Center," her dad said.

"Are there any other kind of beginnings?"

The NBC, as the patients—or "guests," in the center's jargon—called it, wasn't a mental hospital. Not officially, anyway. So it didn't show up on her medical records, an omission that would come in handy later. The place was more of a spa, really. A spa with a locked front door.

But despite its New Age fripperies, the place did her good. Mainly because of her psychiatrist, Dr. Appel, a small and entirely bald man who wore the same threadbare tweed jacket to every session. He never said so openly, but he seemed to regard the center's affectations as a joke. Maybe that was why she liked him. Or maybe it was because of the way he listened to her without judging her, without trying to impose his will on her. In his office she could step out of herself, see the connections between her need to control her eating and her fear of being overwhelmed, never measuring up to her father.

"Fear of failure drives my life."

"You've put yourself in an impossible position, then. All of us fail eventually."

"So what do I do?"

"I must admit I fail to have the answer. Proving my point." He arched an eyebrow.

"Was that a joke?" He smiled, the first time she'd ever seen any hint of emotion from him. "It was, wasn't it? Don't quit your day job, Dr. Appel."

He nodded gravely, the edges of his lips tipping into a smile, and she felt somehow she'd succeeded.

Day by day she relaxed, opened up to him about her fears and feelings of inadequacy. Just naming the emotions helped her enormously. One morning, about ten days before she was due to leave the center, she came down to the little cafeteria where she and the rest of the "guests" ate their meals under the watchful eye of nurses and dieticians. And as she smelled the eggs cooking in the kitchen behind the double doors at the far end of the room, she realized that she was so very hungry.

By the end of her stay at the center she was eating normally again. Though Dr. Appel warned her that they'd never go away entirely, that in moments of great stress, her twin black dogs—anorexia and the depression that circled it—might come back.

By the time she left New Beginnings, she'd decided to become a psychiatrist. She'd also decided to break from her parents. She stopped seeing them, stopped cashing her dad's checks, paid for the last two years of medical school herself. Before residency, she joined an army program that gave her a monthly stipend in return for a promise to join the reserves. Part of her knew she'd signed up to piss off her dad, who'd been a lifelong member of the ACLU and burned his draft card during Vietnam. Not the best reason to join, but the decision worked out. She liked being part of the reserves. As a shrink in Southern California, she saw more than her share of borderline personalities, narcissists and drama queens who suffered mainly from boredom and spent their sessions wheedling for Xanax. Talking to soldiers and vets offered a valuable reminder that some twentysomethings faced traumas worse than having nasty stepmoms.

BUT SOMETIME IN 2006, her second tour in Iraq, she started coming unwound. Just as in med school, her problems increased incrementally. She had trouble sleeping, and when she did she dreamed incessantly about the soldiers she was treating, especially the ones who'd been hurt. She exercised more and more, telling herself she'd sleep better if she tired out her body. She started to count calories in the mess line.

Then she lost Travis. He was a good-looking kid. A good-looking man. Broad-shouldered, not too tall, sandy blond hair. When he smiled, which wasn't often, his eyes crinkled. He could have been Paul Newman's younger brother. His looks shouldn't have mattered, but of course they did. And he was funny. In a laconic, Texas way. One time, she'd asked him his favorite food.

He'd smirked and said, "Barbecue, ma'am. Favorite car, an F-150. Black with a number-eight bumper sticker. Favorite activity, drinking beer. Favorite music, well, I like both kinds. Country and western. I mean, ma'am, when you're born in Fort Worth, and your parents name you Travis, you don't have much choice in the matter. You can fight it, but why bother? Can you guess my favorite hat?"

It was the longest speech Travis ever gave her.

She liked him. She looked forward to seeing him.

She'd thought sending him home was the right move. He wasn't ready to go back to his unit. He'd started to get paranoid, as severely depressed patients sometimes did. He complained that some of the other guys in his bunk were making fun of him. For a few weeks, she tried antidepressants, but they didn't help. She didn't want to force-feed him an antipsychotic like Zyprexa that would make him gain thirty pounds and sleep fifteen hours a day. He'd be branded as mentally ill for the rest of his life. She knew she was running out of time to help him. Her tour was almost over, and he was pressing every day to go back to the field. And the army was so short on frontline guys that they wouldn't have said no. But she knew he wasn't ready. He needed to get away from Iraq, from the heat and the wind and the constant reminders of his dead squadmates. She told him she was sending him stateside, where he could get the help he needed.

But Travis Byrne, private first class, disagreed with her diagnosis. And proved her wrong in the most irreversible way possible. And since the night Travis said good-bye to her and the world with a two-word note, she'd felt herself cramping, obsessing over him. "I failed," he'd written. She felt the same. And after a few months back in San Diego, she decided she needed another mission.

NOW HERE SHE WAS, in Stare Kiejkuty, watching Kenneth Karp beat on Jawaruddin bin Zari. From what she could see, Karp wasn't having much luck. Which meant that he and Jack Fisher would be asking to use the punishment box soon enough. After that, maybe, the fifth cell.

She couldn't stand Karp. With his constant pacing, his tight energy, he reminded her of a monkey. She'd bet he was covered in thick, black hair. And yet he did carry himself with power. He would be an energetic lover, if not a good one.

Ugh. Was she really thinking about what Ken Karp might be like in bed? She'd been here far too long. Like everyone else.

Karp walked out of the interrogation room. He was coming up here, she knew. He liked to work detainees over and then leave them alone to imagine what their next punishment might be. "Let them stew," he said. "Builds the dread." As a psychiatrist, Callar had to agree. Anxiety twisted the mind, forced it in on itself. As a human being, she wasn't so sanguine. Her own dread seemed to be getting worse.

Before Karp could reach the office, she walked into the hall, down the stairs that led to the steel front door of the barracks. When she stepped out, the late-winter sun caught her full in the eyes. She blinked, raised a hand to shield her face.

It was day. She'd forgotten.

16

Seven seventy-two Flores was an oversized Spanish colonial, two stories, red tile roof, thick white walls. In typical Southern California style, it nearly filled its lot. A steel-gray Toyota SUV sat in the narrow driveway along its left side.

The house lay in the heart of the prosperous and placid precincts of northern San Diego. To the west, closer to the ocean, homes were even now selling for millions of dollars. But 772 Flores didn't fit with its neighbors. Blackout shades covered its windows. Brown patches dotted its front lawn. It looked like a foreclosure. But the loss at 772 went deeper than an unpaid mortgage.

Wells parked his rented Pontiac behind the Toyota. He reached for his Glock, tucked it under the driver's seat. For this visit, he preferred to be unarmed.

The front door was heavy and oak, with an old-style brass knocker. A wooden sign proclaimed "Casa Callar." No bell. Wells knocked solidly. But the house stayed dark. "Mr. Callar?"

Nothing. Wells heard faint music from upstairs. Classical, a mournful dirge.

"Mr. Callar?" Wells yelled. "Steven? It's John Wells. I called last night."

He knocked harder. Still nothing. Fine. He was sure Callar was inside. Wells would just have to wait.

He settled into the Pontiac and flicked on the satellite radio, the car's main perk, flipping between the all-Springsteen channel and a couple of the alt-rock stations that played the stuff Anne had shown him on their night together. Death Cab for Cutie and The Hold Steady and the rest. Wells liked the songs, but they were too pretty for him, music for overage children whose biggest problems were drugs and love. Though even Springsteen had gone soft these days. Or just gotten old, the desperate anger of his early albums burning down to a quiet melancholy.

He'd listened twice more to the message Anne had left him, but he hadn't called her. He figured that he'd wait until the mission was over to decide whether to see her again. Right now, though, he missed her, wondered where she was, what she was doing. He hadn't wondered that about anybody except Exley for a long time. And he felt vaguely disloyal. But still he wondered.

AFTER A HALF HOUR, the front door to 772 swung open. A man strode out, nearly running, holding a baseball bat loosely.

"Off my property. I'll call the cops."

You wanted to call the cops, you would have called them, Wells thought. The guy was about six feet, with long arms, skinny and muscular. He looked like a pit bull kept hungry so he'd fight better. A barbed-wire tattoo knotted his right biceps. His hair was short and flecked with gray, his face long and flecked with pain.

"Mr. Callar? I'm John Wells. We spoke yesterday."

Callar cocked his head sideways as if he'd caught Wells lying but couldn't be bothered to argue. He lifted the bat, took a practice swing, a cutting, long arc that stopped just short of the Pontiac's driver's-side mirror.

"What would you do if I put a hole in your windshield?"

"It's a rental."

For a moment, Callar smiled, and Wells could see the man he'd been. Then the smile was gone. Callar walked back to the house. At the door, he tossed the bat aside, turned, looked at Wells. Waved him in.

The blackout shades left the house almost spookily dark. Callar led Wells into the kitchen. Wells could dimly see a chef's island, a brushed-steel fridge, tall, white cabinets. Given the messy front lawn, Wells imagined the house would be chaotic. Furniture upended in the dark, bugs underfoot. But when Callar flipped on the lamp on the counter and filled the room with the cool gray light of a compact fluorescent, Wells saw that the place was clean, plates and glasses neatly stacked in the cabinets.

Wells was reminded of a mausoleum. The house was carefully tended but lifeless, the mirror image of the Northern Cemetery. The great graveyard had been stolen by the living. Seven seventy-two Flores now belonged to the dead.

"Nice house," Wells said.

"My wife had good taste. I'd offer you a drink, but the house is dry."

"Water's fine."

Callar pulled a jug of water from the fridge and leaned against the kitchen counter. He took a long swig and wiped his mouth. He didn't offer the jug to Wells.

"What exactly do you want to know, John? You don't mind if I call you John. Seeing as you've come all this way in your rental Pontiac."

"I want to hear about your wife."

"Rachel. Her name was Rachel. Call her that, please."

This meeting was already stranger, harsher, than Wells could have expected. "I want to hear about Rachel."

"You want the fairy-tale version, how we met when she was a resident and I was a nurse and it was love among the crazies? For our first date we went to a Dodgers-Astros game. Jeff Bagwell hit a foul ball our way and I snagged it. And I'd never caught a ball before in my life, and I wanted it. But I gave it to this six-year-old three seats over because I wanted to impress her. And it worked, even though Rachel told me afterward she knew I only gave the kid the ball to show off. We were married two years to the day after that game. Or you want the real version, how she was dating this ER doc when we met? And she didn't bother to tell me that until a month later, when the guy got up in my face. You want to know how we afforded this house? Shrinks do pretty well out here, all these rich housewives. Plus Rachel got a few bucks when her grandma died. You want to know her favorite color? What she called me in the middle of the night?" Callar had kept his dark eyes locked on Wells for this litany. Now, finally, he looked away.

"You don't care about any of that. Not you or those FBI androids. They look human, but they're not. All you want is how she died, yeah? How she looked when I found her on the bed with a plastic bag on her head? How she smelled after two days alone? Dead and alone? Because she sent me to Phoenix because she knew she was going to do it and she didn't want me to interrupt her. That's what you want to know."

Callar was an open wound, pouring pain out with every word. Yet Wells couldn't escape the feeling that he was watching a performance, *Bereaved Husband of a Suicide*. The guy was too furious to be so articulate. Or too articulate to be so furious. Or maybe he had just had too much time to chew his grief into mush, compose his feelings into this angry melody.

"Whatever you want to tell me," Wells said.

"What I don't get, man, what I don't get is why you're here at all. Seeing as how I told everything to the cops and the detectives. And then two days ago to these robots from the FBI. They left me their card and told me to call if anything occurred to me. If I remembered anything that could be useful in the investigation. Now you show up to kick some more dirt on it. John Wells. You don't have anything better to do?"

"The FBI, they told you what happened. To the rest of the squad." Wells hoping to keep Callar a little bit on track.

"Yeah. Before I kicked them out. You gonna take notes?"

"This is informal. I don't have any authority." Callar had probably guessed as much already, Wells thought.

"I can tell you to get lost whenever."

"Sure."

"Well, that calls for a drink." Callar looked at a cabinet over the fridge.

"I thought—"

"I keep a little something on hand. For special occasions." He clambered onto the counter and pulled open the cabinet, revealing a dozen bottles of Jack Daniel's, the oversized square ones.

"Special occasions."

"Empty, empty, empty . . ." Callar rooted through the cabinet. "Here we go." He pulled down a half-full bottle, the brown liquid sloshing against the glass as though it wanted to escape.

"I didn't offer this to the *federales*, but you strike me as at least half human," Callar said. He slopped whiskey into a glass, stopping only when the brown liquid neared the rim. "This way if anyone asks, you been drinking, I say, just one or two a day."

"Clever."

"Say when." Callar started to pour.

"When." But Callar didn't stop until Wells's glass was as full as his own.

"In for a penny."

"You want to get me arrested for a DUI."

"You? Please." Callar raised his glass. "Got a toast for us, John?"

"Just hoping it's not spiked with rat poison."

"That would be too easy." Callar drank half his glass. Wells followed, wondering how far down the rabbit hole they would go this afternoon.

"Rachel was a shrink. Ever go to a shrink, John?"

The question surprised Wells. "Not really, no."

"Not really or no?"

"No," Wells said, lying. "How'd Rachel end up in the army?"

"The military has these programs, they give you extra cash during residency. You serve when you're done. Money's not great, but the benefits are nice. She signed up third year of residency, wound up in the reserves, and after the war started, she rotated in and out."

"By choice."

"Pretty much. You're a doc in the reserves, especially a woman, you don't want to go into a hot zone, army's not dragging you over. It doesn't look good."

"Tell me more about the two of you."

"First, I want to hear how you got involved in all this," Callar said.

"Last week the CIA director, Vinny Duto, asked me to take a

look. I'm getting up to speed. If you talked to the FBI last week, you probably know as much as I do about the case."

"The FBI didn't have time to tell me much before I kicked them out."

"But you know, seven members of 673 are dead or missing. Professional hits. No leads, no suspects, no motive. The bureau is going on the theory it's probably Qaeda. Qaeda or a detainee looking for revenge."

"And you agree?"

"I can't figure it out. None of it makes sense. But it started with your wife."

"Rachel killed herself," Callar said. "If you read the autopsy, the police report, then you saw. She took that Xanax and she lay down on her bed and put that bag on her head. And she died."

"She have a prescription for the pills?"

Callar sipped his drink. "Sure. She was having a lot of trouble, anxiety attacks, insomnia. Ever since she got back from Poland."

Wells decided to let that thread alone for now. "Police report says she didn't leave a note."

"Maybe she did. Maybe I burned it before I called the cops. Maybe she blamed me for being such a crappy husband."

"Were you a crappy husband?"

"No."

"Was there a note?"

"Listen to me. *Listen.* Nobody could have gotten those pills into Rachel if she didn't want to take them."

"How about the same nobody who's killed soldiers and ops without leaving a clue? Maybe somebody shot her up with a sedative, liquid Xanax, dumped the pills down her throat."

"Or maybe aliens landed from planet TR-thirty-six and killed her and flew off. It didn't happen. She killed herself. You drag it up, rub my face in it."

Wells found his attention wandering to the light sneaking in the edges of the windows where the blackout shades didn't quite reach. He hadn't eaten lunch, and the whiskey was hitting him hard.

"What doesn't make sense to me," Wells said. "Most husbands. They'd want to believe this. They'd want the police to investigate. And if they got any whiff it was real, they'd want whoever did it strung up. But you, you're fighting it hard as you can. And not 'cause you're a suspect, either. The police, FBI, they say your alibi's airtight. You were working in Phoenix the entire weekend. Only got about eight hours' sleep the whole time."

"I want Rachel left in peace."

"Her or you?"

"Both of us."

"Even if someone drugged her and put a bag on her head for you to find."

In the silence that followed, Wells knew he'd gone too far.

CALLAR SUCKED down the rest of his whiskey. "You got a way with words, John."

"I'm sorry. Truly."

"Ought to put my foot in your ass, send you on your way." But Callar didn't. Maybe he was tired of drinking alone. Or maybe, despite all his denials, he wondered what had really happened.

"I have to ask," Wells said.

Callar's half-shut eyes warned Wells to be careful.

"Before she died, Rachel, she get any threats? Did you notice anything unusual? Cars outside the house?"

"Dumb question. But I'll answer anyway. No."

"All right. So, how'd she wind up over there?"

"In 2005 and 2006, she went to Iraq. Four-month tours. Mainly the big hospital there, at Balad, the air base. Evaluating soldiers for psychiatric problems."

Callar broke off. He poured two glasses of water, slid one to Wells.

"She saw a lot," Callar said. "Eighteen-year-old kids, faces melted off. Guys with PTSD so bad that they got locked in rubber rooms. After the second time, she was a mess. Angry. She lost weight. She would hardly talk to me. Then she heard about this new squad getting put together. Six-seventy-three. Dealing with guys they couldn't send to Gitmo. She wanted a job where she could get something back for the red, white, and blue."

"You weren't in favor."

"I thought she didn't know what she was getting into. But she never listened to me. I was hoping they wouldn't take her. She was high-strung after that second tour, and I hoped somebody would notice. But she'd been in Iraq, so she had the clearances. And docs weren't exactly lining up for the work. And shrinks, they know how to fake it. Couple months later, she was on a plane to Warsaw."

"What was she doing?"

"She didn't tell me much. I had the impression they wanted her to make sure they pushed the prisoners to the limit but no further. And to fix them up if they did go too far."

"How did she feel about that?"

"Look. I was only getting snapshots. Talking to her a couple times a week. I think . . . part of her rolled right through it. Maybe even liked it for a while. Then something happened, a few months in, and she hated herself for liking it. And she'd volunteered, so that was worse. She couldn't put it on anybody else."

Callar stopped, but Wells didn't think the story was done.

"Then, near the end, there was another incident."

"Incident."

"Before you ask, I don't know what. Not a clue. But when she got back, she was in bad shape. Taking a whole pharmacy worth of stuff. Ambien, the sleeping pills. Antidepressants. Then Xanax, Klonopin. She was prescribing it for herself and getting docs she knew to give it to her."

"That doesn't prove she killed herself," Wells said. Callar's eyes flickered and his face softened. "All I'm saying is, whatever happened, it came out of something over there. You're sure you don't know what it was."

"Have you not been listening to me? She didn't talk about anything operational. She was a good soldier girl. You want to know what happened over there, check the records. If you can find them. Talk to the rest of the squad, everyone who's left."

"Rachel ever discuss the rest of the squad? Hint who was pushing too hard?"

Now the uncertainty disappeared from Callar's eyes. "One time. She said, 'Steve, you'll never believe what that nasty colonel did today. Ripped out a prisoner's heart. Reached right into his chest. Fried it up and ate it.' What have I been saying? She didn't talk about anything operational. You're just like those FBI dweebs. You pretend to listen, but you don't."

Callar slopped more whiskey in his glass, sucked it down. Though he didn't seem drunk to Wells. The months in this dark house must have turned his liver into an alcohol-processing machine.

"You have a gun?" Wells said. Apropos of nothing.

"Do I have a gun? No."

"Did you ever?"

"Yeah. Put it in a safe deposit a couple months back. Came to the conclusion that a nine and finding your wife dead don't mix. How 'bout you, John? You must be carrying."

Wells opened his jacket to reveal the empty holster. "In the car."

"Not scared of me?" Callar laughed. He drank the last of his whiskey, pushed himself up. "Where are my manners? Lemme show you around."

Callar led Wells up the solid wooden stairs, leaving the light behind. Wells stepped carefully in the dark. Upstairs, Callar opened a door and flicked on another of the ghostly fluorescent lights that he favored. The bed was a modern version of an old sleigh, dark wood and a rounded headboard. The mattress was bare.

"Do you believe in God, John?"

"Used to pray every day. Now I'm not sure."

"I am. I'm sure. It's all void. Sound and fury signifying nothing. An accident of biology. Cosmic joke. Whatever you want to call it."

Wells didn't feel like arguing. "Ever think about opening a window? Let that California sun in? Stop creeping out the neighbors. You know what they called the prison, don't you, Steve? The Midnight House. You've got your very own version going."

"See the stain? On the mattress?"

But the thick white top of the mattress seemed spotless.

Callar flipped on the ceiling light. Still, Wells couldn't understand what he meant. The bedroom was as bloodless as the kitchen. A handful of framed pictures on the bedside table provided the only evidence of life. Callar and Rachel at a baseball game. Callar and Rachel in a rain forest somewhere.

"Pretty."

"Think that makes me feel better?" Callar nudged Wells. "See the stain."

"I don't."

"That's 'cause it's not there," Callar said. "There's nothing left of her. Not even that. Nothing but what I have in my head. And if I leave this house, that's gone, too."

"You'll have your memories wherever you are."

"Then I may as well stay here."

"Let me ask you—"

Callar put a not-very-friendly hand on Wells's arm. "No more. Come on, Johnny. Time to go."

Wells turned to Callar. He had more questions: *Could she have been having an affair? How come you never had kids?* And, most of all, *Were you always this crazy?* But the set of Callar's face left no room for argument.

"When should I come back?"

"When you find the real killer. You and O. J." Callar squeezed Wells's biceps, digging his fingers into the muscle. Callar would be an ugly fighter, fueled by alcohol and rage. Wells let him squeeze.

"This thing you're living, I'm sorry for it. For you. But whoever did this, they're still out there. You can help us. Help yourself."

"Please leave my house."

WELLS LEFT CALLAR'S HAUNTED castle behind. Ten minutes later he stopped at a Starbucks, ordered a large black coffee—he could never bring himself to say *venti*. He found a table in the corner and spent an hour poring over the police and FBI files on crazy Steve Callar, trying to figure out if Callar could have killed his wife. For whatever reason.

But he couldn't have. Not unless he'd figured out how to teleport the six hundred miles from Phoenix to San Diego. During his weekend in Arizona, he'd only been off shift once, between midnight and 8 a.m. on Sunday. The last flight from Phoenix to San Diego was at 9:55 p.m. Callar couldn't possibly have made it.

SO WELLS HEADED UP the 5, leaving San Diego behind and heading for Los Angeles and a red-eye back to Washington. But he made one stop along the way, at a bookstore in Anaheim, where he leafed through a shelf of histories about Germany and World War II, wondering what had provoked Jerry Williams to start reading about the Nazis.

17

When Kenneth Karp stepped into Mohammed Fariz's cell, Mohammed sat in his usual position, rocking back and forth in the right rear corner. He closed his eyes as Karp slid the door shut.

"Come on, dude," Karp said. "You're hurting my feelings."

Mohammed was the forgotten detainee, the second Pakistani arrested during the raid in Islamabad, the seventeen-year-old in the Batman T-shirt who'd shot Dwayne Maggs in the leg and made a fuss on the flight between Pakistan and Poland.

In his month at the Midnight House, Mohammed had been difficult. Some days he read his Quran, prayed on a regular schedule, ate his meals without complaint. But others he spent mumbling to himself and squatting in a corner of his cell. Two days before he had refused his dinner, violating 673's rules, which required detainees to eat every day.

The Rangers called Karp to find out why.

"It's poison," Mohammed said.

"It's the same as we eat," Karp said. Which wasn't exactly true. Mohammed and bin Zari got the leftovers from the base cafeteria. Breakfast was an overripe banana, hunks of bread, and a strange sugary jam. Lunch was toast and soup. Dinner was overcooked mystery meat with soggy rice or french fries that seemed to be made out of cardboard. And the portions were small, a deliberate effort to ensure that the prisoners were always slightly hungry.

But even if the food wasn't gourmet, Karp could promise it hadn't been spiked. He wasn't a fan of giving prisoners LSD or PCP. The effects were too uncertain. Some guys even enjoyed the trips.

Karp picked up the blue plastic bowl that held Mohammed's dinner, lifted a piece of meat to his mouth. Salty, leathery, tasteless, with bits of gristle that had a sandy texture. "Yummy," he said, the meat still in his mouth. He choked it down. "See. It's fine."

He handed the bowl to Mohammed, who tossed it against the wall.

Under other circumstances, that misbehavior would have earned Mohammed a week in a punishment cell. But Karp and the rest of 673 were busy with bin Zari. Karp couldn't deal with another problem.

"Fine, Mohammed," he said in Pashto. "You want to be hungry, your choice." For two days, Mohammed went back to eating, and Karp thought he had learned his lesson. But now he was back in the corner.

IN CIA JARGON, detainees like Mohammed were "dancers." They weren't the most openly resistant prisoners. But their unpredictable cycles of defiance and cooperation made them among the most difficult detainees.

Some dancers were mentally unstable, unable to distinguish fantasy from reality. Others used the technique as a form of passive resistance, a way to incite their jailers. Openly angry prisoners invited brutal retaliation. By alternating—"dancing"—between resistance and compliance, a canny jihadi could slow an interrogation, giving himself time to resist.

Within the agency, the most famous dancer was a Taliban commander who went by the single name Jadhouri. In 2006, a Ranger platoon in Afghanistan captured Jadhouri in an attack on a Talib-controlled village near the Pakistan border. The raid had been routine, except at the end, when Jadhouri ran out of a one-room hut, his hands raised in surrender. Seconds later, a grenade blew out the hut. When the Rangers checked inside, they found fragments of a laptop. Jadhouri had apparently taken the time to strap a grenade to the computer's case before giving up. The Rangers did what they could to recover the laptop, but the explosion had launched it to computer heaven.

Jadhouri was sent to the prison at Bagram, the American air base north of Kabul, where the interrogators took over. For a week, he insisted that the Rangers were mistaken about the laptop. The grenade had blown up accidentally, he said. His questioners lost patience, threatened to send him to Guantánamo, doused him with buckets of cold water. Jadhouri stopped talking. In response, he was kept awake for sixty hours straight. Still, he refused to speak.

Then, on a December Sunday a week before Christmas, a lung-burning wind blowing off the Kush, Jadhouri produced a single piece of toilet paper that became known as the Square. On it he had drawn squiggles and crosses—representing streams and mountains—and written the names of three North-West Frontier villages. At its center, a small X, which Jadhouri claimed represented a hideout used by Osama bin Laden. Jadhouri said he was in regular touch with bin Laden's bodyguards and that he had destroyed the laptop because it held messages from bin Laden.

The interrogators at Bagram viewed the Square skeptically. Still: bin Laden. And Jadhouri must have had some reason for blowing up the laptop.

Unfortunately, the Square itself was too small and badly drawn to be deciphered. Giving Jadhouri access to mapmaking software was unthinkable, so the interrogators made him redraw the map on a whiteboard. When Jadhouri pronounced himself finished, the whiteboard was photographed and the images uploaded to the National

Geospatial-Intelligence Agency, the Defense Department unit responsible for mapping the world.

Two days later, the NGIA's verdict came back. The map was worse than useless. Intentionally or accidentally, Jadhouri's version of the North-West Frontier included roads that didn't exist and a river that seemed to be in Tajikistan. Even disregarding those errors, the target area covered four hundred square miles. Either Jadhouri had a terrible sense of direction or the map was entirely fictitious.

Against their better judgment, the interrogators took one more shot, bringing in an NGIA mapmaker who specialized in central Asian geography. After a day, the mapmaker reported back that the more questions Jadhouri answered, the vaguer the map became. Jadhouri spent two weeks in an isolation cell as punishment.

When he was released, he had a gift for his captors: another square, this one supposedly revealing bin Laden's "true and correct" location. By then even the most humorless of the interrogators got the joke. Jadhouri was returned to the general prison population and encouraged to use toilet paper for its intended purpose. The mystery of the exploding laptop was never solved.

The legend of the Square quickly passed from Bagram to Guantánamo and the rest of the secret prisons the CIA had scattered around the globe. Along the way, it acquired flourishes meant to prove its ridiculousness. In one, Jadhouri had marked the Square in blood rather than ink. In another, the toilet paper was already partially used. And in a third, the fiction wasn't discovered until two Special Operations teams had been put in the air for an attack on the hideout.

KARP DIDN'T FIND the stories funny. The interrogators in Bagram should never have believed such an obvious lie. Even worse, they'd failed to punish Jadhouri properly for embarrassing them. The test of wills between detainees and interrogators never ended. Whenever a prisoner won, even for a single day, his victory encouraged other detainees to resist. Isolating prisoners destroyed that dynamic, one reason that the Midnight House worked so well. Here, detainees couldn't depend on a big group to sustain them.

For interrogations to succeed, detainees had to feel—not just understand but *feel*—that they were beaten, Karp thought. They had to wake up every day knowing that their captors controlled every choice they made. Only then would they tell the truth.

In the years immediately after 9/11, Karp's view had been standard at the agency and the Pentagon. But now Langley and the army had—officially, anyway—backed away from using force or coercion on detainees. At Guantánamo, the FBI's hands-off model was the default. The Feds argued that rough tactics were illegal, made prosecutions impossible, and didn't work anyway. Ill treatment made detainees more resistant, not less. The way to get information was to build relationships with prisoners and reward them for help.

In the FBI model, a dishonest detainee was subject to steady questioning that made him layer lie upon lie on his answers. Eventually, his story collapsed of its own weight. At that point, the agents demanded the truth, and the detainee—knowing that he'd been beaten—gave in. The technique was a classic investigative strategy that detectives in the United States had used for generations.

To which Karp could only say, *What planet are you on?* He had never seen a prisoner who minded being caught in a lie. Arabs and Afghans, especially, loved to tell tales. Catch them lying, break down their stories, and they apologized, smiled, and started all over again.

And only a few detainees could be bribed, in Karp's experience. Most jihadis sneered at offers of books, or better food, or extra time to exercise. Nor were they frightened by the threat that they'd spend their lives in prison, especially not at Guantánamo, where they lived among fellow Muslims. No, they needed to know they would be punished for lying, or refusing to talk. They needed to feel fear. They needed to be broken. Then they would tell the truth. Sometimes.

Anyone who thought that the FBI's tactics would work against jihadis needed to look at American prisons, which were filled with criminals who had accepted long jail terms instead of testifying against friends or relatives in return for shorter sentences. *Stop snitching.* Hell, Barry Bonds's trainer had gone to jail instead of admitting what he knew about Bonds's steroid use. And the guy had won. Eventually, the Feds had let him out. Which was fine, as far as Karp was concerned. Steroid use wasn't a capital crime.

But if the trainer kept his mouth shut for no better reason than to protect Barry Bonds, nobody should be surprised when religious fanatics weren't helpful to their interrogators. When Karp pointed out these inconvenient facts to his counterparts at the FBI, and asked, "So, what do we do with the seventy percent of the jihadis who flat-out refuse to talk?" their answer was, "We lock 'em up and keep working."

That argument had carried the day, more or less. Coercive interrogations had once been discussed at the highest levels of the Pentagon, Langley, and the White House. No longer. The secret charter that 673 had received from the President said only that the members of the unit couldn't be prosecuted. The charter said nothing about *why* such an exemption might be necessary. The people in charge still wanted the information that 673 could provide, but they no longer wanted to know how 673 was getting it. Karp understood. September 11 had faded. Most Americans had forgotten Osama bin Laden existed.

But the threat hadn't changed, Karp thought. Just because Al Qaeda hadn't pulled off an attack on American soil since 2001 didn't mean it had stopped trying. And Pakistan was more volatile than ever. If it fell to an Islamist coup, Al Qaeda would have a nuclear bomb within its grasp. Karp sometimes thought that his mission was to make himself the most hated man in America, because he'd be hated only as long as the threat seemed unreal.

So, Karp counted himself lucky to be at the Midnight House, where he could operate the way he needed to. The top guys at the agency, the army, they *knew* the truth. Even if they would no longer admit it. They knew the United States needed one prison where its interrogators wouldn't have lawyers or the Red Cross watching them.

KARP STEPPED close to Mohammed, stood over him.

"Mohammed."

"Who are you?" Mohammed said in Pashto. "Why do you bother me?"

Karp picked him up, shoved him against the rough wall of the cell. Mohammed's muscles twitched, and Karp wished the kid would fight him a little, come back to earth. But he didn't. His black eyes were dull, his breath bitter, as though something inside him was rotting. He had left Poland, gone somewhere Karp couldn't reach.

"You know who I am," Karp said. "What's my name? Look at me. Tell me my name."

"You say your name is Jim. But I know that's not your name."

Indeed, Karp used "Jim" as his alias with detainees.

"Why do you say that?"

"The others, they tell me."

Karp controlled his surprise. No one else in 673 spoke Pashto. And no one should have told Mohammed about the aliases, anyway, though most prisoners guessed.

"Who?"

"The ones that come when you go. They talk to me. They tell me you stand up too straight."

"Stand too straight? What are you talking about?"

Karp let him go. Mohammed slumped down the wall. When he reached the floor, he raised his head, locked eyes with Karp. He seemed to be back in the cell, at least temporarily.

"Are you a dancer?" Karp said.

Mohammed shook his head.

"You know what I'm asking, Mohammed?"

"No."

"A dancer, that's someone who says whatever comes into his mind, doesn't tell me the truth."

"I tell the truth, sir. Always."

"What's my name?"

"Ishmael."

"Ishmael."

"You're a prophet. Like me."

"You're right," Karp said. "I'm a prophet. And I predict pain for you, you keep this up." He reached for Mohammed—

"JIM."

Karp turned to see Rachel Callar outside the cell.

"I need to talk to you."

Karp seemed about to argue but instead turned and walked out, locking the cell. She led him into the empty unlocked cell next to Mohammed's.

"Doctor," Karp said. "To what do I owe the pleasure?"

"You need to be careful with him."

"How's that again?"

"He's in trouble, Ken. He's got an axis-one disorder, and it's getting worse."

As she'd expected, Karp had no idea what she meant, though she knew he would sooner submit to a night in the punishment box than admit his ignorance.

"Axis one. Schizophrenia, major depression with psychotic symptoms. Severe mental illness. The way he sits in the corner, talking to himself. The way he won't take care of himself. He's coming unglued."

"How would you know? You don't speak Pashto."

"I've picked up a little, the last year. Anyway, it's obvious."

"He could be faking."

"He's not smart enough."

"I've seen more of these guys than you."

"And I've seen more schizophrenics than you."

"Congratulations."

Callar shook her head. Blowing up at Karp wouldn't serve her. Doctors in general and psychiatrists in particular were supposed to stay serene. *I've seen everything, and nothing fazes me.* She'd mastered the drill in residency. She'd even kept her cool in the emergency room one Thanksgiving night when a drunk sat up in his cot and projectile-vomited a mix of liquor-store rum and soup-kitchen turkey in her face.

But now she wished she felt as calm as she looked. This relentless antagonism, not just from Karp but from Terreri and Jack Fisher, was grinding her down. Last night she'd dreamed that she stood atop an endless tightrope, nothing below her, not a net or flat ground or even a canyon, nothing but a black void. Nothing to do but keep walking. And then she fell.

She hadn't had that dream since medical school.

"Ken. Let's just talk it out. Mohammed hasn't given us anything."

"Not yet."

"And when you talk to him, he doesn't make a lot of sense."

"Sometimes."

"And odds are he doesn't have much for us. Given his age, given his probable role in the bombing—"

"We won't know unless we ask."

"This place is incredibly stressful for him. He knows he can be punished at any time. He has no control over his sleep, his eating—"

"It's called prison."

"Even if you're mentally healthy, prison is difficult. And that's if you know how long you're in, where you are. I don't know whether it's genetic or whether he had some serious trauma as an adolescent, but he's in no shape for this place."

"Serious trauma as an adolescent." Karp actually laughed. "Like every other kid in Pakistan. Doc-tor"—Karp made the word sound ridiculous—"this kid shot one of our guys. He's a *terrorist*."

"I'm not saying he's not."

"Good. Then let me do my job. You have an objection, talk to the colonel."

And Karp walked out.

A flush rose in Callar's cheeks. She tilted her head, looked at the chipped concrete ceiling, and counted seconds until her emotions vanished and she turned clear as a plate-glass window. Steve had been right. She shouldn't have taken the job. But she couldn't let it beat her, couldn't let them beat her. She couldn't fail. Not again.

KARP LOOKED INTO Mohammed's cell. The kid lay on his cot, his eyes closed, his chest barely moving. Karp reached for the cell door and then hesitated. The truth was that the shrink was half right. Mohammed didn't belong here. Not because he was crazy, whatever nonsense he was sputtering.

"Axis one, my ass," Karp mumbled in Callar's direction. Trying to assert her authority with this psychiatric mumbo jumbo. Of course Mohammed was stressed out and paranoid. He was supposed to be. He was here for an interrogation, not spa treatment.

No, Mohammed didn't belong here because he didn't know anything. The CIA had traced him to a madrassa in Bat Khela that produced suicide bombers as efficiently as a meatpacking plant turned steers into hamburger. Beyond that, his life was a cipher. Another lost boy in a country full of them.

But they couldn't move Mohammed anywhere, especially not Guantánamo, not until they got bin Zari to talk. Since 2006, the President had said repeatedly that America was no longer holding detainees incommunicado. Technically, he wasn't lying. Technically, Mohammed and bin Zari were even now on their way to Guantánamo. Their stay at the Midnight House was merely a stopover for "processing."

But when Mohammed got to Guantánamo, he'd be given a lawyer. And once he told the lawyer that he'd been held at a secret prison along with Jawaruddin bin Zari, the lawyer would demand to know where bin Zari was and whether his rights were being respected. The United States was in no position to answer that question.

So, Mohammed couldn't be split from bin Zari. And bin Zari wasn't leaving the Midnight House, not as long as he wouldn't talk. So far he hadn't cracked, despite a half-dozen interrogation sessions and two nights in the punishment box. Karp and Fisher were already talking about their next step. Meantime, Mohammed would have to wait. Though Karp's sympathy was limited. Mohammed had been willing to die as a suicide bomber. Three hots and a cot, courtesy of the U.S. taxpayer, was a decent bargain.

MOHAMMED FARIZ'S BAD LUCK had started more or less at birth. He'd entered the world in 1991, the youngest of six children, the product of a pinhole leak in a Chinese condom. His father, Adel, eked out a living ferrying laborers around Peshawar in a battered Toyota pickup.

Adel charged one rupee, about twelve cents, a ride. After gas and traffic tickets, some real, some imagined by underpaid cops, he cleared four dollars a day, enough to rent an apartment in the Haji Camp neighborhood, a warren of narrow streets around Peshawar's grimiest bus station. The eight members of the Fariz family piled into four rooms in a six-story building that now and again dumped chunks of concrete on the heads of anyone unlucky enough to be walking by. Even in the summer, when Peshawar hit one hundred twenty degrees, Nawaz forbade her children from opening the apartment's windows, which overlooked an alley that stank of sewage and stray dogs.

By the standards of Haji Camp, the Fariz family was middle-class. For a decade, Afghans had flooded into the North-West Frontier to flee the Taliban. Many wound up in Peshawar, destitute and desperate. They turned to heroin to salve their misery and prostitution to pay for their heroin. They were nearly all male. The sexual abuse of boys and young men was endemic in the North-West Frontier, in part because unmarried men and women could be killed simply for being seen together.

Prostitution and heroin use were illegal in Pakistan. But the Peshawar police had other concerns. They spent most of their time dodging suicide bombers, and the rest looking for bribes. They rarely came to Haji Camp. By 2003, the neighborhood's disorder had attracted the attention of the self-appointed soldiers of the Jaish al-Sunni, the Army of the Sunni.

The Jaish were a ragged group of young men who called themselves an Islamic militia but were really a street gang, Bloods without the bandannas. Every few months, they descended on Haji Camp for flying raids, their hands heavy with chains and knives. Their leaders carried pistols but preferred not to use them. Guns were too easy. The Jaish wanted blood to flow. Sirens announced their raids, warning residents of Haji Camp to get into their homes. Anyone who remained outside was assumed to be an addict and fair game.

The day after he turned thirteen, Mohammed was caught in a raid. When the siren sounded, he was escaping Pakistan as best he could, playing World of Warcraft at a computer shop around the corner from his family's apartment. To pay for the game, he dragged wheelbarrows of bricks at construction sites. Four hours of work brought him five rupees, enough to play for two hours on a slow computer, or an hour on a fast one. On the night of the raid, Mohammed had found a Shield of Coldarra, which promised him protection from even the toughest monsters. Then the siren sounded.

Around him, boys groaned to one another. "Tonight." "Why tonight?" "Just got started and now this bastard." "Ten rupees down the drain, man."

One boy raised his hand and asked Aamer, the owner, if they could save their games and come back when the raid was over. "What the sign say?" Aamer said. There were seven signs, each painted a different color. They all had the same message, in English and Pashto: "NO Refund EVER."

"But it the Jaish, Aamer. The Jaish come, we should be having a refund."

"What the sign say?"

The boys got up from their keyboards and hurried out. But not Mohammed. Mohammed had his new shield and five minutes left on his hour, and he planned to use both. Somewhere on this level, a

Blessed Blade of the Windseeker was hidden. Mohammed meant to find it. The Jaish needed fifteen minutes to get this far into the neighborhood. Anyway, he was barely two blocks from his house.

Two minutes later, still three minutes left to play, Aamer tugged Mohammed's chair from under him. "Boy, you got to go," Aamer said. "They coming now. Coming quick."

"But—"

Aamer pulled the plug on Mohammed's PC, and the screen went black. Then Mohammed heard the shouting of the Jaish, angry voices rumbling like a motorbike. Close by, a glass shattered and a woman screamed, a high-pitched whine that broke off abruptly—

Mohammed realized his mistake. They'd taken a different route this time, found their way in faster. They were close. "Let me stay, Aamer. Please. *Please.*"

Without a word, Aamer tugged Mohammed's skinny arm and shoved him out the front door. The street was narrow and smeared with crumpled plastic bottles, scraps of wax paper, indefinable bits of metal and concrete. At the end of the block, in front of the halal butcher shop, a man dressed in blue jeans and a black shirt spotted Mohammed and circled a black baton over his head.

Mohammed ran. He could hear the Jaish behind him, heavy footsteps closing on him. They yelled at him to stop, told him they'd show him mercy if he did. But Mohammed was slight and quick and didn't have far to go. He could feel his Shield of Coldarra protecting him. He almost got home.

Almost.

But he slipped. Slipped on a patch of oil invisible in the Haji Camp darkness. Fifty feet from his building. He got up, but they were on him. He tried to punch and kick. But he was small, and they were big and there were five of them. Then the biggest one, the one in blue, clubbed him on the side of the head with a steel baton, and he couldn't fight anymore.

"Whore," the man in blue said to Mohammed.

The five of them surrounded him. He couldn't see anything but their legs and their dusty black sneakers. The soldiers of the Jaish always wore black sneakers. They were practically the only requirement for joining. The men were panting in their excitement, and Mohammed knew what they planned.

"No, I live here, sir," he said.

"You're a whore."

"Please, sir—"

They dragged him into the alley behind his building, so narrow that even the tuk-tuks couldn't fit through it. Above him, a woman, . a black scarf wrapped around her head, looked down from the third floor. He yelled to her for help, but a hand covered his mouth. He pleaded silently for relief, for his father to realize what was happening and come outside. But even at thirteen, he knew Adel wouldn't save him, that Adel was as frightened of the Jaish as everyone else.

The men grew serious. Two held his legs apart and the one in blue pulled down his cheap brown sweatpants. What came next hurt so much that Mohammed thought his insides were on fire. He screamed through the hand on his mouth and kicked his legs as hard as he could. The man didn't stop. The others laughed and one peed on his face.

The man in blue finished, and the other four took their turns. The rest didn't hurt so much, or maybe they did but he didn't care. Before they ran off to find a new victim, they gave him a going-away present, pouring a vial of hydrochloric acid onto his legs, searing their cruelty onto him. In a way, they'd been kind. They could have burned out his eyes.

When Mohammed got home, blood dripped out of him. Nawaz gave him a Coca-Cola. Adel took it away and slapped his face and told him that he'd shamed them all. Three days later, still bleeding, he was packed off to a madrassa in Bat Khela, a town of fifty thousand, sixty miles northeast of Peshawar.

FOR THE NEXT FOUR YEARS, he was given endless hours of instruction in the Quran and the hadith, the sayings of the Prophet. He didn't believe a word. He'd seen the truth of the men who called themselves warriors. His parents never visited. He imagined, hoped, that his mother wanted to see him. But without his father's permission, she could no more travel to Bat Khela than the moon.

At the madrassa, Mohammed rarely spoke. He couldn't be bothered to argue when boys called him stupid. When he talked too much, the scars on his legs burned. He preferred silence. Fortunately, the teachers didn't mind. At night he sat, pretending to study his Quran, on his cot in the whitewashed third-floor hall where sixty boys slept side by side. In reality, he endlessly replayed the night the Jaish had caught him. If only he had quit the game a few minutes earlier . . . If only he had seen the pool of oil on the street . . . If only he'd fought harder. If only . . . But the story always ended the same way.

ON MOHAMMED'S SEVENTEENTH BIRTHDAY, the imams passed the word. Two students were wanted for a "special mission." Everyone at school understood the code. Mohammed asked to join, surprising the imams. They hadn't known he was so pious. Of course, they misunderstood entirely. Without ever hearing the word, Mohammed had become an ironist par excellence. Raped. Blamed for being raped. Disowned by his family. Finally, as punishment, sent to learn from the men who'd trained his rapists.

So Mohammed had decided to buy his way out of the hell of his life by giving himself to his namesake. When the bomb went off, his classmates would call him a hero. In heaven he'd be given a truck-load of virgins to pummel as he pleased. Or else . . . he'd just be dead. Either way, he'd come out ahead.

FOR TWO WEEKS, nothing changed. He went to class, ate, pretended to pray. The other boys didn't say anything to him, but he could see in their faces they knew what he'd agreed to do and they respected him. Fools. One night at dinner, just as he was wondering if he'd been rejected, he felt a tap on the shoulder: *Pack your bags.*

He was taken to a house in western Peshawar. Haji Camp wasn't far away, and Mohammed wanted to say good-bye to his parents, at least his mother, but he knew better than to ask. He expected they'd show him how to make a bomb, but they didn't. Eventually he figured out why: given his life expectancy, why teach him?

On the third night, a mud-encrusted SUV parked in front of the house. A fat man stepped out. Once, in Haji Camp, Mohammed had seen a television show about Japanese men who wore robes and wrestled with one another. Sumos, they were called. This man was Pakistani and wasn't as big as the sumos. But he moved the same way they did, a sidestep waddle. He came into the house and sat next to Mohammed. The couch creaked under his weight, and Mohammed tried not to smile. He could tell the man was important. The man looked at him for what seemed like a long time.

"Do you know me?"

"No, sir."

"I am Jawaruddin bin Zari. Have you heard of me?"

"Yes, sir."

"You know why you're here."

"Yes, sir."

"Are you scared?"

No one had asked Mohammed that question before. He considered. "No, sir."

"Do you understand the mission?"

"Not exactly, sir."

"But you know you will die as a soldier for Allah."

"Yes, sir."

The man patted his shoulder. "Good."

THE TRUCK SHOWED UP a week later. It was empty and shiny. It drove away and came back filled with bags of fertilizer and barrels of oil. The next day the men drove it to a house on the edge of Islamabad. Mohammed had never left the North-West Frontier before. He spent most of the drive with his face pressed against the passenger window.

The house in Islamabad had a television, a treat the madrassa had lacked. Mohammed lay in front of it for hours, watching cricket matches. The men ignored him. They treated him as ignorant and stupid, and he supposed he was.

Mohammed hadn't been told the plan, but he knew he wouldn't be in the truck when it exploded. His death would be a diversion. He would wear a bomb vest and walk as close as possible to the main Diplomatic Quarter checkpoint before blowing himself up. In fact, bin Zari planned to blow the vest himself, via a cell phone, though he hadn't bothered to tell Mohammed.

That final night they ate a simple meal, grilled lamb and diced cucumber and tomato. They prayed together. Mohammed fell asleep in front of the television. He was dreaming of World of Warcraft when a heavy hand shook him awake. Bin Zari, holding a pistol.

"Can you use this?"

Mohammed nodded. At the madrassa, he'd learned the basics of handling pistols. Bin Zari shoved the gun into Mohammed's hand.

"They're coming," bin Zari said.

"Who?"

Bin Zari slapped Mohammed's face. "Stupid. The police. And the Americans." He ran out, and Mohammed heard his heavy steps headed to the roof. Mohammed peeked outside the window and saw a Nissan and a van rolling into the front yard. Men jumped out of the van and ran for the house. Then the shooting started.

He hardly remembered what happened next. Somehow, he got to the big room at the back of the house. But it was filled with fog that burned Mohammed's eyes and nose and mouth. He tried not to breathe, but he couldn't help himself.

He hid under a crate and put his T-shirt over his mouth and waited. An American, a black one wearing a strange black mask, came in. Mohammed lifted the pistol and pulled the trigger. He could hardly see, but he knew he'd hit the black man, because the man fell down. The floor shook when he hit it. Then another man in a mask came in. Mohammed fired the rest of his bullets, but by then he was so blind he could have been two meters away and he would have missed. He threw the pistol away and raised his hands and stood.

The Americans took him and put a hood over his head and gave him to the Pakistani police. He knew they were Pakistani because they smelled like his dad and they yelled at him in Pashto. They put him in a truck and told him he was stupid, a stupid jihadi, and that he'd killed an American and that he was going to a very bad place. And then they hit him. They hit him in the arms and the legs and the stomach with sticks. Two of his ribs came loose and wagged in his belly. He asked them to take the hood off, but they laughed, and with the laughing he was back in the alley with the Jaish, not remembering it but actually back in the alley. Only this time he was wearing a hood.

Later, the truck stopped. They took him out and took the hood off him. They were at an airport, planes all around and a sweet smell. Mohammed had never seen an airplane up close. They were bigger than he imagined, and not as smooth, metal bits sticking from the wings. Bin Zari was there, too. The police took off his clothes and put the hood back on. And then someone stuck him with a needle. The poison ran through his body and into his head and got stuck there. Then they put him on an airplane. Even with his hood on, he could tell when the plane took off.

He wanted to sleep, but he couldn't, and if he closed his eyes he couldn't move at all, like he was inside a box, only the box was made of his own skin. And the scars on his legs itched and itched, but he couldn't touch them because his hands were locked together and it was all happening at once and when he opened his eyes he couldn't see and—

But when he banged his head against the floor, he felt better. So, he banged his head. Finally, the men took off the hood. Bin Zari was next to him in the plane, and he told Mohammed to calm down, that the Americans had them now and they needed to be strong, be soldiers for Allah. The poison would wear off eventually, he said. Mohammed didn't trust bin Zari anymore, but he bit his lip and held himself steady until the plane landed.

THE DAY AFTER HE ARRIVED, they wrapped his ribs up with cloth. Since then they'd mostly left him alone. They were supposed to be human. They looked like people. Two were black, and the rest were white.

One was a woman, and the rest were men. One of them, the one who said his name was Jim, could talk to him in Pashto. The others talked only in English or other languages he didn't understand.

But they all had something in common. They held themselves straight when they walked. Too straight.

In the night now, the djinns came for him and told him that real people didn't walk so straight. These men, the captors, weren't human at all. They were devils, and he was in hell. Mohammed argued with the djinns. He told them he wasn't dead. He couldn't be dead, because he was supposed to die when the belt around him blew up, and the Americans had caught him before he could put on the belt. He told them he knew what dead people looked like. In Peshawar, people died all the time. Mohammed had seen plenty of them. He told them that the Americans were people. They hadn't hurt him since he'd been here. They fed him. They gave him a blanket and the Quran to read.

Sometimes Mohammed could convince the djinns to stay away for a day or two. Then he could eat his food and look around and wonder about Haji Camp, if his friends still played World of Warcraft or if they had a new game. He could almost believe that he might get out.

But the djinns came back. Always. At first they spoke quietly, calmly, and they came only in the night, when he was trying to sleep. But now they stayed all day. They didn't leave when he asked. They told him that if he wouldn't listen, they would put the hood back on and make him drink the poison, nothing but poison, and leave him here forever. He would never die, because he was dead already, never escape this place.

LUCKY FOR HIM, the djinns promised a way out.

18

Wells heard Tonka's barking even before he opened the door of Shafer's house. When he walked in, she put her paws to his chest and licked his unshaven chin joyously.

"Yes. It's good to see you, too."

"You inspire loyalty in one creature, at least," Shafer said from the top of the stairs. His ripped cotton undershirt and plain white briefs somehow managed to be both baggy and revealing. "I'd ask how your flight was, but I don't care. As far as I'm concerned, it's totally binary. You land, it was fine."

"You know what I like about you, Ellis? You make such great small talk."

"We have that in common." Shafer stepped down the stairs, headed for the kitchen. "Come. I need some coffee, and you need to tell me about Steve Callar."

"I'd really prefer you put some pants on."

"My house, my rules."

OVER COFFEE, Wells recounted his conversation with Callar, the darkness inside the house and the man.

"He's crazy enough to be the killer. If only we could find the tele-porter he used to get back from Phoenix."

"And the FBI checked the airline records to see if he flew to D.C. when Karp was killed or Louisiana when Jerry Williams disappeared. They didn't see anything."

"Don't they need a warrant for that?"

"Where have you been? It's a matter of national security. So they send out NSLs"—national security letters—"asking the airlines for help. It's not a demand, it's a request."

"But nobody says no."

"Not in our brave new world."

"When did you turn into a libertarian, Ellis?"

"I just want to be able to get on a plane without being felt up."

"At your age you ought to be happy about it."

"Anyway, the FBI didn't find Callar's name in the records."

"Maybe he drove."

"Maybe. Meantime, we have nothing on him. Or anyone else."

"Have the Feds talked to Terreri and Hank Poteat?" The other two surviving members of 673.

"They're trying to send a team to Afghanistan to interview Terreri, but the army isn't cooperating. Says he's planning an op and can't be interrupted, even for this. They have talked to Poteat in Korea, but he didn't give them much. Like Murphy told us, he wasn't in Poland long. They'd barely started the interrogations when he left."

"What about the registry? You figured out who the missing guys were?"

"I'm making progress. I spent yesterday over at NSA—they run the registry—talking to Sam Arbegan. The head of database analysis.

He couldn't come up with names for the detainees. But he did give me an idea who might have deleted the records."

"How?"

"You want the technical explanation?"

"No, I want it in crayon."

"The registry has multiple layers of security. There's no external access. It's only available over an internal DoD network. Physically separate from the Internet and basically impossible for anyone outside to hack in. So, assume it was someone inside. A couple thousand people can see the database. At Langley, the Pentagon, the prisons themselves. But most of them, the access is read-only. To change records—for example, if a detainee moves between prisons—you have to have what NSA calls 'administrative access.' That's restricted to a few dozen officers at the prisons. The NSA approves them individually. But even they can't delete records. To do that, you have to have something called clearance access."

"And that would be senior people, like Duto or Whitby?"

"Not even them. Really, only the software engineers at the NSA who run the database. On top of that, the registry has a spider, an automated program that tracks the registry. If I look up a prisoner record, my request is permanently stored in the spider, with my user ID and access code. If somebody changes a record, that gets stored, too."

"Deletions, too?"

"That's trickier. Deletions aren't supposed to happen at all. But the guys with clearance access are the same engineers who created the database. They could probably turn off the spider, even though they're not supposed to. But in theory, yes, if the spider stays on, nobody can delete a record without leaving a trail."

"Let me guess," Wells said. "The spider doesn't show anybody monkeying with the database."

"Correct. And Arbegan confirmed the registry doesn't show the extra ID numbers we have. If they were in there, they were scraped out completely."

"Do the guys who ran the database have connections to 673?"

"They're mostly NSA lifers. But one of them, Jim D'Angelo, retired a few months ago. He set up shop on his own, started a company called AI Systems Analysis. Based in Chevy Chase. Tough to find it. Very sketchy information in the Maryland corporate records. Doesn't seem to have a working office or phone or a Dun and Bradstreet report. But I did come across one sentence in an online newsletter that covers the federal contracting business. Last year, AI Systems was hired as a subcontractor for a company called CNF Consulting. Want to guess who CNF's biggest client is?"

"Considering what you told me two days ago, about how Fred Whitby was the guy who ran 673 at the Pentagon, I'm going to go with . . . Fred Whitby, the director of the Office of National Intelligence."

"Ding-ding-ding," Shafer said. "You are correct. Every few months, CNF gets no-bid contracts for technical support for Whitby's office."

"So you think Whitby used CNF Consulting to pay off D'Angelo. For cleaning out the database."

"Looks like it. D'Angelo quits the NSA and right away gets this contract? You have a better explanation?"

Wells didn't.

"Then I asked Arbegan if the database ever showed any unusual outages or problems. When he looked, he found out that about eighteen months ago, during routine maintenance, the spider shut down for half an hour. Plenty of time for somebody inside to delete the records and then cover his tracks."

"But that was way before the IG got the letter with all the

accusations," Wells said. "Six-seventy-three wasn't even finished with its tour."

"Which tells you that whatever happened to the detainees, they knew they had a problem right away. And that they had enough juice to make it disappear."

Wells sat at Shafer's kitchen table, trying to make sense of the picture taking shape. They'd done a fine job eliminating suspects. At least as far as he was concerned, they could write off Jerry Williams and Alaa Zumari. Steve Callar had an airtight alibi.

But Whitby's name kept coming up.

The idea that the director of national intelligence could be involved with these murders struck Wells as bizarre. Those conspiracies happened only in bad movies. And yet the evidence seemed to be pointing toward Whitby.

"What do we know about Whitby?"

"Not enough. He was a congressman for twelve years, served on the House Select." Both the House and the Senate had committees to supervise the CIA and the rest of the intelligence community. "The agency considered him a friend. Supported our budgets, didn't ask too many questions. He lost in 2004, wound up in the Pentagon, a civilian appointee. And, according to our friend Vinny, sometime in 2006 he wound up with responsibility for the secret prisons. Including the Midnight House."

"Why him?"

"Probably because nobody else wanted to touch them."

"So, he got stuck with them."

"Correct. You know, a former congressman, they usually end up lobbying. Playing golf for a living, boring themselves and everybody else to death. This guy is a mid-level appointee at the Pentagon, and out of nowhere he got promoted to DNI. Duto's boss. Something went right for him."

"We have to hit him."

"He's the director of national intelligence," Shafer said. "You don't *hit* him."

"Let's go back to Duto. Find out what he knows. What 673 really got."

"First, I want to talk to Brant Murphy again. With you there."

"I thought you said he's insisting we go through his lawyer."

"He is."

WELLS AND SHAFER STOOD OUTSIDE the unmarked staircase that served as a back entrance to the Counterterrorist Center. Besides serving as a fire escape, the stairs were a shortcut between CTC and the main cafeteria at Langley. They were protected by two sets of double steel doors, built like an airlock and separated by a short hallway.

At the first set of doors, Shafer swiped his ID through a reader, put his eye to a retinal scanner. The red light on the lock beeped twice—and then stayed red. Shafer tried again. Same result.

"What part of all-access don't you understand?" Shafer muttered to the lock.

Along with the agency's most senior officers, Wells and Shafer had "all-access" privileges throughout headquarters. The term was a misnomer. No one, not even Duto, had carte blanche to enter every room at Langley. Most individual offices were key-locked, not electronically accessed. No master key existed, for reasons of privacy as much as security. Officers hated the idea that their bosses could walk in on them without notice. Key locks preserved the illusion of privacy, though in reality, the agency kept duplicate keys to every office and its general counsel regularly authorized searches.

But all-access privileges did allow Wells and Shafer to enter every common area and conference room—no matter how highly classified the section or the program. Now, though, Shafer's access to CTC seemed blocked.

"You try," Shafer said.

Wells ran his ID through the reader, stooped, matched his eye to the retinal scanner. The red light blinked green and the magnetized lock clicked open.

"Murphy blocked me somehow," Shafer said.

"I thought that was impossible."

"So did I."

They walked down the stairs and into CTC itself, looking for Murphy's office. Wells had never been to CTC before. Its size surprised him. Three long hallways held dozens of offices each.

"Busy bees down here," Wells said.

"With all of them working so hard, I'm surprised we didn't catch Osama years ago. Of course, then they'd be out of a job."

"Be nice, Ellis."

The door to Murphy's office was closed. Without knocking, Shafer walked in. Wells followed. Murphy was poring over a report as they entered.

"Excuse me, can I—" Then, snapping the file shut, "How did you get in here?"

"Have you met John Wells, Brant?"

Wells extended his hand.

"You need to leave. Both of you."

"Give us two minutes. It's not about the money. I promise."

Murphy picked up his handset. "Please don't make me call security, embarrass all of us."

"You're lucky it's not about the money, because otherwise I might have some questions about those mortgages of yours—"

"What?"

"Public records. Anybody can find them. Even those dopes at the FBI. Start with your place in Kings Park West. The refi from 2005. My memory's a little fuzzy, but I think it was five hundred thirty thousand? Your wife's idea, I'll bet. 'We're sitting on a pile of cash. Let's live a little. Go to Europe. Take the kids.' Then you had a better idea. Take the equity, double down. Get a vacation place. Eastern Shore. Real estate, in this market, the only way to lose is not to play. The mortgage on that was what, another four hundred? But lo and behold, guess what, six months ago, a year after you're back from Poland, you paid off both mortgages. I'll bet if you ever have to take a poly on that, you've got a story, some rich aunt left your wife a million bucks. But why would you have to take a poly? Nobody's ever gonna notice."

Shafer delivered this recital without stopping for breath. Murphy flushed, faintly, but didn't say a word or move, just held the phone to his ear as if it might have news better than what Shafer had delivered.

"Two minutes, Brant."

Murphy lowered the phone. "Two minutes."

"How many detainees at the Midnight House?" Shafer said.

"I told you, ten."

"That's not what the letter said. To the IG. It said twelve. Twelve prisoner identification numbers. But two of them are gone."

"I don't know what the letter said."

"What happened to the two missing detainees?"

"The letter's wrong. Anything else?"

"What was it like over there?" Wells said. "Did you get along?"

"I went over this already. With the FBI, and your buddy, too."

"Jerry Williams's wife, Rachel Callar's husband, they both told me the squad was having problems. And that something went wrong at the end."

"I can't help you."

"We're trying to save your life, Brant," Wells said. "Why won't you let us?"

"Six of your guys dead and you don't seem worried for your own safety," Shafer said. "A cynic might wonder."

"Full-time guards for me and my family."

"Maybe Duto should pull them," Shafer said. "If you're not going to cooperate."

"Let him try," Murphy said. He stood. "Now you need to leave. Or I really will call security."

"THAT WENT WELL," Shafer said when they were back in his office.

"He'd rather get killed than tell us what happened over there."

"Or maybe he's got nothing to worry about from the killer."

"You think that's possible."

"I don't know. It's time to go at him. I'm going to get Duto to open up his 600s"—the financial disclosure forms CIA employees had to file. "His polys. We don't need a warrant for that. You, you're going to talk to his neighbors. Don't sugarcoat it, either. Tell them Mr. Brant Murphy is under investigation—"

"Ellis—"

"He's telling us to shove it. And he knows we're working for Duto. His ultimate boss. He's got nerve."

"He's got protection."

"Then we'll force it into the open. Whoever's shielding him,

Whitby, whoever, we'll make him come out. He's the pressure point. He's the weak link."

"I don't like it," Wells said. "It feels forced." Though the move made a certain amount of sense. Murphy was acting like he was untouchable. They needed to find out why.

Shafer's phone trilled. "Yes. They're positive?" Pause. "No. I'll tell him. Yes. I'm sorry, too."

Wells knew even before Shafer hung up. "Jerry Williams?"

"Louisiana, Terrebonne Parish. A fisherman found his body today. In the swamp."

Wells remembered Jeffrey Williams, curled on his mother's lap, awaiting sleep, awaiting his father. What would Noemie tell him now?

"They're sure."

"His wallet was in the jeans. And the body had a Ranger tattoo. Looks like he was shot in the head, but they won't know for sure until the autopsy. Bodies in the swamp, you know—"

"Ellis. You're talking about someone who was a friend of mine." Wells felt his gorge rise at Shafer. Then realized he should direct his anger at whoever was behind this.

"Sorry," Shafer said mechanically. "You going to the funeral?"

"I don't think Noemie would want to see me. And you're right. It's time to lean on Brant Murphy. Past time."

WELLS HAD ALWAYS DRIVEN with a heavy right foot. His WRX, a nifty little Subaru that looked like a five-door hatchback but could outrun the average Porsche, only made matters worse. Not his finest character trait, though he'd never had an accident.

He was running at eighty on the Beltway, playing tractor-trailer slalom, when he saw the black Caprice sedan with Virginia plates sneaking up behind him. He figured the Caprice for an undercover statie. He eased off, wondering what the ticket would cost. The Commonwealth of Virginia had raised the price of speeding to extortionate levels.

But the Caprice didn't try to catch him, instead ducking behind an Audi three cars back. Wells peeked again at the mirror, saw a gray Chevy Tahoe sliding in behind the Caprice. Of course, unmarked government vehicles choked the Beltway at all hours. These two might have nothing to do with him. But the way they'd paced him made Wells think they did.

Only one way to be sure. He was three miles from his exit now. Plenty of time to move. If they were on him, he would lose them, get off the highway before they recovered. He tightened his seat belt, feathered the gas, felt the WRX's engine rumble. There. One lane right. Between two eighteen-wheelers. Then into the far right lane, a quick left-right-left around a FedEx van . . . and then he'd see.

He pushed down on the gas, slid the wheel to the right. The WRX reacted instantly. The Caprice matched his first move but then got stuck behind the FedEx van. Wells accelerated and cut left, barely getting by a Toyota Scion. The Scion's angry honk faded behind him as he pulled left and left again to a patch of open asphalt in the passing lane.

And now, no lie, he was having fun, the Subaru weaving through its bigger cousins like a fox dodging a pack of hounds. This stretch of the Beltway had just been repaved—Virginians liked their roads smooth— and it was sticky and tight underneath his tires. For the first time in months, he heard the music of the highway, nothing serious today, no Springsteen: *"He's going the distance/he's going for speed."* Cake.

He boomeranged past a big low-slung Mercedes, resisting the urge to wave. Sixty seconds later, he'd lost any hint of the Caprice or the Tahoe in his rearview mirrors. Easy. Almost too easy.

TWO MINUTES LATER, he swung onto Braddock Road. He was heading for Brant Murphy's no-longer-mortgaged house in Kings Park West, an upscale neighborhood in the city of Fairfax, fifteen miles from Langley. Per Shafer's plan, Wells would knock on neighbors' doors, flash his identification, ask if anyone had noticed anything unusual about Murphy recently. Sudden changes in spending? Late-night trips? Let the neighbors draw their own conclusions. And let Murphy hear the gossip.

He was stopped at a light at the corner of Braddock and Guinea when he heard the helicopter coming in fast and low. He peeked through the windshield, saw it directly overhead. Black, no more than three hundred feet up. Intentionally intimidating, letting him know he was being watched. No wonder the Caprice had let him go so easily.

Then he heard the sirens.

The light changed as the Caprice and Tahoe reappeared. Wells eased the WRX over. Best to settle this now. Spare himself the foolishness of trying to outrun a helicopter.

The Tahoe pulled in front of him, the Caprice behind, boxing him. Two men stepped out of the Caprice. Suits. White shirts. Blue ties. Hands on hips. Federal agents. Or so Wells hoped. Otherwise, he'd made a very big mistake.

19

The Midnight House had five cells. Four were standard prison cells in the basement of the barracks. The fifth was a level down, a single subbasement room. Kenneth Karp had immediately realized its potential.

With a dozen Polish soldiers, Karp and Jack Fisher and Jerry Williams and his Rangers had poured thick concrete walls on all four sides. By the time they were done, the cell was something close to a vault: dark, silent, nearly airless.

Prisoners in the other cells faced all manner of minor indignities and irritations. Karp piped in music while they tried to sleep, sometimes loudly, sometimes so quietly it could barely be heard. He particularly favored Whitney Houston's "The Greatest Love of All," once putting it on a loop for five nights straight, until even the Poles begged him to stop. He and Fisher forced prisoners to stand on one leg for hours at a time, woke them at 2 a.m. for interrogations.

But in cell five, a prisoner was simply . . . left alone. In the void. Monitored by infrared cameras and microphones. Fed at random intervals through a slot in the two-inch-thick steel door, a tasteless gruel in a plastic bowl with a cup of lukewarm water to wash it down. The cell had no bed, only a metal chair bolted to the floor. A prisoner who tried to injure himself by banging his head against the walls lost even the tiny privilege of being allowed to move around the cell. Instead, his hands and legs were cuffed tightly to steel loops embedded in the floor and a hood pulled over his head. Darkness inside darkness. The true Midnight House.

A cell five prisoner could not shower or exercise. He was removed only for interrogation sessions and never told in advance when he'd be taken. The Rangers fired tear gas through the meal slot, stormed in, and dragged him out. But Karp believed that a prisoner should be left alone as long as possible once he'd been moved to cell five. Even interrogation, even Tasers and stress positions and waterboarding, came as a relief from the void.

In fact, cell five was so psychologically punishing that Rachel Callar had forbidden 673 from using it for more than four weeks straight. On this rule, she had refused to waver. A prisoner who wouldn't talk after four weeks of pure solitary confinement could not be broken, only driven insane, she said.

AFTER TWO WEEKS interrogating bin Zari, Karp and Jack Fisher asked Terreri for permission to move him to cell five. Normally, they would have waited longer. The cell was the squad's last resort. They'd used it only twice before. Once it had worked, in just over a week. Once it hadn't, on a Yemeni who'd refused to speak even after four full weeks. They'd had to declare him intractable and ship him to Guantánamo. The Yemeni had been their only real failure, not counting Mokhatir, the Malaysian who'd had the stroke in the punishment box. And the stroke was plain bad luck.

But after running bin Zari through their standard treatments, Karp and Fisher had realized that he seemed to relish them, to view them as a form of combat. They couldn't break him directly. They would have to come at him sideways, hope that he broke himself. The tactic hadn't worked on the Yemeni, who had simply locked down. But bin Zari was smarter than the Yemeni, more social—and therefore, theoretically anyway, more susceptible to the isolation of cell five.

FOR A WHILE, bin Zari didn't seem to mind it. He paced back and forth, regular steps, as if he was trying to measure minutes with his feet. He ran his fingers along the thick pads on the door. He sang. He fell to his knees and prayed. Once he seemed to be reciting an entire cricket match, play by play. He leaned against the door and told him that they would never break him.

They left him for six days. Then they took him out, and Karp promised him that he would remain in the cell until he answered their questions. No threats, no violence. Just the promise of a lifetime in the dark.

His second week wasn't as pleasant. He walked less, talked less. He spent hours each day standing at the door, waiting for any hint of motion outside. He ran his hands along the smooth concrete walls, looking for cracks. He let his food sit for long stretches, though he always ate eventually. Karp was surprised he didn't try a hunger strike. His body temperature rose and fell unpredictably, and his breathing became labored, both signs of stress.

After eight more days, they brought him out again. He'd lost weight. Two weeks of darkness had left his skin pallid, his eyes dull, his lips soft and loose. He blinked in the light of the interrogation room and tried to spit at Karp. But the saliva barely left his mouth.

Karp reached into the bag on the table, brought out an apple and a Swiss Army knife. Bin Zari jerked forward, straining against his chains. Karp sliced the apple slowly. He popped a slice into his mouth. The hunger in bin Zari's eyes was frank and pitiful. His mouth opened, and a thin spool of drool dribbled out before he caught himself and licked his lips.

"Do you have any idea how long you've been in that room?"

Bin Zari was silent. He tried to keep his eyes off the apple, but he couldn't.

"Fourteen days. Two weeks. And yet you look—well, see for yourself."

Karp held up a mirror, gave bin Zari a look.

"It isn't right," bin Zari said. "What you do."

It was the first time bin Zari had complained, the first time he'd shown weakness.

"You can make it stop," Karp said, soothing now. "Just tell us."

"Tell you what?"

Karp finished eating the apple, put the core in the bag. "Who gave you the uniforms and the passes. Who told you how to get through security. Just that. Start with that. And if that's too much, give us one of your safe houses in Peshawar. Then you can stay up here in the light. Have an apple."

Karp reached into his bag, extracted a second apple, smiling faintly, a magician pulling rabbits from a hat. *See? There's no end to them.*

"But I tell you, Jawaruddin, before you decide, think about it. Because some questions we ask, we know the answers. We use those to double-check, make sure you're telling the truth. And if we catch you lying, we'll put you back down there and you'll never get out. No matter how much you beg. The rest of your life. And you won't die soon. We'll make sure of it."

Bin Zari leaned forward—and spat at Karp.

Back into the cell he went. For two days, the burst of hatred he'd summoned in the interrogation room seemed to strengthen him. He went back to pacing, back to praying. But inevitably, his energy faded. He lay on the floor, trying to see through the crack in the door. On the fifth day, he began to pound his head against the wall, a steady chunking that even Karp found awful, madness distilled to a single echoing thud. Terreri sent in the Rangers. They chained him down, put an IV in his arm with a glucose drip to feed him.

AT THIS POINT, Callar protested to Terreri.

"You said he could have four weeks," Terreri said.

"He's lying in his own filth. Deprived of any stimuli. This is how you provoke a complete psychotic break. Irreversible."

"You said he could have four weeks," Terreri said again. "We're nineteen days in. I'm going to give Karp the last nine days."

"What am I doing here?"

"Major, believe it or not, I listen to you. If not for you, I'd keep him in there forever."

"That supposed to make me feel better, sir? Because it doesn't."

Callar walked out of the barracks and into the cold night air, across cracked concrete to the edge of the base. Stare Kiejkuty didn't have much security. An eight-foot fence, a few spotlights, guard towers at the four corners, usually unmanned. It didn't need more. Poland was its own security. There were no Chechens here, almost no Muslims at all. And after centuries of being batted back and forth between Russia and Germany, Poland had finally found a protector it could trust, a protector with no interest in swallowing it whole. No wonder the Poles loved the United States.

Outside the fence, life. Peasants sitting around their kitchens, eating boiled pierogi dipped in runny applesauce. The old ones gossiping about their children's children. The young ones drinking buffalo grass vodka and texting one another—yes, even here—as they looked for their escape, to Warsaw or even farther west.

Did the peasants have any idea what was happening here? Would they care if they knew? No, Callar decided. Two generations before, they'd watched the Nazis feed Jews into ovens. They hadn't protested. They hadn't cared. More than a few had helped. The Poles were not a sentimental people. The tread of foreign armies had stamped the sentiment out of them long before World War II.

Nine days. They'd put bin Zari through hell for nineteen days already. What were nine more? Nine more might break him. It might.

"Nine days," Callar said aloud.

She thought of how she'd gotten here: her decision to join the reserves, her tours in Iraq, Travis's suicide. Along the way, each step had made sense, or seemed to. But taken together, they had the empty logic of a dream.

When they'd signed up for this squad, they'd all been promised two two-week leaves, recognition of the intensity of the work. Callar had taken one, halfway through. The trip had not gone well. Steve loved her, she knew. The blunt truth was that he loved her more than she loved him. He'd grown up in an army family, raised to obey. Unlike most kids, he had accepted the rules without question. His parents had died while he was in community college, his dad of a heart attack and his mother of breast cancer that had refused to answer to chemotherapy. After they were gone, Steve had retreated into himself while he waited for someone new to obey. Probably he should have been a soldier, but the military's machismo didn't suit him. So he went to nursing school and moved to California, where he found his way to the VA hospital where they'd met.

He was a handsome man, Steve, but he'd had only one previous girlfriend, and their relationship had ended badly. *She said I was too in love with her,* Steve said. *That I never said no. I don't understand how you can be too in love.* Rachel hadn't tried to explain. But she knew how his ex had felt.

Still. He was smart and funny in his sly way, a simple and good cook, a considerate lover—sometimes too considerate; sometimes she wanted to tell him to hurt her a little, but she never did because she knew he wouldn't understand—and he supported her without question. He was the opposite of her father, who sucked all the oxygen out of every room he was in, who demanded unending attention as the price of his love. When Rachel went away, Steve wrote her every night, the quotidian details of life on the ward where he worked, misbehaving patients and hospital politics. She cherished the letters, cherished the knowledge that life went on back home. But she hardly wrote back. And he never minded, or if he did, he never complained.

Children would have changed him, she thought. Children would have given him a new focus. He would have been a wonderful dad. But she'd miscarried and then had an ectopic pregnancy and miscarried again, and after that, the docs said she couldn't risk another pregnancy. They'd talked about adoption but hadn't done anything, not yet, so it was just the two of them.

He'd argued with her, really argued, only once, when she'd told him she wanted to go to Poland. He'd warned her: *You're more fragile than you think, Rach. What if it's too much? What then?*

It won't be too much, she said. *And if it is, I can always leave. It's only fifteen months—eighteen, max.*

Please, he said. *Listen to me on this.*

But she'd never listened to him before, and she wasn't about to start.

NOW SHE KNEW how right he'd been. And yet she couldn't tell him. Not over e-mail, not over the phone, not during those unbearable two weeks at home. Not because of anything he would have said. He would never have held his rightness over her, never tried to punish her for her mistake. And not because she'd be breaking every secrecy oath she'd signed, either.

Because she was humiliated at her weakness. Terreri and Karp and the others in the squad saw the bigger picture. They saw that breaking these detainees might help them dismantle terrorist networks that were responsible for the deaths of thousands of people, nearly all civilians, nearly all Muslims.

But she could see only the prisoners themselves, screaming as they were Tased or locked for hours in a box smaller than a coffin. Watching them suffer tore against her instincts and her medical training. But she'd signed up for it, and she couldn't quit. She would finish this tour, whatever it cost her. Just like the guys in Iraq and Afghanistan. The decision to leave wasn't hers to make.

She needed to tell Steve all this, but when she tried to, she couldn't. They'd passed her leave in silent agony. He'd bought Padres tickets for them her second night back, and she'd forced herself to go. After that, she spent most days at home. She made plans with her friends and canceled them. She hardly slept. One night, at 2 a.m., she got into her 4Runner and drove east into the desert to the Arizona border and turned around and drove back, listening to the mad conspiracy theories high on the dial the whole way.

When she got back, she smelled eggs in the pan, onions sizzling, toast browning. In the kitchen, two plates were set, two glasses filled with orange juice. She sat down and watched him cook.

"Breakfast?"

"Sure."

He filled the plates and sat across from her. They ate in silence. She hadn't eaten in two days, and she tried to savor every mouthful, to be present with him and not at the Midnight House. But she couldn't help herself.

"This is great," she said.

"You like it?"

"I do." She shoveled scrambled eggs into her mouth, and before she could help herself she was crying.

"Tell me," he said. "Rach, please."

"I can't."

He turned away from her, went to the sink and poured himself a glass of water. He drank it down before he spoke, still facing away.

"Watching you like this. I can't take it."

"You should leave me, Steve." The baldness of her words surprised her. "I'm no good."

He turned to look at her. Panic was in his eyes. "Do you want that?"

She didn't trust herself to speak. She shook her head.

"I'd die first," he said.

He was desperate to help her, desperate to make her happy. Instead, her misery echoed in him. He couldn't understand why she wouldn't unburden herself to him. And she couldn't explain. She couldn't talk.

She almost laughed at the irony. What she needed was a few hours with Kenneth Karp and his stun gun.

"Why are you smiling?"

"Let me get through this, okay? I promise. I'll get through it. I'll come back to you."

———————

BUT INSTEAD SHE'D SPUN further and further away. Now she was left with nothing but the base around her and the fence in front of her. Then even the fence seemed to shimmer and dissolve. She needed a moment to realize why. She was crying, not a few tears but spigots. She stood and cried until she had no tears left. Then she walked back to the barracks to do her job. To make sure that Jawaruddin bin Zari stayed alive.

AFTER FOUR DAYS LOCKED on his back with nothing but his own mind for company, bin Zari broke.

"All right," he moaned into the silence. "All right. I will tell. Please. I will tell."

Even then they didn't get him. They left him another twenty-four hours. Then the Rangers brought him up to the interrogation room, dressed only in a loose diaper, stinking of his own waste. They pulled off his hood and locked him to the chair and hosed him down.

He was crying when Karp walked into the room, and Karp knew he had won. Karp uncuffed bin Zari's hands and offered him a bottle of water. He tried to uncap it, but his hands and feet trembled uncontrollably. Karp unscrewed it, tipped it gently to bin Zari's mouth.

"It's too much," bin Zari said.

Karp put a hand to bin Zari's head, found the skin hot and clammy. They'd have to get him treated. But first—

"I know," Karp said, soothing now. "I know."

"I will tell you whatever you want to know."

"Of course."

"Things you can't imagine. About the ISI. About Pakistan."

Karp was wary of these grand pronouncements. "Don't lie, Jawaruddin. If you lie—"

"It's true. Please."

"All right." Bin Zari seemed serious. Karp wondered what he could be hinting at. They'd find out soon enough.

"You promise."

"We've never lied to you, have we, Jawaruddin? We've hurt you, but we've never lied."

And, in fact, Karp tried not to lie to detainees. They had to believe that once they decided to cooperate fully, they would no longer be punished.

"That's true."

"If you are honest, you answer our questions"—Karp carefully avoided phrases like "work with us" or even "tell us," for fear they would force bin Zari to confront the reality of his betrayal—"then I promise, not another minute in there."

"A regular cell."

"A regular cell. A shower. A toilet and lights and a bed and solid food. All the things a man should have. Even a radio and a television."

"You promise."

Besides the bottle of water, Karp had brought a briefcase into the interrogation room. He popped the latches, handed over a file. Three copies of a two-page contract, the first in Pashto, the second in Urdu, the third in English, pledging good treatment. No explanation of what bin Zari would have to do in return. Spaces at the bottom for signatures from bin Zari and Karp and Terreri, who had already signed.

The contracts had been Karp's own innovation, and they'd proven brilliant. They were unenforceable and meaningless. But printed on heavy stock with fine legal trippery, they gave detainees the illusion of returning to a world of laws and rules. They announced a partnership, sour but real, between jailer and detainee.

Karp slid a pen across to bin Zari.

"I promise," he said. "Take your time. Look it over and decide."

But bin Zari had already put his shaking hand to the page.

THAT NIGHT, KARP KNOCKED on the door to the first-floor room that Callar used as an infirmary. Bin Zari was inside, a drip carrying intravenous antibiotics into his arm, bandages and ointment on pressure sores that dotted his back and legs. His breathing was slow and labored and his eyes dull.

"He gonna be okay?"

"Should be. Fever's coming down," Callar said.

"When can he talk?"

"You cannot be serious. His infection's still raging."

"Serious as a heart attack."

Callar was through fighting. "Tomorrow, probably. He won't be feeling great, but that's better, right? What we want."

"You're finally getting it," Karp said. He laid a friendly hand on her shoulder.

Suddenly she wanted to kiss him, this man who repulsed her. Put her arms around him and take him back to her room and make hate with him. Compound her degradation by betraying her husband. Sink as low as she could. She fought the impulse down. He was smiling, and she wondered if he'd somehow read her mind. But his attention seemed to be focused on bin Zari.

"Getting it," she said. "Yes. I think I am."

20

In his rearview mirror, Wells watched the men in suits closing on the Subaru. Their hands were belt-high. Holster-high. With the Tahoe in front of him, the Caprice behind, he'd given up his chance to run. He unlocked his doors, lowered his window, put his hands on the wheel.

The guy at his window was maybe thirty-three, medium height, with a blue suit, brown skin. He flipped open his wallet, showed Wells an FBI identification badge.

"Mr. Wells? I'm Agent Joseph Nieves. You need to come with us."

"Am I under arrest?"

"Not at the moment."

"Then you'd best tell me why."

"You're a material witness in a federal investigation."

Material witness was a meaningless term, an excuse to pick him up. *If you felt like talking, you could have called,* Wells didn't say. Professional courtesy. But they wanted to prove they didn't need to show him any courtesy at all.

"I'll come. But I'm driving."

"We'd prefer if you ride with us." Nieves sounded embarrassed.

"You made your point. Don't push it." Though Wells almost hoped Nieves would.

Nieves stepped back, murmured into the microphone in his lapel, nodded. "Mr. Wells, will you give me your word—"

"Yes. Let's go."

THEY CONVOYED NORTH along the Beltway, the Caprice's siren clearing the road as smoothly as a snowplow. At exit 46, they swung east onto Chain Bridge Road, which led to the Langley campus. But they weren't going to the CIA. Just past the Dulles toll road, they turned left, heading for a complex that looked like a typical suburban office park, centered around a large X-shaped building.

In reality, the complex—called Liberty Crossing—was the newest center of power in the American intelligence community. Its low-key appearance was deceiving. The buildings were more concrete than glass, built to survive a truck bomb. A thick-walled guardhouse protected the main entrance, and a hairpin turn in the access road ensured that vehicles would be moving slowly as they approached it. Behind the guardhouse, waist-high steel boluses blocked the road. In block letters, a sign proclaimed: "Pre-cleared visitors only. Visitors without pre-clearance will not be admitted." And an afterthought: "Welcome to NCTC/ODNI"—the National Counterterrorism Center and the office of the director of national intelligence.

The Caprice stopped beside the guardhouse. From the Subaru, Wells watched as Nieves handed over his badge and had a short, heated conversation with the guard inside. Another guard in a flak jacket emerged from the back of the house, leading a German shepherd. The dog trotted around the WRX, poking its nose under the bumpers. "Clear," the handler said. And only then did the boluses behind the guardhouse retract, opening the road to the building.

Disrespect upon disrespect, Wells thought.

———

THEY PARKED in the visitors' spots near the front entrance. Nieves walked to Wells's door. "You holding?"

Wells flipped open his jacket to show his Glock.

"It would be easier if—"

Wells slipped the pistol under the seat. "Just don't try to strip-search me."

He wasn't strip-searched, but he did have to pass through a body-imaging scanner at the entrance. "Standard procedure for all visitors," Nieves said.

"As long as it's standard procedure."

The building had been finished barely a year earlier, purpose-built for Whitby's new agency. Its lobby was expensive, crisp, and high-tech, white walls and marble floors so smooth they belonged on the starship *Enterprise*. Oversized photos of President Obama and Fred Whitby stared down from behind the guard station. Beside them, brass letters proclaimed "Office of National Intelligence: Coordination, Integrity, Transparency." To Wells, the motto sounded more appropriate for a garage that specialized in windshield replacements.

Just past the guard station, Nieves waved a keycard at an unmarked steel door that opened into a long concrete hallway. "This way."

Wells followed Nieves into a windowless square room with a camera in the corner.

"Get you a soda or anything?" Nieves said.

Wells ignored him until he left. After ten minutes, the door opened again and two agents hustled Shafer in. "Whitby's certainly making a point," Shafer said, after they left. "Oh, yes, indeed. How'd they pick you up?"

Wells told him. "You?"

"Outside my house," Shafer said. "No helicopter, but they embarrassed me in front of the kids. Idiots."

Wells closed his eyes and saw Cairo, the mosques and the minarets and the river that hardly seemed to move. "Have you heard anything about Alaa Zumari?"

As far as I know, he's still a fugitive. Unfortunately I can't call your buddy Hani and ask for an update."

"A little intra-agency cooperation."

The job was becoming stranger by the day, Wells thought. Arrested, or not quite arrested, by the director of national intelligence for a mission they were carrying out on behalf of the director of central intelligence.

"We should go to Congress," Wells said. "Tell them they need to appoint a director of planetary intelligence to sort this out."

"Why stop there? I was thinking galactic."

"Universal."

Wells opened his eyes, saw Shafer peeking out through the narrow window at the door. He sat down. A few minutes later he amused himself by flipping the finger at the camera in the corner. Then he stretched, knee bends and shoulder rolls. Finally, he turned to Wells, who hadn't moved.

"Aren't you bored, John?"

"What's the point of being bored?"

"Maybe I was wrong about you. You're more of a Buddhist than I thought."

"Not a Buddhist. Just patient."

"Is there a difference?"

AFTER TWO HOURS, Nieves reappeared. "Come with me." They passed out of the concrete corridor and down a series of halls, each plusher than the next, into a long conference room. This one had windows. And wood-and-leather chairs. And Fred Whitby. Wells hadn't met him before, but his photo was in the lobby, so Wells was fairly certain. Next to Whitby, Vinny Duto.

"Gentlemen," Whitby said. "I'm sorry to keep you waiting." He stood and smiled. Duto followed. Whitby was handsome but smaller than Wells had imagined. With his blue eyes and tiny hands, he looked like nothing so much as an elf in a tailored gray suit.

"Ellis Shafer. And John Wells," he said. "I wish we could have met on better terms. Please, please sit."

"The terms were yours," Wells said.

"I'm sorry about the way you were pulled over. When it became clear you were headed for Brant Murphy's house, my agents felt they had to intercede. It was for your protection as much as ours. One of my men worried you were behaving erratically."

"Your men. FBI works for you now?"

"You can't seriously be pretending to be worried that we're threats," Shafer said. "Even Vinny is too smart to pull that card. I realize you were shining shoes at the Pentagon when John saved Times Square, but you might look it up."

"I know Agent Wells's record intimately," Whitby said. His voice sounded to Wells as though it had been filtered through a garbage bag fresh out of the box. Smooth and shiny and heavy and plastic. "Yours, too. And that is the reason you sit here as my guests—"

"Guests—" Shafer said. At the agency, Shafer had crafted a role as a cranky professor, a sharp-tongued genius. Duto had reached a rough accommodation with him, and with Wells. He let them operate unmolested. In turn, they didn't argue when he took credit for their successes, using them to burnish the agency's luster, and his own.

But Whitby didn't care about the glories of Duto or the CIA. His brief was broader. As director of national intelligence, he ran the entire "intelligence community," the monster that included sixteen agencies in all, with hundreds of thousands of employees and an annual budget of forty billion dollars. He divvied up the money, set priorities, oversaw turf wars. Whitby, not Duto, reported directly to the President. And if Whitby wanted to, he could make life very difficult for the CIA and everyone in it, including Wells and Shafer.

Yet Duto had known all this when he'd asked Wells and Shafer to investigate the 673 murders. He'd told them he would handle Whitby. But Duto had been wrong, Wells thought. For this meeting, he and Shafer would do well not to argue. At least until they saw Whitby's cards.

Beside Wells, Shafer seemed to make the same calculation. He sat back in his chair, patted his stomach like a man with indigestion. Finally he murmured, "So, we're your guests."

"Anyone but you two would be looking at obstruction-of-justice charges right now," Whitby said. "Or worse."

"We're obstructing the FBI investigation?" Shafer said. Quietly, not argumentatively. A man trying to get his facts straight. The performance didn't come naturally, but Shafer was managing. George Smiley as played by Larry David.

"We've got a hundred agents on this—"

"Impressive," Shafer said. "The results, if I may be so bold as to point out, have been a little thin so far."

"If I may be so bold as to point out"? Shafer just needed a smoking jacket, Wells thought.

"You don't know enough to judge our results, Mr. Shafer. We are making progress. We do not need two cowboys disrupting the investigation, disturbing and frightening witnesses. As well as damaging our relationship with a foreign intelligence service that is our ally in the fight against Islamic extremism."

Whitby tilted his head a fraction, shifted his attention from Shafer to Wells.

"Agent Wells? Anything to say? Or you prefer Mr. Shafer to speak for you?"

The unpolluted blue of Whitby's eyes reminded Wells of the tint of deep ice on a New Hampshire lake in January. They were a soldier's eyes. Yet Whitby wasn't a soldier, just a politician-turned-bureaucrat. He presumed to judge men who had taken risks he would never share. He mistook his bureaucratic squabbles for combat. Explaining this to him would be impossible. He would simply stare with those blue eyes, seeing nothing, believing he saw everything.

"Nothing to say," Wells said. "Nothing at all."

WHITBY OPENED THE LAPTOP in front of him, tapped the keyboard. On the flat-panel monitor behind him, a map of Pakistan appeared and a dozen red circles lit up.

Whitby clicked on a circle near Islamabad. A satellite image appeared, a warehouse on a small army base. The photograph was extremely high-resolution, sharp enough to reveal dents on the Jeeps parked beside the warehouse.

Whitby clicked again. The satellite photograph disappeared, replaced with a blurry image of six large bunkers. "From a Predator with the new radar package," Whitby said.

"That's through the wall?" Shafer said.

"Yes."

Beside the image, acronyms and numbers marched down the side of the screen: "5 (PLU/UA) Y 100/300 GS 400 (UR) PTI Med/High RA High AA Medium OTR High."

"Any guesses what we're looking at? Humor me, Mr. Shafer."

"A Pakistani nuclear-weapons depot?"

"No fooling you." Whitby ran a pointer down the list of acronyms, reading as he went: "Five weapons. Plutonium. Unarmed. Yield of one hundred to three hundred kilotons each. Four hundred guards on the site. No heavy weapons. Possibility of Taliban infiltration medium to high. Road access high. Air access medium. Overall threat risk high."

Whitby clicked back to the main map.

"We have similar information for every nuke in the Pakistani arsenal. They have eighty-two weapons now, by the way. We knew they'd been moved around, split up, but we had no idea how much. Seems Musharraf"—the former Pakistani president—"decided that scattered sites would be the best way to save enough weapons to survive an Indian first strike. Now, of course, the Paks have a slightly different problem. As do we."

Whitby pointed out the red circles, one outside Rawalpindi, the other near Lahore. "These two bases are our biggest problem. Both with senior commanders who are sympathetic to the Islamist movement."

"Why doesn't the army move them?" Shafer said. "Or replace the commanders?"

"You know better than that. Every general is his own little power center. And those warheads, they're prestigious. Tricky to ask a general to give up control. Especially one who might have a line to Al Qaeda."

Whitby closed the map. "Mr. Shafer, you're welcome to examine these estimates for as long as you like. At your leisure. I know you're a strategic thinker. And in your strategic"—Whitby's repeated use of the word somehow made it, and Shafer, sound ridiculous—"analysis, is this information precious?"

"If it's accurate, sure."

"It comes from the very highest levels of the ISI. It's accurate. They even took us inside six depots. And we've checked the others with Predators and satellites, and as far as we can tell, they told the truth." Whitby paused. "I don't need to explain what this does for us, do I? Why do you think we bulked up in Afghanistan? Not just to play with the Taliban. We have a QRF"—a quick reaction force—"at Bagram on permanent alert. One of these depots gets hot, we're in the air in fifteen minutes. For the first time ever, we have the Paki arsenal under control."

"A genuine coup," Shafer said. "But please. I'm a bit slow. How does this connect to 673, the murders? Last I checked, none of the detainees at the Midnight House worked for the Pakistani army. Or the ISI."

"I can't tell you. But I promise, this is related to information that 673 developed."

"You promise. Sweet of you."

"It's true," Duto said.

Shafer turned his head to Duto. "How long have you known about this?"

As an answer, Duto coughed into his hand.

And then Wells saw the missing piece. One of them, anyway.

This map was the reason that Frederick Whitby, former congressman, former mid-level Pentagon analyst, had become one of the most powerful men in Washington. The reason he was the director of national intelligence and Duto was at Langley reporting to him. And it had come out of the Midnight House. But the Midnight House had been rotten. If the FBI's investigation into the murders of Task Force 673 went the wrong way, Whitby's triumph would lose its shine.

Shafer got it, too, Wells saw. He lifted his head, a dog on the scent. "Is this why you're obstructing the FBI's investigation?"

"I'm not—"

"You blocked them from seeing the letter to the IG."

"That letter is nothing but rumor. Totally unsubstantiated."

"It's unsubstantiated because you didn't let the inspector general investigate it."

"It has nothing to do with these murders. Whoever's killing those men, a foreign terrorist group, a domestic criminal, the FBI has the tools it needs."

"Does the FBI know you oversaw 673 at the Pentagon?" Shafer said.

"Senior bureau officials are aware of my previous position and don't believe it's pertinent to their investigation." Whitby was tense now, falling into bureaucratic jargon, Wells thought.

"Maybe if they knew about the letter, they'd reconsider."

"Mr. Shafer. You and Mr. Wells have not an iota of authority to investigate these crimes. Director Duto made a mistake in thinking otherwise."

"I made a mistake," Duto agreed. Almost cheerfully. Not even an eyelid twitch.

"We can't risk letting this leak. If the Pakistani public finds out we've been monitoring their nuclear stockpile, there will be riots. The army will face enormous pressure to relocate the weapons. At best, we will then lose our knowledge of where they're housed. At worst, terrorists will try to steal them as they're being moved. And none of this has anything to do with the 673 murders. So, I'm asking you now, don't get in the way. Let the FBI do its job."

"But there's something I don't get," Wells said. Playing the naïf, as they all seemed to expect of him. Whitby turned his frozen blue eyes on Wells.

"You were in charge of 673?"

"In a manner of speaking. I helped set it up. It ran autonomously."

"But you saw the take."

"Yes."

"And you know what tactics they used?"

"It ran autonomously."

"I didn't ask if you okayed them. I asked if you knew of them."

"We're not here to talk about this."

"Bear with me," Wells said. "My question is, how can you be so sure of the information that 673 developed without knowing exactly what they did to the prisoners?"

"The information was incontrovertible. That's all I can tell you."

"Did it come from the missing detainees?"

"What missing detainees?"

"The two who aren't in the system. The two who don't exist."

"I don't know what you're talking about."

"Of course you do. There are twelve prisoner numbers mentioned in the letter. Ten match detainees. The other two don't go anywhere."

"That letter is nothing but rumor. It's quite possible whoever wrote it decided to put in fake PINs to cause this kind of trouble."

"You don't really believe that."

"I am through discussing the letter, Mr. Wells. It should have been destroyed."

Wells wondered if he should push further, bring up Jim D'Angelo, the former NSA software engineer who'd gotten the no-bid contract. Then decided to wait. They still didn't know exactly what D'Angelo might have done for Whitby, or why. They didn't know where Duto stood. They needed evidence, not hunches.

"So, that's it," Shafer said. "We leave it alone."

"You leave it alone."

"And what if somebody picks up the phone, calls us with a tip?"

"You refer them to the FBI."

"And if we happen to stumble on some bit of evidence—"

"You give it to the FBI."

"Got it," Shafer said. "Got it, John?"

"Got it, Ellis."

"So, we're done here?"

"Most certainly."

Shafer pushed himself back from the table. Wells followed.

"Gentlemen," Whitby said. "I'm not sure I've made myself clear. Don't press me on this. Director Duto can't protect you. Your reputations won't protect you. You are to stay away from this investigation. That is a direct order. Understood?"

Wells raised his hand. "Question."

Whitby stared at Wells's upraised arm as if he wanted to chop it off. "Is this funny to you, Agent Wells?"

"I'm just used to a more direct threat. Drop your gun or I shoot you in the head. That kind of thing. I can be a bit slow. And you're being, you know—"

"Vague—" Shafer said. "He's being vague, John. And that's unhelpful. I, too, want to know exactly what's at risk here. Will we be losing our parking passes at Langley? Our per diems on road trips?"

Whitby smiled. And Wells saw that they weren't close to cracking him. "I'll bring you in as material witnesses, hold you until the FBI finds the killers. Worst case, you two get stuck in detention for years and even the agency can't get you out."

Whitby slid a thin, red-bordered file folder across the table to Wells. Wells opened it. Gruesome photographs, a crime scene in Moscow. Wells recognized the men. He'd killed them.

"Murder, plain and simple," Whitby said. "Not a CIA operation. Just a rogue agent, out of control, killing FSB agents. The same man who just went to Cairo and pissed off our closest Arab ally. Make for some interesting reading in the *Post*, wouldn't it? Or *Vanity Fair*. It's more a *Vanity Fair* kind of story, the hero with the feet of clay. And you're in jail, no way to explain yourself."

"The same rogue agent who stopped a nuclear attack on Washington—"

"That didn't happen, Mr. Shafer," Whitby said. "Or did it? It's so highly classified, it's practically a myth. And it's going to stay that way. Could provoke national hysteria otherwise."

"Times Square wasn't classified."

"Times Square was a long time ago. What's he done lately?"

Whitby slid another red-bordered folder to Shafer. "As for you— I've got twenty years of you giving classified information to the French, Israelis, Saudis. Even the Russians."

"Trading. Not giving."

"Was it authorized? In writing?"

"We always got as much back as we gave," Shafer said. "Or more."

"I'll bet I can find a couple exceptions. Those might be tough to explain to a jury. Or the *Post*. Yes. Strikes me as more of a *Post* story. Nothing operatic about this one. Meat-and-potatoes espionage."

Wells slid back the file.

"Director Whitby," he said. "It's been a pleasure to meet you."

"The same. Agent Nieves will show you out."

THAT NIGHT, Shafer and Wells sat high in the upper deck at Nationals Park. D.C. had once been home to the famously lousy Washington Senators. Sportswriters had joked that Washington was "first in war, first in peace, and last in the American League" before the Senators decamped to Minnesota in 1960 and became the Twins.

Now Washington had a new team, the Nationals, itself a refugee from Montreal, with a new name and a new six-hundred-million-dollar ballpark. But the Nationals were no better than the Senators had been. And Nationals Park was three-quarters empty even on sunny days, making it an excellent place to avoid eavesdroppers.

Wells stretched his long legs on the seat in front of him. He and Shafer were in the upper deck, with an entire section to themselves. "So?"

"He can make it messy for sure. He knows how to work the press. Knows your stuff is classified and tough to leak. It really would be a problem if people knew how close we cut it last year. Meanwhile, Whitby goes to town. Bold move. Instead of dancing around your reputation, he attacks it straight on."

"Paints me as out of control and dangerous."

"Thinking you're above the law. Yep."

"How could he be so wrong?"

Shafer laughed. They both knew Whitby's accusations had more than a grain of truth.

"What about you?" Wells said.

"He's got ammo. You see it in context, it makes sense, but if he takes a couple examples, Shafer gave this satellite imagery to the

Saudis, this NSA intercept to the French—it would take some time to explain to a jury. More important, money. Probably all I have."

"And Vinny's locked up tight."

"Looks that way," Shafer said. "Though I have a theory on that."

"You think he set us up."

"I'll tell you when it's all done. I promise. So, what do you think, John? Do we quit? Walk away? Give the man what he wants?"

Wells didn't bother to answer.

"I didn't think so," Shafer said.

Far below them, a Nationals batter—a slim black guy who reminded Wells of Darryl Strawberry circa 1986, tall and lean and quick—stroked a scorching line drive to right field. It spun into the corner, and by the time the Brewers outfielder corralled it, the batter was rounding second, eating up the basepaths with smooth, long strides. The right fielder fired a strike from the corner, but by the time the third baseman got the tag down, the runner had touched the bag for a triple. The crowd, such as it was, cheered.

"Nice," Wells said.

"You used to be able to run like that. Must be hard to get old for an athlete like you. Feel the reflexes go."

"I still have enough left to toss you over the railing."

Shafer squeezed Wells's biceps. "Maybe. How about putting that muscle to good use?"

"Whatever you say, boss."

"We have to go to Jim D'Angelo. As soon as possible. Find out who asked him to replace those names. And why."

"But won't he run straight to Whitby?"

"Not if we play him right."

PART THREE

21

The white Mitsubishi van bumped through the center of Derai, a dusty farm town in the heart of the Swat Valley, one hundred miles northwest of Islamabad. The road through Derai was wide and potholed, lined with swaybacked two-story buildings that leaned on one another as unwillingly as employees at a team-building exercise.

The streetlights were out, and the stores were closed, their metal gates pulled down. The streets were empty aside from an old man slowly pedaling a bike ahead of the van, his skinny brown calves rising and falling under his robe. The only proof of life came from the televisions playing in the apartments above the stores.

Given what they'd seen on the road into Derai, the lack of activity wasn't surprising, Dwayne Maggs thought. Maggs sat in the back of the Mitsubishi, massaging his aching right leg, which hadn't fully recovered from the bullet he had taken two months before. In the front seat were two Delta operatives, both able to pass for local.

A skinny white cat skulked across the road, head low, fur matted by the summer rain that had been pelting down for an hour. The cat ignored the van with the studied nonchalance of a Manhattan jay-walker and disappeared into an alley on the other side of the street, beside a blown-out police station, its windows gone, concrete hanging at odd angles from its walls. The cops had fled across the river, to

Mingora, a bigger and marginally safer town. A gray-and-white cat surveyed the street from between two sandbags atop the station. The cat was probably about as effective as the Paki cops had been, Maggs thought.

Outside Derai, the van turned southeast on the narrow road that dead-ended at their ultimate objective, a tiny farming village called Damghar Kalay. Maggs snuck a glimpse at his watch. Ten fifteen. Right on schedule. On the edge of town, a necklace of lights flickered on a minaret, glistening in the rain-streaked sky.

Aside from the minaret, Damghar was dark. A couple miles beyond it, on the opposite bank of the Swat River, the lights of Mingora glowed. Mingora was the regional capital. With one hundred seventy-five thousand residents, it retained hints of vitality that Derai had lost. Mingora, Derai, and the villages around them lay on a belt of flatland that the icy Swat River had carved from the mountains of the Hindu Kush. With hot summers and plenty of water, the southern Swat Valley was surprisingly fertile, an agricultural oasis. The mountains around it were largely uninhabited, a trackless and beautiful wilderness that in happier times had been called "the Switzerland of Pakistan." Just seventy-five miles north of here, the massive peak called Falaksair topped twenty thousand feet, a stone fist punching through the sky.

Yet the mountains had not buffered the Swat from the upheaval shaking Pakistan. For years, Talib militants had encroached into the valley from their strongholds on the Afghan border, one hundred miles west. By the summer of 2008, their takeover was nearly complete. Police and government officials hunched in their compounds as black-turbaned Talibs patrolled the streets of Mingora, enforcing their own version of sharia—Islamic law—from the backs of their pickups. They taxed store owners, burned girls' schools, beat anyone they suspected of crimes against Islam. In June 2008, they even destroyed Pakistan's only ski resort, at Malam Jabba, twenty-five miles west of Mingora. The Talibs didn't take kindly to frivolities like snow sports. No one would confuse the Swat Valley with Switzerland anymore.

The Taliban's control of the Swat did not yet extend to the main road into the valley. Traffic to and from Islamabad flowed without roadblocks. Still, driving up here was risky, especially for Maggs. All six of the Deltas on this mission had rough brown skin and long black beards and spoke Arabic, Pashto, or both. On the road, they didn't stand out. As a black man, Maggs didn't have that camouflage. The Mitsubishi was a cargo van, no side windows. Maggs had spent much of the trip lying on his seat, invisible to anyone outside.

Behind the van, the other four Deltas followed in George Fezcko's favorite armored Nissan sedan. Its trunk held AKs, Glocks, and a handful of grenades. In contrast, the van's cargo area was empty, aside from a three-speed bicycle identical to a million others in Pakistan—and a black bag that held the most important piece of equipment of all.

THE DELTAS HAD COME in from Bagram a week before. They were good soldiers, tough and experienced. But the fact that they were here at all highlighted the problems the CIA was having in the new world. After rotating for six-plus years through Afghanistan, the Delta ops had picked up the language and looks to blend in. To survive.

Meanwhile, in Islamabad, too many of the CIA's best and brightest were still stuck in the cold war model. They rarely left the Diplomatic Enclave. They told themselves they were cultivating sources inside the ISI and the army. But from what Maggs saw, they got played by their Paki counterparts as often as not. Fezcko, his old deputy chief of station, was the only senior operative who'd gotten outside the wire and put himself in harm's way on a regular basis.

Maggs had to admit he missed Fezcko. He missed Nawiz Khan, too, wished Khan could have come on this mission. But a month before, in July, Khan had been sent to Lahore, on the India-Pakistan border. He'd called Maggs with the news. He didn't have to explain the reason. He was being punished for the success of the raid where they'd caught bin Zari and Mohammed.

Khan had nearly managed to avoid the backlash. His team stayed loyal to him, sticking to the story he'd devised. Only four terrorists were in the house, and all were killed during the attack. No one mentioned bin Zari or Mohammed, much less the Americans involved in the raid.

The physical evidence at the house didn't match the story. But the Islamabad police knew better than to get involved. Truck bombs were the ISI's turf. But anyone at the ISI who knew that bin Zari had been at the house could hardly say so, since aiding the attack he'd been planning would have been the only way to know. Khan seemed to be on the verge of escaping punishment. Then he was told of the transfer.

"Sounds like you got off okay," Maggs said.

"Not so much, my friend. I shan't have my men with me," Khan said in his British accent. "Down there I can't trust anyone."

Maggs heard cars and trucks in the background. He wondered where Khan was. Not his house, certainly. Khan would never call Maggs from his house. "Maybe you ought to take a trip," Maggs said. "See the States. Visa won't be a probem."

"Generous but entirely unnecessary," Khan said. "How's your leg?"

"No more marathons, but not bad," Maggs said. He'd been lucky. The bullet had missed bone and major nerves. His doctor had promised him that if he took his rehab seriously, he could expect a full recovery. Not that Maggs needed an excuse to exercise.

"And how's George?"

"Good," Maggs said. "I'll make sure he knows where you are."

"And our friends? Have you heard anything yet?"

"Not yet. Roaches go in, but they don't come out."

"Roaches?"

"I promise, I hear anything, I'll let you know. It was a wild night, wasn't it?"

"It most certainly was."

"Be safe down there, Nawiz. You need help, you send a flag up the pole, I'll rustle up the cavalry, come get your ass. International incident or no."

"I believe you would. *Salaam alekeim,* my friend."

"Alekeim salaam."

FOR THE NEXT MONTH, Maggs waded through boring assignments, managing security for a congressional delegation, overseeing the installation of new cameras inside the CIA's floor of the embassy, bringing in two new guards. And, of course, rehabbing his leg.

Then, in mid-August, Nick Ulrich, the chief of station, was called to Kuwait for an urgent meeting. Maggs wasn't invited, but he heard through the grapevine that the other guests were the chiefs of station from Delhi and Kabul and two lieutenant generals from Centcom. An all-star cast.

Ulrich was gone a day. When he got back, their operational pace picked up markedly. For two days in a row, Bagram ran up Predators to take out weapons caches hidden in the North-West Frontier. On the third day, Indian security forces arrested four members of Ansar Muhammad, Jawaruddin bin Zari's old group, at a house in Delhi. And Maggs wondered if bin Zari had been broken.

The answer came the next morning, just as he was settling at his desk for his second cup of coffee. Ulrich's secretary buzzed him.

"COS wants to see you."

"Of course."

Ulrich could have called, himself, but he wasn't the type. Maggs walked down the hall, and Ulrich's secretary waved him. Without getting up, Ulrich handed him a sheet of the blue paper used only for the most urgent messages.

"Came in this morning."

TOP SECRET/SCI/CHARLIE BRAVO RED/COS C1 EYES ONLY

    LAPTOP BURIED IN KITCHEN OF HOUSE IN DAMGHAR KALAY, SWAT VALLEY. PROVES SENIOR ISI OFFICIALS HAVE DIRECT LINKS TO PAK TER-RORIST ATTACKS. ISI UNAWARE. TARGET BELIEVED UNGUARDED. CIVILIANS ONLY. LOC/ADDINTEL TO FOLLOW.

    SOURCE: HUMINT (D)

    R/C: 2/5

    IAR

"LOC/ADDINTEL" stood for location/additional intelligence.

"HUMINT (D)" meant that the information had come from a human source, rather than an electronic intercept or another spy agency. "D" meant that the informant was a detainee.

"R" stood for the reliability of the source, "C" for corroboration. Both were scored on a scale of 1 to 5. In this case, the information was considered likely to be accurate even without independent confirmation.

And "IAR" meant immediate action required.

MAGGS HANDED BACK the cable. He had lots of questions. Why were the interrogators sure the laptop existed without independent corroboration? Had this come from bin Zari, or someone else? And why did the coding have a "Charlie Bravo" handle? Charlie Bravo meant that the note had come from Centcom through Bagram. But information from bin Zari should have run through Langley, not the military. After all, he and Fezcko were the ones who'd caught the guy.

"They broke Jawaruddin."

"Maybe," Ulrich said. He was in his early fifties, with a full head of thick, brown hair, a bulbous nose, and a broad, almost stately, chin. He looked like he belonged on an English estate circa 1925, chasing foxes and shooting grouse. He was far from dumb, and Maggs figured he was good in meetings with the ISI and the Pak generals. But Maggs didn't like him, and the feeling seemed to be mutual.

"You want me to put a team together—"

Ulrich raised a hand to cut him off. "Squad's coming from Bagram tomorrow," he said. "Deltas."

"Deltas?" Ulrich was notoriously turf-conscious. Yet losing this assignment didn't seem to bother him. Maybe he knew that the Deltas had a better shot at pulling off the job than his own agents. Maybe he didn't think the laptop was important. Or maybe he'd been told the score and decided not to fight. Maggs couldn't ask. Whatever he was thinking, Ulrich wasn't the type to share.

"Deltas," Ulrich said. "Six. But they'll be detached to us for the assignment."

"Right." Maggs saw now. Technically, neither the Deltas nor any American military forces could operate in Pakistan without the approval of the Pakistani government. After all, the United States was at peace with Pakistan. Legally, anyway. But getting the approval of the Pakistani authorities for this job might be tough. *We need to go up into the Swat and steal a laptop that proves you're all terrorists. Not a problem, right?*

To get around the legalities, the Deltas would be "TR"—temporarily reassigned—and handed over to the CIA, which didn't have to follow the military's rules, for the operation. Maggs understood the logic. But he didn't like it. He would be running six guys he didn't know on a job that was based on intel he couldn't verify.

"Got it," Maggs said. "And I'll be in charge."

"Correct. We're always talking about improving cooperation with the Pentagon. Now's your chance."

"Thanks, boss."

THE DELTAS ARRIVED the next day. The good news was that they were every bit as professional as Maggs expected. They understood that they wouldn't have the usual military backup for this assignment. No air support or Black Hawks to come for them if things got messy. They would get in and out quietly, or not at all.

The bad news was that they didn't have any better read on the intel than Maggs did. They'd gotten their orders the same day as Ulrich and Maggs. Major James Armstrong, the squad's leader, said the source wasn't being held at Bagram.

"You'd know," Maggs said.

"We'd know."

More proof that this tip had come from bin Zari, Maggs thought. But why were his interrogators so sure they could trust him? Maggs wished he could talk through his concerns with Armstrong. But bin Zari's capture remained a closely held secret. Even in Islamabad,

Maggs and Ulrich were the only CIA officers who knew. So Maggs shut his mouth and went ahead trying to figure a way into that house. He would have had an easier time if the agency had decent informers in Damghar. Or anywhere in the Swat. But the CIA's only halfway trustworthy source in the entire valley, the deputy mayor of Mingora, had fled six months before. The Taliban had set a truck tire on fire outside his house and promised him that the next time his head would be inside it. The Talibs didn't know the mayor was an informer. If they had, there would have been no warning at all. They just didn't like him.

As usual, Maggs and the Deltas were relying on technology to fill in the gaps. The NSA sent along a series of fifteen-centimeter-resolution satellite photos of Damghar Kalay, the target village, that showed the exact location of the house, as confirmed by the anonymous detainee. The building was squat, a single story high, forty feet long and thirty feet wide. Construction was typical for rural Pakistan, bricks poorly aligned and the rear wall bulging under the weight of the roof. A medium quake would take the whole house down. A small tractor sat in front, along with the remains of a pickup truck. A second satellite pass picked up a teenage boy and an older man standing beside the tractor, apparently trying to start it up.

Ideally, the house would have been isolated, several hundred yards from the next building. They hadn't been that lucky. The house lay on the southern side of a one-lane cart track that dead-ended at the open fields east of the village. Homes were scattered along the track, divided by low walls. The target was about one hundred twenty feet from its nearest neighbor, far enough that they could approach without being immediately noticed but close enough that a gunshot or even a shout would attract the attention of the neighbors, and eventually of the Taliban.

To get a glimpse inside the house, the agency sent up a Predator equipped with thermal scopes. The scan—taken just before dawn, when the air was coolest and the heat gradients greatest—revealed at least five people asleep in the house, including three children. An exact count was impossible, because the house's interior walls deflected heat in ways that couldn't be precisely modeled.

The next day, two Deltas took a Jeep to Mingora and then Derai and Damghar for visual recon. They came back that night with mixed news. The house itself was easy enough to find. But as part of their creeping takeover, the Talibs had just imposed a midnight-to-dawn curfew on the roads around Mingora.

The curfew further limited their options. They knew they might need as much as an hour of quiet in the house to find the laptop. They'd planned an early-morning raid, figuring on catching the family in its deepest sleep, getting into the house and silencing them before they could react. Even without the curfew, the play was dicey. Anyone awake would see their vehicles. Now it seemed impossible.

They turned Maggs's office into a war room, satellite photographs and thermal imagery on every wall. They spent a day and most of a night puzzling over the photos, considering and rejecting various plans. They debated buying Toyota pickups and black turbans and going in dressed as Taliban before deciding that the risk they'd run into real Talibs was too high. Besides, they had no way of knowing whether the family in the house was sympathetic to the Talibs, the government, or neither.

They considered taking rafts up the river, or driving up and rafting down. Aside from the fact that rafts were obvious, slow, and couldn't be defended, the plan was foolproof. "Let's bring a keg and make it a picnic," Armstrong said.

At one point Armstrong suggested, more than half seriously, that they helicopter in a couple of platoons of Rangers, take over the house, shoot anyone who got close, and helicopter out when they were done.

"Great idea. What do we tell the Pak army when they discover we started a war in the Swat?" Maggs said.

"Assuming they notice? We don't tell them jack."

"And when they bring in their own jets to chase us down?"

"They won't even fight the Talibs. You think they're going to mess with us?"

Maggs had to admit the plan had a certain simplicity. "Too bad we're not at war with them," he said. "It would make things so much easier."

BUT THEY WEREN'T, and they didn't want to go in hot, not into a house that had kids and women and most likely no Talibs at all inside. For a while, Maggs thought the mission might be impossible under the parameters they'd set.

Then he had an idea. It made him queasy. It could easily backfire. But it was the best hope, maybe the only hope, of getting inside the house without civilian casualties.

So he told Armstrong.

"That stuff works? For real?"

"Honestly, I've never used it myself," Maggs said. "But I know we've tested it, and we say it works. And the Russians used it."

Armstrong nodded. "That's right. I remember. Killed a bunch of folks with it, too."

"That they did."

"It's illegal."

"Sure is. Unethical. Possibly immoral, too. Got a better idea?"

———

WHEN MAGGS WENT TO ULRICH, Ulrich shook his head. "This is what you have for me? After four days?"

"Sir. I'll be glad to walk you through the options we considered and rejected." *And if you'd ever been on a mission, you might have some idea what I'm talking about.*

"You believe this is your best bet."

"Yes."

"And Major Armstrong agrees."

"You're welcome to ask him yourself."

Ulrich ran a hand through his thick black hair. "Nothing in writing," he said finally. "If I have to sign for the stuff, I will, but nothing about what it's for. And if it goes wrong up there, you don't hang around. No matter what. Civ casualties, whatever."

"Chivalrous, sir."

"Don't piss me off, Maggs."

The equipment arrived the next day. Via diplomatic courier, naturally. No FedEx for this package. The questions they'd gotten from the engineers and scientists at Langley were entirely technical, about the size and layout of the target. The hypothetical and nonexistent target. Maggs had the distinct feeling nobody back home wanted to know what they were doing.

Meanwhile, the Deltas flew in a workstation from Bagram that used satellite photos to create a three-dimensional model of Damghar, the target village. The building images were schematic, but they were accurately placed and sized, giving the team a chance to practice driving through intersections that otherwise would be nothing more than lines on a map. Chris Snyder, who as team medic had the unpleasant job of using the equipment from Langley, ran through a half-dozen dry runs with it, the last three in complete darkness, before pronouncing himself satisfied.

"We really gonna do this?" Armstrong said on their second day of practice.

"Guess so," Maggs said.

"It's crazy, you know that, right," Armstrong said. It wasn't a question. "There's tough and there's dumb, and we're on the wrong side of that line."

"We don't have to. We can tell Ulrich no."

"The civvy risk is too high."

"We don't even know what's on the laptop. If there is a laptop."

Armstrong shook his head. "We're going, aren't we?" he said.

"Yeah."

"Then we best go sooner, not later. Only getting worse up there. Matter of time before they start blocking roads."

"I was thinking the same," Maggs said. "We go tonight. Supposed to be overcast, medium rain. Good for us. It'll keep people inside, off the roofs."

"It doesn't look good when we get there, I reserve the right to pull out."

"That's the smartest thing anybody's said this week."

TWO HOURS LATER, they loaded the AKs and grenades and Glocks in the trunk of the Nissan. They put the special equipment into the black bag and the bag and the bicycle into the van. Then they rolled.

By air, only eighty miles separated Islamabad and Mingora. But the drive between the cities was a four-hour dogleg through a wall of mountains, west toward Peshawar and then northeast on the grandly named N-95, a winding two-lane road cut from mountain walls.

On the way up, they got stuck behind an old school bus whose white-and-green paint couldn't quite conceal the yellow underneath. Farmers and villagers crowded four abreast on the seats, as children stood on their laps, poking their faces out of the windows. Every inch of the roof was covered with battered trunks and green plastic buckets and tiny wire cages filled with squawking chickens. The bus edged up the side of the mountain, pouring diesel smoke, and the more Armstrong honked, the slower it went.

Finally Armstrong gunned the van's engine and swerved around the bus, which promptly accelerated. As the van reached the bus's midpoint, a pickup truck rounded the blind curve in front of them. In the backseat, Maggs's stomach churned. Watching the pickup come at them was like seeing a bullet in slow motion, the road's geography shrinking second by second.

"Armstrong."

Armstrong laid into the horn.

The pickup truck slowed but didn't stop. The bus inched left. And somehow they fit three abreast on the two-lane road. As the pickup disappeared behind them they came around the corner—and saw that the road widened, creating a perfect passing lane.

"Wasn't even close," Armstrong said.

"Try to save some luck for the mission."

THE SUN DISAPPEARED BEHIND the dusty brown mountains as they made their way down the pass. In the distance they heard the evening calls to prayer being called, mournful sighs that came from everywhere and nowhere at once.

As night descended, the rain started. They passed a pickup truck of Talib militants, who looked at them curiously but didn't try to stop them. An hour later, they reached the concrete bridge that ran across the Swat and connected Mingora with Derai. They were halfway across when Armstrong slowed the van.

"Is that—" he said. "Yeah, it is."

"Oh, man," said the Delta in the passenger seat, Snyder.

At the north end of the bridge, a headless body dangled upside down from a steel pole. Rain dripped off the corpse's arms and shoulders. Its brown skin had been torn to ribbons. Its stomach was distended, swollen like a balloon in the summer heat. Above it, a sign proclaimed "Infidel Whoremonger Thief" in Arabic and Pashto.

"They really are in charge up here, aren't they?" Maggs said.

"And they don't like thieves much," Armstrong said.

"They do that to a thief, wonder what they'd have in store for us," Snyder said.

"Probably best not to find out."

THEY PASSED THROUGH TOWN, passed the old man and the white cat and the bombed-out police station. They made the turn onto the road that dead-ended in Damghar Kalay. Halfway down, the Mitsubishi cut its lights and pulled over. The Nissan followed.

Maggs pulled the bike and the black bag from the back of the van and tucked the bag into the wire basket attached to the bike's handlebars. Snyder slipped a Glock with a silencer onto a specially made holster attached to his thigh, under his dark blue *salwar kameez*. He tucked in an earpiece and strapped a battery-sized transmitter to his chest, then taped a pea-sized microphone to his shoulder. "Copy?" he whispered.

"Copy," Armstrong said.

Then, without even a "good luck" or a "vaya con Dios," Snyder hopped onto the bike and rode toward the village a mile away.

22

One wood. Two iron. Pitching wedge. The totems of a civilization dedicated first and foremost to its own entertainment. The clubs rattled in the blue Callaway bag, protective covers atop their precious heads, as Jim D'Angelo walked down his driveway toward his Cadillac Escalade. D'Angelo was a golfer in the John Daly mode, a meaty man with a jiggly stomach and giant haunches.

"You know, that's a hybrid," Shafer said. "He's a real environmentalist."

"Hope it's got a reinforced chassis," Wells said. He and Shafer were watching the Escalade from a Pepco—Potomac Electric Power Company—van down the street.

D'Angelo got into the Cadillac, put the clubs beside him in the passenger seat.

"Cute," Shafer said. "They get to ride up front."

"That's a man who loves his golf clubs. We doing this here or following him?"

"Here."

Wells rolled up, turned into D'Angelo's driveway just as the Cadillac's rear lights flickered on. D'Angelo honked, at first a quick beep and then a longer blast, as Wells and Shafer stepped out. D'Angelo lowered his window. "You guys got the wrong house—

As they neared the back of the Escalade, D'Angelo reached into his jacket for what Wells assumed was a phone. Retired NSA guys didn't carry. At least Wells didn't think they did. But D'Angelo wasn't going into his jacket pocket. He was reaching higher across his body—

"Jim!" he yelled. "We're agency! CIA!"

D'Angelo stepped out of the Cadillac, holding what looked to be a Glock .40. A lot of pistol. D'Angelo's hands were shaking, but he was so close he could hardly miss.

"Lemme see the other guy, too," D'Angelo said. "The shrimp." Shafer was on the other side of the Escalade.

"Least I'm not an elephant," Shafer muttered. He moved beside Wells, hands high.

"You have a weapon?"

Wells: "Yes."

Shafer: "No."

"Take it out, put it down, slowly."

Wells did.

"Now lie down, both of you."

"We were hoping to do this without making a scene," Shafer said.

"Little late." D'Angelo hesitated, tucked his pistol into the waistband of his green golf pants. The Glock dented his tummy notably. "Shrimp, reach into your pocket, toss me your wallet."

Shafer did. D'Angelo flipped through it, dropped it on the driveway.

"Ellis Shafer. What about you?"

"John Wells."

"Lemme see."

Wells tossed his wallet to D'Angelo, who poked through it without comment and tossed it back. Wells was reminded of what Whitby had said about his reputation. Not so long ago, Wells was treated with respect, even deference, on those rare occasions when he used his real name outside the agency.

But the shooting in Times Square had happened four years before, and—as Wells had asked—the agency had tried to keep his photos off the Internet and refused any and all interview requests. For the first few months, he'd received thousands. These days, he got only a few each month. His career hadn't ended after Times Square, of course, but only a handful of senior officials at Langley and the White House knew what he'd done more recently. And the wheel of celebrity spun so fast these days that a couple of years out of the spotlight made a notable difference in name recognition. A subset of women—and a few men—viewed him almost as a purely imaginary figure, a living James Bond, a perfect projection for their fantasies. Anne had suffered from a mild version of that syndrome, though she'd shaken it quickly.

"Hey, sport," D'Angelo said. "Kick it over." He nodded at Wells's pistol. Wells nudged the pistol toward him. D'Angelo tossed it in the Cadillac.

"We need to talk to you," Shafer said.

"You need to go. I got a one o'clock tee."

Shafer walked toward D'Angelo. "Jim. It's my duty to remind you you're a *database engineer*. You never killed anything in your life more dangerous than bad code. John could have taken your head off if he chose. He was polite and didn't. But don't tempt him. Even without his pistol, he's more than a match for you. Now, please stop wasting time and invite us in."

The speech froze D'Angelo. He stood, hands on hips, as Shafer stepped closer. "Come on," Shafer said. "Chop, chop. Quicker we get in, quicker we get out."

WELLS AND SHAFER SAT on D'Angelo's couch, a black leather sectional, in a living room filled with photos of D'Angelo and his wife, who was nearly as big as he was, and their two sons, who were even bigger. Everything in the house was oversized: the photo frames, the television, the furniture, even the black Lab that sloppily greeted them.

D'Angelo sat across from them, pistol in his lap. "What do you want?"

"You worked for the NSA."

"I can't confirm or deny—"

Shafer pulled a file from his jacket, handed it to D'Angelo. A copy of his personnel record. "Like I said. Quicker in, quicker out."

"Sure. I retired last year. As you already know."

"You were there twenty-five years. Degree from Carnegie Mellon in operations research, went straight to Uncle Sam."

"Sounds right."

"Why'd you leave?"

"Always wanted to start my own business."

"Consult. Work an hour, get paid for a day, isn't that what they say about consultants?"

"They do."

"And it's going good? Even with the economy?"

"So far."

"Good enough that you can play golf on a Tuesday afternoon."

"Listen, whatever you're fishing for, I really do have a tee time. And unless they've changed the rules, you can't operate on American soil, anyway. Which makes this conversation either informal or illegal or both."

"I'll get to it, then."

"And you're not taping this, correct—"

"We are not. Informal. Like you said. So, at NSA, before you retired, you ran the consolidated prisoner registry."

"I wouldn't say I ran it alone. But yes."

"Complicated job," Wells said.

"Sure. Multiple layers of security, levels of access, sites all over the world."

"And comprehensive. Every prisoner anywhere."

"Yes. We were asked to put together one database where the agency and DoD could track everybody."

"Ever hear of an interrogation squad called TF 673?" Shafer said.

"No."

"A black site called the Midnight House? In Poland?"

"No."

"You sure."

"I'm sure."

"Now, see, if you're going to lie to us, you got to be smarter than that," Shafer said. "Of course you know about 673. Their prisoners were in the database, and you managed the database, yes?"

D'Angelo puffed air through his cheeks like a three-hundred-pound chipmunk. "Just get to it."

"Six-seventy-three had ten members," Shafer said. "Now it has three. The others are dead. Know anything about that?"

D'Angelo hesitated. Then: "I heard a rumor."

"That why you freaked out when we got here?" Wells said. "Went for your gun?"

"I didn't know who you were, and you weren't wearing uniforms. It had nothing to do with that unit, 673."

"Maybe you thought somebody was coming for you because of those two detainees you deleted from the system."

"I don't know what you're talking about." D'Angelo pushed himself up. "And you need to leave."

"Another stupid lie," Shafer said. "Six-seventy-three had twelve detainees. But the registry only shows ten. Two of them are gone. And Sam Arbegan, your old boss at Fort Meade, he told me that only four engineers at NSA had systems-level access to the database. You were one."

"So, what?"

"So Arbegan said that the database had perfect integrity. That's what you guys call it, right? He said that it couldn't be changed without leaving tracks. Names could never be eliminated. Told me all about the spider, how it worked. But I guess if you run the thing, you don't need to worry about the rules. That night the database and the spider went down in 2008, you were on duty, right?"

"No idea."

"You were. I checked the records."

"For an informal investigation, you've been working awful hard." D'Angelo raised the pistol. "You're in my house. And I am asking you to leave."

Wells edged away from Shafer. D'Angelo flicked the pistol between the two men, as if he couldn't decide who might be more dangerous. "Back off, Ellis—" Wells said.

"Oh, I will—"

"I'm not playing good cop/bad cop here, I'm telling you to back off. He's scared, and guys like him get dumb when they're scared. He's big and slow, but it doesn't take long to a pull a trigger. We're going."

"Okay."

Wells stood and Shafer followed.

"You're really leaving?" D'Angelo said.

"We can," Wells said. "Or I can tell you what we know, how we know it. And believe me, you'll be interested. Maybe enough to help us out."

D'Angelo looked at the pistol in his hand as if it might have the answer. "And if I don't? You'll go?"

"You think we want to hang out with you? Watch you play golf?"

"All right. Two minutes."

Wells sat on the chair next to the couch, away from Shafer, perpendicular to D'Angelo. "You haven't been read in for any of this, so I'm breaking the law just telling you," Wells said. "But fair's fair. Somebody wrote our IG about 673 and the detainees. Basically said they'd been tortured. This was before the murders started. The IG tried to investigate and got stuffed. Now the FBI's investigating the murders, right? But they don't know about the letter. Or the missing detainees. And we're pretty sure you're the one made those names disappear. But you didn't come up with it on your own. All we want from you is a name. Who told you to do it. Fred Whitby? Vinny Duto? Somebody else? Even further up the chain?"

"I don't understand why you think I know anything about this."

"You were there the day the spider crashed," Shafer said. "Then there's that no-bid contract. If you'd been smarter, you would have set up a real company, done some work, but you got lazy. Anybody decides to poke at that shell of yours, it'll come right down. The Caddy, that apartment in Virginia, I'm guessing you got close to a million. Real money to make a couple of names disappear."

In one smooth motion, Wells uncoiled and sprang across the six feet of living room between him and D'Angelo. He raised his right arm and chopped D'Angelo in the temple with his elbow, snapping D'Angelo's head sideways. With his left hand, Wells grabbed the gun. He kept moving until he was on the other side of the room and only then turned to see the results of his work. D'Angelo slumped in the chair, huffing. He raised a hand to his temple, feeling for blood.

"You hit me," he said, the shocked, aggrieved tone of a third-grader who couldn't understand why the other kids picked on him.

"We're all safer this way. Including you." Wells popped the clip from the Glock and tossed it under the couch.

Slowly, D'Angelo's breathing returned to normal. "That's assault," he said.

Shafer waved his phone. "You want to call the cops, go ahead."

D'Angelo shook his head.

"We are the only ones who have this," Shafer said. "Like John said, the Feds, they don't know about the missing detainees. What happened to the registry. Your contract. And we don't care if they ever find out."

"All we want is to figure out who's killing our guys," Wells said.

"So, be a sport," Shafer said. "Tell us who bought you. Let us get out of here and maybe you still make your tee time."

"And you don't tell the FBI. Or your IG. Or anybody."

"If we wanted to get the FBI involved, we would have already. You know how they play. Or maybe you don't. They come here for an interview. They show you their badges and you talk to them for five minutes. Maybe ten. You tell them the same lie you told us, that you never heard of the Midnight House. Something dumb and obvious. And before you know it they have you on an obstruction charge, or a one thousand and one, even worse."

"One thousand and one?" D'Angelo said.

"You know what that is? Lying to a federal agent. Carries a sentence of up to five years. Even if they don't put you under oath, they can get you for it. And since they don't tape, it's your word against theirs, what you really said. Ask Martha Stewart about the one thousand and one. And she had plenty of money for lawyers." Shafer paused. "So, now you're thinking, *Okay, I'll just keep quiet. Not say a word.* But that's not gonna work, either. There's too big a trail here. Too many connections. Trust me, you don't want the FBI looking at this."

D'Angelo put both hands to his face, rubbed his cheeks. Wells wondered what it would be like to be so big. He imagined he'd be tempted to prod his body constantly, remind himself of its reality, credit himself for adding a few extra inches of padding between his soul and the uncertain world beyond. The true consolation of the flesh.

"I tell you what I know, you'll leave," D'Angelo said.

"Scout's honor," Shafer said. Wells nodded.

"It's simple. The fall of 2008, I was in charge of the registry, like you said. Managing this thing, making sure the prisoners were logged accurately. We had high-level encryption on it. We did not want people playing with names or identification numbers. Once you were in, you were supposed to stay in."

"Whose decision was that?"

"My bosses. They wanted the registry to stay clean. For precisely this reason. Anyway, in September, I got a call, somebody asking me, could I make a couple changes to the registry."

"Changes."

"Deletions. And I said, 'No, anything like that has to come from the director of NSA. In writing.' And my guy, he says to me, 'This is a matter of the national interest.' I said, 'Get it in writing, then.' He said, 'Okay, look, if you do this, I promise we'll make it worth your while.' And I said, 'Yeah, you'd have to pay me like a million bucks to mess with that thing.' I was joking. But he said sure." D'Angelo's eyes widened, as if he still couldn't believe that he'd asked for money, or that his request had been granted.

"Careful what you wish for," Shafer said.

"A million dollars. For ten minutes' work. Less. Look, I was already planning on retiring from the NSA. With my crappy pension. You know, I graduated Carnegie practically the top of the class. I got a job offer from this little company called Microsoft. But I wanted to serve my country. I sure did, too. I served it by sitting in an office writing code for twenty-five years. I didn't realize 'til too late, code is code no matter where you write it. If I'd gone to Microsoft . . . Anyway. I figured this was God's way of evening things out. Only ever since I did it, I realized it wasn't God giving me that money."

"An attack of conscience," Shafer said. "It didn't extend to your turning yourself in."

"No. But I've been waiting, all this time, for somebody to ask."

"Lucky us for being first," Shafer said. "You remember the names of the guys you deleted?"

D'Angelo shook his head. "But they were both Paki, I'm sure of that. One was in his early thirties and the other was like seventeen. I think they were caught in Islamabad. And both booked the same day, and it wasn't that long ago. I mean, not that long before I erased them. Summer '08, maybe."

"And did your guy tell you what had happened to them?"

"He said they weren't around. Which could have meant rendition, but I didn't think so. Because then why go to all this trouble?"

"You figured they were dead."

D'Angelo nodded.

"But your guy, how did you know you could trust him, he wasn't setting you up?"

"I knew he was real. Partly because it was such a weird request," D'Angelo said. "Too weird to be anything but real. I mean, who would come up with a sting like that? The FBI? The NSA IG? Didn't make sense. And I knew the guy was a real op. I mean, I'd met him before. In Kuwait."

"So, what's his name? "

D'Angelo shook his head.

"Come on, Jim. You've been calling him somebody, that guy. No more. We need his name."

D'Angelo was still. Wells wondered if they'd have to come at him again. But then he nodded. "He worked for you guys," D'Angelo said. "I think he still does. His name's Brant Murphy."

Wells and Shafer looked at each other. "We know him," Shafer said. "Who was he working for?"

"He never said," D'Angelo said.

"You're lying."

"It's true. Why would I lie? I didn't ask, didn't want to push."

"But the money, when you got paid, came from CNF. Which gets most of its money from the DNI."

"Honestly, I was surprised to find out it was a DNI contract. Fact is, I always assumed it was Langley that wanted the names gone."

Duto and Whitby. Whitby and Duto. Two scorpions in a jar, Wells thought. Playing a game only they understood.

"Why'd you go through such an elaborate scheme?" Wells said. "Why not just take the cash?"

"When he agreed to the million, I told him to give me a hundred thou in cash up front, the rest through a shell. I wanted the money to look legal. I knew they could do it that way. He said fine. But I was stupid. Should have gone with the cash. Instead, I left this trail."

"Without which you wouldn't have the chance to unburden yourself to us," Shafer said. "Lucky you."

D'Angelo didn't seem to notice the sarcasm. "Anyway, I got the first hundred. I went in, cleaned out the registry. And about six months after I retired, Murphy called, told me there'd be a no-bid contract coming my way. Theoretically, I'm doing database analysis for the DNI."

"So, the money is from Fred Whitby?"

"Yes, but I'm telling you I don't know whether he was in on it. For that, you're going to have to ask Murphy."

"I guess we will."

23

The road into Damghar was muddy but passable, hard-packed by tractors bringing wheat to market. The rain fell steadily, dampening Snyder's robe, cooling his hands. Overhead, the clouds had thickened and the sky was black. He hit a pothole, and the bike dropped under him and nearly skidded out. He slowed, lowered his eyes to the road, tried not to think of the odds they faced, of the thousands of militants holed up in this valley. He'd decided already that if they got pinned down here, he was saving the last bullet in his Glock for himself. He wasn't leaving himself to the tender mercies of the Talibs.

He passed one house, another, and then he was in Damghar proper. The village's buildings were a muddle of crumbling brick and concrete. He swerved around a rusted-out motorcycle engine to find his front tire in a pile of something soft and fetid. The silence was absolute. The place felt more like a half-unearthed ruin than a living village. Even the dogs were quiet. The Talibs had decreed that any dog on the streets could be shot on sight. Like many devout Muslims, they considered dogs *haram*, forbidden. The strays that had survived the first culling had hidden themselves away.

Thanks to the practice on the simulator, the streets felt familiar to Snyder. Without slowing, he turned left, around the mosque in the center of the village, and then left, again, onto the cart track that led to the target house.

Two minutes later, Snyder reached the house. He slowed as he rode by, listening for a television, a baby's cry, a man's footsteps. Any sign of life. But he heard only the hum of rain against the road, the faint squeak of the bike's tires.

He rode another hundred yards before turning back. He'd reached what pilots called V1, the last chance to abort takeoff. He could still go back to the squad. No one would question him. They would go back to Islamabad, try again another night. But once he got off the bike, they'd be committed. If anything happened to him, the rest of the squad would come for him. Then they'd have to fight their way out, and that would be little more than suicide.

He stopped in front of the house, counted backward from five. To the south, thunder boomed. He breathed his fear in deep, exhaled it into the rain. And he went. He set down the bike, grabbed the black bag from the basket. He ran low along the edge of the property, protected by a wall that was a four-foot-high jumble of mud and stone. At the front left corner of the house, he ducked around the tractor, flattened himself against the wall.

He waited five seconds, and five more, listening for movement inside. The house was still. Before his fear could rise, he moved again, creeping along the wall, feeling the the brick against his back. A window was cut halfway into the wall, really just a hole in the concrete. Snyder ducked low and kept moving. As he did, the rain picked up and another thunderclap broke the night, closer this time, though still miles away.

Two nights before, the agency had repeated its thermal scan with the Predator. The people in the house showed up in the same places they'd been the first time around. Two in the back-left corner of the house, three close together in the middle. They couldn't be sure, but the best bet was that Mommy and Daddy were in one room, the kids in another. What really mattered, though, was that they knew which rooms were occupied.

Snyder inched around the corner of the house and dropped to his hands and knees. Behind the house, the wheat stretched high in carefully cultivated rows. The village was a mess, but the fields were immaculate. The rain hissed down, and the river burbled a mile off. A dog barked in the distance. Snyder froze, waited. But he didn't hear it again.

He edged to the window, peeked inside. In the darkness he saw the outlines of a mattress on the floor, a thin sheet covering two pairs of legs. Now, at last, he heard breathing, steady and ragged.

He leaned against the wall, unzipped his bag, pulled out a canister, as big around as a dinner plate, three inches high. A long rubber tube extended from a nozzle on the side of the canister, ending in what looked like a bicycle needle. The needle was the problem. If he threw the tube inside the house, the needle would clatter against the floor. Then Snyder saw the jagged hole in the wall, a foot above the ground, where a brick had crumbled into dust. He knelt down, poked a finger into the hole. It ran the width of the brick. He pushed the needle into the hole inch by inch, as carefully as a surgeon making the morning's first cut, until he'd threaded the tip through. Then he pressed down the panel on top of the canister.

The canister didn't look like much, but its simplicity was deceptive. It had cost the CIA seven million dollars to develop. It held tubes of compressed nitrogen, an electronic flow meter, and two vials. The vials contained a mixture of propofol and fentanyl, two potent anesthetics that were normally given intravenously. Making the propofol inhalable had been the project's most significant scientific hurdle.

Propofol was liquid at room temperature, a chalky white fluid that anesthesiologists called "milk of amnesia." Doctors had used it for decades to knock out patients for minor surgeries. A twentieth of a gram of propofol would put a man to sleep in seconds. Normally, it could only be given intravenously, but by attaching it to a chloro-fluorocarbon compound, the agency's scientists produced a chemical that was a gas at room temperature but retained propofol's anesthetic qualities.

Fentanyl, the other compound in the mix, worked more slowly than propofol but had a wider safety margin. Three agency scientists, all Ph.D.s in toxicology, had experimented with different combinations of the two drugs, seeking a safe mix that would work in less than five seconds. At first they'd tested the gas on dogs and monkeys. But eventually they needed to find out if the gas was safe for human use. Outsiders weren't an option, since trying it on humans, even if they were volunteers and informed of the risks, would be unethical. The scientists organized a do-it-yourself study in their lab in the basement of the Old Headquarters Building, testing it on themselves a dozen or so times, with an agency doctor standing by. Aside from one minor incident—a three-hour coma—the stuff had worked. They'd declared it ready for battle.

As Armstrong had pointed out to Maggs, the idea of knockout gases wasn't new. In 2002, Chechen terrorists took eight hundred fifty hostages in an opera house in Moscow, promising to blow up the building if they were attacked. After negotiations failed, Russian special forces poured fentanyl and halothane, an older anesthetic, into the building's ventilation system. The good news was that the soldiers retook the building without having to fire a shot. The bad news was that the gas killed at least 129 of the hostages.

To reduce the risk of overdoses, Maggs and Armstrong had agreed to use the lowest possible dose, just enough to knock the family out for fifteen minutes. After that the people in the house would have to be, in the dry language of the mission, "mechanically restrained." Bound and gagged.

THE CANISTER HISSED SOFTLY as Snyder pressed the top panel. The engineers at the Directorate of Science and Technology had built it to work without mechanical parts, on the assumption that it would be used in places where silence was essential. The compressed nitrogen mixed with the fentanyl and propofol in a cylinder about the size of a small spark plug. Then the gas poured through the tube and into the needle, which was another marvel of engineering, designed to disperse the gas as widely and quickly as possible. After consulting with aerospace engineers from Boeing, the Langley engineers had designed a series of superfine titanium mesh sheets at the tip of the needle. The propofol and fentanyl molecules bounced wildly off the mesh, careening in every direction as they entered the open air. They filled a one-hundred-cubic-foot room—twelve feet by ten feet by eight feet three inches—in less than a minute.

The hiss faded. A thumbnail-sized LCD on the side of the canister flashed yellow and then turned green, indicating that the gas was flowing freely, no blockages inside the canister or at the tip. Snyder peeked in the window, but nothing inside had changed. He was faintly surprised. He realized that he had expected to see or smell the gas, though he knew it was both odorless and invisible. Then the man in the bed kicked his legs convulsively. Seconds later his breathing changed, slowing and settling, and Snyder knew that the gas had hit him.

He scuttled along the wall to the next window. He peeked inside, saw three pairs of skinny legs. Based on their size, two were children, one was a teenager. And at least one was awake.

"Faisal? Faisal?" a boy said in Pashto, his voice small, querulous. "Do you hear it? Faisal?"

An older boy answered grumpily. "Hush, Wadel. It's thunder only. Don't be a woman."

Snyder couldn't find a crack in the wall. He pulled the second canister from the bag. He flicked a switch on the canister to set the pressure at high and pressed the panel and tossed the tube in the window.

The tube slapped against the cement floor and the gas leaked out with a loud hiss. Inside, one of the kids rolled to his feet. "See it, Wadel?" Steps came toward the window. "There. The snake."

The tube went taut. Snyder imagined the boy must have grabbed it. He held tight, hoping the tube wouldn't tear. The tube stretched—

And then went slack as the boy collapsed, banging against the concrete as lifelessly as a sack of potatoes.

"Faisal?" the second boy, Wadel, said. He stepped toward the window. "Faisal?" He wasn't yelling, not yet, but his voice was rising. "Fath—"

His voice ended. It didn't trail off. It fell dead as suddenly as a radio being unplugged. A fraction of a second later, Snyder heard Wadel's body thump against the floor beside his brother's.

"Guess it works," Snyder whispered. He backed away from the house to be sure he wouldn't get more than a whiff of the gas. He pressed the send button on his transmitter.

"Echo One," he said into his microphone. "This is Echo Five. Target is secure."

"Roger that," Armstrong said.

THREE MINUTES LATER, the Nissan and Mitsubishi rolled up. The Deltas stepped out, popped the trunk of the Nissan, pulled two bags of gear. Two operatives hid themselves inside the Mitsubishi, their silenced Glocks at the ready. If a Talib patrol happened down the cart track and decided to investigate, they had orders to shoot on sight. The other three Deltas and Maggs ran around the house and joined Snyder.

"Nice job, Chris," Armstrong said.

Snyder nodded. Nothing more needed to be said. The five of them pulled on specially made gas masks that had penlights embedded in the rubber above their eyes—enabling them to see without having to carry flashlights—and stepped through the window into the corner bedroom. It was unadorned, not even a rug, just a couple of faded blankets on the mattress. Neither husband nor wife stirred. They were breathing, but slowly, irregularly. Snyder was sure he could smell the gas, though he knew it was odorless. He was glad for his mask. *Do androids dream of electric sheep?*

"Let's get them out before they OD," he said.

They cuffed the man's hands and feet together and taped his mouth shut and his eyes closed and carried him to the room that ran along the front of the house. They repeated the procedure with the woman and then moved into the boys' room.

"Damn it," Snyder said.

Faisal, the smallest boy and the one who'd gotten the biggest hit of gas, seemed to have overdosed. His lips were faintly blue and his chest wasn't moving. Snyder pushed back the boy's eyelids and saw only white. He felt for a pulse and couldn't find one. Finally he picked up a slow thump, barely thirty beats a minute.

He picked up the boy and carried him out of the bedroom and set him next to his parents on a threadbare rug in front of a poster of the hajj, the great pilgrimage to Mecca, and began CPR, five chest pumps and three quick breaths, five and three, five and three, harder and harder. A rib cracked under him, but he didn't stop. *Come on, come on . . .* He hadn't killed this kid. He couldn't have.

Then Faisal coughed. His chest rose an inch, two inches, higher, his heart awakening even as his brain slept. His mouth opened and air leaked out, not a last breath but a first. Snyder pulled away and watched the boy breathe. Armstrong walked in.

"He okay?" Armstrong said.

"I broke his rib, but yeah."

"Then cuff him and tape his mouth."

Snyder wanted to argue, but Armstrong was right. They couldn't let him scream. He laid duct tape over the boy's mouth.

"You watch 'em while we find this laptop," Armstrong said.

"Yessir."

Snyder closed his eyes and wobbled. He sat heavily on the couch and wondered if he'd somehow gotten a lungful of gas.

"You might want to draw your weapon, Snyder."

Snyder reached for his pistol as Armstrong walked out.

THE KITCHEN HAD A TABLE and six chairs, a wooden cabinet full of chipped plates and cups, a propane-fired stove, and—

"Concrete," Maggs said. "They had to have a concrete floor."

Compared to the rest of the house, the kitchen floor was magnificently built, a single solid slab. Henry Task, who at twenty-nine was the youngest member of the Delta team, grabbed pickaxes and hammers and chisels from his bag of gear. Armstrong pulled a metal detector from the second bag. Maggs wondered if a laptop held enough metal to trigger a detector under six inches of concrete. He checked his watch. Ten forty-five already, and they would need at least a few minutes to get through the concrete. They were cutting it close. They had to be over the bridge and out of Mingora by midnight.

Armstrong made a sweep, stopped by the base of the cabinet. "Getting something." Maggs and Task pushed the cabinet sideways. Armstrong waved the detector over the spot where it had stood. "Not much, but it's there," he said. "I hope."

Maggs and Task grabbed pickaxes and started swinging.

IN THE FRONT ROOM, Dad woke up first. Not surprising, as he was the biggest and had gotten the smallest dose relative to his weight. He nodded his head sideways, the first hint of voluntary motion. A few seconds later, he turned on his side. Snyder tried to imagine the panic he must feel. He'd fallen asleep in his bed and woken up somewhere else, his hands and legs cuffed, blind and unable to speak, hearing men grunting in a language that wasn't his. As Snyder watched, he flipped onto his back and thrashed, swinging his legs up and down, looking for any purchase.

"Stop," Snyder said.

Armstrong ran into the room. He straddled the father and smacked him across the temple with the butt of his pistol, twice. The dull sound of metal cracking bone echoed off the concrete. The man groaned through his duct tape and his bound legs swung down.

"Snyder," Armstrong said. "Are you out of your mind?"

"I'm sorry, Major."

Snyder didn't know if he had taken a hit of the gas or was simply exhausted. He'd never failed on a mission before. Then again, he'd never been on a mission like this before.

"Go into the kitchen and stay there."

"Yessir."

MAGGS AND TASK and Bruce Irwin, the fourth Delta in the house, were chipping steadily into the concrete, their pickaxes rising and falling as steadily as the arm of an oil pump. Then Task stopped. "Sir," he said. "I think I felt something."

Maggs knelt down and saw the corner of a black plastic bundle peeking out of the edge of the hole they'd made.

"No more axes. Be a damn shame to put a hole in the hard drive." Maggs and Task lay on the floor and pounded away, trying to enlarge the hole with hammer and chisel. The clank of steel on steel ricocheted through the kitchen. Maggs wondered if the neighbors would hear. No matter, because it was 11:20 already. One way or another, they were leaving soon.

Sweat poured down his face. He pulled off his mask, figuring the gas must have long since dissipated. He hammered away at a seam in the concrete, and the hole widened enough for him to slide his fingertips around the edges of the plastic. He tugged at it, wormed it forward inch by inch, no longer concerned it might be booby-trapped. This valley was its own trap. The bundle slid forward in his fingers, stopped, and then came free.

"Let's go."

Task began to pile the axes back into the bag, but Maggs grabbed his arm. "Forget it, Sergeant."

IN THE LIVING ROOM, Maggs held up the bundle to Armstrong, who raised a fist in silent triumph. They stepped out the front door and piled into the Nissan and the van and rolled out. Through the village. Through Desai. Over the bridge. Onto the road that led out of the Swat Valley and over the mountains. With every mile, Maggs felt himself relax. They'd put their necks in the guillotine, and somehow the blade hadn't dropped.

Then they rounded a corner to start the long climb southwest. And they hit the roadblock.

An extended-cab Toyota pickup sat astride the pavement two hundred yards ahead, a .50-caliber heavy machine gun mounted on a tripod in its bed. Three Talibs stood beside the gun, two more inside the cab. The militants apparently hadn't been expecting to face anyone coming out of Mingora. The .50-cal—actually a Russian 12.7-millimeter TUV—was pointed up the road, away from the van. But as they rolled close, the Talibs swung it around until its muzzle faced them. A man jumped out of the pickup.

"Halt!"

"Major—" Snyder said.

Armstrong stopped the van, raised his hands, looked straight at the Talib. "Nothing fancy here," he murmured in English. "We're just gonna take them out. Maggs. You're going out the back with your AK. You've got to hit the guys on the .50. I'll floor it, crash into the side of the truck."

"Done," Maggs said.

"You ready, Chris?"

"Yessir."

———

SNYDER WASN'T AT ALL SURE he was ready. The TUV had a three-foot barrel and a range of nearly a mile. Up close, it had the power to vaporize skulls. And it was definitely up close. Snyder didn't see how Maggs could get out the back and get a bead on the gunners before they took him and Armstrong out. He began to pray, silently, *Our father who art in heaven, hallowed be thy name, thy kingdom come, thy will be done . . .*

"Cool," Armstrong said, his voice steady as a pilot warning of turbulence ahead.

Behind them, Maggs dropped the safety on his AK, unlocked the doors of the van.

THE TALIB RAN TOWARD THEM, his left hand raised, his right gripping his AK. From the back of the pickup, the gunner put a spotlight on them, its glare nearly blinding.

"Turn back!" the Talib yelled.

Armstrong eased off the gas, lowered his window. The van rolled forward. "Have mercy. We're taking my father to Peshawar, the hospital!" he yelled in Pashto. "He's very sick."

The Talib stood in front of them, lowered his AK. "No exceptions to the curfew. Take him home."

"Please. He won't survive the night. He's in the back. Talk to him. *Inshallah*, you'll see."

As Armstrong spoke, Maggs opened the back door and stepped into the road behind the van. Armstrong touched the gas and the van inched forward.

"I won't tell you again. Turn around."

Maggs stepped sideways and fired a three-shot burst at the gunner on the TUV. As he did, Armstrong floored the gas. The Mitsubishi leapt forward at the Talib in the road. He fired three shots, missing high, and then disappeared with a grunt under the van. The Mitsubishi thumped over him, front wheels and then back, and roared forward.

In the bed of the pickup, the gunner groaned and slumped forward just as he squeezed the trigger. The TUV's burst missed high and wide. The Talib beside the gunner tried to push him aside, but Maggs laid out another burst. The rounds tore into the second man's shoulder and knocked him into the bed of the pickup.

In the passenger seat, Snyder could only watch through the windshield as the van closed on the pickup. He had the distinct feeling that he wasn't actually in the van, that he was watching a movie of the scene rather than living it. At moments like this, time was supposed to slow, he knew. He was supposed to remember the great moments in his life. Instead, a groaning feeling of unreality overwhelmed him—

The van rammed the pickup broadside and crumpled its passenger door, crushing the Talib in the passenger seat instantly. The impact tossed Snyder and Armstrong against their seat belts, which gave a few inches and then tightened and pulled them back. The van's engine block was shoved backward, toward Snyder, as his seat popped forward, forcing his left leg up and out. The engine rammed Snyder's leg and snapped his tibia and fibula as cleanly as wishbones.

As Snyder screamed, the driver of the pickup opened the door and ran through the brush, down the side of the hill, toward Mingora. Armstrong lifted his pistol and shot through the front windshield at him but didn't get him.

Armstrong laid a hand on Snyder's shoulder. "You okay."

"I can't move, Major. My leg."

Armstrong looked down at Snyder's leg, the ankle curled back under the calf in a pose even the best yoga instructor couldn't have managed. Wounded Warrior Six. "We'll get you out."

"Yessir."

Armstrong tried to pop his door open, but the frame of the Mitsubishi was bowed and the door wouldn't come loose. He wriggled out the back of the van, the laptop in hand, as tendrils of smoke began to rise from the front of the Mitsubishi. Snyder shot out his window to get air. He hung his head out the side of the truck and coughed.

Maggs ran toward the pickup as the Talib in the bed of the truck came to his knees. The Talib's AK had gotten caught behind him. He scrabbled for it as blood poured out of the shoulder. Then the Talib gave up and tentatively lifted his hands over his shoulders—

And as he did, Maggs fired a burst and he went down. No prisoners. Not here, not now.

THE NISSAN ROLLED UP and the four Deltas jumped out. Armstrong handed the laptop to Task, the driver, and waved him back into the car. "Task, get around the pickup. If something goes wrong here, you take this and go." He turned to the other Deltas. "Snyder's stuck. Leg's broken. Got to get him out."

The smoke was thicker now, but Armstrong crawled back into the van as the three Deltas tried to pry open the door. Before they could open it, Snyder screamed, a lungful of obscenities that echoed over the valley. Armstrong had him by the shoulders and was tugging him toward the back of the van. Maggs ran to the back of the van, and together he and Armstrong pulled Snyder out as flames rose from the front of the Mitsubishi. Armstrong and Snyder were coughing, and soot covered Snyder's face.

"We got you," Armstrong said.

Armstrong and Maggs and the Deltas carried Snyder to the Nissan, fifty feet past the pickup. Behind them, the van's gas tank exploded. The van jumped six inches. When it landed, its windows were gone and yellow-orange flames rose from its body.

Armstrong nodded at the burning remains of the van. "We won't be taking that home."

"The pickup."

"Let's leave it in the road. Buy us some time. We'll all ride with Task."

"Gonna be as crowded as that bus." Maggs looked at the valley below. Ten miles away, at the edge of Mingora, a convoy of cars streamed toward them in the dark. "I'm gonna fix that roadblock."

As Armstrong and the other Deltas arranged Snyder in the Nissan, Maggs grabbed a grenade and ran for the pickup. The keys were still in the ignition. He turned on the engine and backed up. Metal ground on metal as the pickup pulled away from the van, forming a metal L that blocked the road completely.

Maggs stepped ten feet away and tossed a grenade inside the pickup and dove for the side of the road. He covered his hands from the twin explosions that followed as first the grenade and then the Toyota's gas tank blew and the night turned white.

Thunder broke overhead, as if the skies were applauding. Maggs ran for the Nissan, a hundred feet ahead. When he got there, the trunk was open, holes shot through for air.

"Me or you," Armstrong said, looking down at the trunk.

"Long as it's not both of us. You're taller. Stay in the car." Maggs climbed in and settled himself, shoving aside an AK that was poking into his back. Armstrong slammed down the lid.

———————

THE NEXT THREE HOURS were among the most unpleasant of Maggs's life. The road twisted like a badly designed amusement park ride: *Check out the new Nausea-Coaster.* Rain poured into the trunk through the air holes, soaking him to the skin. And he had no way of knowing if the Talibs were closing. Though maybe not knowing was for the best. He'd find out when the shooting started.

But it never did. And finally, the car stopped and the lid popped open. He stretched his cramped legs but didn't try to move. He shivered wildly. He hadn't realized just how cold he was. In the distance he heard traffic, trucks passing.

"Enjoying yourself?" Armstrong said.

"Putting the black man in the trunk. Racism, pure and simple."

"Believe me, it was no fun up front."

"Where are we?"

"Five minutes from the Islamabad-Peshawar highway, my friend. We made it. Never even saw them. Roadblock worked. Nice job." Armstrong reached a hand down. Maggs waved it off.

"I'm comfy. Wake me back at the embassy."

"Come on, you gotta be freezing."

"Let's just get it done." Maggs wasn't sure why he was protesting. He only knew they'd have to drag him out of the trunk now.

THEY WERE BACK at the embassy before sunrise. Maggs knew he ought to sleep, but he was too jacked. They all were. Even Snyder, with his broken leg. And not just because of the insanity of what they'd just pulled off.

No, they all had the same question.

"What do you think?" Armstrong said, as he unwrapped the plastic that encased the laptop. It was an IBM ThinkPad, an X60. Maggs was no tech, but it looked undamaged to him. It even had its charger taped to the bottom.

"Really hot Paki porn," Task said.

"They have hot porn?"

"No. That's why it's so special."

"Horse porn."

"Horse-dog porn."

"A horse doing a dog? That's just sick. Where do you get that, Task?"

Maggs plugged in the charger, reached for the on button, then stopped.

"What if there's a virus on it, erases the hard drive as soon as we touch it?"

"If something goes wrong, we'll turn it off, unplug it," Armstrong said. "It can't delete itself that fast."

"You sure."

"I'm sure."

They should wait, Maggs thought. But they'd nearly died tonight for this lump of plastic. They'd earned the right to its secrets. He reached for the power button and they watched as the machine sprung to life.

24

"B rant Murphy," Shafer said. "Brant F. Murphy. Know what the F stands for?"

"I can guess."

"This guy's like a bad dream. Everywhere we turn."

"Ellis. You said you don't believe in big conspiracies."

"I'm starting to."

"Me, too."

"Even when Duto put me under house arrest, back in the day, I understood. Didn't like it, but I understood. He had his reasons. But this feels different. Not like some bureaucratic snafu. Tell me I'm wrong."

And yet Wells felt a tingle of what could only be called excitement, the thrill of operating without a net, without the agency behind him. He remembered the months after he had first come back to the United States from Pakistan, when he'd broken out of CIA custody and gone to ground in Atlanta. He'd lived lonely and pure.

Shafer seemed to glimpse Wells's enthusiasm. "The lady doth protest too much."

They sat in Shafer's kitchen, watching Tonka chase squirrels around the oak tree in the backyard. A fat gray squirrel dashed past up the tree and danced on a branch twenty feet above the ground, chittering down as the dog barked furiously back.

"I'll get you a ladder," Wells yelled.

"I know how she feels," Shafer said. "Just hoping for a mistake."

"Are we the squirrels or Tonka?"

"I'm not sure yet."

"I'm starting to miss the jihadis," Wells said. "At least I know what they want. This I don't understand at all. Did Murphy, Whitby, and Terreri really team up to kill everybody in 673?"

"We still need a motive. A couple of million dollars isn't enough. Not split three ways. Not for this."

"What if it was more? A lot more. Say 673 got onto something, some secret account for bin Laden that had fifty million dollars in it. A hundred. Pick whatever number you want. They take the money and then they kill the detainees. The whole squad's in on it. The detainees have to die because if they ever get to Gitmo, they're going to tell their lawyers about all this money. Murphy comes back here, gets D'Angelo to delete the names, so nobody ever knows the detainees even existed. The squad disbands, and somebody has an attack of conscience. Sends a note to the IG. Alleging torture and theft. And Murphy and Terreri don't know who sent it. So, they decide to eliminate the rest of the squad. And Whitby, he's happy with the intel they got, he doesn't want to hear anything else."

Not for the first time, Wells was struck by the enormous gap between the agency's headquarters and its frontline operatives. The lords of the intelligence community sat in their offices at Langley and Liberty Crossing, pretending they were in charge. Until something went wrong. Then they told the prosecutors and the congressional investigators that they couldn't be expected to know exactly what was happening on the front lines.

"Possible," Shafer said. "But let me ask you. Why didn't the letter mention a hundred-million-dollar bank account? Plenty of accusations in there. Why not that? And why cut Whitby in? For that matter, can you see this whole squad killing two prisoners in cold blood? Can you see Jerry Williams going for that? And one more thing. I don't like Brant Murphy, either. But would he murder his own squad? Or anyone else."

Wells tried to picture Murphy putting a bullet in someone. Even ordering a hit. And couldn't.

"Or even Fred Whitby. It takes a certain disregard—a certain coldness—"

"I know, Ellis. Better than you." Wells looked at Shafer. "Or not. I never have gotten the stories, what you did all those years running around Africa. And behind the Wall."

"No, you haven't."

"I think of you as this oldster whose socks don't match, but you weren't always."

"I wasn't," Shafer said. "Maybe there's another explanation for what happened. And it comes from something we keep forgetting."

Wells waited.

"The Pakistani nuke depots. Massive coup. Unless Whitby and Duto are flat-out lying, we got it because of intel that 673 developed. Terreri and Murphy must have known it would get noticed at the highest levels. And that they would have to produce the prisoners who gave it up. But what if those prisoners were dead? Problem. Best solution, make the names disappear. Let the intel stand on its own."

"So, in this scenario the prisoners weren't killed intentionally?"

"Maybe they tried to escape, got shot. Maybe Jack Fisher interrogated them too hard and they died."

"So, these detainees had the list of all the nuclear weapons depots in Pakistan. Where they're located, how they're guarded."

"I admit, that part doesn't work. Crazy as the Paks are, I can't see them giving that info to a terrorist."

"Try this," Wells said. "We kidnapped a Pak general. We got the info on the weapons depots from him, and we killed him accidentally on purpose and we made him disappear."

"And the ISI went along with it? We killed one of their top guys and they didn't care?"

"Maybe they didn't know. They thought he defected." Wells shook his head even before he finished. "It still doesn't work."

"Brant Murphy's going to have to explain it for us."

"We can't get to him. We show up at CTC, he calls Whitby, Whitby calls Duto."

"That's half right, John. We can't get to him *at CTC*."

"You're not saying we go back to Kings Park West."

Shafer nodded. And Wells could only smile.

"Know what I like about you, Ellis? You're as crazy as me."

BUT GETTING TO MURPHY at home proved as hard as getting to him at work. After the murders of Jack Fisher and Mike Wyly, the agency had given Murphy a permanent protective detail. An unmarked van, two guards inside, sat in front of the house around the clock. An armor-plated Lincoln Town Car ferried him to and from Langley. When he had to drive on his own, he used an agency Suburban, also armor-plated. But he rarely went anywhere except the gym. And wherever he went, two guards always shadowed him.

Because Murphy's guards were CIA officers, Wells and Shafer couldn't use any of the agency's unmarked vehicles. Instead, a friend of Shafer's at the FBI let them borrow from the bureau's surveillance fleet, which included everything from bank vans to FedEx trucks to a 1988 Jaguar XJS. They switched cars every day, sometimes twice a day.

They did have one advantage: Murphy wasn't the only one in

Kings Park West who'd bet on real estate. Every fourth house in the neighborhood seemed to be for sale, giving them a good excuse to drive around. They scheduled appointments to visit houses in the early evening, hoping to catch Murphy making a mistake, going for a run or out to dinner without his bodyguards.

But after a week, they were no closer to getting to him or even figuring out how they might. "We need to face facts," Wells said, on the fifth day of their drive-bys. "This isn't working."

"He'll let his guard down," Shafer said.

"Not soon enough. And the guards are in the way."

"We can find a nonlethal way to take them out."

"Long shot, but say we can. Then what? We kidnap Murphy? Where do we take him, Ellis? Your house? It's insane."

"You can always get to people."

"I couldn't get to Ivan Markov. As much as I wanted to. And we're not talking about killing him. We're talking about *interrogating* him. Which means we can't cut and run. It means we need time with him. Which we won't have. And why exactly do we think he's gonna talk to us now? He didn't before."

"We didn't have D'Angelo before."

"Ellis, no matter how many different cars we borrow, we're low on time. Two guys can't run long-term surveillance on a defended target. Especially not here. It's too quiet. I can *feel* people watching me. We're going to get spotted. In days. Not weeks."

Shafer didn't argue.

"It's time to clue the bureau in," Wells said. "Tell them everything. If they knew about the letter and D'Angelo, they might make progress. Or I can go back to New Orleans, talk to Noemie Williams, see if she remembers anything. Or Steve Callar. Or maybe we need to talk to Duto, see if he'll tell us what game we're playing."

"Let's give it a couple more days, see if anything breaks. It's just possible Murphy'll get bored, go for a drive on his own. Or a run, even better."

"Two days," Wells said. "No more."

AND SOMETHING DID BREAK, though it wasn't what Wells had expected.

Three p.m. Saturday, the seventh and final day of surveillance. Shafer was watching his daughter play softball, so Wells was alone. He had just cruised by Murphy's house in a Verizon van. The armored van sat out front, as usual, a red Ford Econoline with two unsmiling men in front.

Then he saw two cars in the driveway of a foreclosure that was the closest empty house to Murphy's. The first was a blue Audi A4 with a vanity Virginia license plate: "SLHOUSE." It belonged to Sandra ("Call me Sandy") Seward, a Century 21 agent who had several listings in the area. Wells had met her during his house-buying excursion. The second was a black Toyota Tercel. Wells had seen it before. Precisely three nights ago, stopping in front of Murphy's house. At the time, it had worn a Domino's Pizza sign on its roof. The driver hadn't gotten out of the Tercel. He'd simply lowered his window, said something to the guys in the van—asking for directions, presumably—and driven off. Wells kept driving, reached for his phone, called Shafer.

"YOU SURE ABOUT THIS?"

"He's doing the same thing we are," Wells said. "Casing Murphy, staking out the neighborhood as quietly as he can."

"Because if you're right, then we have to throw everything out.

Murphy's not involved. The killer's on the outside. Unless Whitby's put a contract out on Murphy. Which makes even less sense."

"I'm telling you, this is the guy."

They decided not to go after him at the house. They had no authority to make an arrest, and if the guy pulled a weapon, they risked getting the real-estate agent hurt and alerting Murphy's guards. Instead, they would have to chance tailing the Tercel. Wells guessed the guy, whoever he was, was staying at a low-rent motel in D.C., a place that would take cash so he didn't have to use a credit card.

They split up, positioned themselves at intersections on Braddock Road, which ran between Kings Park and the Beltway. If they missed him, they would have to alert Murphy's guards to watch for a black Tercel. But Wells much preferred to find the guy himself, figure out who he was, before getting the agency or the Feds involved.

For an hour, Wells sat in a bank parking lot on the corner of Twinbrook and Braddock, watching the lights change. The Tercel didn't show. He wondered if they had lost the guy, or if maybe he'd been wrong all along.

Then his phone rang.

"I got him," Shafer said.

Fifteen minutes later, the Tercel was on the Beltway, Wells and Shafer behind. They crossed the Woodrow Wilson Bridge east into Maryland, then turned north on 295. The driver kept in the right lane at a steady fifty-eight. Probably he was worried about being pulled over in a car with fake plates. But caution made him an easy tail.

At Route 50, the Tercel turned west, into D.C., over the narrow, sluggish Anacostia River. Wells felt a faint thrill as he crossed over the bridge. He would always remember meeting Exley at the Kenilworth gardens, barely a mile from here, on the night that Omar Khadri had called him to New York. *Exley*. He didn't know how to leave her behind. And yet he had. Maybe he just needed a cute New Hampshire cop who would take him on hikes and bust his chops when he retreated too far into himself. Maybe he needed to give that a try, anyway.

Two miles west of the Anacostia, Route 50 became New York Avenue, a rambling strip of liquor stores, strip clubs, fast-food restaurants, and cheap motels. Surveillance here was trickier. Shafer jumped the Tercel, so that they would at least have a chance at him if he made a light that Wells missed.

Just past Montana, the Tercel turned into the parking lot for the Budget Motor Inn. Wells cruised by in time to see the Tercel pull into a spot in front of room 112. Ten minutes later, Wells and Shafer were sitting down the block at a KFC.

Shafer had insisted on buying a four-piece dinner special, giving Wells the dubious pleasure of watching him eat. As he chewed, he spun the drumstick like an ear of corn. Disgusting but efficient, like so much that Shafer did.

"Sure you don't want some?"

"Yes," Wells said. Though he hadn't eaten KFC in a long time and the chicken looked tasty. Terrible, but tasty. If that combination was possible. "When do we call the cops?"

Shafer laughed. A piece of chicken, or some chicken-like substance, flew from his mouth, landing on Wells's hand. "Good one."

"Then could you finish that, so we can go in?"

"He's not going anywhere, and we're not going in until after midnight."

"He could go after Murphy before that."

"This guy's careful. He's not moving until he's sure."

"Then I'm going home for a while, pick up some things."

"Like what?"

"Are you really asking me that? In the middle of a *restaurant*?"

"It's a KFC."

"Things we might need."

"And it's finger-licking good."

"Do not lose him, Ellis. You lose him, I might use those things on you."

"You promise?"

Wells took the rest of Shafer's chicken and left.

THE BUDGET MOTOR INN didn't have a lobby. It had a waiting room, like a doctor's office, if the doctor worked in Mogadishu. Wood-grain veneer on the walls and thick bulletproof glass protecting the front desk. A sign taped to the inside of the glass explained, "Credit cards or cash only. No checks. No exceptions." The guy behind the glass was in his late twenties, black, with a shaved head and Urkel-sized black glasses. He barely looked up from his battered copy of *Fight Club* as Shafer and Wells walked in.

"You want one bed or two?"

"We don't want a room," Shafer said. He held up his CIA identification.

"Lemme see that."

Shafer slid the badge under the glass. The guy frowned at it, handed it back.

"CIA? You expect me to believe that?"

"Yes."

"You're not allowed to do anything on American soil."

"Everybody's a lawyer."

"As a matter of fact, I'm hoping to go to law school."

Wells pulled out his own CIA identification, held it against the glass.

"John Wells? Mr. Times Square? Seriously?"

Wells nodded.

"Where you been since then?"

"Hanging out on the beach," Wells said. "Those fruity drinks with the umbrellas? Mai tais?"

"For real?"

"But now he's back," Shafer said. "And he's better than ever. And he and I have business with the guy in room 112. Anything you can tell us about him?"

"You cannot be serious."

Shafer slid two hundred-dollar bills under the glass. "For your college fund."

"It's law school." The guy pecked at the ancient keyboard on his desk. "You're gonna be disappointed. He's registered under the name Michael Jackson."

"He show ID?"

"Doesn't say here, but probably not. You don't have to if you pay cash up front and put down a three-hundred-fifty-dollar deposit. More than the whole room's worth."

"We're going to say hi to him," Wells said. "All we're asking is that you ignore him if he calls you when we knock on his door."

"What if he calls the cops?"

"He's not calling the cops," Shafer said.

THE TERCEL SAT in front of room 112, as it had all night, empty spaces to either side. Even with an RV taking up five spaces, the motel's parking lot was only half full. But New York Avenue was alive with Saturday-night traffic, SUVs cruising by, pumping rap from behind tinted windows. A D.C. police car slowed as it rolled past, the cop inside looking curiously at Wells and Shafer. They ignored him and kept walking, and he disappeared. Wells didn't want to be here for his next pass.

The noise from the street covered their approach. Wells loosened his jacket but left his pistol in his shoulder holster. He and Shafer were going in cold. They needed this guy alive. Wells reached 112 first, flattened himself against the wall, two big steps from the door. The window shade was drawn, the room silent and dark, lacking even the glow of a night-light.

Shafer stood fifty feet away. Wells counted five and nodded at him. Shafer walked noisily to the door, rapped his knuckles against its faded red paint. "Henry!" he shouted. "That you, Henry?"

No response.

Shafer knocked again, harder. "Henry! Come out, you two-timing prick!"

"Get lost!" a voice inside yelled back. Wells had heard it before but couldn't place it.

Shafer hammered away like a woodpecker on meth. Inside, someone stood up and shuffled to the door. "I'm not Henry," the voice said, more calmly now. "Please go away."

"Henry! I'm gonna call the cops!"

The door opened a notch, still on the chain. "Henry's not here." The tip of a pistol poked through the gap between the door and the frame. "And you need to leave."

"I am sorry," Shafer said. "So, so sorry." He raised his hands and stepped away.

The pistol disappeared and the door swung shut—

But even as Shafer backed off, Wells was moving. He rocketed forward, popped his shoulder into the door, carrying himself back to those crisp fall afternoons at Dartmouth. Two decades gone now. He'd been quick enough then to speed-rush from the outside, tearing

342 | ALEX BERENSON

past linemen and tight ends on his way to the quarterback. He wasn't that fast anymore. But he was fast enough.

His shoulder hit the door and he felt the chain pull taut and then snap loose, the screws that held the fastener popping out of the wall. The door made solid contact with the man inside, and Wells got low and kept pumping his legs—*never stop moving your legs, that's where the power comes from,* Coach Parker always said. The guy on the other side of the door grunted and went down, and Wells swung open the door and stepped in.

THE ROOM WAS DARK, illuminated only by the glow from the parking-lot lights outside. The man inside sprawled in the narrow aisle between the bed and the wooden chest of drawers that sat against the wall. Wells still couldn't see his face. The man scrabbled back, groped for his pistol.

Wells leapt down on the man. As he landed, slamming chest against chest, he saw the face of his enemy.

Steve Callar.

Wells's shock was so complete that for the first time in his life he dropped his guard during a fight. Callar took advantage. With his free hand, his left hand, he clubbed Wells twice. Wells sagged but held Callar's right arm, the one that held the pistol. Callar heaved his body convulsively and tossed Wells off. They lay sideways beside each other, close enough for Wells to see every pore on Callar's face, smell the sweet-sour whiskey on Callar's breath. Then Callar rolled on top of Wells. Wells rolled with him, trying to use his momentum to flip Callar another one hundred eighty degrees and put him on his back. But the space between bed and dresser was too cramped and instead they got stuck side by side again.

Wells chopped at Callar's face with his right forearm, the trick that had worked on Jim D'Angelo. But he didn't have the momentum, and anyway Callar was fighting with a rage that Wells couldn't match. Wells outweighed Callar by at least twenty pounds, all muscle, and yet Callar was giving him everything he could handle—

Before Wells could finish the thought, Callar twitched sideways and pushed his left leg between Wells's legs and drove his knee into Wells's testicles.

The agony was so enormous that Wells couldn't move. Tears filled his eyes, and the air came out of his body. Somehow he kept his grip on Callar's right arm as Callar tried to tug down the pistol. Callar grinned at him, a hard, crazy smile, and began to wrench his arm free. Wells was holding on with his left hand, his weak hand. His strength was ebbing. In a few seconds more, Callar would have him. Callar felt it, too. His grin widened.

Wells saw the opening.

He shifted his legs to block Callar from kneeing him again. And he hooked his right thumb into Callar's mouth and pulled back Callar's cheek. Callar's face twisted and he snapped his jaws shut, trying to bite Wells's thumb. But Wells pushed his thumb in farther and tugged until Callar's cheek tore—

Callar screamed, a desperate bleat. He thrashed his legs and swung his head sideways and scratched at Wells's face, long fingernails clawing into Wells's face, as Wells pulled and Callar's cheek tore further—

When he had done as much damage as he could, Wells pulled his thumb out of Callar's mouth and made a fist and slammed it into Callar's jaw, a miniature uppercut. He hit Callar once, twice, and a third time, and then shifted his grip to wrap his hand around Callar's neck, Wells's superior strength taking over now. He clenched Callar's neck tighter, tighter. Callar's face turned red and his eyes rolled up and foam mixed with the blood running from the corner of his mouth and—

THE LIGHTS FLIPPED ON, and someone pounded on Wells. Shafer.

"Don't kill him, don't, don't."

Wells rose to his knees and straddled Callar's chest and relaxed his grip. Callar's mouth opened, and the blood burbled out of his torn-up face. Wells and Shafer watched him breathe. Then Shafer grabbed the pistol from his limp right hand. Wells picked him up and put him on the bed. Shafer pulled two sets of cuffs from his jacket and locked Callar's wrists together and then his ankles. The adrenaline evaporated from Wells, and he sagged against the wall.

"We need to go."

"No," Shafer said. "Rooms 111 and 113 are empty, and there's no sirens."

"That's Steve Callar."

"Yeah. I've seen his picture. He doesn't look much like it now."

"I don't get it."

"You should go in the bathroom, get yourself cleaned up."

WELLS FLICKED ON the fluorescent lights and saw a berserker in the bathroom mirror. A thick, red trail of blood, maybe his own, maybe Callar's, streaked down under his eye. Spit and phlegm covered his cheeks. Wells turned the tap and dabbed at his face until the washcloth was red. Traces of blood lingered, but he looked mostly human. He pulled down his jeans and boxers and winced as he touched his swollen testicles.

Shafer opened the bathroom door, holding a bottle of peroxide and a box of Band-Aids from the first-aid kit in the car. His jaw slipped open as he saw Wells poking at himself.

"Now's really not the time, John."

"Funny, Ellis."

"Next time wear a cup." Shafer tossed Wells the bottle and the Band-Aids, grabbed a towel, and left. Wells patched up his face as best he could and pulled his pants back up and walked shakily into the bedroom.

"He's gonna need stitches," Wells said.

"Stitches? You just gave him a new mouth. He's gonna need a face transplant, like that French lady." Shafer pressed at the bloody gash on Callar's face with the towel.

"It's not that bad."

"Remind me never to get in a fight with you."

"You need reminding of that?" Wells put a hand on Callar's shoulder. "I still can't see how he got to his wife."

Callar groaned and stirred. Wells stepped away, drew his Glock, tried to keep his hand steady. Callar's eyes blinked open. He poked his tongue though the hole in his face.

"You found me."

"Saw you cruising the neighborhood," Wells said.

"But you didn't know it was me. Until you got here."

"That's right."

"Anybody else know? FBI? Or is it just us chickens?"

"It's over now, so why don't you tell us what happened?" Shafer said. "Why you killed your wife and everyone else. And how you got from Phoenix to San Diego and back without anyone noticing."

Callar laughed, a huffing laugh that turned into a vicious cough. Blood and spit exploded from his mouth, and a gob of phlegm landed on the television on the dresser.

"I've been telling you all along, and you still don't get it," he said. "My wife killed herself."

Then, finally, Wells understood.

25

The video had been shot with what looked like a pinhole, through-the-wall camera. The image quality wasn't great. But it was good enough.

On-screen, Jawaruddin bin Zari stood beside another man, tall, in his early fifties, in a neatly tailored suit. A trimmed black beard framed his face. Maggs knew him immediately. They'd met once before, at the embassy. Abdul-Aziz Tafiq, head of the ISI. Arguably the most powerful man in Pakistan.

Maggs wondered if the video had been spliced or faked. The NSA's techs would have to check. But to his eyes it seemed authentic. Given the risks of the meeting—for both men—whatever had brought them together must have been crucial, an issue that could only be resolved face-to-face.

The terrorist and the security chief were in what looked like an empty office. No window or desk or phone, just a table and a couple of chairs. An on-screen clock recorded the date and time: 14 Dec. 2007, 6:23 p.m.

"*Salaam alekeim.*"

"*Alekeim salaam,*" Tafiq said. "My friend, you asked to see me. Here I am."

"I wanted to be sure this message came from you."

"It does." Tafiq paused. "So? Can you?"

"How many bombs have I set over the years?"

"You missed the general."

"That was more complicated. And Pervez is fortunate."

"This won't be easy. Her car will be armored. Police in front and behind."

"Leave it to me. She'll hardly be moving. Those streets. And she can't help herself. Waves to the crowds like the woman she is. As long as I have the route."

"You'll have it."

"And the details of her security. Whatever you can give me."

"Done. She cannot survive."

"OH, MAN," MAGGS SAID to Armstrong, who'd been translating the conversation from Pashto. "You're sure about this?"

"I'm sure."

Only one *she* counted in Pakistan. Benazir Bhutto. And she hadn't survived. No. She'd been assassinated on December 27, 2007, in Rawalpindi, after a rally for her political party, the Pakistan Peoples Party. Another chance for peace in Pakistan destroyed by violence. The killer, or killers, were never caught.

A murder condoned—not just condoned but set in motion—by the chief of the ISI.

ON-SCREEN, bin Zari put a friendly hand on Tafiq's arm. "Don't worry," he said. "She won't."

"And your men?"

"Whoever you like. With connections or no."

Meaning, Maggs presumed, that bin Zari was asking Tafiq to decide whether the assassins would be known members of Islamic terrorist groups or sleepers unknown to any intelligence agency.

"No connections," Tafiq said. "But make sure they're expendable. In case there's pressure from the Americans and we must find them."

"Done," bin Zari said. "As for the money—"

"You should do it for free. You hate her more than we do."

"As for the money."

"Half tomorrow. The rest when it's over."

"Done."

The two Pakistanis leaned in, hugged. And the screen went black.

26

"Your wife killed herself," Wells said. "So you killed everyone else."

"Someone finally gets it."

Wells looked around, seeing the room for the first time, eleven feet square, the ceiling barely seven feet high and mottled with brownish stains. A light fixture poked like a pimple from the beige stucco wall behind the bed. Callar must have sat in rooms like this for weeks on end, in San Francisco and New Orleans and Los Angeles, plotting his mad revenge.

Wells ran a hand over his face and came away with a thin trail of perspiration and blood. Callar watched him with flickering eyes.

"Nice, isn't it?"

"I've seen less depressing torture chambers. Really."

"It does have HBO."

"You stay here when you killed Ken Karp?"

Callar shook his head. "Down the street. Believe it or not, this is a step up. No bedbugs. Who's your buddy, John? Didn't do you much good in the fight."

"I'm Ellis Shafer. Why don't you tell us what happened?"

"Why don't you tell me?"

"Fair enough," Shafer said. "Stop me when I make a mistake. You didn't know exactly what happened over there. But it was bad. Hard on your wife. And she wouldn't quit. You asked her to come home, but she wouldn't."

"She wouldn't even take her second leave."

"Finally, the tour ended. Rachel came back to California. Got even more depressed. Wasn't working. You couldn't help her. She wouldn't talk to you about it. She was the doctor, you were the nurse."

"I couldn't even get her out of bed. She lay there all day. Every day. A couple weeks before she died, I called her folks, asked them to come down from L.A. Didn't tell them exactly what was wrong, but they knew it had to be something serious or I wouldn't have called. She'd only seen them once since she had her breakdown in med school. A few minutes before they got to the house, I told her they were coming. She didn't say a word, just got dressed, put on makeup," Callar said. "They got to the house and she put on this act, went out to lunch, told them she was fine. She came home and told me if I ever did anything like that again, she'd leave me on the spot. She said her life was her life, she didn't want anyone to know what was happening, and especially not her parents."

"Not a healthy attitude. Especially for a mental-health professional."

"I could have tried to have her committed involuntarily. In California we call it a fifty-one fifty. But she would have run rings around the cops. Probably would have wound up having me committed instead."

"But you still loved her."

"More than anything. You know, I wanted her from the first moment I saw her in the emergency room. It really was like that. And it never went away. The way she held herself, the way she could look at a patient, a sick one, a real crazy, size him up, put him at ease right away, just putting a hand on his shoulder."

"A real crazy," Wells said.

"Outside the hospital, she was funny. Smarter than I was. I guess we were never really partners, and maybe I should have minded, but I didn't. My whole life, people been telling me what to do, and it never bothered me."

"Rachel say what happened over in Poland?"

"Around the edges. She told me she thought that Murphy and the colonel were skimming. And something bad happened at the end. But I didn't know what. She never said."

"Then she sent you to Phoenix. Did you know what she planned to do?"

"I wasn't sure." Callar ducked his head to his shoulder, wiping at the blood trickling down his face. "No, that's not true. I knew. But I hoped I was wrong. Anyway, like I told you, she never listened to me."

"And when you got home, she was dead."

"That's right."

"She leave a note?"

"She said she was sorry. That I'd be better off without her. That she failed."

"She say how?"

"No. 'I failed.' That was it. And these twelve numbers. All ten digits long."

"Did you know what they were?"

"I thought they were those 'prisoner identification numbers.' She'd mentioned them."

"So, you hid the note from the cops," Shafer said. "And a couple weeks later, you sent the letter accusing Murphy and Terreri of skimming. And for good measure, you accused the squad of torture."

"Pretty much. I wanted a real investigation. There were enough details in the letter. I figured someone would have to look into it."

"But you were wrong."

"I figured somebody would call the house. Ask to talk to her. They didn't know she was dead at that point. And when they found out, I figured it might make them wonder even more about the letter. But after a couple of months, I realized nobody cared."

"You decided on your own action."

Callar grinned. Blood dripped off his chin and onto the dark blue blanket beneath him. Wells wondered if the owners of the Budget Motor Inn had chosen the color because it hid bloodstains.

"Do you remember where you got the idea?" Shafer said.

"Indeed I do. She had one picture of the squad. Taken close to the end. Except for her, they all looked happy, believe it or not. Smiling, arms around each other. Wearing these cowboy hats. She was off to one side. She was smiling, too, but I knew she was faking it. The way she was holding herself, with her arms folded. I looked at that picture. Looked at it and looked at it. And kept imagining Rachel not being in it. And then I found out that those two Rangers had died in Afghanistan. And I imagined them not being in it, either." Callar looked at Wells. "Remember that movie *Back to the Future*, when we were kids?"

"Sure."

"So in that movie, Michael J. Fox, he's got this picture of his family. And when he goes back to 1950-whatever and messes up the way his mom and dad are supposed to meet, the people in the picture, they start to vanish. Because he's screwed up his own birth, see? And one day I saw the same thing happening to Rachel and the Rangers in the 673 picture. I mean, I didn't imagine it. I *saw* it. I knew what I had to do. I just saw that picture entirely blank. It only seemed right."

"You have the photo with you?"

"In my backpack."

Wells rummaged through, found it. The members of 673 stood in front of an anonymous concrete barracks. Everyone but Callar wore cowboy hats. In the center, Murphy and Terreri held up a painted wooden sign that read, "Task Force 673, Stare Kiejkuty: The Midnight House." Callar was in the group but not of it. Her smile was pained, her face tilted slightly away from the camera, as if she was looking at something the others had missed. A ghost on the edge of the frame.

"Why not just go after Terreri? Or Terreri and Murphy?"

"I blamed all of them. I didn't know exactly who did what, but I knew everybody was dirty. It wasn't my job to make distinctions."

"It was your job to kill them," Shafer said. "With an assist from whoever killed those Rangers."

"That's right." Now that he wasn't talking about Rachel, Callar's voice was flat, remorseless.

"What about that posting on the jihadi Web site after Wyly and Fisher were killed? The one that said it was revenge for the way we treat detainees?"

"I knew at some point you guys would put the murders together. I was hoping to jump in front, misdirect you."

"You figured out how to post it in Arabic?"

"I had time, the last few months. It wasn't that tough. Lot of cutting and pasting."

"The banality of evil," Shafer said. "We could discuss the morality of collective punishment with you, but there wouldn't be much point."

"No, there wouldn't."

"What about the fact that your wife killed herself?" Wells said. "I don't like Brant Murphy, either. But he didn't hurt your wife. And you said she had a breakdown in medical school. Maybe this would have happened no matter what."

A growl escaped from Callar's ruined mouth. "Easy," Shafer said. Callar tugged at his cuffs. Wells imagined the steel shearing, as if Callar's anger could bestow superhuman powers. But nothing happened, and finally Callar gave up.

"Nobody hurt her?" he said. He spat at Wells. Then laughed, a high screech that bounced around the room, wrapping around Wells like a spiderweb of madness. "They broke her. She went there as a doctor. She came back as a torturer. That's how she saw it. They made her see what she was capable of. Don't you see, that's why she posed for that picture? That's why she saved it. To remind herself that she was no better than anyone else. That she was worse. She was a *doctor*."

"They took her will to live," Shafer said.

"That's right. She had that breakdown fifteen years ago, but she was copacetic for a long time. So, don't put this on her. Not on her."

Wells wondered, *Did she know how much you loved her?* Though maybe it didn't matter. Either way, she'd killed herself.

"Ever done anything like this before, Steve?" Shafer said.

"Anything like this? You mean, murder? No. This is a first."

"You're a natural."

"It's not that hard. If you can handle a gun. The tough part is not getting caught. Especially in this case, a bunch of different cities. But I was careful. I had money saved up, and Rachel left more. I quit work and figured out where everybody lived, and I cased them out. I drove everywhere, bought different cars in every city, stayed in motels like this. But now that you know it was me, you'll find the traces."

"How come you didn't start with Terreri and Murphy?"

"By the time I figured out what I wanted to do, Terreri was over in Afghanistan. And Murphy, I figured if I hit a guy high up in the agency, somebody would put it together. The way I did it, I got a long way before anybody figured out what was happening."

"Tell us about the first murder."

"That was Karp. He was the easiest. Bad habits. Left him vulnerable."

"How'd you get to Jerry?"

"Lucky for me, he was drinking pretty hard. I set up on the street with a twelve-pack around the corner from that bar he liked. Took a couple days, but sure enough he came by. I asked him if he wanted a beer. I'd met him in the bar, so his guard was down. He had about five. I offered to drive him home. I'd bought this old Jeep Cherokee with tinted windows. He got in the front and I went in back and blew off his head. Drove the body out to the swamp and dumped him."

Wells stood, looked around the room for something sharp, something heavy.

"Please do," Callar said. "You'd be doing me a favor."

"Sit down, John." Shafer patted his arm. "Sit."

Wells sat.

"But you didn't think it through," Shafer said. "You left the CO and the XO. And now they're defended."

"I would have gotten to Murphy if you hadn't found me." Callar lay on his back, spoke to the ceiling. "Any more questions, gents? Or is this where you call those FBI cyborgs and turn me in?"

"You're sure you don't know what happened at the end over there? Or the specific intel they got?"

"You're going to have to ask Murphy and the colonel." Callar sat up again. "I don't suppose you'd be willing to uncuff me, give me a minute with that Beretta of mine? One round would do. Spare us all the indignity of a trial."

"Maybe we need some indignity," Wells said.

Shafer stood. "Maybe. Step into my office, Mr. Wells."

UNDER THE FLUORESCENT LIGHTS of the bathroom, Shafer outlined his plan.

"You're insane," Wells said.

"Then let's call the FBI, be done with it. Like we should have already. Whitby will drop Callar in some rathole and that'll be the end of it. We'll never know what happened in Poland. We'll have no leverage at all. This is our best shot."

"Duto didn't ask us to figure out what happened over there, Ellis. He asked us to figure out who was killing the squad. Which we have."

"Somebody needs to know who those detainees were, what happened to them. If only to tell their families. Somebody needs to find out what was going on at the Midnight House. What *we* did. Even if there aren't going to be any trials."

"What if Murphy won't bite? Would you really go through with it?"

The look in Shafer's eyes was answer enough.

AN HOUR LATER, Wells parked his Subaru in the driveway of the vacant house in Kings Park West where he had spotted Callar's Tercel. He unholstered his pistol, tucked it under the seat.

He walked down the driveway and along the road toward Brant Murphy's house. He was wearing only a T-shirt and jeans and holding his hands at his shoulders. As he reached the property line of the house, still fifty feet from the front door, a spotlight from the van caught him. He stopped walking, raised his arms over his head. The guards stepped out of the van, hands on their holsters.

"John Wells?"

"Yes."

"Down on the pavement."

Wells dropped to his knees. The guard stepped closer.

"Lie down."

"I need to talk to Brant."

"Lie down, Mr. Wells. That's an order."

Wells lay down, prone, arms above his head like he was a kid playing at Superman. He was tired of having strangers point guns at him. But then nobody had made him come over here.

The guard stopped six feet away. He had shiny black eyes and a long narrow chin and a halo from the spotlight behind him. He reminded Wells of a Jesuit priest in a seventeenth-century Spanish painting.

"What are you doing here?"

"I need to talk to Brant."

"I'm afraid that's impossible."

"I've got no gun," Wells said. "If I'd wanted to hurt him, believe me, this isn't how I'd go about it. I've got a message for him, and it's urgent. Frisk me and tell him I'm here to see him. Please."

The guard glanced up at the house. "Stand up and raise your shirt." Wells did. "Over to the van. Slowly. When you get there, put your hands against the passenger door."

At the van, the guard frisked Wells, slowly and expertly, squeezing his legs, working down from thigh to ankle and then back up. Wells hoped the guard wouldn't go too high. He was still throbbing from Callar's knee.

"Sit down."

"Tell him his life is at risk," Wells said. "And that he shouldn't call anyone until he talks to me."

The guard walked up the driveway.

TWO MINUTES LATER, Murphy emerged, holding a flashlight. The guard stood beside him, his pistol trained on Wells's chest.

"I should have you brought in right now," Murphy said.

"Good news. Shafer and I, we know who's after you."

"Prove it."

"Give me five minutes."

358 | ALEX BERENSON

"Come on, then." Murphy stepped back up the driveway.

"It's better if we do this outside."

They walked side by side down the empty street, the van trailing, in what was without doubt the strangest meeting ever held in Kings Park West.

"What happened to your face?" Murphy said.

"The guy, the killer, he's in custody. Not far from here."

"You're full of shit, John."

"I'm completely serious."

"How come I haven't heard, then? When was he arrested?" Murphy stopped, put a hand on Wells's arm. "Who has him in custody?"

"At the moment, Ellis Shafer."

"You personally found the killer."

"Ellis and I, tonight, yes."

"And have him."

"Ellis does. The guy was casing your house. You were next on the list."

"You are going to be very sorry you woke me up at two thirty in the morning for this."

"Look at me." Wells waited until he had Murphy's attention. "It's no joke. So, the good news, we have him. There's bad news, too. The bad news is this is very personal for him, and he's willing to die. And you, Poland was as close as you ever got to the front lines, so you don't know what it's like, that mind-set. But I'm telling you that a man who's willing to die is unstoppable. Especially if he's patient. I mean, if you're the President and you have an unlimited budget and a thousand Secret Service officers and you never go anywhere that hasn't been vetted first, maybe you have a chance. But you're not the President, Brant. This is all the protection you're going to get. In a year or two, you'll have less. The agency'll take it away bit by bit. It's expensive. People forget. But this guy, he won't forget. He'll wait and wait. Then he'll hit you. I wouldn't bet against him."

"I'm calling Whitby right now. Have you brought in."

"Sure. Only one problem." They were at the crux. "You do that, Shafer's gonna let him go."

"You wouldn't." Murphy grabbed Wells's arm, leaned in close. He looked around, side to side, his eyes darting, as if the killer might even now be lurking behind a tree or under a car.

Behind them, the van stopped. The Jesuit guard opened his door. "There a problem, Mr. Murphy?"

"No problem," Murphy said. He hissed at Wells, "You'd let him go? Knowing that he's killed Americans? Soldiers? Our operatives? You'll be an accessory to murder, spend the rest of your life in jail. You'll—"

"Shafer can't help it if this guy overpowers him."

"I'll tell everyone what you said."

"And I'll deny it."

Murphy stopped. The only sound was the low grumble of the Ford's engine.

"So let him go. We'll find him. The FBI—"

"Hasn't had much luck so far."

"This is gutless," Murphy said. "*You're* gutless. Hiding behind this man. You want to threaten me, threaten me yourself. Not this."

The words stung. Wells had never been called gutless before. And he'd never had cause to think of himself that way. But tonight he did. Because Murphy was right. Wells should never have let Shafer use Callar this way.

But Wells had come too far to back off now.

"I guess I must not like you much," Wells said.

Murphy rubbed his face and squeezed his eyes shut. He opened them, as if he hoped to find himself back in his bed, this nightmare over. But Wells stood in front of him. "Just tell me what you want," he said.

"The truth. About the missing detainees. About what happened at the Midnight House. Ten days ago, Whitby showed us this incredible intel. The location of every nuclear weapon in Pakistan. That's a coup. He said it came from you, from your squad. So, how come no one will give us a straight answer about what happened over there? How come the IG's investigation got zapped? How come Jerry Williams's wife says he wasn't the same after he got back?"

"That's all."

"That is all. No notes, no tapes. Just the truth. Then we hand this guy over for whatever justice the people of the United States of America see fit to dispense."

"Even if I tell you, it won't do you any good."

"Maybe it'll do you some good, Brant. Maybe it'll set you free."

"You're quoting me the lobby?" When the original CIA headquarters was completed in 1961, the chief at the time, Allen Dulles, had inscribed a proverb on a wall in the lobby, John 8:23. *Ye shall know the truth and the truth shall make you free.*

"Look, you must have killed them, those two detainees, otherwise you wouldn't have paid D'Angelo to zap their records. That was a big mistake, and you knew it was risky, but you did it anyway. And the only explanation is that you had to have them gone because they were dead. So, why don't you just come clean? I swear, Brant, I'm not wearing a wire. Your guys frisked me."

"You think that's what happened? You think we killed our prisoners. Got what we needed from them and disposed of them. War crimes."

"Maybe it was an accident."

"You know what, John? I'm gonna tell you after all. Outside of Whitby and Terreri and me, you'll be the only one who knows the truth. And then you can decide who to blame."

27

By the time Rachel Callar walked into Terreri's office, the rest of the squad was there. The room stank of cigar smoke. Eight men, eight cigars. Even Jerry Williams, normally a health nut, was puffing away.

"Major."

"Colonel. I see you have a fire drill planned."

"A pleasure as always," Terreri said, waving his cigar at her. "Can I offer you one?" He nodded at the wooden box on his desk. "Cubans. From this store in Warsaw. I'm picking up a few dozen before we go home."

"Congratulations. Who's watching Jawaruddin and Mohammed?"

"Fatty and crazy aren't going anywhere," Murphy said. "We figured they could use some time alone."

Callar knew Murphy wanted to rile her. Yet she could hardly resist the bait, putting a finger in his chest and telling him to shut up, that those were human beings downstairs and she didn't care if Jawaruddin had given them the keys to Fort Knox and Osama bin Laden, too, and—

She breathed in deep, reached for the place where she was in control. She knew it existed, though she needed a map to find it these days.

"I don't think it's a good idea to leave them alone."

"Then go keep an eye on them," Murphy said.

"Enough," Terreri said. He reached for a cardboard box from under his desk, pulled out cowboy hats in all shapes and sizes.

"We've all worked hard all these months. I know it's been tough. But it's paid off. This is what Jawaruddin bin Zari has been hinting at for the last couple weeks. We recovered it four days ago in Pakistan. Karp and I are the only ones who are supposed to see it, but I figure we all deserve a look. But you'll only see it once, so watch closely. And it goes without saying, this is beyond classified."

He clicked on his laptop. On the flat-screen television across the room, the video of bin Zari and Tafiq began to play.

TWO FLOORS DOWN, Mohammed Fariz sat on his cot, his eyes closed, his legs folded under him. He looked almost peaceful, but he wasn't. The djinns were with him constantly now.

They didn't yell at him anymore, and for that he was grateful. They didn't yell because he'd agreed to do what they asked. He understood them now. They were his friends, the djinns, his only friends. They helped him see.

Every day, the Americans walked Jawaruddin down the corridor past Mohammed's cell. And every day Mohammed saw that Jawaruddin wasn't Jawaruddin at all. A devil had put salt in his mouth and seeped into his blood through his throat. He seemed to breathe, but he didn't. The Jawaruddin-devil was in charge here. The Americans pretended to hold him, but really they worked for him. He could leave anytime. Every time Jawaruddin walked by Mohammed's cell, he said hello, and the words made Mohammed's teeth hurt so much that he wanted to pull them out. But Mohammed didn't say anything at all. He just nodded and smiled. The djinns told him that if he nodded and smiled, his teeth wouldn't hurt. The djinns explained everything. They came in the night and talked to him.

They showed him how to unscrew the metal leg of his cot, how to sharpen its edges against the bed frame each night while the guards slept. They showed him that if he stood on his cot he could use the leg as a screwdriver to loosen the grate that covered the air duct in the ceiling. The screws were rusted tight, and for a week Mohammed worked them, inch by inch, tearing up his fingers. He wondered if the Americans would notice, but the djinns told him not to worry, that the Americans didn't pay attention to him anymore. Finally, the night before last, the screws came loose and he took off the grate and stood on his tiptoes and looked inside the vent.

The tube above was a dark tight metal hole, too small for an average-sized man to fit. But Mohammed wasn't an average-sized man. He was an underfed teenage boy, 1.6 meters—five-four—and sixty kilograms—one hundred thirty pounds. He reached inside the vent. Less than a foot above the ceiling, it connected with a cross-tunnel that ran above all the rooms and cells in the basement. Mohammed screwed the grate back on and lay down and closed his eyes and waited for the djinns to tell him what to do next.

MODERN AMERICAN PRISONS DIDN'T have ventilation systems that extended directly into their cells. But this wasn't a modern American prison, and until 673 arrived, these cells weren't used for long-term confinement anyway. Misbehaving Polish soldiers were hauled in for a week or two and then discharged or transferred to larger bases for more serious punishment. And central heating was a necessity in Stare Kiejkuty, where the temperature regularly dropped below zero in the winter.

When 673 took over the barracks, Jack Fisher had seen the vents.

He'd given the Rangers standing orders to check them once every two weeks, make sure the prisoners didn't tamper with them. Mohammed's cell was due for another check. In four days.

AS MOHAMMED READIED HIMSELF for his mission, bin Zari lay two cells away on his cot, hands folded behind his head. He could almost believe he'd dreamed those weeks in the torture chamber. The antibiotics had taken care of his pneumonia. The blisters on his skin had healed. He had no scars, no broken bones. His insides had nearly recovered, the woman doctor told him. Even the most sympathetic lawyer might not believe his story.

These Americans had defeated him without leaving a mark. He wanted to be angry at himself for breaking, but he couldn't. He'd sent dozens of believers to their deaths, helped them strap explosives to their bodies and blow themselves into eternity. But in truth he'd helped those men, offering them the briefest burst of earthly torment in return for the perpetual bliss that Allah granted his martyrs. What the Americans had done to him was something else, endless pain unrelieved by death. No one could beat that room.

Since he'd agreed to talk, they'd treated him decently. Then again, he hadn't given them reason to hurt him. In the last few weeks, he had thought of going back on his word, giving them fake names, addresses, plots. But he didn't know how much they knew. And if they put him back in the torture cell, he would shed his skin like a snake, thirsty and desperate as the blood poured off him. They would take him to the brink and bring him back, over and over, until his mind snapped.

The day before he broke in the torture room, its walls had turned into living crepe paper. He'd needed a few seconds to realize he was seeing roaches, thousands of them. They scuttled across the floor and over his skin, crawled into his mouth and nose and even his ears, scuttling along, their touch dry and quick. They weren't real. He knew they weren't real. They had bomb belts, tiny and perfectly formed, strapped to their shells. Bin Zari had enough sanity left to know that roaches didn't wear suicide bombs, that the stress of being chained to the floor for days on end was making him hallucinate. But they *felt* real. He saw them and heard them and suffered their touch on his skin. And he knew that if he stayed much longer in the cell, he would lose what was left of his mind.

Whenever he thought about lying to the Americans, he remembered the roaches. Maybe he was a fool. Maybe the Americans would go back to torturing him after he'd given up his secrets. But he didn't think so. They'd offered a clear bargain all along. Give us what you know, and we won't hurt you.

He'd realized something else, too, something he should have figured out months before. He could turn his weakness into strength. The most important piece of information he had might be more dangerous for them than for him. Let them find the videotape with him and Tafiq. Let them play it at a tribunal at Guantánamo. Let the world see it. The Americans would know once and for all that their supposed allies in Pakistan could not be trusted. The ISI would be forced to declare its allegiance openly.

But he couldn't tell them about the tape right away, or they might not believe him. He gave up other information first to prove his reliability. Each day they debriefed him. They were pleasant to him now. They gave him bottled water whenever he wanted, and he ate what they ate now, no more gruel.

In turn, he gave up safe houses in Peshawar and the North-West Frontier. He even gave up the cell that Ansar had put together in Delhi to work on an attack against the Indian parliament. In truth, bin Zari had always doubted the ability of the men they'd assigned to that job, so the information was less valuable than it appeared. He let them think he was broken, an act that wasn't hard to pull off, since he was, more or less. Then, when the interrogator who called himself Jim asked about the ISI, bin Zari sprang the trap.

"Of course we were close to the ISI."

"Senior officers."

"In some cases."

"Did you communicate regularly?"

"Yes. In fact—" Bin Zari broke off. "I've answered all your questions. But this I can't speak about."

At first Jim smiled, joked, cajoled bin Zari to talk. But after an hour of questions, Jim grew irritated. Finally, he ordered the Rangers to take bin Zari back to his cell. "No supper," he said. "Take tonight, sleep, and wake up ready to talk."

The next morning, Jim appeared outside bin Zari's cell carrying a tray. He tilted it so bin Zari could see what it held: three biscuits and a bowl of honey. The sweet, hot smell of the biscuits filled bin Zari's nostrils, made his mouth drip. Bin Zari wondered where they'd come from. He'd not seen food like this since they'd captured him.

"You must be hungry after missing supper," Jim said. He dipped a biscuit into the bowl of honey, ate it carefully, one small bite after another. "Remember, in the other cell? How hungry you were?"

Jim dipped the second biscuit into the bowl. "So, you'll tell me what you meant, about the ISI?"

"I can't."

"You don't get to decide. You answer my questions, or I'll put you back in that place. Just as soon as I've eaten this breakfast."

"You promised."

"And you promised to be honest with us, Jawaruddin."

"Please."

Jim seemed to lose interest in the conversation. He kept eating. And when the third biscuit was gone, he turned away.

"That's it, then," he said. He didn't even seem angry. "I'll send the soldiers for you. Please don't fight."

"Don't."

Jim began to walk away.

"All right," bin Zari said.

Jim stopped.

"I'll tell." Bin Zari explained that he'd once taped a meeting that showed him talking over a terrorist plot with a senior member of the ISI. He refused to disclose the details of the meeting, saying that Jim wouldn't believe him. "You'll think I'm lying, and I fear what you'll do," he said. "You must see it yourself."

He'd stored the video on a laptop, and hidden it at a farmhouse that belonged to distant cousins of his in the Swat Valley. They didn't even know it existed, he said.

"Why make this tape?" Jim said.

"In case the ISI ever decided to betray me. Or Ansar Muhammad."

"If you're lying—"

"I'm not."

"And you can show us where to find it?"

"Yes."

That evening, Jim came to his cell holding a Quran. "For you."

Bin Zari didn't thank Jim. He hadn't fallen that far yet. But he took the beautiful book, with its gray cover and intricate silver filigree, gratefully.

That night, as he read, he wondered what the Americans planned to do with him. Would they find the laptop? And if they did, would they send him to Guantánamo? Or simply kill him? He no longer cared.

But he knew that in the next world, Allah would see fit to torture these Americans, just as they'd tortured him. For eternity. No matter how much they begged for forgiveness, how loudly they screamed their mistakes. For this vengeance Jawaruddin bin Zari prayed as he read his holy book.

MOHAMMED PEEKED THROUGH the bars of his cell. The corridor ran forty feet, past four side-by-side cells. Mohammed was housed in the second cell, Jawaruddin in the fourth. Past Jawaruddin's cell the corridor ended in a concrete wall. On the far end of the corridor, two gates controlled the entrance to the cell block. A pair of chairs were positioned outside the gates. Usually a guard or two was stationed there to watch the corridor, an American during the day, one or two of the others at night.

But for the first time in Mohammed's memory, the chairs were empty. *Now,* the djinns told him. *Now.*

Mohammed squatted low and flipped the cot up against the wall under the vent. He unscrewed its sharpened leg, careful not to slice his palm open on its edges. When it was loose, he touched its blade with the tip of his thumb and was pleased to see blood rise from his brown skin.

He pulled himself up the side of the bed and squatted on its edge. With his free hand, he loosened the screws that held the vent. A bigger man would have knocked over the cot, but Mohammed's lack of size worked to his advantage. The cover came loose. He pulled it free and jumped down. He left the cover on the floor and peeked out the front of the cell. Still no guards.

It's time, the djinns said.

BIN ZARI CLOSED his eyes and tried to sleep. Though for some reason that little monkey Mohammed was scraping around his cell. Normally

Mohammed didn't say much, just stared whenever bin Zari walked by. Bin Zari wished the Americans would send the boy to Guantánamo or back to Pakistan. Wherever. He was strange, and bad luck. A fierce sour smell came off his greasy, tangled hair, and his eyes were black stones that gave no hint of what, if anything, he might be thinking.

Bin Zari knew Mohammed wasn't responsible for their original arrest, but he blamed the boy anyway. He'd never been close to being captured until that night in Islamabad. "Little monkey," he yelled. "What are you doing?"

UPSTAIRS, THE VIDEO WAS DONE.

"Remember it," Terreri said. "You're never gonna see it again. I shouldn't have shown it to you, but we are a team, we've always been a team, and we will always be a team."

"Even you, doc," Fisher said.

"I feel so much better now," Callar said.

"What happens next, Colonel?" This from Jerry Williams.

"We're going home," Terreri said. "Unless you want to stay awhile while, hang out in Poland."

"Sir, that's not what I meant." Humor wasn't Williams's strong suit. "I meant with the prisoners."

"Yes, Muscles, I know. Hasn't been decided. What you just saw, that could cause a lot of problems with the Paks. Only a few people back in D.C. even know about it. Even fewer know how we got it. And they don't want Jawaruddin to get to Gitmo and start bitching about how he's been treated. 'Specially if along the way he mentions the video. And we can't exactly send him back to Pakistan, either. So, it's complicated."

"We ought to leave them here, let the Poles have 'em."

"Personally, I wouldn't care if they spent eternity and a day downstairs. But no, they won't be staying here. When we go, the Midnight House is done."

"We oughta just kill 'em," Fisher said. He looked around the room. "I'm serious. Much easier."

Terreri puffed his cigar, blew a perfect ring. "You mean it, don't you, Jack?"

"That man downstairs is a human roach."

"You're sick," Callar said.

"All your complaining, you've been here every step," Fisher said. "Little late to be holding your nose."

"Wish I could agree with you, Jack," Terreri said. "But that's not how we do."

"You sure? One hundred percent? If I went downstairs right now and did it myself, I'll bet none of you would turn me in."

"I would," Callar said.

"Would you, now, sweetheart?" Fisher stepped toward her, blew a stream of smoke in her face.

"Enough, Jack," Terreri said. "Do you understand me?"

"Yes, Colonel."

"Good. And on that happy note, let's go outside, take a couple pictures. Something to remember when we're old and gray."

DOWNSTAIRS, MOHAMMED PULLED HIMSELF atop the cot, wormed his head into the vent. The tube was cracked and rusted, the air inside hot and stale. He wanted to pull out his head. He wanted to lie on the floor and close his eyes and sleep. And wake up in the room in Haji Camp he shared with his brothers, wake up before the Jaish had touched him. He was so tired.

But the djinns didn't care about his excuses. They had chosen him for the mission. As he wavered, their voices rose, a cacophony of curses and threats, filling him until he couldn't breathe. *Go on*, the djinns said. *Leave it behind.*

Mohammed balanced himself on top of the cot. He pushed himself into the vent and found the cross-passage that ran horizontally through the ceiling of the cell block. To his right, the passage led to the front of the block and the guard station. To the left, it ran toward the rear wall and Jawaruddin's cell.

Left, the djinns whispered. *Left*.

Mohammed put the knife into the passage to his left. He reached for the ridges of metal where the ventilation pipes had been welded together and pulled himself left, pushing the knife before him. For a moment he was stuck, and then he wriggled his shoulders sideways and freed himself and squirmed forward with the syncopated twists of a snake. He slid over the vertical vent that dropped into the cell beside his and wriggled along until he reached the fourth and final cell. In the cell below, he heard Jawaruddin. He looked down and saw Jawaruddin's bulky body through the grate. "Monkey. Are you up there?"

Now, the djinns said. *He's the devil. The devil, the devil, the devil. And if you don't do what we say, you'll be the devil, too.*

Mohammed dropped down and kicked through the grate and slid out.

IN THE CELL BELOW, bin Zari looked up almost in awe as Mohammed's feet emerged from the vent. "Crazy monkey. Where did you think you were going? Trying to escape?"

Bin Zari reached out and tugged at Mohammed's legs and pulled him down. Centimeter by centimeter, Mohammed's belly and neck and head came out of the grate. His arms were over his head, the last part of him to emerge—

And so bin Zari had only an instant to react when Mohammed's arms came free and Mohammed's right arm swung down at his face with something that looked like a lightning bolt wrapped inside his brown fingers. Bin Zari grunted and twisted his head and let go of Mohammed—

But he was too late. The sharpened edge of the cot leg caught his left eye and tore through the lid and the cornea and into the meat of the eyeball. Bin Zari lifted his arms and tried to scream, but Mohammed shoved the leg deep into his brain, and before bin Zari knew what had happened the pain spread from his eye to everywhere and nowhere and he couldn't hold himself and—

He collapsed beneath Mohammed, dead before he touched the ground.

BUT MOHAMMED AND THE DJINNS weren't finished. Mohammed slashed at Jawaruddin's face and belly until the big man's guts covered the floor of the cell and his nose and ears lay stacked on what was left of his chest. *Now eat*, the djinns told him. *Eat.*

"No," Mohammed said aloud.

Then we'll never leave you alone.

But Mohammed had the answer for that. He wiped the cot leg as best he could against bin Zari's blanket. When the blood was gone and he could see the edge of the blade he'd made, he tilted back his neck and tore at himself. The cutting wasn't easy. The blade was dull now and he wouldn't have imagined his poor, wretched body would fight its own destruction so desperately. But the djinns were quiet at last. So he cut and cut until his own warm blood covered his hands and his chest and washed him clean.

28

We took pictures for a while and sat outside and had a couple beers. Then we came back in and found the bodies. Callar did. She went downstairs, and we heard her screaming."

Wells and Murphy had circled the neighborhood as Murphy explained how bin Zari was captured and tortured and finally broken. How he'd told them about the laptop. How the Deltas had found the computer in the Swat Valley. And what it had held.

Somehow they wound up sitting on the driveway where Wells had parked his WRX. The two agency guards watched from the van.

"So who killed them?" Wells said. "Jack Fisher?"

"No. Mohammed."

"The boy?"

"He snuck into bin Zari's cell through the overhead vent and killed bin Zari and then himself. They were alone for close to an hour. Plenty of time."

"How?"

"A blade from his cot leg. Must have made it at night when the Polish guards were sleeping."

"You're sure Fisher didn't do it."

"Why would I lie? Guy's dead. And we could see what happened.

Mohammed unscrewed the grate in his cell, got into the heating system, crawled across to bin Zari's cell. Anyway, if you'd seen the bodies—" Murphy shook his head. "Bin Zari was torn up like wild dogs had gotten him. His body was in about eighty-five pieces. And Mohammed had bled out so badly. We practically needed waders to get to him. He was still holding the knife."

"But it was convenient. Since you didn't know what to do with them."

"It was a nightmare. The most important prisoner since Khalid Sheikh Muhammad, more important, and this crazy kid offs him because we got sloppy. Lazy. We were there too long, all of us. We've been fighting this war too long."

"Did you ever figure out why Mohammed did it?"

"No reason. Kid was nuts. Psychotic. Callar thought so all along."

Psychosis, insanity in all its forms, was the thread, Wells thought. The madness had traveled from Mohammed Fariz to Rachel Callar to her husband like a kids' game of telephone. If kids played telephone anymore.

Murphy reached into his pocket, withdrew a canister of Copenhagen. He extracted a wad of dip the size of a knuckle and stuffed it in his lower lip. "I'm not sorry we did what we did to Jawaruddin. We had to break him. But he shouldn't have died that way, and Mohammed shouldn't have either."

Wells wasn't interested in hearing Brant Murphy's opinions on right and wrong. "You found the bodies. Then what?"

"Must be hard to be perfect, John."

"Finish your story so I can tell you who I caught and get out of here and never have to see you again."

Murphy spat a stream of dip into the driveway. "It was Terreri who realized what we had to do. Terreri and Fred Whitby."

"Whitby knew that the tape you'd gotten from bin Zari—"

"Would make his career. Once-in-a-lifetime stuff. All along, he told us to do whatever we wanted to the detainees, long as the take was good and we didn't leave marks. If they didn't have scars or burns or missing fingers, nobody would care. That was the way Fred figured it. And he was right. But two dead bodies, especially in that condition, that would be hard to explain. Either we were negligent or just plain murderers."

"You had to make them disappear."

"We bought a couple of bank safes in Warsaw. We chopped up the bodies. Bin Zari was pretty well chopped up already. We put the pieces in the safes and borrowed a Polish military helicopter and flew out a hundred miles over the Baltic Sea on a cloudy night and dumped them. Boom. Boom. Problem solved."

Wells didn't trust himself to speak. Americans. Soldiers. Tossing human bodies away like garbage.

"Nobody on the squad protested," Wells said.

"The only one who would have was Callar, and she wouldn't speak to any of us by that point. But there was still one loose end to clear up."

"The prisoner numbers."

"I flew home. I'd met D'Angelo a couple times and I had a feeling about him, that he could be bought. At least rented. He was the kind of guy, always going somewhere fancy, getting somebody else to pick up the tab."

"Takes one to know one."

Murphy spat dip, another long stream.

"And he cleaned the database," Wells said. "Jawaruddin bin Zari and Mohammed Fariz were never in U.S. custody. But he got too cute on the payoff."

"We should never have agreed to the paper trail."

"There's something I don't understand," Wells said. "The video with bin Zari and Tafiq. Wouldn't it be less valuable without bin Zari to authenticate it?"

"I get why you'd think that. But follow the chain. Don't you think the ISI would do anything to keep that video secret?"

Now Wells saw. "We made a deal with Tafiq. Keep the video secret in return for access to the Paki nuke depots. Benazir Bhutto was murdered, and we know who's behind it, and we haven't told anyone."

"I believe the term is *realpolitik*. We make the tape public, Pakistan goes crazy. Total anarchy. Sure, the ISI is dirty. They killed Bhutto, they fund terrorism. They're despicable. But we can manage them. Those nukes are all the Pakis have. Without them, Pakistan's got nothing on Bangladesh. They don't have oil, and we've had about enough fighting in Muslim countries for a while. All we want is to keep an eye on those nukes. The rest of Pakistan can rot."

"Justice for Bhutto."

"Good one, John." Murphy's grin revealed the flecks of dip between his teeth. "And Tafiq, he knows, the video comes out, the Pakis string him up. He tries for exile, who's going to take him? Not the French. Not the Arabs. Not even the Russians. He'll be stuck someplace like Somalia. He wants to make sure the tape stays in a vault somewhere. What's he going to do? Tell us he was misquoted, he wants to see bin Zari to talk it over? He knows it's real."

"And he assumes bin Zari's still alive. Somewhere in custody."

"Correct. Everybody wins."

Wells was silent. The pieces fit together now. The mystery solved. Yet ash filled his mouth. There would be no justice here, not for Benazir Bhutto, not for Jawaruddin bin Zari or Mohammed Fariz. Maybe not even for the members of 673 who had died at Steve Callar's hand.

"You know all this for sure, or are you guessing?"

"Only the principals know for sure. But I saw the video, and I know about the nukes. The connection's there. The greatest good for the greatest number."

Murphy sounded cheerful now. He'd received a great gift, the chance to confess his sins without facing punishment. Without even chanting a dozen Hail Marys. The chance to rub Wells's face in the reality of power politics at the highest level.

"Now I've told you everything. Time for your side of the bargain. And please don't say it's some government hit squad. I wouldn't know whether to piss myself or slap you across the face."

"One last question. You said the principals know. Who would that include?"

"I would think all the obvious names. The President, the Vice President. The head of NSC and the SecDef. Whitby for sure. Duto, probably."

"Duto?"

"I'm guessing, but this kind of deal, don't you think they ask the DCI for his opinion?"

Duto's fingerprints were everywhere now, Wells thought. Only one thread left to unravel. Had Duto known about the dead prisoners all along? Had he set Wells and Shafer on the trail knowing even before they started what they would find?

"Did you tell Duto what happened to bin Zari and Mohammed?" Wells said.

"Of course not. The squad and Whitby were the only ones who knew."

"Could he have found out some other way?"

"You'll have to ask him yourself."

"I'll do that."

"So," Murphy said. "A deal's a deal."

"It's Steve Callar."

"That's impossible."

"He already confessed."

"But he was in Phoenix—"

Wells explained.

WHEN HE WAS DONE, Murphy nodded. "I see it," he said. "Callar wore down. We got rough, and she couldn't take it. We all knew she was depressed. Karp asked Terreri to send her home, but Terreri wouldn't. He was stubborn, said we needed a doctor, and unless she requested a transfer he wouldn't give it. And then at the end, finding the bodies sent her over. She told us we were all murderers, just like the Nazis, that she was going to report us. Terreri told her to go right ahead, betray us. She spent most of the last two months in her room. She kept telling us how she'd failed, how all of us had failed. Terreri would have sent her home by then, but the tour was practically done. Yeah, I see it."

"But you couldn't care less."

"She knew what she was getting into. No one's fault but her own that she freaked out. She comes home, offs herself, the coward's way out. Then her whack-job husband decides he deserves revenge. On us. Like we're responsible for her mental problems. I never laid a finger on her, never even raised my voice to her. You want me to feel sorry for her? I don't think so."

"That's one way to look at it."

"There's another? Lemme guess. Poor little Rachel *felt* more deeply than the rest of us. Oh, the humanity." Murphy stood. "The bad guys in this are Jawaruddin bin Zari and Steve Callar." He walked down the driveway. "It's time for me to go home."

"Don't you want to know where Callar is?"

Murphy gave him a mocking salute. "I leave him to you. I trust you'll do the right thing. You always do."

WELLS STAYED CALM on the surface roads, but when he reached the Beltway he pushed his foot to the floor and the WRX rocketed through the Virginia night. A childish escape, but it was all he had. For the first time in months, Springsteen filled his ears: *"And there's a darkness in this town that's got us, too . . ."* "Independence Day." The song's hero was getting ready to move away, leave his life behind. Wells wondered if he had the strength to do the same.

Back in room 112, he found Callar and Shafer watching HBO, an early-season episode of *The Sopranos*. Callar's cheek had bled through all the towels and most of two pillowcases, but he looked oddly comfortable as he grinned at Wells.

"Come outside with me," Wells said to Shafer.

They sat in the WRX as Wells recounted what Murphy had told him.

"We make it official, he'll be in custody the rest of his life," Shafer said. "We'll call him a material witness. An enemy combatant. He'll never get a trial. We'll never let that video come out."

"Maybe."

"Definitely."

"Then that's how it's going to be. If the President makes that choice and signs those orders and Callar's lawyers can't get a judge to look at the case."

"There's another way."

"No. Ellis, you're the one who told me we needed to get the answers."

"That was before I knew what they were. We go back in there and give him his one bullet. He'll do it. I know he will. It's all he's been talking about."

"No."

"It'll be easier. For him and for us."

Wells gripped the steering wheel tight. "Easy is what got us here. We're following the law this time."

"And when the law fails?"

"I'd rather see the law fail than put my own judgment ahead of it. It ends here."

"At the Budget Motor Inn."

"That's right."

Wells stepped out of the car, walked into the room. Callar looked up from the television. "I want to see my wife."

"Not tonight," Wells said. "Tonight we're taking you in."

Wells wasn't expecting a happy ending, and he didn't get one.

To be sure that Whitby wouldn't be able to make Callar disappear, Wells and Shafer brought him directly to Langley from the motel. In the days that followed, the FBI and Justice insisted that Callar had to be formally charged so the murder cases could be closed. The CIA and Defense argued that a trial, or even an indictment, would cause a media frenzy that would bust open the deal that the United States had cut with the ISI. Anyway, Callar wasn't contesting his guilt, so a trial would be pointless.

Whitby stayed out of the fight. He was holed up with the defense lawyer he'd hired the day after Wells and Shafer brought in Callar. The lawyer, Nate Marmur, was a former solicitor general who specialized in cleaning up these messes, cases where guilt and innocence hardly mattered, or even existed.

The argument festered for a week. Then the President stepped in. Callar would plead guilty to four counts of murder in federal court in New Orleans for killing Jerry Williams, Kenneth Karp, Jack Fisher, and Mike Wyly. He would avoid execution, instead spending life in prison.

Callar initially refused to agree to the deal and demanded a trial. He relented after being told that if he didn't agree, he would be held at sea for the rest of his life held in the brigs of American aircraft carriers. He was also promised, in writing, that he'd be allowed to visit his wife's grave once every other year.

The plea agreement, which was unusually short for a federal criminal case, said only that Callar's wife had killed herself after working with the men on a secret deployment. The murders were revenge for her suicide. Task Force 673 and the Midnight House were never mentioned. After signing confidentiality agreements, the families of the four men were brought to FBI headquarters and allowed to see a redacted version of Callar's confession and the physical evidence against him.

A week after Callar pled guilty, Whitby resigned as director of national intelligence, saying that he wanted to spend more time with his family. The President accepted his resignation with great regret and named Bobby Yang, an assistant deputy director of operations at the CIA, to replace him. Articles in *The New York Times* and *The Washington Post* explained that Yang's appointment showed that Vinny Duto had beaten back Fred Whitby and retaken control of the American intelligence community.

Murphy resigned from the CIA the same day, his twenty-third anniversary at the agency. He and Whidby joined Strategies LLC, a K Street lobbying firm that specialized in representing defense and private security companies. Jim D'Angelo was never charged for erasing the names from the NSA database, though he was barred from future federal contracting work, the slightest of slaps on his oversized wrists.

THEN ONLY DUTO, Shafer, and Wells were left. A week afer Whitby's resignation, Duto invited Wells and Shafer to his office. They arrived to find Duto holding a bottle of Dom Perignon and three glasses.

"I wanted to thank you," he said. "All your hard work."

"Don't rub this in our faces, Vinny," Wells said.

"Aren't you wondering if I knew what happened to bin Zari and Mohammed?"

"I'd break your jaw, but you're not worth the punch."

"I had no idea. So help me God. I mean, the deal with the ISI, yes, I knew. And there were rumors that the Midnight House, at the end, something was wrong. But I didn't know what."

"If you didn't it's only because you didn't want to," Shafer said. "Protect yourself from the scandal."

"Don't be such a cynic, Ellis," Duto said. "Karp and Murphy never told me, and Whitby shut me down after we got that letter."

It was at these moments that Wells felt his limits most keenly. These raw power games left Wells cold, and so he refused to play them. That attitude was a strength, but a weakness, too. It left him as a pawn for men like Duto.

"So, you called us," Shafer said.

"I knew, I wound you up, you wouldn't stop spinning until you solved the case."

"And you figured the answer had to be bad for Whitby. Whatever it was. Otherwise, he wouldn't have gone to so much trouble to interfere."

Duto twisted the champagne cork until it exploded across the room. Bubbly sunlight poured from the bottle. He poured the glasses full. Duto was in an expansive mood, Wells saw. His triumph filled the office like fog. Wells didn't think he'd ever be able to drink champagne again.

"From the beginning, I should have been more involved with the Midnight House," Duto said. "I knew we had to be in the mix, but I didn't like the setup. Thought it could all blow up."

"You figured, let the Pentagon handle it."

"Then they hit the lottery, find this tape. And Fred Whitby rides it all the way to DNI. You think that's good for the agency?"

"Now Whitby's gone," Wells said. "You're right back where you belong. Top of the anthill."

"Justice has been served, John. The killer caught. Congratulations. Have a drink. Well deserved."

"A couple years ago, after China, I was so beat up. Exley, she told me, if I wanted to quit, I could. No one would judge me. Back then I thought, *I can't. I can't be weak.* But now I'm strong enough to be weak. I quit, Vinny. Effective immediately."

"John—"

"Because it's not about being weak. I'm sick of this game, that's all."

"Is this about Exley? I wouldn't count on her taking you back."

Exley. The magic word. Just hearing her name when he wasn't prepared was enough to suck the air out of Wells's lungs. "This has got nothing to do with Jenny." Which was true in the strictest sense. Wells still hadn't called Exley; he was headed for New Hampshire. Though everything was always about Exley. "This is about the stench coming off you. This is about the Midnight House. And that we know who killed Benazir Bhutto. And we're not going to do anything about any of it."

"Okay. You're in charge, John. You're the President. What do you do?"

"I go public."

"And when there's riots in Pakistan? And the nukes go missing?"

"We have to do something. We can't let the ISI get away with murder."

"What if we could do something? What if *you* could do something?"

TOO LATE, WELLS UNDERSTOOD that Duto had been leading him down this path all along. The floor seemed to twist under his feet. Was this what Duto thought he'd become?

He put a hand on Shafer's skinny shoulder. "Did you know about this?"

"Can't swear to God, because I'm an atheist, but no."

"I'm going to forget you ever asked me this," Wells said to Duto.

Duto sipped his champagne. "You said it yourself. The ISI, they're getting away with murder. And Tafiq is at the heart of it."

"It doesn't even make sense. We have a deal with him. Why would you want to get rid of him now?"

"We'd rather have someone we can trust running the ISI."

"And killing the guy in charge is the way to get there? *No.* I'm not an assassin, Vinny. I came here to quit. My stuff's packed. I'm getting out of this swamp."

Wells wasn't sure whether Duto was testing him or this offer was genuine. He no longer cared. More than anything, he wanted out of this office, out of this whole sick business.

"No problem. You'd have to quit. You couldn't be connected with us at all, not for this."

"Good-bye, Vinny." Wells looked at Shafer. "If you had any guts, you'd come, too."

Wells turned away, walked out of Duto's office, slammed the big wooden door behind him.

But he couldn't get away fast enough to escape the director's last words. "Don't kid yourself. You'll be back."

And the Lord said to Moses, "This is the land of which I swore to Abraham, Isaac, and Jacob, 'I will assign it to your offspring.' I have let you see it with your own eyes, but you shall not cross there."

—Deuteronomy 34:4